Praise for *In Another Life*

"In this lovely novel, Johnson shows us the redemptive power of love and second chances through the ages. Evocative of *Outlander*, *In Another Life* is a thrilling combination of romance, adventure, and history."

—Margaret Dilloway, author of *Sisters of Heart and Snow* and *How to Be an American Housewife*

"Delicate and haunting, romantic and mystical, *In Another Life* is a novel with an extraordinary sense of place. Fans swept away by Diana Gabaldon's eighteenth-century Scotland will want to explore Julie Christine Johnson's thirteenth-century Languedoc."

—Greer Macallister, author of *The Magician's Lie*

"Johnson's heartbroken researcher wends through the lush landscape and historical religious intrigue of southern France seeking the distraction of arcane fact—but instead, like the reader, is transformed by the moving echo of emotional truth. An imaginative, unforgettable tale."

—Kathryn Craft, author of *The Art of Falling* and *The Far End of Happy*

"The dark days of thirteenth-century Cathar persecution in France reach out long fingers to intrigue and bewitch in Julie Christine Johnson's immersive depiction of past and present in this atmospheric novel of love, loss, and reincarnation."

—Tess ontfort mystery series

IN
ANOTHER
LIFE

JULIE CHRISTINE JOHNSON

sourcebooks
landmark

For Brendan

Copyright © 2016 by Julie Christine Johnson
Cover and internal design © 2016 by Sourcebooks, Inc.
Cover design by Laura Klynstra
Cover images © svaga/Shutterstock, Yolande de Kort/Trevillion Images

Published by Sourcebooks Landmark, an imprint of Sourcebooks, Inc.
P.O. Box 4410, Naperville, Illinois 60567-4410
(630) 961-3900
Fax: (630) 961-2168
www.sourcebooks.com

Library of Congress Cataloging-in-Publication Data

Johnson, Julie Christine.
  In another life / Julie Christine Johnson.
     pages cm
  (pbk. : alk. paper) 1. Widows--Fiction. 2. Americans--France--Fiction. 3. Man-woman relationships--Fiction. I. Title.
  PS3610.O3575I53 2015
  813'.6--dc23

2015011192

Printed and bound in the United States of America.
VP 10 9 8 7 6 5 4 3 2 1

Historical Note

 ight hundred years ago, a vast territory of fiefdoms stretched between the Pyrénées Mountains, the Massif Central, and the Mediterranean Sea. The region was united by *langue d'oc*—the linguistic precursor to modern Occitan that is spoken throughout southern France and Catalunya in northern Spain. Languedoc, as the area is now known, was largely independent of the French kingdom to the north. It was here that a new faith based on ancient Gnostic traditions took shape. That faith came to be known as Catharism and its followers, Cathars.

The Cathars believed if one's earthly life had not fulfilled its purpose in a worthy manner, the soul would be condemned to a perpetual cycle of rebirth, trapped in a corruptible body, until God declared the soul redeemed. Heaven was a release from the hell of reincarnation.

Catharism differed radically from the social and moral code of the Catholic Church, and in the twelfth century, the Church declared Catharism a heretical faith. Yet the Cathars continued to grow in number and influence. Until January 1208, when, on the border between Provence and Languedoc, a murder changed Europe forever.

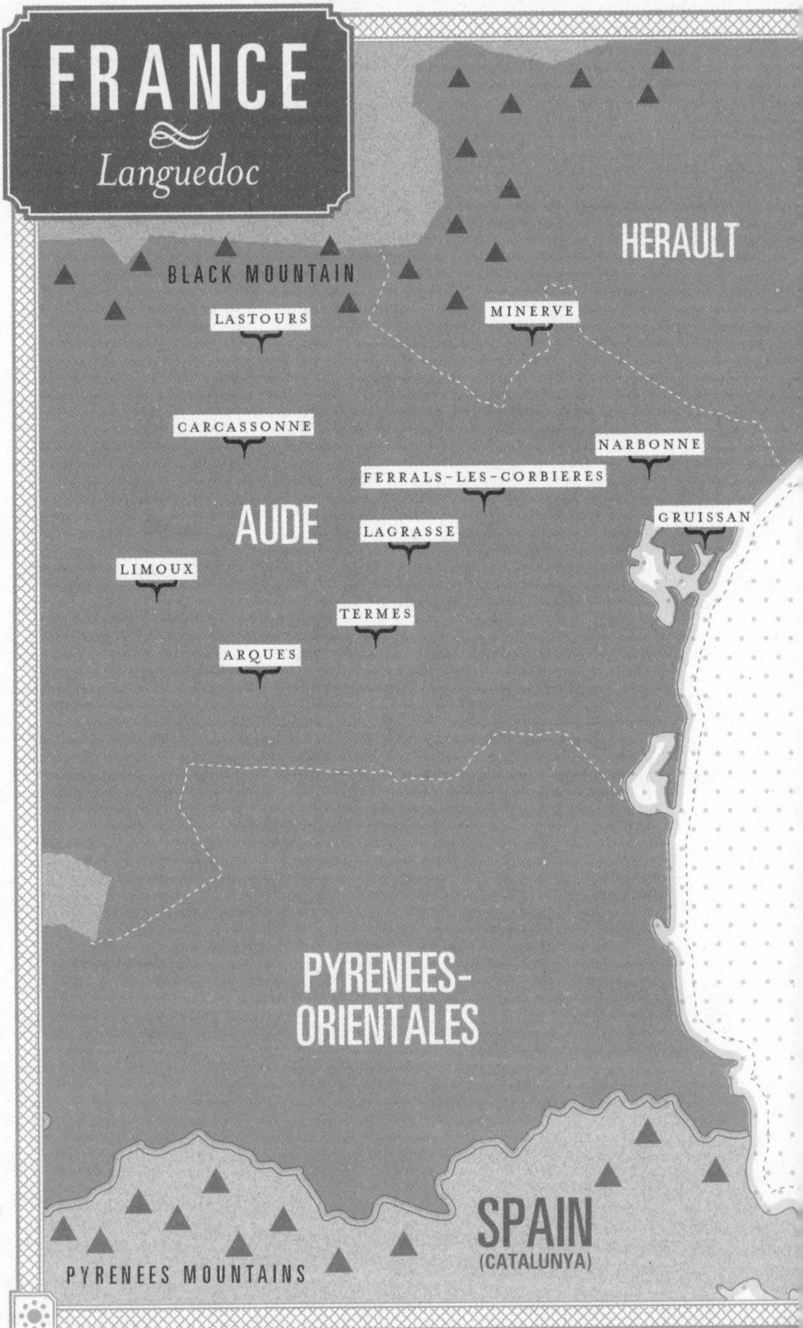

FRANCE

Languedoc

HERAULT

BLACK MOUNTAIN

LASTOURS

MINERVE

CARCASSONNE

NARBONNE

FERRALS-LES-CORBIERES

GRUISSAN

AUDE

LAGRASSE

LIMOUX

TERMES

ARQUES

PYRENEES-
ORIENTALES

SPAIN
(CATALUNYA)

PYRENEES MOUNTAINS

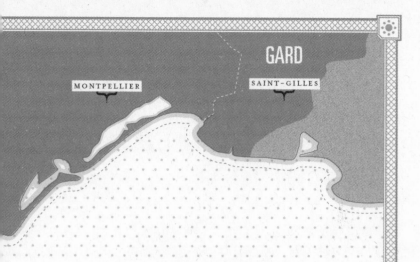

GARD

MONTPELLIER

SAINT-GILLES

MEDITERRANEAN SEA

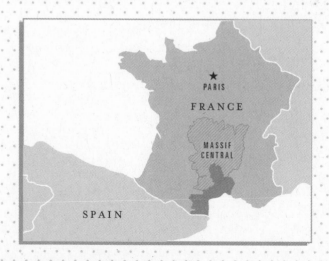

★
PARIS

FRANCE

MASSIF
CENTRAL

SPAIN

Part One

···

Our dead are never dead to us,
until we have forgotten them.

—GEORGE ELIOT

···

PARIS-CHARLES DE GAULLE AIRPORT, OUTSIDE PARIS—WINTER SOLSTICE, PRESENT DAY

*E*ighteen months after her husband's death, Lia Carrer returned to Languedoc like a shadow in search of light.

From inside the airport terminal's glass atrium, the gray blanket over Paris looked no different from the Seattle sky she'd left behind. But the City of Light was not her final destination. The high-speed train known as the TGV departed directly from Charles de Gaulle and would carry her five hundred miles south to Narbonne in fewer than five hours.

Once aboard the TGV, Lia sank into her reserved window seat. Echoes of jet engines and loudspeakers reverberated in her head, but the sounds of train travel—doors opening and closing with a pneumatic whoosh, air slamming between passing cars—reassured her that her journey was nearly over. She was back on solid ground. Soothed by the slight swaying motion of the moving train, Lia gazed out the window and allowed France to absorb her.

As winter-brown valleys gave way to the rocks and rises of the Massif Central, anticipation thrummed in her heart. On the other side of this vast expanse of extinct volcanoes and stony plateaus lay the storybook settings of Provence and the wild and lonely beauty of her beloved Languedoc. She imagined summer's scouring heat on the scrubland valleys of the Pyrénées and winter's wild storms along the Mediterranean coast.

It was December 21, the last of the darkest of nights. Lia hadn't consciously intended to arrive in France on this day, but the timing seemed auspicious. She'd always thought of winter solstice, when the pale hemisphere tilts again toward the sun, as a time of rebirth. Perhaps this journey was her rebirth. At the very least, it was forward motion.

Golden dusk was fading to deep blue as she collected her rental car from the Narbonne train station. She drove the final miles to the small town of Minerve on an empty highway through dark valleys where medieval ruins stood at the inter-section of Roman roads. The soft drone of conversation on a Europe 1 call-in show and the occasional reminder from the disembodied GPS voice kept her company. Lia's journey ended when she stepped inside Le Pèlerin, a stone house at the edge of the village, perched high above the Cesse River.

Three years before, her dearest friends Rose and Domènec Hivert had purchased a crumbling ruin in Minerve, twenty miles north of their farm in Ferrals-les-Corbières. Naming it after the peregrine falcons that swooped and hunted through-out Languedoc, they'd transformed Le Pèlerin into a *gîte*—a vacation rental—to supplement their income as farmers and winemakers. *Pèlerin* also translated as *pilgrim*. When Lia called needing refuge, Rose offered up the cottage for her use until she could sort out her next steps.

Lia dropped her bags and kicked off her shoes in the foyer. "That's me," she announced to the dark, still house. "The pilgrim in search of a home." Entering Le Pèlerin, she had the sensation of walking into a nest tucked in the hollow of a tree, sheltered and calm. A lamp sitting on a narrow table just inside the door cast low light through the square passageway between the kitchen and front room. She hadn't been to Le Pèlerin since Rose and Domènec finished the remodel, and what she saw made her hum with pleasure.

The entryway separated the kitchen and dining room from the snug front room. Timber beams crossed the low ceilings, and plush, mismatched rugs in deep reds and blues were strewn across stained pine floors that had been polished until they shone. She walked around the front room, running her hands along the rough plaster walls that would hold in warmth on chilly days yet keep the house cool and fresh during the intense Languedoc summers. On the far end, logs were piled inside the fireplace built from river rock; all she need do was touch flame to the kindling to start a roaring fire. Domènec had emailed the day before she left Seattle to assure her that Marie-Françoise, a woman from the village who kept an eye on the place, would stop in to turn up the thermostat before Lia arrived. And indeed, the radiant heat under the stone floors in the kitchen warmed her stocking feet.

In three days, her friends would return from an early Christmas celebration with Domènec's parents in Perpignan. Until then, Lia was alone.

She trembled with weariness. Lugging her bags to the loft bedroom was more than she could manage, so Lia left them at the foot of the stairs, unpacking only a change of soft clothes and the small bottles of shampoo and body soap she'd stashed in her carry-on.

The claw-foot bathtub was wide and deep enough to fit two comfortably: utterly impractical, a waste of water, and the most wonderful sight Lia could have conjured at that moment. She turned the hot water on full and nudged open the cold tap; the reluctant water pressure meant she had some time before the tub filled. She stripped and padded naked to the kitchen. After twenty-six hours in the same clothes, the cool air was a refreshing kiss on her gritty skin.

A three-quarter moon lit the long room and pulled her toward the far end, where a long table sat before a wall of windows. Feeling weightless with fatigue, Lia thought she might float through the windows to the terrace and the Cesse River canyon beyond. But her bleached reflection halted at the glass.

Angles defined her body where there once had been curves. Shadows pressed against her ribs, the hollows of her cheeks, and her sunken eyes. She touched her belly and the sharp point of a hip. She was bone and muscle, hard and flat. Grief had eaten away the lush curves of her breasts and the sweet rise of her belly that Gabriel had loved to caress.

It had been so long since she'd really looked at her reflection. She'd avert her eyes from the floor-to-ceiling mirrors in the yoga studio and keep her face tilted toward the sink while she washed her hands in the bathroom down the hall from her office. She'd worked hard to disappear, to become a ghost.

Now, her body shimmering white against the cold glass, Lia saw how tightly she held herself, as if hardening her muscles would somehow steel her heart from pain. Eighteen months since she'd had an appetite. Eighteen months of going through the motions. She'd drifted through a life that had no rails to grasp for balance.

The lassitude had caught up with her on a warm day in October, when Seattle's skies glowed Tuscan blue and the scent of dry leaves rose in the air. The dean of the history department at Cascade University, where she'd served as an adjunct professor of European and medieval history, called her into his office, shut the door, and informed her that the department would not renew her contract after fall quarter. Her recent student evaluations had been grim, and she'd fallen behind on department committee work. The dean had previously hinted at a tenure-track position if Lia would just complete and defend her dissertation within the following year. But after Gabriel's death, her dissertation on the role of reincarnation and the afterlife in Cathar theology sat unopened on her hard drive. It took someone else making a decision about her life to propel Lia into finally making a few of her own.

She backed away from the glass with a curse of surprise but stopped as something white flashed just beyond the window. In the space between heartbeats, she saw the face of a man. Moonlight revealed fierce dark eyes and the etched planes of cheekbones. A seeping black streak marred the left side of his face, running from his temple down his cheek to the corner of his mouth. The palm of a hand came into view, reaching toward her. Her own hands flew up and smacked the glass as adrenaline, warm and electric, seared the weariness from her bones.

A screech ripped through the air, and the vision reassembled itself into something other than human. On the bough of an umbrella pine that clung to the side of the cliff perched a raptor. The breeze lifted the feathers of the bird's underbelly, and the moon bleached them white. His brown head tilted, and his amber eyes lit on Lia's naked form. Keeping her movements small, she looked around for something to cover herself. A chenille throw sat folded on a low, upholstered chair in the near corner. She edged toward the chair, her eyes on the bird outside, and clutched the blanket.

With the throw draped over her shoulders like a cloak, Lia turned the lock, pressed down the handle of the French door, and slipped onto the terrace attached to the stone face of the house.

She'd encountered a Bonelli's eagle two years before during a birds-of-prey demonstration at Château de Peyrepertuse. Once the emperor of Languedoc's skies, the Bonelli's eagle faced extinction in France. To see one in the wild was a once-in-never chance. Tears welled in Lia's eyes as she realized what a gift she'd been offered.

"What brought you here?" she whispered to the eagle as it watched her from his perch on the swaying bough.

In reply, he shifted his weight and showed Lia the profile of his fierce head and hooked beak. Then he spread his wings, and she gasped at the span of feathers, bone, and sinew that measured six feet from tip to tip. He launched from the tree, the whoosh of his wings more a sensation than a sound, and was swallowed by the night.

Leaning over the iron railing, she peered into the black depths below. The river whispered and the wind answered as it swept through the scrub, but the moonlight revealed only vague shapes. She slipped inside the door and locked it behind her.

"Lia, you need to sleep," she said to the empty room.

The sound of her voice broke the spell, and she heard rushing water. The hot bath beckoned, as did the wine that filled a rack on the kitchen counter. Domènec and Rose had stocked it with bottles of their vigorous estate blend of Syrah, Grenache, and Mourvèdre. Lia pulled a bottle from the rack, took a glass from the cupboard, and, with a free finger, gathered the corkscrew from the counter.

A layer of steam drifted over the tub, and water rippled just below its edge. Lia turned off the taps, letting an inch or two drain out while she lit the candles arrayed on the windowsill and opened the bottle. The wine was so opaque, it appeared black in the low light. She sank into water just shy of scalding, holding the glass above the surface, and stayed in the bath until the heat and the wine quieted the clamor in her head and dissolved the aches in her body.

Wrapped in a lavender-scented towel, she climbed the stairway to the loft tucked under the timber-and-plaster roof. A wall heater clicked and sighed as it radiated warmth into the deep, low room. The towel fell to the floor, and as she slipped between the down duvet and the cotton sheet, the bedding gathered her in a soft embrace. Sleep found her at last.

NEAR MINERVE, LANGUEDOC—WINTER SOLSTICE, 1208

In a cave scoured deep into the limestone above the Cesse River, Raoul d'Aran shook with fever. He sat huddled with his hands tucked under his armpits as a chill wind needled through his sweat-soaked wool cloak. With his remaining strength, he clenched his heart around his hot rage. But it was the grief that threatened to overcome his reason as images spilled across his fevered vision. He saw the villagers trapped in the church of Saint-Maurice, felt their bodies crushed against the wooden doors, heard their fists pounding on the shutters, and his nose burned with the smoke that filtered into the sanctuary.

"Paloma." Raoul released his wife's name into the shadows of the cave. "Oh, my girl." He panted and tried to swallow the sobs that pushed against his throat. "Wait for me," he prayed. "I'm nearly there."

The night deepened, and the scrub and stone around him sank into the dark. Raoul's face dropped to his bent knees, but he jolted awake when his rough cloak scraped the gash on his cheek. Cursing through clenched teeth, he touched the wound; his finger came away black with blood. He retched at the stench of rotting flesh and spit into the earth beside him. The violent motion caused his vision to swim, and he moaned in pain. He lost the struggle with consciousness, and his breathing slowed until the rise and fall of his chest was nearly imperceptible.

His fever dream brought him to a river where willow branches stretched to the shore. At the sight of water, his legs buckled, and he fell to his knees. He plunged his head below the river's surface, gasping and spluttering as the icy water filled his belly. Retreating to a shallow pool a few feet away, Raoul scrubbed the grime from his face and hands. The moonlit water reflected the bruises of fatigue under his eyes and the wound on his face that had sealed in a thick, black line.

The water rippled, and a dimly lit room with a long table and a floor of smooth stone floated into view. A figure entered the tableau and approached Raoul without hesitation. As the details of the apparition sharpened and fused, he saw a woman, her bare skin luminous in the low light. Her long hair curled around her shoulders in an amber veil. His eyes traced the outline of ribs beneath the swell of her breasts, the hollow of her hips, and the carved muscles that rippled down her thighs to the ridge of her knees. The woman stopped just short of the window, revealing the full relief of her face, and Raoul started back in shock. Then joy coursed through him as though a flock of goldfinches had taken flight under his skin.

"Paloma," he breathed in wonder and leaned closer. The red-brown curls were not his wife's gossamer blond, and the eyebrows and lashes were distinct in color and shape, but Paloma's silvery-green eyes, the color of olive leaves, looked out from a face formed by the same delicate curves. She was as beautiful and distant as the moon.

Stepping backward, the woman's gaze met Raoul's. Her mouth opened as if to scream, her hands shot up, and her palms struck the glass between them.

"Paloma?" He pressed his hand flat against the cold pane, but a trace of wind ruffled the water, and the scene disappeared.

In the cold cave, Raoul's clenched hands released, and a thin chain bearing a silver pendant streamed from one fist. The pendant fell flat in the dirt. It was a cross with an open center and three bound points on each side: the Occitan Cross, the symbol of the Languedoc resistance. The necklace had once belonged to his wife. *Paloma.* His chest rose as his lungs sought the cool air. His chest fell and did not rise again.

Outside the cave's entrance, countless stars pricked the night with icy light. A great raptor landed with a murmur of wings at the cave's entrance and paced on three-pronged talons. Its keen eyes picked out the black mass of a man huddled in the blue shadows, his head slumped against his chest. With a cry that tore into the sky, the bird flew away from the specter of death.

LE PÈLERIN, MINERVE—DECEMBER

A path of sunlight fell through the skylight to the polished pine floors and tracked across Lia's bed, pouring white light over her. She burrowed deeper, but thirst and heat pulled her from the harbor of sleep. Her hot skin clung to the damp sheet, and her tongue swelled inside her rough mouth. Her head clanged with the effects of three-quarters of a bottle of the Hiverts' potent Corbières wine. Lia sat upright and kicked away the duvet. Shading her eyes, she stood on the bed and cracked open the skylight. Cold air rushed in, smelling of wood smoke and frost.

Downstairs, she filled the coffee press with scoops of Italian roast. Her last infusion of caffeine had been at least twenty-four hours before, and she whimpered with relief as the aroma bloomed under the hot water, the grounds black and thick like soil after a heavy rain. Filling a large mug nearly to the brim, she took a tentative sip and then a deeper swallow, relaxing as the caffeine constricted the blood vessels pushing knives of pain into her temples.

At the windows overlooking the Cesse River, Lia stared out at a world that had been a black void the night before. Flocks of bleached clouds gathered in a cerulean sky, and winter's diaphanous light glinted off the traces of mica in the limestone of the canyon's sides. She stepped onto the terrace enclosed by wrought iron. Below, the cliff sheared away to the riverbed, and a thin ribbon of turquoise shimmered as the Cesse traveled south.

Turning to face the house, she saw a handprint etched into the glass door like a white tattoo. Each line of the palm, each whorl of the fingertips, was outlined like a spider's web. Setting the coffee mug on a small table, Lia hovered her hand over the window; the fingers of the print extended far beyond hers, and the palm dwarfed her own. It was a man's hand.

Last night's vision of a face marred on one side came to her just as a ray of sun hit the palm print and evaporated the fine lines. Lia stayed outside, staring into the river canyon, until she could no longer feel her bare toes.

She retrieved her laptop from upstairs and sat at the kitchen table, skimming through the emails she'd received since leaving the States. The last one, its subject line written in Occitan, caught her eye. It had arrived just as her plane was rising into the sky above Seattle.

My dear Lia,

My heart rests easier, knowing you will soon be in the embrace of friends here in Languedoc. I went to Ferrals-les-Corbières recently in search of that outstanding Mas

Hivert wine, and Rose Hivert gave me the news that you were returning to France.

Lia's head filled with the warm voice behind these words and the anguished memories of her first encounter with Father Jordí Bonafé, archivist at Cathédrale Saint-Just et Saint-Pasteur in Narbonne.

Three days after Gabriel's death and in deep shock, Lia had insisted on going through with a presentation at the Institut de Recherche Cathare—the Institute of Cathar Studies—in Carcassonne. Rose and Domènec had pleaded with her to cancel, but at the time, the lecture had given her a reason to continue breathing.

Father Bonafé had approached her after the talk, and over coffee, he offered words of solace as she spilled out her grief. In the week that followed, as the investigation unfolded and the details of transporting Gabriel's body to his family's home in Mexico were arranged, Lia spent many hours in the comfort of the priest's office at the cathedral and in the cool, quiet archives below.

She returned to Father Bonafé's email. He continued with additional poetic words of condolence and caught her up on the gossip in Languedoc's small world of medieval France researchers. Then the tone of his message changed.

Rose told me your teaching contract has not been renewed. It's an unfortunate decision by your university, but I hope your enthusiasm for your research has not diminished.

I know the circumstance of our meeting is painful to recall; please forgive me for bringing it up. But your lecture at the institute and the questions you raised surrounding Pierre de Castelnau's death and the origins of the Cathar crusade are things I haven't been able to set aside.

Since that night, I've wondered if your theories might not be possible. What seemed like legend carried through time on the flimsy backs of folktales and rumor now appears plausible as history. I wonder if you're still pursuing this research.

When you are rested from your travels and ready to visit Narbonne, I hope we can meet.

Lia drew her legs into the chair and rested her chin on her knees. Why was the priest wondering about all of this now? Yes, she had her doubts about the true nature of Pierre de Castelnau's assassination—the event in 1208 that spurred the bloody Cathar Crusade. She'd been pursuing this tangential line of research before Gabriel's death, but her doctoral adviser had swooped in and pulled her back, warning about lack of credibility in anything that smacked of medieval conspiracy theories. The recent popularity of books and movies that mentioned the Knights Templar, the powerful military order of medieval religious crusaders, and their connection to the legend of the Holy Grail threatened to reduce serious research to swords-and-castles pop culture.

And indeed, modern Languedoc had become newly captivated by the tragic story of its medieval countrymen, conquered eight hundred years earlier by those legendary Knights Templar and the Catholic Church. A tourist industry had sprung up around the theme of the Pays Cathare—Cathar Country. Summertime found Languedoc's compact roads filled with camper vans and cyclists traveling the Route des Cathares between castle ruins and the ancient fortified villages that were still vibrant with commerce.

Lia had relented to her adviser's demands, agreeing that any change of direction would mean starting her dissertation over nearly from scratch; she couldn't afford the distraction, not when she was so close to the end. She'd mentioned her thoughts about Castelnau's assassination during that lecture two summers ago as a rhetorical aside, to show there was still so much about Cathar history that remained unknown and probably unknowable.

She replied to the priest in Narbonne, giving him her cell phone number. Lia couldn't resist any mystery Languedoc offered.

LE PÈLERIN, MINERVE—CHRISTMAS EVE

*T*wo days later, Lia emerged from the cocoon of the cottage for the first time since her arrival. She'd needed the time alone to begin the transition from one life to the next. Le Pèlerin's refrigerator and pantry were full, and the fireplace and the books had been enough to fill the short days. But for Christmas, Rose and Domènec had planned a quiet weekend of celebration with their small family and insisted Lia be with them.

Her eyes watering in the frigid air, Lia walked the short distance from the cottage to a shared garage and tossed an overnight bag onto the passenger seat of the Peugeot. The car's heater blasted warm air through the chilled interior, and the stereo speakers carried news of the world, both of which Lia snapped off to enjoy the winter silence. Her memory found the road south to Mas Hivert, Rose and Domènec's farm and winery outside Ferrals-les-Corbières.

Forty-five minutes later, she turned into the drive. She'd just raised her hand to knock when the front door opened and a pair of coal-black noses shoved through the gap. Silky, golden bodies pressed into Lia's legs, followed by a pair of toddlers chirping for her attention. Amid the chaos of barking dogs and children's voices, familiar arms embraced her. Rose drew her inside the light-filled kitchen, which was thick with the scent of sage, and held her while four-year-old Joël and two-year-old Esmé clung to her legs.

"You can't know what this means to me, to be here again," Lia whispered in her best friend's ear. She leaned away, her hands on Rose's shoulders. "Your hair. Rose, you look amazing."

Rose rubbed a hand across the bare nape of her neck, where tight coils had once brushed her shoulders, and fluffed the back of her pixie cut. "I did it. The big chop. It was getting ridiculous, driving to Montpellier every month to get the locs tightened. These two keep me running around enough as it is." She bent down and scooped up Esmé. The little girl reached for Lia, and Lia buried her face in the child's cinnamon-brown ringlets, inhaling the strawberry-jam sweetness of her skin.

Domènec's rusting Land Rover rattled into the driveway moments later. He thumped up the back steps and into the kitchen, hugging a woven basket crowded with packages. "The entire village was shopping at the *épicerie*," he groaned as Rose and Lia unloaded his arms. "I didn't think I'd make it out alive. And here is our Lia at last."

After welcoming her with a kiss on each cheek, Domènec herded the circus out of the kitchen. Rose and Lia emptied the basket and piled the bounty on the counter: olives from a coop-erative in nearby Bize-Minervois, *fleur de sel*—sea salt—from

Gruissan, aged sausages, mustard laced with Armagnac, and duck breast wrapped in butcher paper.

As Lia poured Cara Cara oranges into a large, emerald-green bowl, Rose patted her behind and said, "A couple of days here, and we'll fill out those cheeks." She danced around the counter before Lia could slap away her hand. Lia flipped up a middle finger, and Rose blew a kiss across the counter. She withdrew a loin of lamb from the refrigerator and elbowed the door shut. "Besides, you're not a guest," Rose said. "You're family."

Lia had arrived in the United States as a freshman at Brown University, one of the few without family to help move her into the dorm. She didn't know a soul in the States, and she wore her loneliness like a suit of armor. When asked where she was from, Lia would shrug and say, "Africa and Europe. It's a long story." It took too much effort to explain that Papà had been raised in an enormous, cluttered clan north of Venice and that Maman had been an only child, a daughter of Languedoc. Lia kept secret that her parents had been physicians for the same relief agency in Africa, that they'd met in Mogadishu, fallen in love, married, and had a little girl—Lia—who grew up thinking of Somalia as home.

It was too painful to tell how, when she was twelve, a bomb blast at a refugee camp had killed her parents and ended her childhood. She'd been forced to leave Somalia, shuffled like a card into the deck of her father's family in Italy, spending summers with her maternal grandparents in southern France until a scholarship brought her to an American university. She landed with an accent no one could place and a tangle of amber curls that barely covered the chip on her shoulder. Lia felt she'd lived everywhere but belonged nowhere, least of all amid a crowd of loud American teenagers. By the time she realized that her dismissive reply made her seem pretentious, her reserve had been mistaken as haughtiness, and her looks posed a threat to her dorm mates, she'd already spent that first semester alone.

Turning up in January from New Orleans with a posse of sisters and aunts, Rose Chouteau moved in her skin with a ballerina's grace and had a laugh Lia wanted to live inside. Rose claimed her, knocking the "I am a rock, I am an island" attitude into Providence Harbor. She promised to teach her to knit if Lia would teach her Occitan, the old language of southern France and northern Spain that Lia had spoken at home with her mother and in France with her grandparents. Rose spoke flawless French with a molasses drawl, but as her Occitan vocabulary grew, they fell into speaking their secret language together. Years after they'd graduated, Rose married a wine-grower who brought her to his home in Languedoc-Roussillon.

"César, Cloé! *Laissez ça tranquille!*" Rose snapped at the golden retrievers, who'd trotted into the kitchen following the scent of lamb. Without further command, the dogs sank onto squares of sunlight on the tile floor. "How are you, Lia? Really?" she asked, switching to English. Occitan had been their secret language in the States, but in France, they fell into English when they were alone. Lia knew that Rose, tucked away in the Languedoc countryside, ached to speak her native tongue.

"I'm still a bit numb," she admitted. "Between jet lag and my usual insomnia, the last few nights have been rough." The words to describe the flash of a man's face, the exhilarating sight of the Bonelli's eagle, and the imprint of a palm on the window stopped in her throat, caught somewhere between the absurdity of the images and the desire to hold them secret until she could explain them away as jet lag and fatigue. She joined Rose at the kitchen island and began slicing red potatoes and turnips into quarters to roast alongside the lamb. "But being here, sur-rounded by this place I love…" She waved the knife, taking in the sweep of the view from the kitchen windows. "My heart and head are opening again. If I finish my dissertation and get through the defense, I can look for a permanent position here." She smiled as Rose sent up a small cheer. "There's something I need to tell you," Lia said.

Rose pressed the pilot switch for the oven, and the gas ignited with a soft whoosh. She leaned against the counter. "What's happened?" she asked.

"I heard from the attorneys in Montpellier just before I left Seattle. It's been a year and half, and the police still have no leads on the Mercedes. They're setting aside the investigation until new evidence comes to light. Which it probably never will."

"Oh, Lia."

She'd known it was coming. Gabriel, a professional mountain bike racer, had died alone on a road just a few miles from the finish line of the Tour d'Arques. His body told one story: he'd somehow been thrown clear of his bike, and the landing had shattered the upper vertebrae of his spine. The paint chips on his bike and the pieces of headlight scattered on the pavement told another: a late-model black Mercedes had flattened the bike's carbon and aluminum frame. It wasn't an easy car to miss on the back roads of the Pyrénées, but the Mercedes had vanished. Left behind were Gabriel's broken body, a trail of tire marks on the tarmac, and his mangled bike.

"Maybe it's for the best," said Lia. "Closing the investigation, I mean. I think it's time I move on with my life."

"What about the lawsuit?"

Lia continued chopping, the whacks of the knife punctuating her words. "The attorneys insist we still have a solid civil case against the Federation." No one could explain why Gabriel had veered from the trail in the hills, emerging onto the road over half a mile away from the designated juncture. But the question of how a car had entered the closed-off highway during the race had led to a lawsuit against the Fédération des vététistes—the Federation of Mountain Cyclists—which had sponsored the three-day race through the foothills of the Pyrénées. "Honestly, the longer this goes on, the more certain I am that Gabriel would be against this lawsuit. The Federation nurtured him from the beginning. Money can't tell me the truth about what happened. It won't bring him back. I have Gabriel's life insurance, and once the condo sells, I'll have that too. I don't need anything, Rosie. I'll sort out the details later."

"Honey, I don't mean to push. I know the money can't replace Gabriel, but it could let you find the life you want."

"The life I want?" Lia set the knife on the counter and laid her palms flat to steady herself. "I'm not even certain what that is. My heart is shattered, and my career is in shambles." She gripped the counter. "I don't know if I came here to start over or to run away."

"Right now, the why isn't important. What matters is that you came home. And Le Pèlerin is yours for as long as you need." Rose met Lia's declarations with stern affection.

"Be careful." Lia winked, trying to lighten the mood. "I may take you up on your offer."

Commotion in the dining room signaled an end to their few moments alone. Domènec and the children returned, Joël sporting a streak of soot on one cheek and a Lenten-like smudge between his eyes. Domènec slipped an arm around his wife's waist, and Rose slipped back into French.

"If there's dirt, Jo will be sure to find it." She licked the pad of her thumb and bent to swipe at the soot on her son's face.

"*Chérie*, the fire is blazing away, thanks to my helpers here," said Domènec. "I'm taking the kids with me to pick up those vine trellis locks from Alain."

"On Christmas Eve?"

"Vines don't take holidays."

Rose rolled her eyes at Lia and kissed her husband. "Jo and Esmé need a nap before dinner," she said. "Just be back by four."

Domènec clicked his tongue, and the dogs scrabbled to attention, eager to be on the move again. The women followed and bundled Joël and Esmé into their car seats in the rear of the aging Land Rover, while the dogs panted and smacked their tails against the cargo door. The children blew kisses, and Domènec pulled away with a honk and a wave. Rose and Lia retreated to the quiet kitchen.

Rose arranged the lamb loin in a large cast-iron casserole and slid the dish into the hot oven. "How about some tea?" She shook a container of loose-leaf Assam.

"Please. Strong and black," Lia said. "I'll need help to make it to bedtime without a nap."

They moved to the front room, where the fire snapped and hummed. Rose poured the steaming tea into two mugs and added milk and two cubes of sugar to hers. Lia left her tea to cool on the low table in front of the sofa and tucked her legs beneath her.

"I worry about you in the cottage all by yourself," Rose said as she peered over the rim of her mug. "Not that it's not safe in Minerve. I just hate the thought of you alone."

Lia gave a Gallic shrug of her shoulders, the gesture reminding her of her mother and grandmother as much as her sea-green eyes did when she looked into a mirror. "Alone is just what I need to be. I can take this time to finish my dissertation and figure out what to do next." She picked up her tea and blew across the hot surface. Then it dawned on her. "You have someone for me to meet, don't you?"

Rose dropped her eyes, but she couldn't hide a small grin of conspiratorial pleasure.

"Oh God, Rose, the thought of meeting anyone now, of trying to explain my loss and my life... I can't bear it."

"I know, honey. I just worry about you closing yourself off from the possibility. What you had with Gabriel was precious. But that doesn't mean you won't love again."

"What's his name?" Lia asked to have something— anything—to say.

"Raoul," Rose replied. "Raoul Arango. He's a winemaker from Spain. Dom met him last year when Raoul inherited the old Logis du Martinet down in Lagrasse."

"If it were anyone else but you, *ma copine*, I would be pissed." Lia clutched her mug, worrying her fingers on the handle. So often Rose was able to voice the thoughts that Lia was too afraid to admit. And Lia wasn't ready to admit that she didn't want to be alone.

"He's crazy beautiful to boot."

"You're hopeless." Lia pushed her feet against Rose's legs, giving her a gentle shove.

Rose yelped and raised her mug high to avoid spilling the hot liquid. She squeezed Lia's toes with her other hand. "Maybe it's because I know your type, but there's something about Raoul that reminds me of Gabriel." Rose watched her carefully, as if worried that she might have gone too far. Lia offered a small smile to show her it was all right. "He lost his wife and children a few years ago in some sort of accident," Rose continued. "The kids were twins, just toddlers, about Jo's age, I think." She shuddered. "I'm not sure what happened, but it must have been terrible."

Unspeakable sorrow sank into the air between the two women, and they fell into their own thoughts.

Lia's greatest regret since Gabriel's death was having no children of his to cherish. She couldn't begin to make sense of how a man bore the loss of his wife and children, but she didn't think she was capable of helping anyone else with their pain. If grief was the price of love, maybe it was better to remain alone.

"I'm not ready to meet anyone, Rosie," she said again after a long, full silence.

"I know. I won't push, I promise. But Raoul and Dom have become friends, so if I invite him to our midwinter party, don't think I'm trying to set you up. We just want our friends to be together."

Lia sighed in mock exasperation, but Rose's phone trilled, and the moment of sisterly intimacy was broken. Lia returned to the kitchen to give Rose some privacy, and in the bright light of day, surrounded by the farm's cheerful bustle, her sorrow faded, along with the images of the man and the eagle.

NARBONNE—JANUARY

*T*he holidays came and went, the new year arrived, and finally, Lia received a call from Father Jordí Bonafé. On a fresh morning in mid-January, she drove to Narbonne and parked just outside the center of town. Early for their ten o'clock appointment, she wandered the small city's boulevards and through its squares, rediscovering favorite haunts.

Winter might return to deliver an icy slap at any time, but an exuberant sun found a way to leapfrog the season into spring, and it beamed white-gold through the bare branches of the chestnut and plane trees that lined the translucent waters of the Canal de la Robine. The tramontane wind had swept down from the Massif Central during the night and scoured the clouds from the sky before rushing out to sea, leaving a brilliant blue stillness in its wake.

Lia walked into the covered pavilion of the *marché*. Fish caught before dawn released aromas of the sea that mingled with the scent of vanilla-sweet crepe batter on a hot griddle and the sultry whiff of cumin and cardamom as spice merchants opened their bags. A tiny patisserie stood tucked between the long, refrigerated cases of a cheese-monger and a vendor of cured meats. The shop specialized in the pastries of Catalunya, the territory just across the Spanish border that shared so much of Languedoc's history and culture, and Lia made her last purchases there. She meandered from the pavilion and across the canal to the Place de l'Hôtel de Ville.

The Gothic facade of the Palais des Archevêques loomed over the open square and pulsed gold in the morning light. A café at the far end came to life as waiters, sullen with sleep, removed chairs perched upside down on tabletops. Waiting tourists sat down the moment a table was cleared, lifting their elbows as an irritated waiter swiped a damp rag over the surface and smacked down small pots of sugar and shakers of pepper and salt.

Lia took a seat on a low wall surrounding the preserved stretch of the Via Domitia, the oldest portion of the Roman road that had passed through southern France. The monument was set at one end of the square, a perfect perch to watch Narbonne greet the day. From her basket, she took out a small stainless steel thermos of coffee and a tender, yeasty brioche.

She filled the thermos cup, and when she brought the steaming coffee to her lips, she saw him at a table on the edge of the café's patio. Wearing a black suit and a pale lavender dress shirt, he sat with one arm stretched across the back of a chair and a black leather loafer resting on the opposite knee. An espresso and a croissant sat on the tiny table before him like props on a stage set. A breeze funneling through the passage lifted his golden-brown hair. Sunglasses shielded his eyes from the glare of sunlight on wet stone, sunlight that glinted off a platinum watch as he raised the miniature cup to sip his coffee.

He glanced at the watch and stood, his suit falling into place over long limbs. Even the most insignificant gestures—placing coins on the table, smoothing his jacket—were sensual, and from behind her sunglasses, Lia's eyes lingered over his trim, graceful frame. Imagining toned muscles underneath the elegant, bespoke suit, she bit her lip against a rush of desire.

The stab of guilt that followed her body's yearning dimmed the brightness of the day. The coffee tasted sour, and the brioche had staled in the cool air. Lia turned her back on the café and dumped the black coffee on the cobblestones. Standing, she brushed crumbs from the front of her loose, gray wool trousers.

"Lia Carrer?" She glanced over her shoulder, and surprise became an awkward self-awareness. She wondered if she had coffee breath or crumbs on her face, and she resisted the urge to touch her hair, lick her lips.

"Pardon me for disturbing you." The man from the café removed his sunglasses to reveal ebony irises ringed by bands of gold. "I'm Lucas Moisset, a freelance photographer. I was working for the Federation of Mountain Cyclists that day, in Arques." His broad Languedoc vowels were clipped by a Parisian inflection. "I recognized you from photos. I am so sorry for your loss."

Lia flinched. Her mouth opened to repeat the canned reassurance she offered to everyone. But she found she couldn't say "Thank you" or "It's all right." All she could manage was "What a strange coincidence."

"I'm also a mountain bike enthusiast," he said. His gaze drifted over her like he was searching for something. It made Lia more uncomfortable than if he'd merely ogled her. A roué she could shut down and walk away from. But he seemed sincere. "I was devastated by what happened. Everyone connected with the circuit had such great respect for your husband."

This softened her. "You're kind to say that about Gabriel," she replied. "I should be prepared for memories to come from the most unlikely places now that I'm back in Languedoc." She wondered if she should recognize Lucas Moisset, if they'd met before. She would surely remember so striking a face.

He pulled a thin wallet from the inner breast pocket of his jacket. "My studio is here in Narbonne. If there is anything you need, call me at any time." He handed her a business card.

It took a moment to recognize the watermark of the bird etched behind his name: a peregrine falcon. The same shape as the brass plaque that bore the name of her cottage in Minerve. *Pèlerin*, a pilgrim who makes a journey to a holy place; *faucon pèlerin*, the majestic bird of prey that haunts the Languedoc skies. *Moisset* meant *falcon* in Occitan.

"Very clever play on your name," she said.

Lucas tilted one corner of his mouth. "Of course, you speak Occitan. I recall reading that you're a professor of medieval history. And that you have family roots in the area?"

Again, Lia dug around in the jumbled cabinet of her memory. Maybe she'd met him the day of the accident. Those hours— from the moment she saw the ambulance pull away from the finish line in Arques where she waited for Gabriel to arrive and her heart exploded in horrific premonition, until she collapsed at the hospital when he was pronounced dead on arrival—were a blur.

"My mother was raised in Languedoc," Lia confirmed, feeling vulnerable with this stranger who seemed to know so much. "But I'm no longer a professor. Just an eternal student trying to finish her doctoral dissertation." She closed her hand over his business card. "And if you'll excuse me, I have an appointment." She picked up the basket and wrapped her arms around it, creating a barrier between herself and Lucas Moisset. "No, of course. I understand." He placed his sunglasses back on the bridge of his nose; her somber face was reflected in the lenses. Lucas extended a hand, and in reflex, Lia met it with her own. Her hand felt lost in the firm grip of his smooth skin and fine bones, and the connection lasted just a moment too long. Then Lucas released her. "Take care, Lia." He walked in the direction of rue de l'Ancien Courrier.

A couple dressed in matching calfskin coats and sleek leather boots approached the Roman monument where Lia stood, alone and exposed, as she watched Lucas disappear into a passageway. They trilled in Castilian Spanish, ignoring her. Behind them, three men in business suits, their polished loafers clicking on the paving stones, discussed a marketing plan in rapid-fire French. They broke around her like a wave.

The heels of Lia's boots tapped in staccato rhythm as she walked into the covered Passage de l'Ancre. Her destination was Cathédrale Saint-Just et Saint-Pasteur, the centerpiece of Narbonne's medieval past. She detoured into the Jardin des Archevêques to catch a breathtaking glimpse of the cathedral's mighty flying buttresses before returning to the fourteenth-century cloisters. Pulling on the cathedral's door, she entered the nave with her eyes closed. Only when the door clicked shut behind her did she open them. The full grandeur of Saint-Just et Saint-Pasteur rose before her.

Lined on either side by dark wood choir stalls and stone pillars, with a vaulted ceiling that loomed 130 feet above, the immense chancel exuded somber weight. High in the upper walls, windows of jewel-toned glass glowed. Someone coughed, and the sound reverberated through the vast expanse. The echoes sank between cracks in the stone floor.

Clinging scents of incense and candle wax wafted over the ancient layer of mold. A small, dark-haired woman wearing a floral print dress and a pink apron—she could have been anywhere between thirty-five and fifty-five—polished a panel of filigreed walnut. A bell sounded, sonorous and slow, tolling ten times.

Lia passed unnoticed behind the chapels and into a hallway leading to the drab administrative offices. A cup of coffee steamed on the front desk, but the outer area was empty. She waited a heartbeat before skirting behind the counter and tiptoeing to the corridor. She peered in both directions, but there was no sign of the cathedral's Cerberus: secretary Madame Josephine Isner, who guarded the cathedral's inner sanctum with a hair-shirt personality and a whip-sharp tongue. Lia seized the moment and quick-stepped down the short corridor to the right. The fluorescent lights reflected dully on the white-and-tan-checked linoleum floors.

She rapped on a low door marked *Abbé J. Bonafé*. It opened immediately, and she found herself in the embrace of a short, corpulent Catalan priest who smelled of old books and aftershave.

"Lia, *ma fille*." The tension she'd carried from her encounter with Lucas Moisset in the Place de l'Hôtel de Ville dissolved at the sound of Jordí Bonafé's warm and welcoming voice.

"Father Bonafé." She stooped to kiss each cheek. "It's wonderful to see you again."

He held her at arm's length, and the sparkle in his nut-brown eyes stilled. "You're too thin," he said. "But lovely as ever."

He led her into his office, where the sun cast spotlights across overflowing bookshelves and a massive oak desk. An ancient computer hummed in the center of the desk, and manila file folders were scattered across the ink blotter, nearly burying a turquoise rotary phone and an outdated intercom. Just to the left of the door, a wing chair upholstered in worn brocade and a sofa set behind a low table formed a small sitting area. The office was exactly the same as the first time she'd seen it two summers before.

"Nothing ever changes here—not you, certainly not this cathedral. It's so reassuring," she said.

"Yes, well, if more people in this heathen country worshipped, perhaps there would be enough money to renovate this heap." Father Bonafé huffed. Motioning Lia to the sofa, he settled into the chair with a sigh. On the table stained by round water marks sat a tray with two cups and saucers, a teapot in the shape of an elephant, and a delft-blue platter covered with a yellow linen cloth.

"Now, for the more immediate problem—filling out your flesh." Chuckling, he rubbed his palms together and folded back the cloth. Placed in two neat rows on the platter were a dozen golden *xuixos*, a deep-fried pastry filled with custard, the specialty of Father Bonafé's Catalan hometown of Girona. The aroma of cinnamon and browned butter was a sensual mix of comfort and seduction.

With a groan, Lia pulled a wax paper bag from the basket at her feet and handed it to the priest. She'd purchased a dozen *xuixos* at the Catalan bakery. "I see we share the same predilection for sinful pleasures."

He peered inside and clapped his hands in delight. "These are from Iolanda's stall!"

"Perhaps you can offer those instead of a Communion wafer," she teased.

He selected a pastry from the tray and nibbled with an affected delicacy before setting it on a saucer.

"I'm not nearly so restrained," she said and bit a *xuixo* in half, one hand underneath the pastry to catch the oozing cream. Crystals of sugar clung to her lips, and her eyes closed as the intoxicating mix of fat and sugar melted on her tongue. One heady taste was enough.

"Have you come home for good?" Father Bonafé asked as he filled their cups. She waved away his offer of milk and chased the brazenly sweet pastry with bitter black tea.

"Is this my home?" she mused. "Somalia has only the ghosts of my parents and childhood memories. Papà's family hates that I'm alone and so far away, but if I returned to Italy, there would be an endless stream of second cousins and family friends I'd have to meet. Potential suitors," she added in response to the priest's questioning look. Lia leaned into the cushions piled onto the sofa and balanced her cup and saucer in one hand. "The only place that answered when I asked myself 'Where do I belong?' was here. Languedoc. I had to get out of Seattle, Father. There's nothing and no one for me there."

"It seems that in America, death is viewed as something almost shameful, not spoken of in polite company," said Father Bonafé. "I don't sense much respect for the ritual of mourning."

"There is an expectation that you must pick up and move on," Lia agreed. "People stop calling after a while. But I don't blame them. No one wants to be around a young widow. It's just too sad." Her gaze drifted to the windows and the cloisters beyond. "I've spent all these years considering how the Cathars viewed the afterlife, their belief that souls are reborn to play out their destinies on earth. Yet I've always considered reincarnation as some sort of primitive mysticism," she said. "But now that this has happened to me again—losing someone I love before their time—the Cathars' sense of the continuity of life seems so full of hope. There's always a chance for redemption." She turned back to Father Bonafé. "How is reincarnation any more farfetched than heaven and hell?"

The outer corners of the priest's eyes crinkled in a canny smile, but to her relief, he didn't offer pat guidance. Hers was a question without an answer.

Lia's hand shook as she set her cup and saucer on the table, and she hugged a small pillow to her chest. She wasn't sure if she was speaking as a researcher to a fellow scholar or as a grieving widow to a man trained to offer comfort, but it no longer seemed to matter. The borders between personal anguish and scholarly interest dissolved in this storied setting.

"For a long time, I wanted to believe in their world," she said quietly, squaring the pillow on her lap and smoothing its embroidered surface. "I prayed that Gabriel waited for me in some in-between place, and he'd find a way back to me." To her dismay, tears burned her eyes. "Ah, damn. Just when I think I'm done with the crying." She pushed the pillow aside and pressed a paper napkin against each eye. "I can't carry that anger with me, Father. No more than I can carry around the belief that Gabriel will come back."

"So there's no room in your heart for a life beyond this, Lia? Either the heaven I peddle or the reincarnation and redemption that your beloved Cathars preached? No hope that you will see your husband again in some other world or time?"

She pressed her lips together and made tiny rips in the napkin. Without looking up, she said, "It's not lost on me, as someone who rejected God long ago, that I've made it my life's work to study a mystical faith, and yet I have no beliefs of my own. No way to frame my own grief with rituals of remembrance and letting go. Perhaps that's why I've felt so lost." She crumpled the napkin and met Father Bonafé's eyes. "But no. There is no life but this."

The room was still except for the hum from the aging computer. Lia took the opportunity to change the subject.

"The one thing I do know is that I have to face my dissertation." She grimaced. "I'm too late to save my job but hopefully not too late to salvage my dignity." Lia mentally crossed her fingers. "I'm hoping you can help me access the archives at the Institute for Cathar Studies. There are documents there I need to see, but I've been trying to make contact for days and no one returns my calls or answers my emails."

Father Bonafé cleared his throat and placed his cup and saucer on the table. "Lia, it's been kept out of the press, but the institute is nearly kaput." He made a slicing motion across his neck. "Funding dried up during the recession, and the government has no means to bail it out. The trustees fear that once the institute declares bankruptcy, its holdings will be auctioned off to private collectors to pay its debts."

"What?" Lia sat upright, knocking her knees against the coffee table. The bone china clinked in delicate protest. "This is a disaster. Father Bonafé, I have to get in there to use those materials. I need to see the originals—the Internet and reproductions can only take me so far. Oh my God. I'm so close to finishing, and now this."

The priest held up a hand. "Not to worry, my dear scholar. We've determined the collection will not fall into the hands of strangers. A few trusted archivists in Languedoc-Roussillon will guard the institute's holdings until a permanent solution can be found. And this is between you and me. We'd rather the public not know just yet."

Lia sank back. "Is that kind of distribution legal?" she asked.

"Well, it's not technically illegal." Father Bonafé lifted the teapot lid and peered inside.

His studied nonchalance sounded a distant alarm in Lia's

mind, and she held out her hands in mock approbation. "So I should assuage my conscience knowing those artifacts will be safely tucked away here and there? How will I find what I need? Who's on this list of 'trusted archivists'?" She was surprised at the snap in her voice.

He didn't reply, and her question dropped between them in a stalemate. She wondered if behind his stony stare, Father Bonafé regretted confiding in her. But she pushed on. "Is the cathedral receiving anything from the archives?"

The priest topped off his cup and took his time sipping and swallowing his tea. At last, he nodded.

"Father Bonafé." Madame Isner's tart voice crackled into the room over the intercom. "The rector would like to see you as soon as you have a spare moment." The intercom whooshed and snapped, signaling the secretary still had her finger on the button, awaiting a response.

"I'll be right out, Madame Isner," the priest replied.

"And would you please inform your guest that sneaking into back offices is quite against protocol? This is why we have a waiting area. Visitors should be prepared to wait." Claiming the last word, Madame Isner silenced the intercom.

Father Bonafé pulled a face at the machine and then winked at Lia. "I swear she can see through these walls."

He walked her down the hall and through a back exit to the sunlit cloisters, bypassing the vexed secretary. Once outside, he said, "Lia, there are documents in the institute's archives that have escaped notice. The administration has been far too focused on staying afloat to keep up, and they've had to dismiss most of an already meager staff. I'd hoped to enlist your assistance in sorting through some recent acquisitions and transcribing the original Occitan."

A frisson of anticipation vibrated in her belly. "That email you sent... What did you write?" She dug around in her bag and retrieved a Moleskine notebook. "Here, the line was so perfect, I wrote it down: *What seemed like legend carried through time on the flimsy backs of folktales and rumor now appears plausible as history.*" She slapped the notebook against her open palm and shifted on her feet. "Father Bonafé, have you found something related to Pierre de Castelnau?"

The noncommittal shrug and the shifting away of the priest's eyes in the seconds before he replied shot a tendril of doubt through Lia's excitement. "It's too soon to say. Once the materials are in my possession, I'll be in touch." He placed a hand on her arm. "And please, call me Jordí. I insist, Lia. We're talking as friends and historians, not as priest to parishioner."

She wasn't ready to be dismissed, not just yet. "Father— Jordí—the idea that someone would remove priceless documents from the institute, even if the goal is a noble one, I just... This secrecy feels wrong." He answered with a weary exhalation that said nothing and meant everything, but Lia pressed on. "Those documents belong to the French people, to French history, not hidden away in a church basement or someone's cellar."

"A church basement?" Her friend bristled at the suggestion that the cathedral's subterranean library was a mere basement.

"Sorry, that was petty. But these materials should be available to anyone who applies to view them through the proper channels."

"Lia, you must trust me on this." His brown irises, which so easily melted with laughter, had hardened into petrified wood, and his singsong, Spanish-accented French became clipped with tension. "If private collectors cannibalize the institute's archives, we may never see those materials again. The fewer people who know, the better it is for the integrity of the collection. Now, I must run." He said his farewells and left her standing in the sunshine and yet in the dark.

Lia crossed the cloisters and returned to the empyreal nave of Saint-Just et Saint-Pasteur, trying to sort her aching curiosity from her professional disquietude.

LE PÈLERIN, MINERVE—EARLY FEBRUARY

*A*n email from Lucas Moisset arrived at the end of January, through the portal of Lia's LinkedIn profile, just as the sharp memory of their encounter had dulled to a lingering curiosity. She scanned the message quickly, then took a breath and a seat to reread it. Once again, he caught her off guard.

Dear Lia,

I hope you're well. Again, I offer my apologies for taking you by surprise in Narbonne. It occurred to me after we met that you'd be an ideal collaborator for a project I'm working on, so I have a business proposition for you. I could explain it over the phone or in another email, but it would be easiest in person, since it involves your research (which I'd like to

hear more about) and my photography. Could you meet me
Friday for dinner?

She clicked Reply but sat with her fingers poised on the key-
board for many long minutes, unable to respond. Finally, leaving
the cursor blinking on a blank window, Lia pushed back her
chair and changed into her running gear. Maybe pounding her
feet against the pavement would deplete her anxiety. The diver-
sion worked—until she returned from her run an hour later,
only to see her computer waiting on the dining room table.

Before she had time to change her mind, she sat in her sweaty
clothes and quickly started typing.

Bonjour, Lucas.
    Thanks for the email and dinner invitation. I'd be
delighted to talk about my research, though you should be
careful what you wish for. I'm likely to bore you to tears.
Dinner Friday would be

She paused, staring off into the distance. Having dinner with
a man she found so attractive would be nerve-racking. It would
feel wrong. It would be a relief.

"It's just dinner, Lia," she muttered as she typed *lovely* to end
the sentence. Then she hit Send.

Two emails later—he hadn't asked for her phone number,
and she hadn't offered—they'd agreed to meet at La Cauquilha,
a seafood bistro in Gruissan, at eight o'clock. Then she booked
an appointment at Salon Anouck in Narbonne.

NARBONNE—FRIDAY AFTERNOON

Lia rushed from the medieval alleyway off rue Littré to the

Place de Verdun. From the busy boulevard Gambetta, she darted through the crowds until the doors of Salon Anouck appeared before her.

Inside the salon, quiet murmurs of stylists ministering to their clients wafted through the warm, softly humid air. Ushered into a plush chair in the foyer, she was offered a glass of wine or something hot to drink. As much as she would have liked the wine, she opted for green tea. Lia planned to drive straight from the salon to the restaurant in Gruissan. The receptionist relieved her of the garment bag that held her change of clothes, assuring Lia it would be waiting in a private changing room after her hair and makeup session.

This salon visit was long overdue. For months, Lia had done little more than pull her tangle of curls into a low chignon and brush a wand of mascara across her upper lashes. She'd borrowed a couple of cashmere sweaters and wool and silk trousers from Rose, to replace the fleece and denim that had been her Seattle uniform. But she'd refused to care any more than that.

Yet she'd become acutely conscious of her haphazard appearance since arriving in France. She was surrounded by sublime people whose elegance seemed effortless yet studied. The women were sleek and shiny as mink, their skin flawless and polished; the men had manicured hands and left clouds of sweet tobacco and orange trailing behind as they passed.

Comparing her rough presentation to the women around her, Lia was reminded of how her mother could look poised and cool in surgical scrubs in the relentless African heat, while her untamed daughter carried the desert sand and city mud on her clothes and smeared across her tanned cheeks. Her grandmother had tried, during those summers Lia spent in Limoux after her parents died, to nurture the sense of style she declared innate in all French women. But Lia, a grieving and bewildered preteen struggling to assert her independence amid the gaggle of Italian cousins, had insisted she was African. Not French, not Italian, but a white child of Somalia. And now, she wanted nothing more than to be embraced by the Languedoc culture and to make it her own.

Once seated in a reclining spa chair, Lia surrendered to the ethereal music drifting from hidden speakers. She dozed in the heated chair, its built-in roller gently pulsing up and down her spine, while her hands and feet were massaged and her nails painted. Then she moved to a stylist's station, where a young woman with a short cap of black hair set in finger waves washed and conditioned Lia's hair, leaving her in a cloud of jasmine and musk.

Moments later, a woman arrived, dressed in a fitted black top with a mandarin collar and slim black capris, her shining blond hair pulled into a severe ponytail high on her head. The woman placed her finely manicured hands on Lia's shoulders. She introduced herself as Élodie, the stylist who would bring some order to Lia's hair and see to her makeup. They exchanged a few cursory pleasantries as Élodie stood behind her, considering Lia's curls and split ends. She separated and pinned up Lia's wet locks and made some styling suggestions, to which Lia readily agreed, but then, mercifully, their conversation ended. Lia closed her eyes again and imagined the evening ahead. Her nerves were knotted tight at the prospect of dinner with Lucas.

An hour later, Élodie spun Lia's chair to face the mirror, and all thoughts of dinner evaporated from Lia's mind. She hardly recognized the woman facing her. Her hair had been blown into gentle waves, parted on one side and tucked behind her ears. The light caught its natural shades of brown, amber, and gold. Élodie had perfected the art of barely there makeup, and Lia's skin and eyes shone with life and light she hadn't seen since before Gabriel's death.

Those eyes filled with tears as pride and loneliness washed over her. After cooing and dabbing away Lia's tears, Élodie swept a soft brush over Lia's neck and face and whisked off the silky black sheath. The raven-haired assistant returned to lead Lia to a private room at the back of the salon, where she slipped into a clinging wrap dress of dark teal jersey with a plunging neckline and stepped into tall heels with delicate straps crisscrossing her ankles.

She took stock of her mood. She'd told Rose about the encounter with Lucas in Narbonne and of tonight's meeting, but she'd downplayed the photographer's looks and skipped over his charisma. Unsettled by the thought that she was betraying Gabriel by having dinner with another man, she reminded herself again that it wasn't a date.

So why the new dress, the heels, the makeup, the hair? she asked her reflection.

And her reflection replied, *Because you're alive, Lia. Forgive yourself for that.*

She folded her other clothes into a shopping bag, picked up a pashmina wrap from the padded bench, and turned her back on herself.

Lia parked outside Gruissan's medieval center and stepped carefully across the loose gravel lot to a covered passageway. Following the passage to its end, she emerged at the foot of rue de la République.

Lucas waited for her outside the restaurant. He wore black wool trousers and a gray button-down shirt, with a cashmere sweater the blue-gray of the winter sea draped over his shoulders. From his widened eyes and half smile, she knew she'd made an impression. Her ankles wobbled in her heels...or was that her heart skipping a beat? They exchanged cheek kisses, his fingers encircling her forearm.

"Lia. You look beautiful."

She'd intended to be aloof and untouchable, but with one gesture, he'd made her feel as self-conscious as a teenager on her first date.

Lucas held the door open, and she entered La Cauquilha. Clatter from the open kitchen, the clink of flatware against china, and the buzz of conversation bounced off the cozy bistro's Grecian-blue ceilings, shell-white walls, and polished wood floors. Nearly every table was occupied, and several heads turned at their entrance.

A waiter, wearing a spotless white shirt and a black apron that draped to his shoes, swept by with plates of food cascading down one arm. He acknowledged them with a cheery "*Bonsoir, madame, monsieur*" and tilted his head to his left, indicating an empty table in the far corner. Lucas said something to the waiter out of Lia's earshot before ushering her to the table, one hand touching the small of her back.

A trio of votive candles set in glass bowls filled with sand sparkled on the table. Lucas pulled out her chair and waited for her to sit before taking his seat. Servers dipped in and out to fill their water glasses and deliver a bread basket.

"I'm so glad you came," Lucas said after their orders had been taken.

"Did you think I wouldn't?"

"I wondered if you'd think it was too soon."

Before she could ask "Too soon for what?" the sommelier appeared at their table with a bottle of Blanquette de Limoux and presented it for approval.

"I thought this almost-spring evening called for a celebration," said Lucas. "Do you mind if we start with sparkling wine?"

"Of course not," she replied. "Blanquette is one of my favorites."

He nodded to the sommelier, and the discreet ceremony proceeded. The first taste was offered to Lucas, who deferred to Lia. She drank in the wine's bouquet of white blossoms and nectarine and swirled its bracing effervescence in her mouth.

"It's perfect." She smiled at the sommelier. He filled their flutes and set the bottle in the bucket of ice and water that rested in a stand beside the table.

Lucas raised his glass. "To winters that feel like spring," he said.

She touched her glass to his. "To fresh starts." They danced around what had brought them together with chatter about the restaurant and the delightfully warm weather and compared notes on their favorite Languedoc wines.

At last, Lia smoothed her hands across the linen tablecloth. She'd had enough of small talk. "So tell me about this business proposition. Your email was cryptic, but you got my attention."

Lucas rested an elbow on the back of his chair, his other hand toying with the stem of his wine flute. Watching him, Lia thought of that old Carly Simon song her parents used to play. They mangled the American accent with their French- and Italian-inflected English, but she still remembered the line about a man walking into a party like it was a yacht. Lucas had that same inscrutable self-possession.

"It's simple, really," he said. "Several months ago, a colleague and I submitted a proposal to a British publishing company for a book on historic Cathar sights throughout the Languedoc region. You know, one of those glossy, coffee-table books with lots of panoramic shots of castle ruins at sunset, snowcapped peaks in the distance?"

Lia nodded, smiling. She had such a book, one of the few things she'd saved from her parents' home. She'd perused it so many times, the spine was cracked. The photographs brought her to the places she loved, no matter how far away she might be.

Lucas continued. "The proposal was accepted, and the publisher offered us a contract, but my coauthor—a historian who was writing the text—pulled out a few weeks ago. A family situation I won't go into. And it turns out, in all these months, he'd hardly written a thing. I still have a few months of layout and design ahead of me, so it's not a crisis yet. But with an early summer deadline for the first draft, it may soon be."

Lia remained still, hoping for and dreading what she knew he was about to ask.

"After I saw you in Narbonne, I pulled up as many of your articles and transcripts of your lectures as I could find online, even your course syllabi." He sat forward and pressed his palms together. The distance between their faces could be measured in inches. She inhaled his cologne and the mint of toothpaste on his breath. "I realized I could never have collaborated with this other historian. What little he'd written sounded straight out of a tourist's guidebook. He's not even French. Lia, there's no one who can capture the Languedoc spirit, who can take dry facts and make them come alive, the way you can. You know this place—its languages, its secrets."

The waiter arrived with their starter plates of mussels with rouille and grilled octopus on saffron rice. As they ate, Lucas described the contract he'd negotiated, and the sums of money floored Lia, accustomed as she was to the pittances paid by academic presses. She laughed and held up her hand to stop him. Her mind was whirling.

"This is a lot to get my head around. I'm supposed to be finishing my dissertation." She thought of the boxes of research she'd sent ahead from Seattle, of the cursor flashing on her blank computer screen. But to work on a living project that would be in the public's hands within a year, not forgotten on a shelf along with all the other dissertations… "Tell me more," she said.

Lucas took his time outlining the book and his vision for the editorial content, patiently answering Lia's many questions. The text accompanying his photos would tell the history of the villages and Cathar strongholds spread across the Aude and Hérault Valleys, the Black Mountain range, and the foothills of the Pyrénées.

Their conversation was interrupted again, this time by the presentation of their entrées of seared tuna in a shiitake sauce. Lia tasted and approved the aged Provençal rosé made with the obscure Tibouren grape that she'd selected as their dinner wine.

"What could I say to convince you to work with me on this book? If we approached the publisher, made them aware of your work, I'm certain they'd grant us an extension. You could finish your dissertation and pick up the book when you're ready."

Lia's ears rang with the words *we* and *us*. She drained the rosé from her glass and glanced around the restaurant. Couples sat with their heads bent toward one another in murmured conversation, sipping wine and slipping knives through succulent fish. She caught her and Lucas's reflections in the large front window. Lean and elegant, so finely dressed, they looked as though they belonged together.

The appearance of the waiter in the reflection brought her back to the table.

"How is your meal?" he asked Lia.

"It's perfect."

The waiter dipped his head and glided away.

"About that dissertation." She nodded as Lucas lifted the bottle, offering to pour her more wine. "I'd been writing about the nature of Cathar religious beliefs, particularly the afterlife and their belief in reincarnation, but since Gabriel's death…" Lia adjusted the linen napkin in her lap, buying a moment to steady herself. "It's become almost too personal. As though I need to come to terms with my own feelings about death and an afterlife before I can keep writing about the Cathars." Caught between an ache to talk about Gabriel and the need to bind her grief tightly, she opted for a change of subject.

"My regret now is that I didn't start with the question of how and why the Cathar Crusade began. I'm so near the end of this dissertation, and I have to finish the work I started, but I can't get my mind off the murder of Archdeacon Pierre de Castelnau." She sliced through tuna as pink as the rosé in her glass, unaware that Lucas had gone completely still, his eyes cold as iron. "He was murdered in January 1208," she said. "In the midst of mediating a land dispute between Raymond VI, the Count of Toulouse, and Hugh de Baux, the Viscount of Marseilles. History has it that Castelnau was ambushed on his way to parley with the viscount, supposedly by a mercenary of Toulouse's." She bit into the silky flesh of the seared tuna.

"Toulouse was a known Cathar sympathizer," Lucas said in a clipped tone. "The Church was trying to give his land to a rival. What greater motive could there be for Castelnau's death?"

Lia was shaking her head before Lucas had finished speaking. "Toulouse wasn't that committed to the Cathars. He just liked their economic policies. To the Cathars, the Church represented unmitigated greed. The sympathizers—those wealthy landowners and nobility like the count—tolerated the heretics because they didn't demand tribute like the Church. Toulouse wanted to keep his subjects happy, but even more than that, he wanted to keep his wealth in place. And in turn, the Church loathed the Cathars for their rejection of tithing and papal taxation." She was beginning to warm up to her theories. "The Vatican had been after the Cathars for years. They hired mercenaries—knights even—to wreak havoc in Languedoc villages and terrorize the heretics or anyone who seemed friendly with them." She held up her knife, stabbing at the air to emphasize her point. "Then Pierre de Castelnau, the pope's own appointed emissary, is murdered by a known sympathizer, the Count of Toulouse? It's much too convenient a coincidence."

Lia took Lucas's wrinkled brow and silence for confusion and set down her knife and fork to explain. "I believe the Vatican was looking for an excuse to launch genocide," she said. "The Cathars declared themselves free from the earthly chains of greed and wealth. They believed in the equality of men. And of women. That's what the Catholic Church feared: loss of money and loss of power. The Church and its lackeys, the Knights Templar, used Castelnau's murder to declare war against the so-called heretics. His death broke the stealth campaign against the Cathars wide open. I think the Church orchestrated Castelnau's assassination, but I want to know why they chose someone as highly placed as the archdeacon. Was it merely because his death would attract so much attention? Or was he murdered for something he knew, not just for who he was?"

To her surprise, Lucas set his napkin on the table and pushed back his chair. "Would you excuse me for a moment?"

He was gone before she had a chance to respond.

SAINT-GILLES, PROVENCE-LANGUEDOC BORDER—JANUARY 1208

*L*ucas Mauléon approached the church from the southern
end of the square. He waited in the shadows, observing
the low front of the great abbey and its three portico doors.
Two cats bounded across the square, one hissing as it chased the
other, feral toms fighting over scant scraps. Otherwise, it was
quiet. It was only days past the darkest hours of the season, and
dawn was slow to come, but soon the church bells would ring
for the sunrise service of lauds.

He crossed to the abbey's central portico, where the dual
handles of iron were unchained, and pushed against one half
of the door. The polished wood whispered as it glided over
worn stone.

Archdeacon Pierre de Castelnau stood before the altar with

his back to the entrance, smoothing an embroidered cloth across a low wooden table where the bread and wine of the Eucharist would be arranged. White bursts of air trailed his movements as he chanted.

"Reverend, would you spare a moment for a blessing?"

Castelnau yelped and spun around, the heavy gold chains at his neck clinking. "Goodness, man, you startled me." He clutched at the ermine borders of the cloak he wore over his black soutane and drew them closed.

"You should be more careful." Lucas walked toward the altar with a measured pace. "These are uncertain times. You never know who might wander in uninvited."

The archdeacon sniffed and covered his shock with a smirk. "If I'd known you were coming, I would have arranged for a more gracious reception." He smoothed his robe and his tone, attempting to regain control. Squinting into the dim light of the nave, he asked, "But why are you wearing Toulouse's coat of arms? Is it possible that you've switched allegiance from the king to a renegade count and I hadn't heard?"

Letting the question hang in the air, Lucas bent to retrieve a long, slim knife from his boot scabbard. He traced a slow arc in the air, and Castelnau flinched as the silver blade gleamed in the candlelight.

"What is the meaning of this? How dare you brandish that weapon in God's own house?" Then his eyes bulged, and his mouth opened and closed as he struggled for his voice. "It's true." His gasp echoed in every corner of the sanctuary. "I was warned that Plessis would betray me, but I never believed he would condemn me to death."

Lucas hesitated at this last pronouncement. Only he and his commander, Philippe du Plessis, knew of the mission that brought him south, so close to his boyhood home. Who had betrayed them to the archdeacon? But he could spare no time for reflection. Betrayal wouldn't change what he'd promised to do or had been promised as a reward. The command had been given, and his hand belonged to those who wielded the most power. Hesitation would mean failure.

His shadow grew as he strode forward, and it vanished as the two bodies met. He clasped Castelnau around the back of the neck, bearing down on the space between muscle and bone, and drew the archdeacon to his chest in a tight embrace. The older man struggled as the knife caught on the thick fabric of his wool robes, but his limbs went rigid when the blade sunk deep into his flesh. Castelnau clutched at Lucas with one hand, babbling in pain. "I have seen the spirit of God," he wheezed. "They are not heretics. They are the Trinity."

Lucas withdrew his arm and released his grip on the archdeacon's neck. He moved away as Castelnau slumped to the ground, unaware of the rectangle of white that dropped from the archdeacon's hand and slid underneath the altar. He peered into the shadows of the nave, his nostrils flaring.

Then he sank to one knee beside the priest, wiping the red blade on the fur lining of the archdeacon's cloak. Castelnau's eyes opened. A bubble formed at his lips, then burst, and a thin trickle of blood ran down his jaw. He blinked once and was still. Lucas bent an ear to the archdeacon's mouth and held his own breath as he listened.

Satisfied, Lucas replaced the knife in its scabbard and straightened to his full height. His long stride carried him to the door, where he paused, his head cocked. Hearing only the scratches of mice in the straw, he pulled up his hood and opened the door. But he remained in place, allowing the door to close before him. Then he slipped back into the shadows of the nave.

With silent steps, Lucas moved toward the squat figure crouched beside a column to the left of the altar. Approaching from behind, he pressed the blade of his knife against the exposed skin above the cowl of the monk's robe. The rotund young man froze. The knife's edge kissed the rolls of fat on the back of his neck, and Lucas imagined the skin parting like a ripe peach. He bent over and encircled the soft chest with one long arm. The monk gave off a rank miasma of fear.

"Whatever you saw and heard, it was enough, wasn't it?" He spoke in *langue d'oc.* "There's no reason to kill you." The monk wobbled his head. "You'll wait until dawn. Then you will ring the church bell as for lauds. You'll ring until the entire village is here to see the slain body of the archdeacon. You will tell them that as you approached the church, you saw a man running away. And that man was wearing the coat of arms of the Count of Toulouse. Speak, so I know you understand."

"I saw your surcoat. You are Toulouse's man." The monk's voice emerged as a squeak.

"What is your name? You aren't from the region."

"J-Jordí Baltasar B-Bonafé," he stammered. "Of Girona, Catalunya."

"You will live to bear witness to what happened here today, Jordí Baltasar Bonafé of Girona, Catalunya. I will guarantee your safety if you do as you are told. Do you understand?" Lucas laid a hand on the young man's shoulder and squeezed, his fingers displacing fat as they ground into the monk's collarbone.

The monk gasped in pain and nodded rapidly to signal his assent.

The nave carried no sound of Lucas's thick leather soles crossing the aisle, no sound of the door closing behind him.

❧

A thin strip of gold lined with rose etched the Luberon range to the northeast. Dawn was near. Lucas strode down the sheep tracks that led from the village walls to the fields beyond.

Achille whinnied at his approach. Lucas caressed the horse's forehead, and the courser pressed into him, nosing in his cloak for a hidden piece of bread or carrot. He held the great horse by the neck and shuddered.

He'd killed before, of course, but as a Templar knight—a Soldier of Christ—on the battlefields of the Fourth Crusade in Anatolia, far from home. There too he'd seen the faces of those he was about to slay, but they had shown neither fear nor bewilderment. His victims were soldier-warriors, as he had been, merciless in their frenzy to survive and slaughter. The sword blade, the knifepoint, or the ax head could have been turned against him, and his opponent never would have hesitated. On a battlefield, hesitation meant certain death.

Pierre de Castelnau was different. He'd been unarmed, a man of God, and he had not surrendered in silence. *I have seen the spirit of God*, Castelnau had gibbered in his last moments. *They are not heretics. They are the Trinity*. Lucas shook his head. The nonsensical moaning of a dying man mattered not.

Achille huffed his restlessness, and his front hooves pawed at the frozen ground; it was time to leave. Lucas removed his cloak and the tunic underneath. He folded the red cloth embroidered with a twelve-point cross into a small bundle, pressing it tightly to his chest to flatten the material before shoving it to the bottom of a saddlebag.

He'd worn the pilfered cloak in anticipation of being seen; Toulouse's coat of arms would be enough to implicate the count. A witness saying he'd seen a man bearing the symbol of the House of Toulouse leaving the church where Castelnau had been assassinated was a welcome opportunity. And he had a name, a frightened monk known as Jordí Bonafé, who may prove to be useful beyond ringing a church bell in alarm.

The stallion's ears sprang up as the pealing of bells ripped through the serene meadow. Private triumph rippled through Lucas. He had done as commanded and could claim his reward. The new sénéchal of the Aude and Hérault Valleys, the most powerful keeper of the law in Languedoc, grabbed the pommel of his saddle, stepped into the stirrup, and swung a leg over the horse's back in one confident uplift of his lean body. Before this new year grew much older, Lucas—who had abandoned his Occitan name, Moisset, to become the French soldier known as Mauléon—would appear in his former Languedoc home, victorious at last.

With a glance at the eastern sky, Lucas pressed his heels into Achille's side. Man and horse sped toward Paris.

BISTRO LA CAUQUILHA, GRUISSAN—FRIDAY EVENING

Lucas returned to the table a few minutes later, the stray locks of hair that fell across his forehead separated and damp as though he'd splashed his face with water. He regarded Lia calmly but gave no explanation for his abrupt exit.

"Thanks for showing interest in my research," Lia offered in awkward apology. She'd obviously made some sort of gaffe, but she had groped through their conversation while he was in the bathroom and couldn't figure out where she'd gone wrong. "It's not often I find someone willing to let me drone on about dualist theology or Vatican intrigue."

"It all sounds like the making of a great conspiracy theory," Lucas replied. The corners of his mouth lifted, but the smile did not reach his eyes.

"Yes, I know." She sighed dramatically, hoping for levity.

"The dark and mysterious Knights Templar make for bestselling novels and blockbuster movies. But behind every cliché, there is an element of truth, isn't there? Otherwise, the legends wouldn't work."

"It was a long time ago," Lucas said, considering his half-finished meal. His voice was so soft, he seemed to be speaking more to himself than to her. He looked up, and the gold flecks in his irises glinted in the light of the low-hanging pendant lamp. "I should have asked how long you plan on staying in Minerve."

"I don't have a time frame," she replied. "But my dearest friends are close by, and my father's family is just a few hours' drive away. My life's work surrounds me. There doesn't seem any place I should be but here. I'll need to sort out somewhere permanent to live, but for now, Minerve is home."

"I imagine Languedoc is full of distressing memories."

She cast a glance around the restaurant to avoid the emotion she was certain her eyes betrayed. "Maybe it was wrong to have come back to the place where Gabriel died. But I have to forgive France for his death. Too much of my soul is here. Gabriel's soul is here." She stopped, aware she was sharing her most personal longings with a man she hardly knew.

Lucas placed a hand on top of hers, and she froze at the startling intimacy of his warm skin. "The Cathars believed a tragic death could condemn a soul to the hell of rebirth on earth instead of passing to eternal paradise," he said. "It's natural to hope to see your husband again."

Lia sucked in her ire and embarrassment. "Wow. That's one hell of an assumption. I'm researching a belief in reincarnation, not hanging my heart on a fantasy."

Behind Lucas, flames roared up from the open kitchen, and the diners around them gasped. A chef shook a pan over the stove and tossed prawns in the flambé. In the moment before the flames died out, Lia pulled away her hand and hoped the low light hid the flush on her face.

"I shouldn't have pried." He spoke slowly, breaking the tension. His hand remained on her side of the small table, his tapered fingers reaching toward her. "It was a ridiculous thing to say." A passing waiter cleared their dinner plates, breaking into his apology. They refused the dessert menu. Instead, Lucas ordered a ristretto, and she asked for a cappuccino.

The hands on the square copper clock behind the bar pointed out the time on its numberless face: almost eleven. It seemed impossible that three hours had passed.

After dinner, they entered the maze of confined streets that coursed through Gruissan's medieval center. Lia thought she'd parked in a lot off avenue Général Azibert, but when they crossed the perimeter road, the lot was nowhere to be found.

"I'm certain it's not far. Really, I can find my way from here."

But Lucas wouldn't hear of Lia wandering around Gruissan alone. He was unhurried, but she felt ridiculous. How could she have lost her way? Continuing along rue du Fort, they passed a restaurant overlooking the salt marshes. A few kitchen staff and waiters stood just beyond a side door, shifting their feet in the cold and burning through cigarettes with short, intense drags. Within moments, she and Lucas emerged in an open space familiar to Lia, since she'd driven onto its gravel surface a few hours before.

Several cars filled the lot, but they walked straight to her Peugeot, Lucas's hand still on her back, a rudder to steer her body. Whether she led the way or he knew the direction, Lia didn't want to know.

When Lucas took his hand away, an imprint of heat remained on her skin. She pressed the Unlock button on the key fob. The car chirped twice, and the lock released with a click. Lia turned back to Lucas, her arms crossed over her torso, clutching her tiny purse. "Thank you."

"It was my pleasure," he replied. A breeze gusted in from the sea and sent dried leaves and scraps of paper scuttling between the cars. "I take your research seriously, Lia. I hope you don't think I was trying to belittle your work earlier."

"No, of course not."

Lucas tucked loose strands of hair behind her ear, and his hand skimmed her cheek before falling away. His touch thrilled her and stirred up longing and loneliness. He reached around her and opened the car door. "Good night. Drive safely."

In her rearview mirror, she saw him watching, motionless, as she drove away.

Lia's dreams that night flickered like an old movie reel. Gabriel flew past on his bike, spinning toward danger. Lucas stood on the other side of the road, silently holding out his hand.

A third man appeared by her side. A scar ran down one cheek, inflamed and red, ugly in the bright light. But his eyes were warm. He opened his mouth, and his lips formed her name, but she couldn't hear his voice. He too extended a hand to her but looked sharply away. A Mercedes bore down on them, and the sound of screeching tires filled her ears.

She woke with a throbbing head. The sheet was soaked with sweat, and she shivered as her damp skin cooled and the memory of the dream returned. She whispered Gabriel's name over and over, an incantation of sorrow, until sleep took her away at last.

CARCASSONNE—MID-FEBRUARY

*D*ull light and stagnant air sank heavily into Carcassonne's
dreary streets. Lia paced in front of the shaded windows
of the Institute for Cathar Studies, her cell phone pressed
against her ear. Through the glass front doors, she could hear
the institute's phone ring and ring, her call echoing in the dark,
unattended space. The sign on the locked front door stated the
institute was closed indefinitely.

She was also waiting on Father Bonafé—*Jordí*. He'd left a
message on her phone late the night before, long after she'd
gone to bed, his first contact since her visit to Narbonne the
previous month. He'd assured her someone would be at the
institute to open the doors for them at 9:00 a.m.

Jordí hadn't given any details about the last-minute

arrangements, but she dared to hope it was an opportunity to see documents few knew existed—and to be a witness to their safekeeping. She'd driven from Minerve in a state of shaky anticipation. But it wasn't only from excitement at seeing the collection. A few days following their dinner in Gruissan, she'd called the cell number on Lucas's business card.

"Let's talk more about this book," she'd said. He sent web links of sample layouts. Lia's excitement for the project began to build when she saw how skillfully his photographs captured Languedoc's craggy beauty and the haunting Cathar ruins. Light warmed or chilled the stone, depending upon the time of day and season of the year; he'd conveyed the intensity of the sun and wind by showing the timeless natural world interacting with man-made antiquity. Her mind was already crafting the accompanying text, weaving a narrative of fact with the living, breathing past.

Early that morning, it struck her: Lucas and Jordí should meet. She'd left a rushed message on Lucas's voice mail: "I know it's last minute, but could you meet me at the Institute for Cathar Studies in Carcassonne today? There's someone I'd like to introduce to you. Afterward, we could head up to the Cité for those interior shots you need of the basilica. Just a thought. Call me."

And he had, while she was in the shower. She listened to his message, holding a towel closed with her arms. "I can be there, Lia. But who is this 'someone'?"

She laughed when her return call went straight to his voice mail. "Tag, you're it," she said in English, then continued in French, "I'm so glad you'll be there. It's my friend Jordí Bonafé. He's the archivist at Saint-Just et Saint-Pasteur. Meet us at noon." She knew Jordí would never allow a stranger into the collection, but they could all meet later, after she'd viewed the archives, and have some lunch.

She had tapped out a quick text message to Jordí: Sorry, short notice. Invited photographer Lucas Moisset to lunch. Noon, Institute. Explain later.

Neither man had responded before she left for Carcassonne, an hour's drive southwest of Minerve. But a text beeped through the endless ringing of her call to the institute. She disconnected the pointless call and opened the message, cursing as she read the text: Won't make it today. Can't reach contact at ICS. So sorry, try again soon. Fr. Jordí.

Frustrated, she walked back to her car and tossed her laptop bag onto the Peugeot's backseat. Once behind the wheel, she punched out a message to Lucas: Don't come to town. Institute closed. Meet me at basilica.

Lia slammed the car into reverse, peeling out of the institute's parking lot, the Peugeot's tires squealing on the wet pavement. She steered out of town and up to Languedoc's most famous site: the medieval fortress city perched above Carcassonne.

SAINT-GILLES, PROVENCE-LANGUEDOC BORDER—JANUARY 1208

The young monk crouched behind a carved column, hidden in the shadows of the nave, his knuckles stuffed in his mouth to stifle a scream. His knees, bent against the cold stone, shot nails of pain down his shins. Round and dark, Jordí Bonafé had arrived in Saint-Gilles from the Sant Benet de Bages monastery in Catalunya only days before.

He heard the church door snick shut. Whispering a prayer for courage, Jordí rose on shaking legs and shuffled to Castelnau. The monk fell to his knees before the archdeacon, flinching at the naked expression of horror in the dead man's open eyes, the pain in his twisted mouth. Blood pooled around the upper half of the body, coagulating in the cold air of the nave. Jordí hoisted his bulk and stumbled to the altar, where he uncorked a small vial of olive oil and upturned it against his thumb. He returned to the slain priest's side and knelt by his head.

He closed the archdeacon's eyelids and anointed them with blessed oil, speaking the words to send his soul to eternal rest with God. "*Requiem aeternam dona eis, Domine.*" It was not the extreme unction the slain papal legate deserved, but Jordí could do no more.

When he made the sign of the cross over the archdeacon, Jordí saw that the man's right arm was bent beneath his body at a severe angle. It was one indignity he could correct. He grunted as he rolled the body onto its side, and the archdeacon's sodden cloak pulled away from a pool of blood with a wet sound. Jordí's gorge rose in disgust, and bile stung his throat, but he tugged the crooked arm free.

Castelnau's hand fell with a hideous thump onto the step below, and a leather pouch unfurled in his palm. The finely tooled calfskin glowed warmly in the candlelight, though the edges were stained red. Using two fingers, Jordí removed the spoiled pouch and laid it on the step away from the body and the blood.

The archdeacon's other arm was flung wide, his hand empty. Jordí crouched behind him and lifted his shoulders, silently asking God's forgiveness for this morbid curiosity. There was nothing underneath the priest.

He lowered the body carefully, cradling the head until it came to rest on the stone tile, and moved Castelnau's arms to his sides. Blowing air through puffed cheeks, he looked around the altar and into the nave. The shadows were shifting from black to gray as the first thread of light seeped in the eastern window high above the altar. He shuddered at the memory of the knife against his neck and the low voice growling in his ear. Jordí prepared himself to lie, for how could he admit he'd been too great a coward to do more than witness the murder of Archdeacon Pierre de Castelnau? He would say he'd been sent on an errand by the archdeacon and only saw a man fleeing the abbey. A man wearing Toulouse's coat of arms.

A triangle of cream caught his eye. Jordí crossed the dais, grimacing at the stiffness in his legs. With the toe of his sandaled foot, he pulled the scrap out from the bottom edge of the silk *broderie* covering the altar.

It was a folded sheet of vellum bearing a red wax seal, but the wax was cracked and the seal split in two. The missive had been opened. Jordí pressed the two halves of the seal together until they formed an image of a standing bear in profile. He retrieved the leather wallet from the step and saw that another insignia had been branded onto the leather flap. This seal showed two knights riding one horse, encircled by a border of Latin words: *Sigillum Militum Xpisti*. The seal of the Soldiers of Christ. Although the bear meant nothing to him, Jordí recognized the symbol of the Knights Templar, and it filled him with a sense of doom. Blood throbbed in his ears, a drumbeat that said, *Leave it be, Jordí Baltasar Bonafé. Leave it be.* He knew he should drop the letter and let wiser heads take over this horror.

He opened the sheet.

Heavy, scrawling Latin text nearly filled one page, but the correspondence bore no salutation or signature, only a date: December 1207. At the bottom, a different hand had penned two lines in delicate script. As Jordí absorbed the words, his heart pounded so hard he couldn't swallow, and his hands were clammy with sweat.

A rooster crowed in the distance, and another answered. Weighed down by shock, Jordí collected the bloodied leather pouch from the side of Castelnau's corpse and found the spot behind a grand column where he'd witnessed the assassination. There, a stone tile had shifted under his feet as he'd crouched in terror. He wiped the pouch on his robe and tucked the vellum inside.

Working a fingernail between the loose mortar and stone, Jordí pried up a corner of the tile, and the rest of it broke free. He dug out a hollow in the dirt below and buried the leather pouch in the cold space. After replacing the tile, he trod over the stone, using his bulk to press it level with the others.

He passed down the aisle and melted into the blackness behind the altar. A few minutes later, the church bell began to clang. First in a slow, steady peal, and then faster, losing rhythm, its notes of panic sweeping across the village and into the plains beyond.

CARCASSONNE—MID-FEBRUARY

*M*ore than three million tourists swarmed over the Disney-like facade of Carcassonne's medieval Cité every year. Lia preferred Languedoc's lonely, ruined citadels, with their shattered stones and hollow towers and courtyards overrun with brush, haunted by the ghosts of Cathar history and legend. Yet she admitted, as the celestial vision of the Cité rose from the fog above Carcassonne, the vast fortress was magnificent. Its intact walls, turrets, and towers had endured hundreds of years of battles and occupation to become one of France's greatest cultural treasures.

Although muted sunlight had clambered through the layer of fog to warm the gray walls, clouds thickened as the morning moved on, and the Cité was shrouded in mist. The trinket shops were open for business, but their doors remained closed against the chill. Lia skirted past a group of tourists disembarking from a bus with German plates and sought out the Basilique Saint-Nazaire et Saint-Celse.

The nave was empty and cold. Votive candles flickered in aisle chapels—the only sign that worshippers had been here before her on this somber morning. Despite the eerie silence and jumping shadows, the massive nave enchanted Lia anew. Its arched ceiling was vaulted by six enormous spans that led east to the choir, where glorious panels of stained glass towered over the altar. Long pews formed rows that disappeared into the dark.

Lia edged down a row near the vault of Saint-Pierre and sat beside a column that stretched to the ceiling, huddling in her down jacket. She closed her eyes and calmed her mind until her breathing slowed. She heard footfalls but didn't turn, certain it was a tourist. She dreaded catching anyone's eye, wanting only to remain in the quiet space of her meditation. The steps faded.

Moments later, footsteps whispered again across the basilica's tile floor, breaking her concentration. A warm current of air ran between her feet, carrying with it the scent of pine and warm hay. This time, her skin tingled. She rose and slipped past the column, entering the dark aisle of chapels along the western wall.

From the pillars on her right, a figure appeared. It was a man, not much taller than she but with a powerful build. As black as a shadow, he moved swiftly toward her. He wore a hooded, black wool sweater, stretched and torn, and jeans worn at the knees. His heavy boots were caked with mud. Suddenly, he was before her.

"Paloma," he said, reaching out.

Lia drew back in alarm. "I'm not Paloma." Her sharp voice ricocheted off the stone and tile.

"You were followed here," he stated in a low and soothing voice, as if she were a child or a frightened animal in need of calming. "You're not safe."

It jolted her to realize he was speaking in Occitan, the ancient language of Languedoc. His hooded face, his torn clothing—he was clearly mad. Although rattled by their bizarre exchange, Lia responded in the same calm tone, hoping to send the man on his way.

"I think you have me confused with someone else. But it's all right. Just leave me to enjoy this peaceful place." Her hand closed around the phone in her pocket, and she wondered if she could dial 17 for the local police without looking at the screen. Yet she didn't move away. A small voice chimed from deep inside her, *You're safe.*

Air streamed through the vast space again, but unlike before, there was no warmth, no scent of summer. It was icy cold. The candles set in candelabras flickered, and several winked out as if invisible fingers had pinched their wicks. A door banged against the wall, followed by footsteps striding across the stone floor. Instinctively, Lia looked toward the sound, but no one appeared.

When she looked back, the man had his shoulder pressed against a small, wooden door set inside the chapel wall. She heard the soft scrape of wood against stone, and a fug of cold, moldy air poured from the open door.

"He's inside the church. You must come with me." She backed away, but in a motion so fluid she had no time to react, the man was behind her, one gloved hand over her mouth. "Paloma," he whispered in her ear. "I am asking you to trust me. Please. Now."

The iron vise of his arm wrapped around her chest, clamping her arms to her sides, and he propelled her toward the darkness.

"Watch your head," he said, and absurdly, Lia ducked, passing into a black space. The man pressed in behind, and she heard a click. She knew she should fight back, but claustrophobia paralyzed her reason. The blackness was so complete, Lia felt suffocated.

"Let me out," she moaned, staggering backward on watery knees. Then she shoved past him in a frenzy of fear and groped at the wood in front of her, searching for a handle. "I can't breathe!" she screamed. Her horror at being trapped in this enclosed space subsumed her fear of this delusional stranger.

"It's just a short distance to the outer door." The calm voice was meant to soothe her mania, even as strong hands pinned her arms to her sides. Only hope of a way out kept her from flailing against him with fists and feet.

The man took the lead as they plunged down a corridor, one of Lia's icy hands clenched in his warm fingers. Her elbows brushed against the sides of the passageway, and the top of her head skimmed the ceiling. They were in an impossibly small space. Panic gripped tighter at her throat, and her every thought was a shriek. They pressed through the darkness, turning corner after corner for an eternity, until he stopped abruptly and Lia collided with his solid back. She heard a thump. He backed into her hard, and she was pushed farther back into the corridor. Sanity slipped. Again a thump. The man grunted with effort and cursed.

"Please, please, please," she whispered, collapsing to the earth. It was damp and reeked of sealed tombs and forgotten places. Then he was in front of her, his hands touching her shoulders as he searched for her face in the dark.

"I need you to stand up and move back. This door hasn't been opened in a long time, and it's wedged shut. Please, I promise I will get you out."

Lia clung to the wall as she half stood, half crawled backward. A loud crack reverberated, and a sliver of light appeared. A shadow shifted, blocking the light, and there was the sound of wood splintering.

Light flooded in and, with it, cold, sweet air. The wind howled through, churning up the earth at the exit created in the stone. The man continued to kick at the wood of the broken door until the hole was wide enough to pass through, and then he lifted her to her feet. Lia pulled out of his grasp and reeled over the threshold, gasping raggedly for air. He came to her side and laid a hand on her back.

"Don't touch me." Lia jerked away.

He removed his hand but remained beside her, waiting until she calmed. The wind cut through her sweater, and her bare hands shook as she zipped up her jacket. The knitted scarf that had hung loosely around her neck was gone.

At last, he pushed back his hood, revealing a pallid face that was split on one side by a scar. It ran red and angry from his left temple to the corner of his mouth, recently—and badly— healed. Her broken mind strained to make a connection.

"You're not safe here," he insisted. "Follow the path back into town. I'll find you there."

For one wild moment, she thought he was Gabriel. Those deep brown eyes regarding her with love and sorrow made her want to reach out and... With a shudder, she dropped her head into her cold hands. Then a shift in the air pulled her head up again. Thick, moist air flowed from the wreck of the doorway they'd exited through, colder than the chill wind that blew her hair into her face. She was alone.

Lia stood on the edge of a cliff just outside the Cité's walls. The overcast sky hung heavy with a coming storm over the valley of vineyards to the south. Across the Aude River, Carcassonne huddled in the dim light, a gray, crumbling carcass of past glory. The rush of traffic on the distant A9 and an occasional wailing siren from the city's streets assured Lia she was still in the present world. She pulled her phone from her pocket, but the screen was blank. She pressed the power switch and waited until the familiar apple symbol showed gray against the black void. No reception. Not a single bar.

In the stillness, Lia began to doubt what had happened in the basilica. The man's sudden appearance, the stranger who was so disturbingly familiar, was upsetting enough. But with his disappearance, reality shook free of its tether, and she considered the possibility that she was losing her mind.

As she leaned over the edge, she braced herself against a boulder that jutted into the air. A hair's width of a trail was just visible on the far left edge of the cliff, created perhaps by wild animals and enlarged by humans. Cigarette butts, a cracked Kronenbourg bottle, a discarded tennis shoe, and condoms were scattered alongside. Lia scooted over the edge on her behind, her toes straining. Her feet touched down, and she inched sideways along the eroding dirt path.

Once on solid ground, Lia looked back, but the ledge where they had emerged from the basilica was out of sight. A flash of white and brown sparked at the corner of her vision. A bird of prey looped and swirled on an air current, folded its wings, and dove into the vineyards below. Lia watched the place where it had vanished, but the bird did not reappear. She continued down the path, and soon she emerged on a gravel road that led to a sidewalk of chipped and broken cement.

She crossed onto a side street she knew in the small city, walking past the open garage doors of an automotive repair shop, a plumbing supply store for contractors, a grimy *tabac*. Men in blue coveralls or sweatshirts and denims stopped their work to watch. There were a few leers and some friendly smiles, but no one troubled Lia. The sight of their humble figures and the sound of their mellifluous French or melodic Arabic was a balm poured over her frayed nerves.

A familiar shape with lean shoulders and a crown of dark gold hair appeared half a street ahead. She picked up her pace. "Lucas!" she shouted. Abruptly, he veered left into a passageway. Lia followed. It wasn't a through street but an alley that ended in a low brick wall with a closed wooden door set inside. She faltered and stepped back. She'd had enough of low, close spaces.

Lia's feet carried her in the direction of the signs pointing south—*Centre Ville*, the center of town. The streets widened to allow the passage of cars, and soon she was forced onto the sidewalk. She approached the entrance to a hotel, where several taxis waited.

A taxi driver took her to the lot near the Cité where she'd left her car just a few hours before but a lifetime ago. She sat in her car, watching the thick clouds gather in a downy layer across the horizon. Finally, she called Lucas.

"Lia! I tried calling, but your phone was out of service range. Where are you?"

"I'm—" The cold weight of fatigue pressed down on her. "I'm sorry, Lucas, I think I'm coming down with the flu… I'm chilled and feverish. I just need to get back to Minerve."

His hesitation lasted two heartbeats. "No, of course, take care of yourself. I have plenty to do here."

"Are you at the basilica?"

"Yes. I've been waiting for you."

"It's just that I thought…" She looked around the parking lot. Her Peugeot, two taxis, and four large tour buses were the only vehicles. Of course, Lucas could have parked elsewhere, but this was the closest lot to the Cité's entrance.

"Lia?"

"Nothing. I'm not making any sense." Lia wanted to be far away from Carcassonne and this bewildering day. "I'll call you next week? Again, I'm sorry. I hope I haven't wasted your time."

As she pulled away from the citadel grounds, the pregnant skies opened and the rain burst forth.

MAS HIVERT, FERRALS-LES-CORBIÈRES—TWO DAYS LATER

*L*ia coasted down the drive to Rose and Domènec's house, sighing when she saw it already crowded with cars. She'd avoided large gatherings, preferring the isolation of Le Pèlerin, the anonymity of wandering alone in cities and citadels, or the comfort of Rose's company, where nothing had to be explained to be understood.

She'd almost canceled today. The ordeal in Carcassonne had exhausted her courage. Lia had spent the next day bundled in a sweater and sweats, curled under blankets on the sofa before the fire, hands wrapped around a mug of tea; she couldn't get warm or breathe deeply enough. She replayed the scene in the basilica over and over, bewildered that she hadn't fought back, unable to make sense of the conflicting emotions of panic at being trapped and trust in the stranger who'd held her.

But this was the Hiverts' annual midwinter fete, their last chance to relax and unwind with friends and family before the round of obligatory wine conventions, followed by spring's intense work in the vineyard, consumed their days until summer. There was no question but that she would be there—she was family.

Winter had returned overnight. There was a silvery tinge to the sky, and the air shimmered with frost. As she walked around the house to the kitchen door, the first cool feathers of snow floated down. Her heart soared, and despite her urge to run from the gathering, Lia felt festive and hopeful.

The kitchen was warm and alive with cooking and children. A roasted goose rested on top of the stove, the golden-brown skin of one leg poking from underneath the loose cover of foil. Etta James crooned from speakers mounted high in the wall. A young woman Lia didn't recognize sat in the corner nook coloring with Joël, Esmé, and two other toddlers.

"Did you see that?" Lia set a basket on the counter filled with her homemade chocolate chip cookies, a bag of Italian-roast coffee beans, a bouquet of hothouse flowers, and a bottle of single malt Scotch.

"See what?" Rose was pitting a bowl of Lucques olives, but she tilted a cheek to receive Lia's kiss.

"Snow!" Lia said the magic word, and the children popped up in their seats to peer out the windows into the frosty yard.

"Snow!" they squealed in unison, clapping their hands and bouncing on their sturdy, squat legs.

"Where is everyone?" Lia opened the glass door of an antique cherry cupboard and retrieved a vase from within.

"The men are out hunting," Rose said. "They stayed up until

the wee hours drinking, but they were up before dawn to scare away pheasants and wild turkeys with their hangovers. I predict within an hour of dinner, they'll all be snoring on sofas."

Lia set the vase—now full of salmon-pink, crimson-red, and cream Gerbera daisies—in the center of the kitchen table and opened her arms to the children's warm bodies. Esmé curled her tiny limbs around Lia's, sinking into her hip, while Joël stood on the seat of his chair and clasped her free arm, eager to show off his coloring book.

"Hello, I'm Lia," she said to the young woman whose arms were full of two toddlers begging to go outside to play in the falling snow.

"Hello," the teen replied, disentangling a small fist from her hair. "Do you remember me? I'm Céline Hivert, Domènec's niece. This is my brother, Jack." She tugged her braid free from the small boy's clutch and smoothed the silky brown hair of a cherub-cheeked girl beside her. "And our cousin, Charlotte."

"Céline?" Lia had last seen her two years before, when Céline was a shy adolescent. She'd blossomed into a lithe teenager in the way that French girls seemed to enter adulthood: wise to the world, already confident in their beauty and charm. Her and Jack's father was Domènec's brother, Jean-Luc. And baby Charlotte was the daughter of Domènec's sister, Marie.

Seeing this small tribe of children and the gracious Céline tore at Lia's heart. Here was a family, complete—siblings and cousins, fostered by loving aunts and uncles and grandparents. It was a joy she and Gabriel had once hoped for.

"Céline is our angel." Rose broke her pensive moment with a slam of the oven door. "The kids adore her, and thank God, they obey her."

Céline stood to give Lia a kiss hello, but further conversation was impossible in the din of the children's voices. Lia helped her dress the squirming brood in parkas, hats, gloves, and tiny Wellington boots and watched as they ran shrieking outside and snatched at the falling snow, Céline close behind.

Once the kitchen was empty of joyful noise, Rose sighed and slipped into English. "We've got a full house."

"I've been preparing myself for the onslaught," said Lia. "But I'm not certain I'm ready for this."

"If you need a break, you know you can walk away. Your room is ready."

"Just keep me busy." She squeezed Rose's arm in gratitude. "What can I do?"

Rose showed her a mound of bread dough resting on the counter. "Do you mind tackling the knead? I assembled the dough but realized I need to make the gravy."

"I'm your girl," Lia replied, relieved to have a task to busy her hands and quiet the nervous chatter in her mind. "Remind me again who will be here," she said as she washed her hands.

"Well, you know Jean-Luc and Jacqueline and the kids. Marie wasn't certain if Paul would come—things have been touchy for them lately. I think he's really trying, but it's tense. Poor little Charlotte, she wants to please them both." Rose paused and snipped off a trio of bay leaves from a tiny potted plant on the counter. "Domènec's parents…where are they? Napping, probably. Greta and Nicolas from the village. Do you remember them from the party we had two summers ago—" She stopped and looked up with a stricken face. That summer's night was the last time they'd all been together before Gabriel died.

"Rose. You don't have to watch what you say around me. Any memory of Gabriel is a good one."

Rose nodded, but her eyes shone with tears.

Lia kept the conversation going. "I remember Nicolas was besotted with a blond Danish goddess who towered over him by at least a foot. They're still together?" Tacky bread dough coated her hands. She continued to gather the pile in a heap, beginning the process of transforming the sticky mess into a silken ball.

"Yes, and getting married in the summer, despite our best efforts to change his mind. She hates getting dirty, for Chrissake. Marrying a farmer."

Lia pressed the heel of her hand into the dough and pushed away. "So that's everyone?" she asked, trying to sound nonchalant. And failing.

"No, honey," Rose replied. "Raoul came out this morning to join the hunting crew." She glanced at Lia, watching for a reaction.

Shaking her head, Lia heaved an exaggerated sigh and winked at Rose. They fell silent, lost in their tasks and thoughts. Nina Simone began singing "O-o-h Child," and they sang along, Rose's contralto harmony sliding beneath Lia's soprano melody.

Lia's hands fell into that familiar, ancient rhythm of knead, gather, quarter turn, knead. She thrust the heel of her hand forward, over and over, sweat collecting around her hairline. Shaking out her arm, she switched sides and began again. She caressed the dough into a ball and set it inside a large ceramic bowl, rolling it gently in the olive oil that had pooled at the bottom. As Lia placed a linen towel over the top, commotion erupted outside the kitchen door.

Laughter and shouting preceded the hunting party's entrance. Thumps and thuds followed as they removed their muddy boots, heavy flannels, and down jackets in the outer room. Domènec entered the kitchen with a brace of pheasants in his hand and a triumphant smile on his windburned face.

"The men have returned. We will not starve," he announced.

Jean-Luc and Nicolas followed, shaking snow from their

hair and rubbing their chilled hands. They greeted the women with kisses and apologies for their muddy clothes, now steaming in the warmth of the kitchen, releasing aromas of tobacco, burning leaves, sweat, and a hint of Cognac. Being surrounded by these men who were so vibrant with life stung Lia with acute loneliness.

"You are not cleaning those in here." Rose stood with arms akimbo. Domènec, holding the birds behind his back, leaned in and kissed her full on the mouth. "*Arrête*—stop!" She melted into a smile.

Jean-Luc took the pheasants, insisting he was the only one who could clean them correctly. He collided with two more men on his way out the door. From the tangle of tired limbs emerged Domènec's brother-in-law, Paul.

Behind Paul stood a man with his head tipped back in easy, full laughter. The kitchen's bright light revealed a scar, partially covered by a shadow of stubble, that ran from his hairline to the corner of his mouth. This was the scarred face that had flared like a candle flame in her window on winter solstice. This was the man who had led Lia through her own personal hell in Carcassonne's basilica and then disappeared.

Lia watched the scene before her as if from a distance—voices faded, motion slowed. "My God. It's you."

In the commotion, no one heard her whisper.

Then the man's brown eyes met hers and widened, and the laughter emptied from his voice and face.

Part Two

···

Le cœur a ses raisons que la raison ne connaît point.
The heart has its reasons that reason knows nothing of.
—BLAISE PASCAL

···

MAS HIVERT, FERRALS-LES-CORBIÈRES—SAME DAY

ia!" Paul appeared before her. He clasped her shoulders with his meaty hands and enfolded her in a crushing hug. His greeting broke the spell, and a cacophony of voices rang as the children exploded into the kitchen in a swirl of snow and barking dogs. Rose and Céline released the children from their zipped jackets and tight boots, while Domènec passed around bottles of cold beer, and Lia busied herself with the mulled cider that simmered on the stove.

As she set a mug of spiced cider on the counter, she scanned the room, but the man had slipped away. Movement beyond the window caught her eye, and she saw him heading toward the barn with a shotgun over his shoulder, the action open and muzzle pointed toward the ground. If he was cleaning the gun, he'd be out there a while.

She had to endure the gauntlet of embraces and chatter in the kitchen, but as soon as she could, Lia slipped out to the mudroom and stepped into a pair of Rose's boots. She waved to Jean-Luc, who'd set up a pheasant-cleaning station on a concrete apron beyond the back patio, and ran through the thin layer of snow.

Inside, the barn was warm and lit by a series of pendant lights hanging from a loft ceiling, and the air was thick with the scent of clean hay and the musk of horse. At the end of a long corridor that ran between the stables, the man leaned over a wooden door, caressing the muzzle of Domènec's beloved bay, Django.

Lia pulled up short, remaining in the shadows, but the door closed behind her with a thump. The man's gaze followed the sound, and he stared at her for a long moment. As he approached, she saw that he was slightly changed from the man she'd met in Carcassonne—older, wearier somehow. His eyes were the same—deep brown and flecked with green and gold—but the skin around them was lined in white, crinkled from squinting into the sun. Soft feathers of gray graced his temples, and strands of silver shot through his close-cropped brown hair. Lia felt again the heart-stopping sensation that she was standing before the ghost of her husband.

"You could be no one else but Lia," he said, extending his hand. "The prodigal daughter returns. Welcome home. I'm Raoul Arango."

Her arm seemed to move of its own accord. She saw the white flash of her palm, felt the sting run from her hand up her arm as it smashed into the side of his face. The crack of her slap echoed through the barn. Tears stung her eyes.

"*Jesucrist*," he swore in Catalan.

"I'm claustrophobic, you son of a bitch!" She swiped at her face with the back of her hand, smearing angry tears.

"You're also insane." His fingertips touched his cheek, and his tongue probed from the other side. His baffled look gave her a moment of triumph and wonder at her own strength. "What was that for?"

"*You're shitting me,*" she spit in English.

Raoul scowled at the ugly hiss; she guessed that even if he didn't understand the words, he grasped their meaning.

"Two days ago?" she continued in French, biting her sentences into chunks. "The basilica? Raving like a madman and shoving me into a tunnel? Who the hell *are* you?" Her voice rose, and she heard the scraping of horse hooves on cement.

"*Valga'm Déu,*" he cursed again in Catalan and scrubbed a hand over his face. "What are you talking about?"

"Do you really not remember?" The anger waned, and bewilderment poured in. "Carcassonne? You called me Paloma."

Raoul stilled at the sound of the name, unwilling or unable to answer. Then he pinched the bridge of his nose as if pushing back a headache.

The side door flew open, and Nicolas entered, stamping the snow from his feet. "Oh, hey! Didn't know anyone was in here. I've been sent on an ice mission." They stared at him. "Just here? In the freezer?" Nicolas jerked a thumb at the large chest freezer humming in a corner.

Raoul broke away from Lia without a word.

The two men pulled bags of ice from the freezer, and as they left the barn, Nicolas tossed a glance over his shoulder at Lia, his eyebrows raised. "Lia, *tu viens?* Are you coming?"

"*J'arrive.* I'm on my way," she replied.

The sounds of snuffling horses, the wind whistling through a crack in a window, and the slow drip of water on cement began to filter through as the pounding of blood eased from her head.

FERRALS-LES-CORBIÈRES—FEBRUARY 1208

The moon rose as Raoul descended to the Orbieu River valley. It was early evening and cloudless; the sunset cast a faded vermilion glow across the scrubland plain. Already the days were lengthening toward spring, but as darkness fell, a wise traveler would be making haste toward shelter. Only a few miles lay between him and his home—he would reach Lagrasse by supper.

Leaving Montpellier later than he'd planned, he bypassed the main road for the hidden byways and sheep trails. News of the archdeacon's assassination by a hired mercenary of the Count of Toulouse had spread west from Saint-Gilles a month before, and rumors of retribution by the Catholic Church followed swiftly behind. Strangers speaking *langue d'oïl*—the language of the French kingdom to the north—had become an increasingly common sight. They traveled on horseback in small groups, openly armed and looking like the soldiers Raoul supposed them to be.

His nostrils flared at the scent of smoke. With the slightest pull of her reins, Mirò stopped. She tensed under Raoul's thighs and fluttered out a questioning whinny. Raoul gathered a handful of forelock and rubbed her mane. "I know, girl, I know," he soothed the disquieted horse.

Taking note of the wind's direction, he turned to see if he was still alone on the rocky trail and out of sight of the main road. He lingered a moment before he gave Mirò's flanks a minute squeeze and flicked the reins to leave the brush for the wide road that led straight to Ferrals-les-Corbières, the last village before his home outside Lagrasse.

Inside the walls, Ferrals-les-Corbières was silent. Daub huts clustered against the great tower like mushrooms on a log, but despite the persistent, acrid odor of smoke, their thatch roofs were still intact. Farther in, stone-and-timber structures offered more security and warmth but no more signs of life than the peasants' lean-tos. Raoul dismounted and followed an alley to the tiny central square that opened before Saint-Genès, Ferrals-les-Corbières's compact, square chapel.

There he saw several men and women carrying buckets of water from the village well into the chapel, while others emerged from its interior bearing loads of wood or stone. They worked with grim determination, the fronts and sleeves of their tunics and smocks soaked with water or sweat despite the chill. It was then he noticed that the arch above the chapel's portal had been shorn in half. Black soot stained the sand-colored brick around the edges of the open door. The missing door, Raoul realized. It was nothing more than clumps of charred wood.

He heard a click and a low whistle. Looking up, he saw a man descending a ladder set against the chapel wall. At his warning sound, those on the ground turned toward Raoul, and work came to a reluctant halt. They glared at him with sullen expressions, the whites of their eyes in stark contrast to their soot-covered faces.

"I'm Raoul d'Aran of Lagrasse," he said, opening his hands to show he held only the reins to his horse. "I'm returning home. What happened here?"

A few snorts followed his question, and most of the villagers went on with their work. An elderly man too feeble to lift the heavy buckets shuffled to Raoul's side, leaning heavily on a cane as though it were a third leg.

"Jaufres Belengers?" he croaked.

"I know old Jaufres," Raoul replied. "His sons run sheep on my land."

The old man nodded, satisfied Raoul was trustworthy. "Jaufres is my cousin. Tell him Tibout wishes him good health, but not so good he outlives me." He laughed, a high, wheezing sound full of phlegm, and placed a bony hand on Raoul's arm to steady himself. "Where have you been that you are not home on this cursed night?"

"I had business in Carcassonne," he lied. "I'm a winemaker and merchant." The latter was true, but it was not his vocation that had taken him away from the village.

"Misfortune can befall a man on these roads after dark."

"I'm sorry for the misfortune here," replied Raoul. He wasn't in the mood for a grandfather's lecture. "But the village doesn't appear damaged beyond the chapel. The fire started inside?"

"No misfortune, this." Tibout spat a glob of gray mucus just beyond the toe of Raoul's boot. "Evil hands set this fire."

A wiry man, perhaps ten years Raoul's senior, snapped his head up from where he was crouched at the well. His cheeks sunk around nearly toothless gums. He hissed at Tibout and threw a glare at Raoul that was thick with contempt.

"It's the French," the old man continued, heedless of the warning. "Since Toulouse had the pope's man killed, Languedoc has become a French soldier's playground."

Raoul needed no further explanation. This hadn't been an accident of candles left unattended, a flame snatched by the wind and tossed at the wooden roof and door, but another sign that revenge for Castelnau's murder was rippling in faster and faster waves through Languedoc's villages. Even as the count proclaimed he was innocent of any conspiracy, the alleged criminal had been torn apart by a mob, and rumors moved from murder to war. Castelnau's assassination had lanced the boil of Languedoc resistance; Paris and Rome would clean the wound of heretics by fire. Raoul walked toward the chapel and was met halfway by the man who had warned the others of his approach from his perch on the ladder.

"You should move on, retake the road to your family. The old man is right. Misadventure follows the solo traveler."

"I can tell you what happened here," said Raoul, ignoring the admonition. "A small band with swords and shields but no coat of arms arrived in the morning after most men had gone to the fields or vineyards. The strangers rounded up the women and old ones here," he said as he swept his arm around the small square. "One or two started the fire in the church, and the others stayed outside to frighten the villagers. By the time you saw the smoke and could return, the riders had fled in the other direction. Am I correct?"

The man folded his arms against his chest and squared his shoulders, looking oddly vulnerable yet determined. "They told the women, 'If there are Cathars among you, banish them, or we'll return to burn them out.'"

Raoul gave a quick tip of his chin to show he understood, that he'd heard it before.

"If they are after heretics, why would they destroy a Christian church?" asked the man, his voice low to hide it from listening ears.

"Forget reason, my friend. It isn't just a religion they want to destroy; it's our land they want to possess."

Raoul left them to pour water on the remaining hot ashes in the church. They could rebuild the roof if the interior frame wasn't badly damaged. Otherwise, the ruined structure would stand as another in a growing collection of crumbling, smoking warning signs that war was coming to Languedoc.

MAS HIVERT, FERRALS-LES-CORBIÈRES—EARLY EVENING

*I*n the kitchen, Rose was giving orders in the final, hectic moments before dinner was served. A platter with ceramic bowls of tapenade, mustards, and relishes sat on the counter. Lia added small saucers of sea salt and two pepper mills and slid the platter onto one palm, calling up her front-of-house skills from waiting tables during her undergraduate days. With her free hand, she opened the pocket door that separated the kitchen from the dining room.

The sound of laughter and music carried from the great room, where the stone fireplace was ablaze with snapping logs. But the dining room was hushed and empty. Lia guided the door closed behind her. Roman blinds of dark wood were tilted to filter the bright reflection of the snow, and the massive walnut table glowed in the low light. Turkish rugs covered the distressed and sanded pine floor.

She set the tray on a buffet next to two decanters of dark red wine and made her way around the table, distributing the condiments. Rose's artfully mismatched dishes and linens added whimsy to the comfortable room. Pinecones dipped in silver paint graced the place settings, and a name card was tied to the base of each pinecone with red ribbon. The names had been printed in metallic gold ink. Lia exhaled in exasperation to see her assigned place was next to Raoul's.

Just as she reached for her name card, there was a muffled thump at the door. She opened it, and Domènec backed in, holding an ice bucket in each hand and linen towels draped over his arms.

"Care for the first taste of champagne? Vilmart 2004 Coeur de Cuvée."

Lia took one heavy bucket and placed it at the far end of the table while Domènec set down the other and lifted up a dripping bottle. With a deft hand, he removed the capsule and cage and gently twisted the bottle until the cork released with a soft hiss. Lia had two champagne flutes ready. Domènec poured a small amount into each and let the froth settle before filling the glasses.

"To midwinter and the promise of spring," she said, tilting her delicate flute. He tapped his glass lightly against hers. Aromas of pear and ginger wafted from the flute's graceful bowl, and citrus bubbles laced her tongue.

"Divine," she pronounced.

"It's not bad," Domènec agreed, grinning at his understatement. "Let's not tell the others. There's really no need to share this."

"I have no problem with that," she said, laughing.

Comfortable in each other's silence, they relaxed in the

gracious quiet of the room. Lia leaned over and picked up Raoul's place card. Domènec swallowed quickly.

"I meant to introduce you when we got back to the house, but Raoul disappeared."

"How well do you know him, Dom?"

"I don't know a lot about his past," he admitted. "He was raised in a winemaking family in Catalunya and inherited the estate in Lagrasse. That's what brought him out here less than two years ago. I guess it wasn't long after you'd gone back to the States." He stepped over to the windows to peer at the dusk waxing blue against the blanket of snow. "Do you ever get a feeling about someone? From the moment I met him, I felt I'd known Raoul forever. Something about him reminds me of Gabriel. There will be a gesture, or the way he stands, and I..." Domènec turned with the same stricken look on his face Rose had given her earlier.

Lia nodded briefly to show him it was all right, she understood; inside, she vibrated. Of course, she'd noticed the resemblance. "Do you know how he got that scar?" she asked.

Domènec pressed his lips together and gave a quick shake of his head. "He hasn't said anything about it, and I didn't want to pry. I think it must be related to his family's accident, but I know only that they died several years ago, someplace along the Hérault coast." He joined her at the table. "We don't talk about much outside of farming and winemaking. He's very private. Content enough, I suppose. But lonely, I'm certain."

The spell cast by the shadows quivering in candlelight and Domènec's somber words released something in Lia that she'd been trying to ignore since Carcassonne. She set her glass down carefully, ran her finger around the wafer-thin rim, and asked, "Do you believe in ghosts?"

True to his gentle nature, Domènec didn't raise an eyebrow

at her non sequitur. He pulled a chair away from the table, motioned for Lia to sit, and sat beside her. "I'm a son of Languedoc," he said with a smile. "And a lapsed Catholic, like most French of our generation. The stories of ghosts and restless spirits are more a part of my soul than the catechism. What's on your mind, Lia?"

"Just before Gabriel died, I'd been researching visions the bereaved have of deceased loved ones. I wanted to show the connections between the Cathars' beliefs in reincarnation and the Christian story of the resurrection. Some Biblical historians believe the disciples' grief over Jesus's death was so profound, they had visions of him after the crucifixion. And in the retelling, the myth of the resurrection became accepted fact." She picked up her champagne glass but set it down again, fidgeting. "Visions of the dead are actually quite common. Heartbreaking, really."

Lia met Domènec's eyes. His brows were knitted in confusion and concern. "I kept hoping it would happen to me, that I'd see Gabriel, have another chance to talk to him," she continued. "It never did, of course. Maybe because I know too much about it. I know visions of the dead are simply products of a broken heart."

"But if they offer comfort?" Domènec began.

"I guess the mind will go the way it wants."

They listened to the muffled voices bumping against the walls around them, the laughter and music that filled the house with love.

"I met Raoul two days ago," she said. "In Carcassonne. I didn't know it was him, didn't realize it until he walked into the kitchen earlier. I can't even tell you what happened, really. But he thought he knew me." She wasn't ready to admit she'd seen him before Carcassonne, as a disembodied face suspended in her window.

Domènec tilted his head, trying to follow her disjointed story. "He's probably seen a photo of you around here. We've certainly talked about you enough."

"Was his wife's name Paloma?"

"I believe so." He nodded slowly. "Yes."

"Have you seen a photo of her?"

"No, but…Lia. I don't understand."

She emptied her glass and pushed it away. "He called me Paloma. He thought I was her."

"Lia, no. That can't be. Raoul's solid. I don't think—"

The door from the kitchen opened. At the same time, a pair of shrieking children fell into the dining room from the great room beyond, trailed by a man on all fours wearing a Mardi Gras mask in the shape of a tiger's head. There was a near-collision of little bodies with Jacqueline's knees as she entered from the kitchen, carrying a platter heaped with baked white beans. Within moments, the dining room was filled with bodies in motion and voices raised in laughter. Domènec's protests were lost in the din. Lia left the place cards as they were.

LAGRASSE—FEBRUARY 1208

Raoul and his stableman worked together to remove his saddle and bags from Miró, wipe the cold sweat from her flanks and belly, and see the horse fed and watered. Leaving his servant to tend to the saddle, Raoul nearly collided with Paloma in the dark corridor outside the stable. His wife stood wrapped in a wool cloak, shifting her slippered feet on the wooden floor. Iset, their Lévrier bitch, now too old to hunt, sat beside her mistress, smacking her long, hairless tail in joyous percussion.

"Little dove," Raoul whispered, drawing Paloma to his chest. "You should have waited inside." He had been away only three days, but relief at finding his family unmolested and his home intact poured into his fierce embrace. His wife gasped but laughed when he released her.

"You'll crush my bones to dust, Sénher d'Aran." She slipped her arm through his as they passed from the stable through a short breezeway to the warm dining hall. "I had supper held for us. Constansa has taken Bertran and Aicelina to bed, but it was a struggle. Bertran was determined to remain awake until you arrived."

Her soft chatter soothed Raoul through a meal of hot potage and cold pheasant. They drank red wine made from his estate's Carignane grapes. Finally, Paloma fell silent and sat back into the chair's embroidered cushions, perhaps sensing the food and wine had restored in Raoul what the journey had taken away. He knew she waited for his news.

"The king's men, the pope's men—whomever they give their allegiance to—burned the chapel in Ferrals-les-Corbières today. I passed through the village not three hours ago."

"Segui de Bles brought us the news late this morning," she replied, naming a trader Raoul often employed to transport his own wine as well as the wine he imported from Spain. "He'd passed a group of five riders heading west, perhaps ten miles outside Ferrals-les-Corbières. He'd seen other fires on his journey from Toulouse—and not just churches, but whole villages... What's to become of this place, Raoul?"

He rolled the smooth-fired cup between his hands as he considered what he could and should tell his wife. "Manel is on his way to Paris. He's been appointed to replace Pierre de Castelnau as papal emissary." He looked up at Paloma's sudden intake of breath. "He's asked me to meet him there in three weeks' time."

"Raoul, no."

"I must. What Manel learns in Paris must be heard in every corner of Languedoc; I can carry the news south quickly. My cousin is risking his life for us, little dove. For us and a country of strangers."

"As are you."

"Yes."

Paloma gazed into the fire. In profile, Raoul saw her gray-green eyes shining with tears. She blinked once, twice, and the tears were stemmed by resignation.

"And what of Manel?" She took a deep swallow of her wine.

"He doesn't know how long he'll remain in Paris. He serves entirely at the behest of the pope." More than this, he would not tell her—for her safety as well as Manel's.

It was no secret that Manel de Perella had been plucked from the seminary at Sant Benet, not far from his Catalan home, to serve as a translator in the Vatican. But now Raoul's gentle, golden-haired cousin was headed straight into the lion's den. He would be the eyes, ears, and mouth of Pope Innocent III in the clandestine Council of Paris, whose constituency numbered just three: Manel de Perella, papal emissary; Arnaud Amalric, the powerful abbot of Cîteaux; and Philippe du Plessis, commander of the Knights Templar.

"He was forced to feign one of his spells to halt the riders conveying him north long enough for me to find him in Montpellier, but he fares well and sends his love to you and the children."

Standing, Paloma smoothed her skirts and pulled the shawl around her shoulders. "I'll wait for you. Don't be long." She touched her husband's shoulder and walked down the dark hall, Iset trotting beside her.

Raoul stretched his legs toward the fire and leaned his head against the tall back of the carved oak chair. Here, the flames provided warmth and light from the safety of a stone hearth. In the hands of mercenaries and Soldiers of Christ, they would be used to ravage his adopted homeland.

I'll wait for you. Don't be long. His wife's words forebode a future Raoul saw in the writhing flames. A future where he, a merchant from Catalunya, would make a spy of his cousin and refugees of his wife and family while he fought to keep the independence of Languedoc.

MAS HIVERT, FERRALS-LES-CORBIÈRES—SAME EVENING

*A*s the meal unfolded, Lia was spared from having to look at the man sitting to her right except to pass the platters of food. She ate little and spoke even less, content to listen to the conversations pulsing around her. It was restful to be removed from the banter yet still sit within this circle of friends and family. Her frayed nerves settled as the evening wore on.

Raoul was subdued as well, until he and Domènec—one on each side of her—began to speak of the vineyards and of their wines. Then the startled and sardonic man from the stable transformed into an earnest, even playful, farmer.

The vines had transitioned from the full flush of harvest to winter dormancy, but pruning was well underway. Throughout Languedoc, laborers—many from Portugal and Spain—were moving through the fields with their shears, cutting and tearing away the unwanted canes from the vines and trimming those they would keep. Their red, chapped digits poked out from fingerless gloves and wove delicate branches around the fruiting wires. As the men spoke of their vineyards, Lia pictured the whole of the Languedoc region trimming, wrapping, tidying, and waiting for the first hint of new growth.

Domènec and Raoul finalized their plans to leave on Monday for VinoMondo, an invitation-only wine conference in Barcelona. Specialty buyers from around the world descended on the Hotel DO: Plaça Reial to taste privately with select winemakers from France, Spain, and Italy. Rose explained to the table how important the convention was for small producers to build their markets in Europe and abroad. Domènec's earthy, brooding Corbières wines were always in high demand.

After Barcelona, the men would head straight for Nice to attend Vins du Sud, the massive wine show with hundreds of wineries from southern France spread out over acres of expo halls. There, Domènec would share a booth with eight other producers from the region who were being nurtured and promoted by their exporter. Raoul's own wines were several years from being ready to market, but he'd assist Domènec in the arduous presentation and glad-handing process during the conventions and make connections of his own.

Domènec stopped the flow of the meal and the conversation to make a toast in thanks for his guests and this shared celebration of midwinter. The room hummed again as soon as they clinked glasses in the center of the table.

"Lia, *à la tienne*." Raoul chimed his glass against hers. He used the familiar pronoun, denoting a particular intimacy.

"Who were you running from in the basilica?"

Something between longing and sorrow flickered in Raoul's

eyes for a moment and then vanished. "I'm sorry, I don't know what you're talking about." But his fingers tensed around the bowl of his wineglass, and in that tiny movement, Lia read the truth. She looked away to see Rose staring at her. Rose couldn't hear their conversation, but Lia was certain their grim expressions told a story of their own.

"We have so much to talk about." Raoul's voice was so close to her ear that it seemed to be coming from inside her head. "But not here." The left side of his face was illuminated by the candlelight. Lia swore she could see the faint outline of her palm on his cheek, and with a slight shudder, she recalled the force of her slap.

"Where have you come from?" she whispered, afraid he would fade away or vanish in a wisp of smoke.

He touched his scar gingerly, as if expecting to feel pain.

"I was hoping you could tell me."

❧

Midnight approached, and Rose's exhaustion showed in the pinched corners of her eyes. Lia sent her off to a hot bath and bed. In the dark, quiet kitchen, she checked the stove burners and swept the floor, pretending for a moment this was her home.

Exhausted children were carried to bed, their grandparents crept upstairs soon after, and the others assembled in the living room for quiet conversation or games of chess, but Lia craved fresh air. She was in the foyer off the kitchen, tucking her feet into boots, when she sensed a presence behind her. Startled, she spun around.

"Care for some company?" Raoul asked.

The blanket of snow squeaked beneath their feet as they walked. Tiny crystalline flakes sparkled in the faint glow from the house. The breeze soothed Lia's flushed skin and sent up puffs of snow faeries conjured by starlight.

"It's so lovely," she said as they entered the vineyards just beyond the dormant kitchen garden.

"Like another world," Raoul agreed. He made a strange sound, as though a laugh had caught in his throat and emerged as a sigh, and knocked snow from a tangle of unpruned vines. The powder cascaded in a shimmering cloud.

They continued up a row of vines, gaining elevation as the land sloped into the hills above the house, and emerged onto a clear stretch between vineyards that was wide enough for a tractor to pass through. Straight ahead, the path ran up into the hills and was lost in rock and garigue. To their left, it descended to a *cabanon*—a small stone shed where Domènec stored tools. They walked there in silence.

Her anxiety at being alone with Raoul had ebbed over dinner as the conversation revealed an empathetic farmer. But the questions Lia had been aching to ask since he'd entered the kitchen dried in her mouth. She probed cautiously at the other emotions surfacing in her heart: the first shock wave of astonishment when she saw Raoul in the kitchen; the anger at having been trapped in a tunnel; the tender understanding of how grief can warp memory. And entwined with all of these: breathtaking desire. In that frozen moment, Lia felt their fragile connection strengthen, as if unseen hands were repairing a frayed rope stretched between them.

Raoul brushed away the light dusting of snow from a bench that sat against the shed, and they perched on its edge. Across the hectares of vines, the lights still burning at Mas Hivert and in the village of Ferrals-les-Corbières glittered. Breathing in air fragrant with wood smoke, Lia found her voice.

"Domènec and Rose have been singing your praises since

I arrived in December," she said. "But it hadn't occurred to Dom to pry into your personal life, much to Rose's annoyance." His faint smile thrilled her. "They said you just appeared in the neighborhood one day…" Her words dangled in the air, but Raoul tugged at his gloves, ignoring the invitation to explain. Still, Lia plunged through the opening she'd created. "I know the pain of losing your life partner, but I cannot fathom the heartbreak of losing children. I am so sorry."

"It was a long time ago."

A gust of cold air pulled at her hair like the fingers of a ghost, tossing it across her face. Lia tucked the loose strands into her coat collar. "Your wife's name was Paloma," she said. Raoul winced, as though the sound of her name caused him physical pain. "What were your children's names?"

"Bertran was my son," he replied. "Aicelina was my daughter."

His simple declaration broke her heart. There is no other way to say your loved ones are gone but *was* and *were*. "Those are old Occitan names."

"My wife was from Languedoc, like your family."

"Do you have family in Languedoc still?"

"No. There's no one left." His answer was a door clicking shut. Quiet, but final.

"Do you know what it was like to see you walk into the house earlier today?" Lia pressed on. "I felt my sanity slip."

His jaw worked, the tension causing tiny pulses as his teeth ground together. "I knew you the moment I saw you," he said at last. "I have memories of you that seem so very old… like something I knew in another life." Raoul paused, and Lia waited for more. But he seemed lost in those memories.

"My first night at Le Pèlerin, I stood in front of a window, looking at my reflection," she said, breaking the thin silence. "A man's face appeared out of nowhere, his cheek gashed and bleeding. Then the face disappeared, and I realized it was some trick of light. It wasn't a man but an eagle sitting on the railing. Or so I thought, until I saw you in Carcassonne."

Raoul opened his hands wide. They spanned his thighs and then gathered into loose fists. "I remember what happened in the basilica," he said. "But I can't explain it. I thought it was a dream." He turned his face to her. "I'm sorry."

The haunted look she'd seen in the medieval Cité was almost but not quite erased. Lia longed to touch his scar, to smooth her fingers across the rough patch of skin. "I know how it feels to miss someone so much that you're certain if you let go, you'll shatter into a million pieces," she said. "Sometimes I hear a voice or a laugh, or I see someone from behind, and for a split second, I think it's Gabriel. Then I remember. It's the most horrible feeling, isn't it? The remembering. It can make you crazy."

Raoul nodded. "I'm trying to make sense of the images that keep running in my mind. I don't know if they're memories or dreams, if they're real or hallucinations. Or if they even belong to me. It's like remembering someone else's life."

He ran a hand over his cropped hair and rubbed the back of his neck, a gesture so like Gabriel's.

A stream of wind sent a veil of snow cascading from the *cabanon*. Lia shivered in her down jacket. Her toes ached, and her face was numb and heavy with cold.

"You look frozen. Let's get back." Raoul stood and offered his hand.

She stepped forward and caught her toe on a stone, tilting into him. They were nearly the same height, yet she felt small against his chest and shoulders. Raoul tipped her gently away, cutting short Lia's soft-focus vision of a kiss that could have so easily come after her stumble. She followed his footsteps through the rows of vines to the house, where a few windows still glowed upstairs and shadows moved behind curtains.

Raoul opened the back door for her but didn't follow her in. "It's getting late, and I've got a dodgy drive home through this snow." He stood before her with his hands in his front pockets.

With tension and attraction balanced on the same taut wire, Lia didn't know how to say good night. She was certain he'd read her mind when he said, "I need some time to think this through. I can't absorb any more tonight."

He leaned in to kiss her cheeks, and Lia's head moved to each side in an automatic response.

"*Dors bien*," he whispered into her hair. "Sleep well. Everything will be more clear in the light."

⁘

When Lia woke the next morning, it was to a quiet house and the bright light of a sun high in the sky. After a quick rinse of her face, she descended to the kitchen. As she waited for the kettle to boil, the note on the island caught her eye.

Sleepyhead. So glad you got some rest. We've all bundled off to Mazamet. Heaps of food in the fridge. Leftovers tonight. Text when you get up. We'll be home before dark. XOXO Rose

Plans had been made over dinner the night before to spend the day sledding and cross-country skiing at Black Mountain. Lia had begged off, preferring to remain inside looking out at the snow rather than covered in its damp cold.

The morning stillness was captivating. The syncopated drip of melting snow as it fell from the eaves competed with the ticking of the mantel clock in the dining room. The snow had transformed the landscape from sharp lines of limestone and granite and barren fields of pruned vines to soft curves and mounds of white.

Lia wandered through the empty house, sipping from a mug of hot coffee. In a small alcove set off from the main room, built-in shelves held treasures from her friends' years of traveling and living abroad. They'd met in Chile, where Domènec was working the grape harvest and Rose was teaching French and English in Santiago. At first glance, they were an unlikely couple—the tall, urbane American and the robust French farmer—but just weeks after Domènec brought her to Languedoc to show her his family's vineyards, Rose set her high heels on a high shelf, rolled up her sleeves, and became his winemaking partner as well as his wife.

On one shelf, a bouquet of dried lavender dropped tiny purple buds. Lia snipped off a sprig, crushed it between her fingers, and drew in Languedoc's musky scent. Next to the bouquet sat a framed photograph taken two summers before. In it, she stood in the circle of Rose and Domènec's arms, her face glowing with happiness, her gaze on the photographer—her husband, Gabriel—whose shadow spilled into the frame. The Lia in the photograph had no idea what pain awaited her just days away. Lia ran a finger across the glass, lingering on Domènec's face.

In the kitchen, she stretched her legs on the window seat, replaying the previous night's conversation as she took in the white expanse of vineyards beyond.

Sleep well, Raoul had said. *Everything will be more clear in the light.*

But in the white light of day, there was no clarity, only confusion. A bubble of anxiety rose in her chest, and her lungs drew tight. Raoul's words haunted her. And he was gone. He and Domènec would leave in the morning for Barcelona. Two weeks. She could wait two weeks.

She set down her coffee cup and closed her eyes, imagining the single flame of a candle, the focal point of her meditation practice. Within the candle rose faces of the men who consumed her thoughts. The reawakening of her physical self that she'd felt in Lucas's presence had embarrassed her, bringing feelings of guilt for wanting to be desired again. She'd danced into that circle but pulled away, repelled by her own vulnerability. His polished beauty, the gleam of a Breitling on his wrist, and the glint of gold in dark eyes that regarded her with an almost raptor-like hunger…that wasn't her. It wasn't the kind of love that could honor what she'd had with Gabriel. The man she ached to see was Raoul—to smell the wood smoke and pine that lingered on his skin, to learn more about his past and if she might fit into his future.

Longing to be with another man has nothing and everything to do with my love for you. She spoke to Gabriel from the warm peace in her mind, and in return, she heard the sweet sound of Gabriel's voice telling her to go on. *Go on? What do you mean? Go on and leave? Go on and love? Go on without you?*

Lia lifted her head and opened her eyes. The light had shifted to the west. The coffee had gone cold. She wanted to be back at the cottage, alone with her thoughts and her books. She wasn't ready to face Rose's concerned, questioning eyes or to explain to Domènec why she thought Raoul had mistaken her for his dead wife.

She rinsed out her cup and assembled a cheese sandwich, eating it upstairs while she packed her bag and stripped the sheets from her bed. After a quick shower, Lia was downstairs again, teasing the snarls out of her wet curls with her fingers. She began to write below Rose's message but thought better of leaving her words where anyone could read them. She'd text her from the road.

Lia followed the tracks left by the cars that had departed down the long driveway hours earlier. Road crews and the bright sun had cleared the snow from the highway, and she was able to relax her tight grip on the steering wheel. But these wet roads would freeze to black ice. She hoped the skiers would be on their way home soon.

The next two weeks slipped away as February melted into the wet grasp of March. Lia found excuses not to meet with Lucas in person, feigning a cold and then an extended research trip to Montpellier, but their work continued via email, and she was grateful for the distraction.

Domènec came back to his family and vineyards, while Raoul continued on to Paris to meet with an American importer. A bubble of disappointment burst inside Lia at the news, but she resolved to wait, respecting Raoul's wish for more time and acknowledging her fear of losing the tenuous grip on her equilibrium. She had come to Languedoc to find herself again, not to lose what little sense of her spirit she still held.

LAGRASSE—MARCH

*S*itting outside a café on the pedestrian rue de la Promenade, Lia pulled the long skirt of her sundress to her knees and stretched out her legs to absorb the soft spring sun. She sipped her coffee, eyes hidden behind sunglasses, willing each shadow that turned the corner to be Raoul.

There were times when Gabriel was on an extended tour that Lia was certain he'd been injured, and panic would overcome her reason. Then the unspeakable had come true when they were only miles apart. As she fretted over Raoul, Lia realized how fragile she remained. But beneath the fragility was a potent anger. Her greatest vulnerability—the fear of losing someone she loved—had surfaced just as she was beginning to heal and hope. She never wanted to feel that vulnerable again.

"Damn you, Raoul." Her phone, sitting on the table beside the saucer, trilled in response.

"Hey, girl. I've missed you." Rose's cheerful voice restored some of the light to her mood. "It's been pretty quiet out your way these past few days."

"Oh, Rose." Little-girl tears stung her eyes.

"Lia. Honey." Rose shushed a child's laughing voice. "What's wrong?"

Lia poured out her truth. She told Rose of the immediate connection she'd felt to Raoul, sharing as much of their conversations as she could without dipping into that scary well of visions or the episode in Carcassonne. She shared her hurt at having opened her heart only to be met by a wall of silence.

Her friend listened, murmuring words of comfort in Lia's shuddering pauses. When Lia ran out of words, Rose said, "I know I'm a soft touch for stray souls, but Raoul has attached himself to our hearts. There's something about him that I want to protect and heal. It's how I feel about you, how I felt the first time I saw you at Brown. I can't deny that I schemed to ignite a spark between the two of you."

"Am I ready for this?" Lia asked. "Am I ready for sparks?" She wanted to see him, with an urgency that was desire mixed with fear. "How do I know the difference between loneliness and love?"

There was a pause, and then Rose said, "Nana just picked up the kids. Why don't you meet me here and we'll go for a drive. Just get out for a while. Play tourist. Talk."

Thirty minutes later, Lia pulled into the driveway of Mas Hivert, where Rose was deadheading the geraniums clustered in pots on the front steps. Rose walked to the driver's side and tapped on the glass. "Scoot over, I'll drive," she said when Lia powered down the window. "There's something I want to show you."

Bemused but ready for a distraction, Lia lifted herself over the gearshift and settled into the passenger seat. "Should I put on a blindfold?" she joked as Rose folded her long legs into the car.

"No, silly." Rose connected her seat belt. "But you have to trust me. Who knows what we'll find?" She squeezed Lia's knee. "Honey, you open me to the beauty of this place that I seem to miss just keeping the business and the babies together. I can't tell you how happy I am to have you nearby. If I think on it too long, I start hearing my sisters and wonder what the hell this city girl is doing in France's back forty, married to a winemaker who has to stand on his tiptoes to kiss me." Rose's laugh rumbled from deep within. "I love my life, I love this country, but sometimes I ache for home. Being with you again makes me realize I just needed a piece of home nearby."

"Time and again, you've saved me, Rosie. The thought I might never have returned to Languedoc because of the memories…" Lia inhaled deeply. "That I might have missed being with you, Dom, and the little ones—I almost can't bear it. And after just three months, I can't imagine being anyplace else."

"Then make a life with us here."

That made Lia smile.

"That's what I want more than anything," Rose said. "To see you smile."

"I have to be in Termes by two," said Lia. "I'm meeting that photographer at the château to do some work on the book." The guilt that she'd said nothing to Rose of her conflicting feelings about Lucas stabbed Lia right where her friend's hand held her leg.

"We're not going far" was Rose's cryptic response. She backed the car out of the drive.

Less than ten miles from Mas Hivert, heading back in the direction of Lagrasse, Rose pulled onto a small, one-lane road. She chattered as she drove, gossiping about this farmer and that, until Lia realized she was talking about Hermès Daran, the former owner of Logis du Martinet—the vineyard estate Raoul had inherited outside Lagrasse. Lia wondered vaguely how far away they were from his home.

"You should have heard them, nattering away like old women, wondering what would happen to the land since Hermès had no family to assume the estate. When Hermès got too old to maintain the vines and too stubborn to update his equipment, you knew they were all calculating the lowest price they could offer him for the land." Rose sniffed in disgust. "But the French are nothing if not determined when it comes to inheritance. Somebody knew something about a distant Spanish cousin. And suddenly, there was Raoul."

"Wasn't he living here already?" Lia interrupted. "Dom said his family died somewhere along the Hérault coast."

Rose's mouth opened, closed, and she shook her head. "I don't really know, Lia. Maybe they were on holiday. There's so much I just don't know."

They turned from the highway onto a narrow lane where the tarmac thinned and ran out. The track was paved in patches of cobblestone and bordered on either side by low rock walls and a riot of broom shrubs, juniper, cypress, and holm oak. Sheltered from the wind and facing the western sun, pockets of purple dwarf iris and orange wild orchid could be seen. As the car tires rumbled over the cobbled lane, the fragrance of thyme and damp earth wafted through the open windows.

Two hundred feet in, they arrived at a large gate of forged iron bars set between square pillars of stone, the only opening in the high brick wall that surrounded the estate. The gate gaped wide, and as they drove through, Lia noted the small camera placed near the top of the right-hand pillar, discreet but not hidden. Behind the house, rows of vines marched up the hillsides in neat hectare plots. The property seemed abandoned. Scarcely a sound could be heard, as if the earth itself had stopped breathing.

The *longère*—a low, single-story house with deep-set windows—stood in a clearing, backed by sloping vineyards. It was made from limestone, the same as Le Pèlerin—another ancient structure salvaged and rebuilt, its traditional character preserved while making it comfortable for modern living. Rose inched along the gravel lane past the glassed-in sun porch on the northeast end, stopping the car just short of the massive oak door in the center of the front facade. There was something so familiar about the house. The sense of déjà vu left Lia feeling as though she were floating slightly above the earth.

"What is this place?" Lia trailed behind Rose, who walked resolutely to the front door and knocked. Rose held up a finger, listening.

Lia hung back, wandering through the small front garden. Tendrils of newly green wisteria crept up the outside wall—last year's dead growth had been trimmed away. The first perennials poked through black loam in window boxes, and the flower beds had a fresh layer of straw to keep them warm through the chilly, early spring nights. A hopeful heart had foreseen a season of flowers, and gentle hands had prepared the soil.

"No one home?" she asked when Rose stepped away from

the door. They walked around the side of the house, where a stand of oak shielded the west side from the fierce summer sun.

"Someone's here." Rose pointed upslope to a late-model Range Rover parked beside the winery. The winery had been dug deep into the hillside, resembling a barrel sliced in half and laid flat on its cut side. It was tall enough to permit a truck and trailer full of grapes to back into its entrance.

A chattering of starlings erupted from the far side of the winery, and a four-legged whirling dervish of terra-cotta red tore around the corner in gleeful chase. Rose curled the tips of two fingers just inside her mouth and blew a short, sharp blast. The dog went still, pointing. Then it flew toward them.

"Isis, come here, girl." Rose knelt down, and the sleek greyhound crashed into her, wriggling, snuffling, and panting with glee.

"I take it you two know each other," said Lia. Isis charged up the hill, barking.

"She was found wandering on the property last September, covered in mange, no collar. She's such a rare thing, we were all certain someone would miss her, but she's not even micro-chipped. No one ever came looking."

Tucking her arm through Rose's, Lia said, "Thanks for getting me out of the house."

"Don't thank me just yet." Rose grinned.

They followed Isis toward the winery. The dog stopped and ran back halfway to bark at them, impatient with their progress. She led Lia and Rose to a small door set in a rounded frame. The handle gave easily, and the women stepped inside. Isis raced past, her happy shouts echoing off the brick walls, and disappeared into the dark chasm between two enormous tanks.

The cool air was blanketed by the thick, yeasty scent of fermented fruit. A row of tall, stainless steel tanks disappeared into the dark recesses on one side, and a motor hummed somewhere out of sight. Lia and Rose walked by a low room filled with three rows of wooden barrels, Lia's heart thudding as they passed deeper into the cavern. Even though the ceiling loomed high overhead, the dim light and heavy air triggered her claustrophobia.

From deep within the building, a door slammed, followed by the sound of running footsteps, which seemed to emanate from the walls themselves. The source of the footsteps appeared as a boy of nine or ten zigzagged through the tanks with Isis in pursuit. He pulled up fast when he saw the women.

"Oh, hello," he chirped. "You're who Isis was carrying on about!"

It took Lia a moment to realize he was speaking English, with an accent that told of boarding schools and neckties worn at the dinner table. The bangs of his blond hair feathered over his forehead in imitation of a preteen pop star, and the cuffs of his jeans brushed against sneakers that had been all the rage when she was his age—the famous white swoosh glowed in the shadowy dark, set against neon-orange nylon. Lia smiled, feeling ancient.

"I'm Rose, and this is Lia. We're friends of the owner's. Is he about?"

"I'm sorry, how rude of me," replied the boy of ten-going-on-thirty. "I didn't think to ask if you spoke English. But you do, so that's brilliant. Do you speak French too? I'm quite fluent. I mostly translate for my mum. She's hopeless, but Dad gets on fine. I'm Charlie. Yes, everyone's in the cellar. Did you know this used to be a hideout in medieval times? The cellar has secret passageways that go deep under the hills—people used to hide out here. I bet there are bones. Dad won't let me explore by myself, but Raoul might take me later into some of the rooms. Wait here, and I'll find them." As soon as his torrent of words ceased, Charlie rushed off again, Isis at his heels.

"Raoul?" Lia grabbed Rose by the arm, pulling her around.

"He got in last night, Lia."

"What the hell? I can't believe you brought me here without telling me."

Raoul and a tall, lean man came around the row of tanks, Raoul gesturing, absorbed in conversation. The men stopped at one of the tanks, oblivious to Rose and Lia.

How does a heart stop and race at the same time? Words left her, replaced by desire, anger, and a sudden shyness. Lia wanted to turn tail and flee before Raoul saw her.

As if hearing his name, Raoul looked up. A light set low in the floor illuminated his face, and it became the face in the basilica. His gaze was piercing, his scar a dark slash of shadow. Something about the tilt of his head, the taut way he held his body, and Lia saw Gabriel shimmering inside him. Lia wanted to stay. She wanted to leave. She wanted to throttle her friend.

Rose grasped Lia's hand, whispering, "Trust me." With her full voice, she said, "Raoul, welcome home! Lia and I were just headed to the *marché* in Lagrasse, so I thought I'd drop off that refractometer you'd asked to borrow." She went boldly forth, extending a hand to the stranger. "Hello, I'm Rose Hivert."

"What serendipity, Madame Hivert," said the Englishman as he took Rose's hand. "I'm Charles Robb. I own the Robb Group. We have several fine dining restaurants in the UK and China. I'm on a mission to spread the word about Languedoc wines, and I assigned myself the dreadful task of visiting wineries. I'll be at your estate this afternoon, as a matter of fact. I made plans to visit Mas Hivert when I saw your husband last month at VinoMondo. You make one of the best old vine Carignane I've had. And you've met my Charlie?" The boy now stood quietly by his side. Charles placed a hand on his son's shoulder, and the boy leaned in, his blond head only slightly above the hip bone of his father's long leg.

"We have. Isis seems delighted to have found a kindred spirit." Rose beamed a smile at the boy, who returned it with a gap-toothed grin. "And thank you for the kind words about our wines. My husband's great-grandfather planted those vines before the First World War. We'll bottle the one-hundredth vintage next year." Rose looked expectantly at Lia, who stepped up and held out her hand to Charles Robb, avoiding Raoul's eyes.

"Hello, I'm Lia." To Rose, she said, "We should leave these men to their conversation."

"Oh, no," replied Charles Robb. "We're finished up here." The Englishman withdrew a small silver case from inside his jacket pocket. He slid it open and presented Raoul with a cream-colored business card. "I'm grateful for the grand tour. The barrel samples were outstanding. As soon as you have bottles ready for tasting, please contact me. I'll make the trip with some of my staff. I'd welcome any excuse to leave London for the south of France. In the meantime, I'm happy to take the remaining Martinet *vin du pays* off your hands. We'll sell it as a house wine until you're ready to launch the rebirth of the winery." He spoke with the easy confidence of a man accustomed to knowing his plans would be carried out to the letter.

His son shook hands with Raoul in a charming imitation of his father before kneeling to embrace Isis. From Rose and Lia, Charlie allowed the French custom of kissing cheeks, blushing despite his dignified mien.

"Well, this works out perfectly," said Rose. "Lia has an appointment in Termes later, which is in the opposite direction, so if you're headed to Mas Hivert, I'll ride with you and show you the way." She spoke to Charles, ignoring the daggers Lia was throwing with her eyes. They all followed Rose as she led the way out of the winery, and then she, Charles, and Charlie were waving good-bye.

As the Range Rover pulled away, Rose glanced back; it was all Lia could do not to raise her middle fingers. Lia wondered if even this exit had been a setup, if Rose had known that Charles Robb was stopping first at Logis du Martinet. Admitting she wanted nothing more than to be alone with Raoul, Lia blessed and cursed her meddling friend.

She sighed and faced Raoul. But he was focused on something distant, perhaps considering the pile of deadwood he'd left to burn, perhaps searching for an escape from this awkward moment.

LOGIS DU MARTINET, LAGRASSE—SAME DAY

I can imagine what you must be thinking," Raoul said. He wore a plain white T-shirt, blue jeans, and leather work boots bleached pale brown by the Languedoc sun.

Lia fought the urge to place a hand on his arm, to feel his bare skin, to make certain he was real. Instead, she sank onto a stone bench that sat next to the winery door.

"Can you? Tell me." She folded her arms across her chest and gripped her elbows, willing herself to breathe.

"That I stayed away after the conferences to avoid seeing you."

Lia paused before answering. Her throat ached with anger and helpless desire, and her nose stung from weeks of tears. "That thought did cross my mind."

"I wondered if that was really you inside the winery or if I was seeing ghosts again," he said. She looked up to see him smile, a gesture to lessen the awkwardness.

"It's really me," she said.

"Would you prefer to talk inside?" He motioned to the winery door. "There's no shade here, and I've got chilled wine in the cooler."

"Charlie said the winery has hidden corridors. I'd rather not take the chance of repeating our adventures in the basilica." She returned his smile, sharing a joke to show she was willing to let Carcassonne go. For the time being. "Besides, the day is too beautiful to be indoors. It's hard to believe we're still in winter."

He sat beside Lia but didn't touch her. "It's hard to believe we never finished our conversation," he said.

Her thoughts pounded in staccato beats, but she waited for him to continue.

"Lia Carrer." He said her name with such certainty, and in that instant, her heart fell open.

It's all right. I understand. I think I'm falling in love with you too… streamed through her mind, and Lia felt a sudden hysteria, alarmed that she might have said the words aloud. When she saw that Raoul's expression hadn't changed, she relaxed. Her unbidden thoughts had remained unspoken.

"Lia must be short for…?"

"Natalìo, in the old Occitan tradition," Lia said. "Natalìo Cloutildou Carrer. But I could pronounce only *Lia* as a little girl, so Lia it stayed."

"And Carrer? That isn't Occitan."

"It's from my father's family in northern Italy. But Béatris, my mother, was raised in Limoux." When Lia named the town on the Aude River, in the foothills of the Pyrénées, Raoul glanced at her, surprise clear in his eyes. "Do you know Limoux?" she asked.

He shook his head, dismissing the question. "My uncle took me hunting in the Haute Vallée once. We must have stopped in town for supplies or to spend the night. It was a long time ago."

It was a long time ago. How many men were going to use that excuse to not explain things to her? Two felt like it was becoming a pattern. Raoul's vague response threatened to close the door, leaving her on the outside of his past. He'd shut her out once before with those words, just as Lucas had in Gruissan.

"At first, I was relieved you'd left town." She spoke to the forest in front of them, not trusting what she might see in his face. "What happened in Carcassonne, the things you said at Rose and Dom's... *'I have memories of you that seem so very old... Like something I knew in another life.'* That's what you told me. You don't just toss out those words and then disappear, unless you regret saying them."

"Lia, I am so sorry. I thought I was giving you space. I thought..." Isis reappeared, and Raoul took her finely sculpted head between his hands. She sat on her haunches and looked at him with her trusting doe's eyes. "Never mind what I thought," he said. "I owe you so many apologies, but let me start with this one." In profile, Raoul's scar seemed to fade in the balm of lemony light. "You said you knew how it felt to lose your life's partner. I was an ass for not reacting to that, for not telling you how sorry I am. I'd be honored if you'd tell me about Gabriel."

By acknowledging the widow Lia would always be, Raoul had acknowledged her whole person. The memories of Gabriel would hurt forever, but there was proof she didn't have to bear the pain alone. Raoul understood the inexplicable grief. He released her to accept what she'd felt Gabriel telling her just a few weeks before, on that snow-filled day: *Go on, Lia. Go on in love.* A quiet magic shimmered in the pastel glow of spring.

"I was in the first year of my graduate program at Cal Berkeley," she said. "Gabriel was just starting to make a name for himself in the mountain-biking circuit. It was a *coup de foudre*—love at first sight. We were married before I started classes that fall. No wedding, just a simple ceremony.

"We were still in Berkeley when Cascade University offered me a teaching position in the history department. It was a steady income while I finished my dissertation and a place where Gabriel could train. We'd been there for two years when he was killed."

"Yet you came back here, to these memories, instead of starting over someplace new?"

"This is home," she said quietly. "You must understand that."

"I do," Raoul replied. "I'm just not sure I had the choice to return."

"Maybe I didn't either."

They sat in silence. Lia's phone chimed with an incoming text, and she glanced at the screen.

Waiting at the citadel. How far out are you? the message read.

Lia weighed the cost of ruining the fragile moment by leaving against the possibility of breaking their delicate truce by expecting too much too soon.

"I'm meeting a colleague at Termes for a project I'm working on," she said. "I'll be late if I don't leave now."

Raoul walked Lia to her car, shyness falling over them like a shadow. Lia opened her door, and they both spoke at once.

"Please come to dinner."

"Can I take you to dinner?"

She laughed. "Ladies first. I know it's a long drive, but would you come to dinner tomorrow? You probably know most of my story, but I still know so little of yours."

"What time? What can I bring?"

"Let's say seven. Bring a bottle of your wine."

"It'll have to be a barrel sample. It's months away from being bottled."

"All the better. I'll be able to say I knew this wine when…"

They traded phones, punching their numbers into the other's contact list.

"I haven't done this in a very long time," Raoul said, resting a hand on the frame of the open car door.

"This?" she asked. "What is this? What are you doing?"

With his free hand, he lifted the sunglasses from her face and tilted up her chin. Lia felt weightlessness and desire fluttering, tingling, radiating from deep inside, and she heard a small voice encouraging her not to question or doubt but to believe and accept.

Their mouths met, and she tasted salt in the hollow above his lip and breathed in his aroma of sweat and sage and the musky pine of his soap. Her hands hovered near his waist. She was afraid if she touched him, she wouldn't be able to let go.

Raoul drew back. "When I first saw you at Mas Hivert, standing there in the kitchen like you were waiting for me, I hoped and feared you had the answers. That's why I stayed away. I didn't know which I wanted more: to understand or to stay in the dream."

"Answers to what, Raoul?"

But he looked past her into some distance she couldn't follow. "I've been waiting for something to happen since I arrived in Lagrasse, someone to show me who I should be," he said.

At last, she understood his evasive ambivalence. Raoul was trying to reconcile his bewildering loss of identity after his family's deaths with the man who'd carried on, surviving.

"When I woke, I was," he finished.

The fine hair on her arms and the back of her neck rose. "'When I woke, I was,'" Lia echoed. "You sound like Adam coming to life in the Garden of Eden. But I understand. I feel like I've been sleepwalking since Gabriel died. Who are you when the other half of your soul is cleaved away?"

Raoul stared at her a moment and gave his head a small toss, as if clearing away an unwanted thought. He brushed her cheek with the back of his hand and lightly kissed her forehead.

He waited until she'd buckled herself into her seat and then reached for her hand through the open window. "*À demain.* Until tomorrow." He squeezed her hand and stepped toward the winery.

"Hey, my address—you don't know where I live!" she called after him.

He walked backward, away from her. "Le Pèlerin, in Minerve, right? I helped build that house."

It wasn't until she was back on the road that she thought to wonder what he'd meant.

CHÂTEAU DE TERMES—THAT AFTERNOON

"I could meet you halfway."

Lia stopped at the familiar voice and tilted her head, raising her hands to block the sun. From his perch on a low wall, Lucas must have watched her hike up the winding path to Château de Termes, the magnificent ruin perched high above the tiny village of Termes. "No, you've got the best view. Save me a spot. I'll be right up."

The path wound around the back of the castle and rose gradually to meet the steep, grassy sides. She passed a young family sitting on their raincoats to protect their backsides from the damp that lingered in the grass, enjoying a picnic. Lia absently picked through their accents and the few words she could hear. *Dutch? Afrikaans?* She skirted the south side of the castle.

A modern staircase of treated wood led her up several feet to a platform. From there, she found a corkscrew stairwell, its steps worn down and slippery from millions of feet over hundreds of years. Without handrails to grasp, Lia ascended the tight space with wary steps and a pounding heart. In a matter of moments, she emerged into bright light. The walls surrounding the courtyard radiated heat from the late-afternoon sun.

Lucas leaned against a rampart, his hands in his pockets. A thin cashmere sweater fit him snugly, and wool trousers flowed without a wrinkle to cuffs that just touched his brushed, charcoal suede loafers. A Nikon fitted with a zoom lens hung around his neck, and the camera bag sat on the wall beside him. His dark-blond hair ruffled slightly in the breeze.

"And here I thought photographers wore khakis and combat boots," Lia teased.

"And here I thought academics wore tweed and tortoiseshell glasses," he replied, his glance skimming her bare shoulders. Aware of the low-cut neckline of her sundress, Lia wished she'd put on her sweater before leaving the car. What had she been thinking, wearing this dress to meet Lucas? She quivered at the memory of Raoul's hands on her skin, his warm mouth opening to hers.

"I thought maybe you'd decided not to come." Lucas's voice snapped her out of thought, and a warm flush of embarrassment replaced the flutter of pleasure.

She joined him at the wall, uncertain what to do with her hands. Crossing them over her chest seemed defensive, bracing them behind her too suggestive. She tucked them in the pockets of her dress, mirroring him. "I made an unexpected stop in Lagrasse. A friend just got back into town, and I wanted to say hello."

"It's good to know you're feeling better—that flu bug was a nasty one."

Remembering just in time that she'd used illness as a way to avoid seeing Lucas, she said, "It was just a cold, nothing serious. This warm spell seems to have cured me."

He'd turned his attention to adjusting his camera and didn't seem to notice her discomfort. "Yes, hard to believe we're still in winter," Lucas answered, snapping a zoom lens into place.

Lia started in surprise. She'd said the same words not an hour before to Raoul. She managed only "It's beautiful" in reply.

And it was. From their vista at the ruined walls, the Termes Gorges gaped to the west, and the foothills of the Pyrénées marched steadily southward. The mountains wore a cloak of dazzling snow, but a pale-green fuzz of new growth and the white, pink, and orange blossoms of flowering plants covered the Corbières Valley. Yet there was a cool, fragile current underneath the warm air, a reminder that the tramontane wind could still rip through, swelling the rivers with rain and turning newly planted fields to mud; there was nothing settled or predictable about spring in Languedoc.

"It didn't make much sense to ask you to tramp through these sites with me until the weather cleared a bit. I got some outstanding shots with the snowfall. I'll send you the digital file. There's a night shot of Quéribus under the full moon I'd like to propose for the cover. Just let me know what you think." He snapped off several shots of the valley. "All right, Professor. I'm ready for my history lesson." Lucas raised the camera to his eye and directed the lens at Lia.

She turned before he could capture her on film and walked to the center of the open courtyard, relieved to talk about something she knew and understood. They made their way through the Château de Termes, Lia revealing its history as Lucas recorded what was left of its past.

The citadel had witnessed one of the most decisive victories of

the Cathar Crusade: a four-month siege that ended in late 1210
when the embattled Cathars—those who had not succumbed
to starvation or dysentery—surrendered to the notorious Simon
de Montfort, conqueror of the Cathars. As she recounted the
facts that were so familiar to her, Lia's mind drifted back to
Raoul, to the few strange and tender moments they'd shared
and what she imagined—hoped—would happen when they
met tomorrow night for dinner, like a normal man and woman
getting to know each other. She was grateful for the breeze that
pushed her hair over her face, covering a secret smile.

Two hours later, they arrived at the main entrance of the
fortress, where the museum and gift shop were housed.

"I'm parked near the river," Lia said.

"I left my car on the east end of town."

She stepped away but paused, working over a thought. "That
day in Carcassonne," she said. "When I called you to say I
wasn't feeling well and had decided to go home?"

Lucas lifted his chin in acknowledgment.

"I was certain I'd seen you in the city center, walking ahead
of me. Yet when I called, you said you were at the basilica."

"I never came into town that day." Lucas lowered his sunglasses over his face, and Lia saw only her own somber reflection. "You must have seen someone else."

Lia pulled at her lower lip with her teeth and looked past
Lucas to see another couple emerging from the visitor's
center. "Sure, I must have," she said, the false note of brightness in her voice landing flat on the brick beneath their feet.
"I'll write up my notes and send you the text to format, and
we'll meet next week?" Lia leaned in and offered Lucas each
cheek for a quick kiss, normal between colleagues, expected
between friends. She was relieved that he'd shifted his camera
bag into one hand and held his Nikon in the other; she was

saved from having to shy away from the touch of his hand on her skin.

"Of course," he agreed, and Lia moved in the direction of her car. "How goes the quest into Cathar Crusade conspiracy theories?"

Lucas stopped her with his question. She sighed and turned back, her eyes narrowed at the slightly mocking tone.

"I thought you said you took my research seriously."

"I do, Lia. Of course I do. This just seems like a waste of your time. Historical record will never tell us who Castelnau's assassin was."

"Historians are first and foremost detectives," she volleyed back, thinking of those archives in Carcassonne she still hadn't seen and of Jordí, who seemed to be too busy of late to meet with her. "It's a constant chase after red herrings, but you can't stop believing the truth will find its way."

"The truth may lead you to things you'd rather not see, Lia." The finality of Lucas's statement nearly knocked her off her mental footing.

"I wouldn't argue with that," she replied. "But fear is no reason to quit seeking the truth."

The tension rose between them, heavy with expectation, but Lia was tapped out. With a shrug and a wave, she left the shadow of the building, emerging into the sun of the cobblestone street beyond.

LE PÈLERIN, MINERVE—WEDNESDAY EVENING

*I*t was after seven; dusk was falling. Lia gathered her hair into a low ponytail and twisted it into a chignon. She decided on a sleeveless gray chiffon blouse that draped low, crossing loosely in front to tie on one side, and a pair of black jersey wide-legged pants. Her feet were crisscrossed by the thin black leather straps of low sandals.

After tenting foil over the roast chicken, she took a cool glass of Lirac Blanc to the terrace. Clouds had pushed in from the sea and lingered in the southeast, where they grew into shifting towers of black and gold. To the north, the light was as clear and bright as spun glass. The breeze sharpened, and the air held the musk of impending rain.

Lia heard the soft thump of a car door shutting and walked

inside, pausing to light the candles on the table. The doorbell chimed low and resonant. Inhaling deeply, she checked her reflection in the mirror above the hall table, tried to still her heart and her hands, and opened the door.

"Lia, hello." He stood on the doorstep, the picture of elegance in a sky-blue button-down, caramel corduroys, and a dark blue sweater draped loosely across his shoulders.

"Lucas. This is a surprise. What are you doing here?"

"I was shooting some video outside Caunes-Minervois and thought I'd see if you were home." His excuse rolled out as finely woven as his sweater. "I should have called first. But it occurred to me just as I was passing Minerve to stop in."

"How did you know where I live?"

"You told me the cottage was Le Pèlerin." He pointed to the brass plaque attached to the stone wall.

Did I? Lia couldn't recall telling him anything other than she was renting a house in Minerve.

"I know it's last minute, but would you care to have a drink? Or dinner? The new bistro in the village is getting great reviews."

"Lucas, I'm sorry, I'm expecting someone." The oven timer sounded. She glanced inside. "Just a moment." Lia dashed to silence the chiming alarm and opened the oven door to see that the white flesh of the potatoes had crisped to a golden brown. She switched off the heat. When she turned back, he stood in the kitchen threshold.

She watched as Lucas took in the place settings, the candles, and the centerpiece of tulips. His body seemed to ripple; his irises deepened to seal black.

"Were you really just in the neighborhood?" Lia asked.

"You caught me," he said, opening his hands in concession. "I wasn't far, within a respectable detour distance. But yes, I went out of my way to see you."

"Why?"

"Why?" he repeated with a smile, as if the answer were obvious. "Because we're creative partners, and I want to know you better. Because I was hoping to take you to dinner."

"Even though I've told you I'm not ready to see anyone?" The moment the words fell out of her mouth, she wished for a rewind button.

"Apparently, you've changed your mind." He nodded to the waiting table.

"You're assuming this dinner is a date."

"You don't owe me an explanation, Lia."

"You're right, I don't."

"But I'm here." Lucas waved a dismissive hand toward the table. "He isn't."

She burst out laughing. "Uncle," she cried in English.

He gave her a puzzled look. "*Oncle?*"

"It's just an expression," she continued in French. Lucas moved into the kitchen to stand beside her. "It means, 'Enough, you win.' You should have been a lawyer, Lucas. You have the perfect reply for everything."

The discreet aroma of his cologne exuded an ancient scent of vetiver and sandalwood. Lia pushed away the sudden, unbidden image of her body pressing into his, her face buried in his neck. The room fell into shadow as the sun dropped behind the canyon. She switched on a small lamp that sat at the end of the kitchen counter and refilled her wineglass. Lia lifted the bottle over another glass, but Lucas shook his head.

"I haven't been completely honest with you." His voice softened, losing its flirtatious tone. He leaned against the center island and crossed his ankles. For a man about to make a confession, he looked relaxed and confident.

"What do you mean?"

"Two years ago, I went to your lecture at the Institute for Cathar Studies. That's when I first heard you talk about Castelnau's death. But you also spoke about the Cathar belief in reincarnation and the fluid nature of the afterlife. You spoke so beautifully about the history of Languedoc and the spirits that roam this region."

Of course she remembered. It was the lecture she'd given three days after her husband's death, the same night she'd met Jordí Bonafé. "It wasn't a large crowd," she replied. "I'm certain I'd recall having seen you there."

"I came late and left early. After you spoke, I knew I'd heard all I wanted to."

"Why didn't you tell me this before?" She set her wineglass on the counter.

"There didn't seem to be a right time. I didn't realize until I looked you up the next day that you were Gabriel Sarabias's wife, and the coincidence shocked me. I'm sorry. It must bring back painful memories."

"Why are you telling me now?"

"I was afraid I'd lose your trust if you found out I'd been there."

Trust. A word she felt she had to learn the meaning of all over again. Raoul, the man who set her spine tingling, seemed to be playing a cat-and-mouse game; Lucas appeared when he wasn't expected, always with a lifeline extended to her. She glanced at the screen of her cell phone. No texts. No calls. Seven had long since passed. Lia willed Raoul to arrive. Did she imagine it, or had his Jeep roared past the cottage a few minutes before, leaving behind the fumes of second thoughts?

"My invitation to dinner is still open," said Lucas. "Though whatever you've made smells delicious. I'm guessing by the way you keep checking the time that your guest is late. He's a fool for missing this."

"Would you excuse me for a moment?" Lia slid the phone from the counter, letting it drop into her palm. She stepped onto the terrace and closed the door behind her. Raoul's voice answered, but it was only a brusque request to leave a message.

"Hey, it's Lia. It's getting late. I'm a little concerned about you. Don't worry about dinner. I'm…stepping out for a bit. Just give me a call when you get a chance." She disconnected the call. "You really aren't coming, are you?" she murmured to the blank screen.

Lia closed her hand over the phone and regarded the man standing inside. Desire and devotion were written clearly on his face and in his dark eyes; he'd treated her with nothing but kindness and deference. But honesty? There were layers to Lucas that covered some central truth.

"Bistro La Candela, isn't it?" Lia asked when she reentered the dining room. "I've been meaning to try it out." She blew out the candles flickering on the table.

"That's the one. Let's walk down."

OUTSIDE LE PÈLERIN—THE SAME EVENING

Raoul drove slowly past the cottage, taking in the bronze BMW parked just outside. He caught a glimpse of a tall, lean man with dark blond hair passing over the threshold of the open front door. He drove into the village and circled back; the car remained in front of the cottage. This time, however, Le Pèlerin's door was closed.

"Lia," he said aloud. He considered going straight to the front door to be greeted by her tawny beauty. He could feel the silk of her skin, smell the lavender and sea bound in her hair, hear the richness of her voice that warmed as it rose to her throat and emerged husky and low from her lips. He ground his teeth

at the thought of leaving her with Lucas, but instinct told him
it wasn't time for a confrontation. He drove on.

Raoul had awakened less than two years before as a man
fully formed in a world that was not unfamiliar. His hands
knew the motions and the required skills. He could drive a
truck and a tractor; he understood motors and electricity, a
toothbrush, a computer. But he had no recollection of when
and where he'd learned to live in this present that had quietly
waited for him. He'd surfaced as a winemaker with his name
on the title of a vineyard and only his dreams for memories.
Raoul knew every inch of the vineyards he now worked,
every hillock and slope, though the forest had disappeared in
some places, grown tall and dense in others. Yet he felt like a
half-empty vessel, moving forward with intuition but no sense
of direction.

He drove out of the village, toward the river canyon, and
parked the battered Jeep on a dirt track used by farmers to
access the vineyards north of Minerve. He sat, hands kneading
the steering wheel, and listened to the shuddering wind that
rose from the canyon and ran its fingers through the oak and
cypress that lined the river. Their branches groaned and scraped
against one another, adding their lamentation to the rage that
built in Raoul. Imagining Lia standing close to the stranger, her
body angled toward him, listening, laughing, the man tucking
a stray curl behind her ear, Raoul's fists clenched. His vision
narrowed to a pinpoint as he remembered.

A few weeks before Christmas, he'd been in a bar in Narbonne, enjoying a late afternoon pastis with Domènec. Coming back from the restroom, he'd seen a man alone at a table, gazing out the window into the descending darkness. In that instant, the air had filled with the stench of smoke and burning flesh; images of fire and charred bodies poured into his vision. He'd had to lean into the wall for support as the floor swayed beneath his feet. When Raoul's head had cleared, he'd seen the front door closing on the man's heels. On impulse, he'd followed and watched as the stranger drove away in a bronze BMW.

Since that moment, he caught himself looking over his shoulder, starting at sudden noises, struggling with insomnia, on guard against an inexplicable malice. When he could sleep, vivid dreams with movie-set images of medieval Languedoc, full of burning buildings and screeching raptors, plagued him until he woke with dread in his gut.

The night of the winter solstice, a different vision came: a woman, emerging naked and ghostly from a dark room, impossibly beautiful, with eyes belonging to his beloved wife. Knowing she was in danger, Raoul reached out, but the woman dissolved into blackness. Another dream followed not long after. He found himself in the basilica in Carcassonne's fortress city, helping her escape from a danger he couldn't name, one that vanished when he'd returned to search inside the church. He woke with the certainty he'd been dreaming of some other life. Until Lia had appeared in the kitchen at Mas Hivert.

She was real in the present and yet somehow a part of his past. As was the stranger from the café, the stranger who had started the nightmares Raoul couldn't escape, the same man who had entered Lia's home. How were they connected?

Raoul wandered a dark corridor with a light at the end that grew fainter and more distant the longer he walked.

The muted phone vibrated against his heart. He listened to Lia's message. Ten minutes later, he stood outside Le Pèlerin.

The village was silent as Lucas walked her home. They'd discussed nothing personal during their meal of duck breast and foie gras with truffles—only their book project. Bending their heads over his iPad, working through a bottle of full-bodied Fitou, they'd studied Lucas's photographs, and Lia had typed notes into her phone, which had given her an excuse to check for a call from Raoul. None had come.

On her doorstep, an unsettled fog of awkwardness and dread drifted around Lia. She inserted her key into the lock and turned to Lucas.

He cupped her face in his smooth hands and traced a line from her earlobe and along her jaw to her mouth with a long finger, a gesture that left her feeling delicate and treasured. He drew her up and settled his lips against hers. She didn't resist his sweet, cool mouth, but the kiss was wrong. He released her face, and the warmth of his hands lingered on her skin. She eased back against the door, grateful for its solid weight.

"I've wanted to do that since I saw you sitting on the wall in Narbonne," he said.

"We're colleagues, Lucas," Lia replied. "*Shit*," she hissed in English. Then, in French, "I shouldn't have let you kiss me."

"It's what two people who are attracted to one another do."

"You assume I'm attracted to you?"

"Can you tell me honestly that you aren't?"

"I can't work on this book with you and have this—whatever this is—between us."

"Then I'll take that as a maybe." His tone was playful, but he hadn't stepped back—she fumbled for the door handle behind her. Lia could take the easy way out and tell him she thought she was falling in love with someone else. But that was too close to the truth, and it was a truth that startled her. It was another step on the path of letting go of the past. Of letting go of Gabriel.

"I'll call you."

"You'll call me," he echoed in a hollow voice. "Of course." He pulled car keys from his front pocket. "I hope so. We're on deadline."

"Lucas."

"I can't compete with an empty table, Lia." He nodded to the cottage as if they could see through the stone and timber to the abandoned dinner inside. "Let me leave with some dignity."

And so he left. She shut the door behind her and heard the bass rumble of the engine as his car came to life. It faded as Lucas drove down the hill and away from Minerve.

Lia dropped her cell phone and keys on the hall table just as a gust of wind slammed a wooden shutter against the house. The crash nearly sent her out of her skin. She raced through the kitchen to the glass wall that overlooked the terrace, secured the windows, and stepped outside to fasten the shutters. Each gust of wind brought needles of rain—a downpour was only moments away. Just before closing the glass doors and wooden front from the inside, she faced the oncoming storm.

He sat on the far edge of the terrace, perched on the iron railing, as he had in December. His feathers appeared black against the bruised sky, and the wind pushed at them from behind, but the eagle stood firm. "*Mon aigle,*" she whispered, her heart hammering. "*Ne me quitte pas*—don't go." She took a tentative step forward. The eagle opened his beak wide but made no sound. She whimpered in awe and took another step.

Balancing with the grace of an acrobat, he lifted from the railing and let the wind take him away. When the rain hit, she heard a high, piercing cry.

Raoul had stayed in the shadows watching the house, waiting for their return.

As the kiss unfolded just feet from where he hid, he felt the pieces of his mind disassembling, the past and the present falling in shards of glass to the bottom of his soul. He heard his wife's voice and felt her body, as vulnerable as the dove for which she'd been named.

"Our souls can cross time, Raoul." Paloma curled into his chest, fitting perfectly in the circle of his arms, as she tried again to explain the Cathars' vision of the afterlife to her nonbelieving husband.

And yet, eight hundred years after his precious Paloma, Bertran, and Aicelina had burned alive in a church in Gruissan, eight hundred years after a fever had burned him alive in a cave not far from where he now stood, Raoul had returned. If only he could understand why.

He dissolved into the darkness and left Le Pèlerin—and Lia—behind.

LOGIS DU MARTINET, LAGRASSE—THE NEXT DAY

*L*ia parked the Peugeot behind Raoul's Jeep, but she sat inside the car for several minutes after turning off the engine. The house and winery appeared sealed up and foreboding, gray brick against gray clouds. The wind had shoved in from the Mediterranean, and the air was thick with impending rain. In the distance, a thin smudge of smoke rose lazily into the overcast sky; Raoul was burning something in the fields beyond the winery. The pungent, ashy odor of smoldering vines wafted down from the slopes and drew her out of the car.

Her phone, tucked in the back pocket of her jeans, chirped with an incoming call. She fumbled for it, squinting at the screen: *Lucas*. She groaned and switched the phone to silent.

Once more into the vineyard, Lia quipped silently to stifle her anxiety. As she climbed the slope, past canes sprouting tiny fists of new green buds, the first drops of rain began to fall.

Raoul stood at the head of a row of vines, one hand pressed into a thick end post, watching the dying fire. Isis sat at his feet, her tail the color of iron-rich earth slapping the ground. She scooted toward Lia, grinning with her long, white teeth. Lia knelt down, and her open arms were filled with wriggling dog.

"I shouldn't have come," she said, holding Isis's face away from hers. "But I was worried when you didn't show or respond to my call." Even as she said the words, Lia cringed at how shrill they sounded. "Now that I know you're fine, I feel so foolish." She prattled on, filling the space that loomed between them.

"It was rude of me to not call," he conceded. "I owe you an explanation, Lia, but I won't lie to you. It's an explanation you may not want to hear."

She rose to standing, and Isis collapsed at her feet. "Try me."

"I did come by last night. But you had company."

Lucas. Dammit.

"That was a coincidence, Raoul. He's a photographer, and we're working on a book together. He just stopped by…" Her sentences were choked. Even though she spoke the truth, her words rang hollow.

"From the looks if it, you're doing more than just working together." Raoul glanced away, but not before she saw glinting anger. "I saw more than I wanted to. So I left."

Embarrassment and rage filled her in equal measure. Her face flamed, and her temper flared. "You spied on me? Oh, this is rich."

They stood apart, trying to work through the other's misunderstanding. Then Lia stepped forward and wove her fingers into his hand where it rested on the post.

"Two days ago, you said you'd been waiting for someone to show you who you should be. You *kissed* me. Can we go back to that moment?"

"Lia." He drew her hand toward him, and she moved a step closer. "There is more I need to say. I am real. Real as you, real as this stone and these vines. But this"—he turned her hand up, tapping his fingers in the middle of her palm—"this flesh is arbitrary, temporary. I am of this world, but not of this time. Not completely."

"What are you talking about?"

"I'm talking about another life. I believe you and I may have known each other in another life."

"You aren't making any sense."

"You're an expert on the Cathar faith. Tell me what the Cathars believed about death and the afterlife."

She pulled her hand from his in exasperation. Why would this history matter now? "The Cathars believed that death doesn't always mean the end to the soul," she replied. "They believed the soul of someone who died tragically could remain in some sort of suspended afterlife, seeking resolution through perpetual reincarnation." Back on familiar academic ground, her voice and hands steadied. "But these are myths, Raoul. Religious superstitions, just like Christian miracles and saints." The rain began to intensify.

Lia recited, "'*When I woke, I was.*' That's what you said to me, but I thought you were talking about waking from the grief of losing your wife. My God. Don't tell me you're talking about reincarnation?"

Raoul lifted a shoulder in a maddening half shrug, neither conceding nor disagreeing.

"Reincarnation?" Lia repeated, her voice rising to a near-shout. She clasped Raoul's wrists, forcing him to look her in the eye. "Is this what you are telling me?" Her mind raced as he nodded slowly, firmly, incredibly. "That is madness. Cruel, ridiculous madness." Lia dropped his hands and stepped back.

Raoul held her gaze, but his face was dark and hard. She could see the sorrow in his eyes, but it was the disappointment that hurt the most.

"I can't do crazy, Raoul," she said. "I've lost too much to waste my heart like this."

As Lia walked to her car, she ached to hear him say, "Stop, Lia. Don't leave." But no voice spoke, and she didn't look back.

Lia stopped at the foot of the drive, out of view of Logis du Martinet, and pulled out her phone. She needed to see some-one who didn't know Raoul or Gabriel, someone who could be objective about her heart. If it hadn't been for the previous night, she might even have called Lucas.

She cursed as Jordí's recorded voice answered her call. She nearly hung up, but when the phone beeped, she let out in a rush, "Father Bonafé, Jordí, I need to see you. Any chance you're around today? I'm headed to Narbonne now. Please call."

Her phone rang as she waited for a convoy of trucks to pass before merging onto the road. "Of course I'll meet you, Lia," said Jordí. "Wherever, whenever you need." She scribbled down the address of a bistro off rue Mazzini and sagged with relief over the steering wheel.

The sobs broke free as she pulled onto the highway.

NARBONNE—SAME DAY

Lia arrived in Narbonne feeling raw and displaced. The city seemed all but abandoned as the Narbonnais congregated in cafés and restaurants to wait out the spring tempest that had blown in from the Mediterranean. The aroma of onions in butter, the musty scent of damp wool, and the reassuring sound of laughter enveloped her in the foyer where Jordí waited. The maître d' led them upstairs to a quiet table on the mezzanine.

"You were upset when you called. What's happened?"

As she searched for the words to explain her morning, Lia realized she had to start from the beginning, which was Carcassonne and the terror of the corridor in the Basilique Saint-Nazaire et Saint-Celse. Everything seemed to tumble forward from that day.

"Yes, what can I bring you? Something to drink?" An aproned waiter dropped a basket of sliced bread on their table, his gaze roaming the mezzanine as he took stock of the other diners. Lia ordered a bowl of onion soup without looking at her menu. The priest ignored his as well and asked for beef cheek braised in red wine—the house specialty. He also ordered a bottle of Cabardès red. The waiter nodded absently, picked up their menus, and moved to the next table.

Re-creating scenes as fantastic as a fever dream, Lia told Jordí of the stranger who had approached her in the nave of Saint-Nazaire. She relived the disembodied footsteps echoing on the stone floor and the descent into the basilica's bowels. How the stranger had shoved her through a suffocating corridor, insisting they were being followed, only to abandon her on the hillside above Carcassonne. Agitation sifted across the priest's face as she spoke, but he remained silent.

A passing waiter brought their wine, opened the bottle, and poured the deep-violet Cabardès. The moment he left, Lia drank half her glass. "Winter solstice, the night I arrived, I thought I saw a face in my window. A man's face, with a scar on his left side, here," she said as she swept a finger across her cheek. Jordí blanched, and his irises swelled, but still he said nothing, and the words continued to pour from Lia. "But it was some sort of optical illusion or crazy vision. I went outside, and there was a Bonelli's eagle sitting on my terrace, so close I could've touched him. He was one of the most magnificent things I've ever seen.

"Here's where it really gets strange, Father. Jordí," she corrected herself. "Two days after Carcassonne, the man from the basilica showed up at Mas Hivert. He's a winemaker friend of Domènec's. At first, he acted as if he'd never seen me before, claiming not to remember anything about Saint-Nazaire. But we talked and he…we…" Heat slid over her face. The priest gave her a curious look; her flushed skin said more than her stammered words. "I realized his was the same face that had appeared in my window on solstice night." Lia sat back, a little scared but filled with relief at having finally told her story.

"Does this man have a name?" Jordí asked.

"Raoul Arango."

At the mention of Raoul's name, Jordí gripped the table's edge, his knuckles turning white from the pressure. His reaction told her enough: their paths had intersected. And this seemed no more improbable to Lia than anything else she'd experienced since December 21.

The waiter appeared with their meals, and Jordí was spared from having to respond. He took time slicing his portion of tender beef nestled in a pile of baked conchiglioni and mushrooms and sat back, closing his mouth around a forkful of meat and vegetables.

Lia dipped her spoon into the large bowl before her and stirred the soup, releasing steam, before asking, "Jordí, how do you know Raoul?"

The priest finished chewing and then set his knife and fork to rest on the side of his plate, taking Lia's question in measured stride. "I knew of him a very long time ago," he said. "He went by d'Aran then. I wasn't around to know what became of him after…" Jordí's voice dropped, and he spoke as though Lia had vanished from the banquette seat. "He was killed before he could—"

Lia's harsh laughter cut short the priest's hushed musing. Her resigned acceptance vanished. "*Killed?*" She leaned forward and said, "Pardon my language, Jordí, but *what the fuck?*"

He grimaced at the English words, understanding the curse. Then the priest turned up his palms as if to offer her the answer. Swallowing a wave of nausea, Lia pushed away the bowl. She gasped, and the gasp became incredulous laughter. Shoving back from the table, she glanced around, reassuring herself the sane world was still having a civilized lunch.

Jordí breathed in deeply and exhaled his answer in a hushed voice. "I don't know when he left this earth, Lia. But he walked it still in 1208."

The clattering of dishes, the rumble of conversation, the comforting buzz of normal life receded into the distance.

"*Twelve*-oh-eight," she echoed. "This can't be."

"I'm sorry. I know this is so hard to understand." She could almost hear him clucking in sympathy. "A lost soul has found you."

"Please, stop." Lia held up her hand. "Let me think." Her glass shook as she lifted it to her lips and drank. "You're telling me that this man I'm falling in love with"—the priest's eyes widened—"yes, falling in love with, despite myself… You're telling me he is eight hundred years old?" She forced a laugh, but it was empty of mirth.

Jordí's words came back to her: *I knew of him a very long time ago.* Fear chilled the heat of her frustration. "Who are you, Jordí?"

"I attended seminary at Sant Benet with Raoul's cousin. He was a dear friend of mine once." Jordí hung his head, toying with the knife by his plate, his own meal forgotten. His words took a moment to sink in.

"I don't believe what you're telling me," Lia said. But she already did. It was a truth she'd tried to ignore since the night she'd arrived in France: the past had caught up to her, bringing another life with it.

The priest sat in silence, letting her sort out the thoughts and emotions that barreled through her mind and pounded into her heart. At last, he spoke. "Lia, let me tell you a story."

The rain had stopped while Jordí spun out his tale, and the bistro settled into the deep of the afternoon. A few diners murmured over their late lunches, and the waitstaff congregated at tables just outside the entrance, smoking and chatting. Some were enjoying a beer after their shift, while others prepared for the evening with small cups of thick, black espresso tempered by cubes of sugar.

"You witnessed Castelnau's murder," Lia said in a flat voice. The wall between her head and her heart crumbled as she tried to reason through what the priest had laid before her. "I'm a fool to accept a word of what you've just told me. And yet I believe you. Or at least I'm willing to play along."

"I'm asking you to trust your instincts and accept the impossible," he conceded.

"It was you who identified the assassin as a man of Toulouse's? History has it Castelnau was ambushed outside of Saint-Gilles, near the river."

Jordí toyed with his fork, running his finger along the pointed tines. "I didn't tell anyone I'd seen the assassination. Only that I'd seen Toulouse's man fleeing from the church before I found the body."

"What? Why? If you'd said that much, why not tell the whole truth?"

"I was terrified that if word got around I'd witnessed the murder, I'd be next. At the very least, I'd be banished from the church for having stood by and let it happen." He stabbed the fork into the linen tablecloth. "And you and I both know what happens to history along the way. Facts are only as good as the proof. But the man was wearing a red tunic with a twelve-pointed cross. The symbol of the House of Toulouse."

"So, you just watched Castelnau die." It wasn't a question, but Jordí responded all the same.

"I was a coward. Yes. Weak. Stupid. I didn't even understand what I was seeing when I read the letter."

"What happened to that letter?" she asked.

Jordí shook his head. "I never reentered the abbey, and I left Saint-Gilles not long after. I thought many years ago to seek out that stone, but the church has been destroyed and rebuilt so many times. If the letter was ever found, history has buried its secrets."

"And you remember nothing of what you read? A date? A signature? Anything?"

The priest squinted, peering through the haze of his memory. "I don't recall a date or if it was signed. There wasn't even a seal, just a simple sheet."

Lia sighed her disappointment. "What was it Castelnau said before he was attacked? 'It's true. I was warned that Plessis would betray me.' Is that it?" Jordí nodded. "Who warned Castelnau?"

"History has sealed that path," Jordí said, lifting his shoulders and raising his hands. "Castelnau knew the man who killed him, that was for certain."

Lia repeated the archdeacon's words, turning them over in her mind. "Castelnau must have meant Philippe du Plessis," she said. "He was the commander of the Knights Templar when the Cathar Crusade was declared." Lia sat back, exhaling a low, soft whistle. "And you really told no one what you'd heard?"

"The name meant nothing to me at the time," Jordí said. "I was just a country monk training to be a priest. A few days after the murder, one of Raymond's men bragged he'd killed Castelnau. And he was killed by a mob immediately after. That's as far as the trail went. Within weeks, Pope Innocent declared the crusade. The details of who had killed Castelnau or why no longer mattered."

"How does Raoul fit into this?"

Jordí pulled at his shirt collar and smoothed his palm over the feathery strands of hair on the back of his head.

"Raoul d'Aran's wife was Paloma Gervais, the daughter of a wealthy wine merchant in Limoux. She and Raoul had two children, a son and daughter."

Lia's heart pounded. "Bertran and Aicelina," she said. *Limoux. Paloma's father.* She recalled Raoul's strained expression when she mentioned her grandparents' village.

"Yes, how did you know?"

"Raoul told me their names. I didn't know he was talking about a family from the thirteenth century. What became of them?"

"Sometime after the burning of Cluet in July 1208, she and the children were sent to hide in Gruissan. In December, they were found out and arrested and sent to the church of Saint-Maurice, where villagers accused as heretics were trapped inside. The church was destroyed by fire on December 18. It was assumed Paloma and the children were among the dead."

She shuddered. She'd read many accounts of the torture and murder of innocents during the Cathar Crusade. Years later, the Spanish Inquisition would garner infamy, but those interrogation and torture techniques had their roots in Languedoc's castle dungeons and churches.

"Why wasn't Raoul with them?"

Jordí shook his head, his eyes downcast. "That I don't know. I never met the man. I heard rumors that he led some sort of resistance movement to warn villagers and landowners of the coming doom, encouraging them to rise up against the Knights and the Church. Raoul d'Aran had the ear of Raymond of Toulouse, who defied the Church for many years, until—"

"Until it became obvious it was a hopeless cause," she finished. After years of openly supporting the Cathars, even after being excommunicated by the Catholic Church for the murder of Castelnau, the count turned his back on Languedoc and joined the crusade to crush the heretics and end the south's fight to remain independent from France. "How did Raoul die?"

"Lia, it's all lost to history."

"The scar." She touched her face.

Jordí lifted his shoulders in a gesture that could have been a shrug or a sign of agreement. "A festering wound in those days could mean blood poisoning. Sepsis could take a man in a day or two." He patted his chest and his side pockets. He brought out a phone from the depths of his coat and squinted at the screen. After tapping out a text reply, Jordí clasped his hands together on the table. "Lia, I apologize. That was the indomitable Madame Isner, wondering where I am. I'm late for a parish finance committee meeting. I must leave you now, but can we resume this conversation tomorrow morning?"

Lia gaped at him, uncomprehending. Leave now? In the

middle of this impossible story? "Where do I fit into this, Jordí?" she asked. "Why has Raoul come into my life?"

"I believe his reincarnation is a sign that he has something to atone for, some part of his story to resolve. But I think those are questions you must ask Raoul."

"I have one last question before I let you go," Lia said. "Do I look like Paloma?"

Jordí's expression was inscrutable, but his brown eyes took on that wooden glare she'd seen in his office in January. "I couldn't say." He pushed away from the table and stood. "I never met Paloma. Now, I really must go."

SAINT-GILLES, PROVENCE-LANGUEDOC BORDER—FEBRUARY 1208

One month after the murder of Archdeacon Pierre de Castelnau, Jordí Bonafé labored up the steps leading from the abbey's crypt to the nave. At the head of the stairs stood Abbot Bonnín, the head of the monastery at Saint-Gilles. He'd left for Narbonne shortly after Jordí's arrival, assigning the young monk the chore of waiting on the visiting Cistercian archdeacon. It was only Jordí's role as Castelnau's acolyte that found him in the nave on that freezing January dawn. Bonnín returned days later to find his parish in an uproar and the novice priest nearly mute with shock.

"Brother Bonafé, here you are." Bonnín heaved up his belly and tucked his thumbs into the wide strip of black felt that spanned his generous waist. "You have a visitor."

Jordí paused at the top step as Bonnín moved aside, and a second figure stepped into view. He was horrified to feel the warm gush of urine flow down his leg as his bladder betrayed his fear. Before him stood a tall man with honeyed hair and black eyes. Pierre de Castelnau's assassin.

"Brother Bonafé, allow me to introduce the sénéchal of the Aude and Hérault, Lucas Mauléon. He has been sent from Paris to meet with you." Bonnín stepped aside. Jordí blinked, looked from one man to the other, and snapped his gaping mouth shut. The last time he'd seen this sénéchal, the man had been wearing the twelve-pointed cross of the French crown's enemy, the Count of Toulouse.

"I've come to offer my regrets for your ordeal," said Lucas. A smile flickered and vanished. "And to escort you to your new residence. You will continue your priestly training in Narbonne."

"Narbonne?" Jordí kept his trembling hands folded inside his robes. The sharp odor of piss singed the air, and he prayed the rot-sweet scent wafting from the crypt would overpower it. "What of the abbey?"

"Your superiors thought it best to relieve you of the burden of all you witnessed here."

"Witnessed?" choked Jordí. He cleared his throat and started again. "But it's over. The man confessed and received his judgment before God. I wish to remain in Saint-Gilles."

Mauléon's face remained closed to the monk's pleas. Bonnín watched the two men with detached curiosity. He wanted the scandal removed from his abbey, and if the Church and the law felt it best to reassign the rotund young monk, so be it. "Come, men, it stinks in this nave," he said. "We'll break our fast and send you on your way."

Jordí excused himself, wanting to be rid of his soiled garment and catch his breath. He couldn't meet the sénéchal's eyes when he returned a short while later, his few things packed in a satchel of thick wool. He was trapped.

Mauléon rushed through the morning meal offered by the abbot and insisted on retaking the road soon after, aiming to arrive in Lunel by dusk. But Jordí begged to make one more visit to the abbey to offer a prayer for their journey.

Alone, Jordí entered the church. As he genuflected, he glanced around the nave; it was empty. He hurried up a side aisle toward the choir. His errand took only a moment. Before he emerged from the portico to the outside, he smoothed the thick cloak he wore over a clean cassock, willing his hands to cease their shaking.

The sénéchal flashed a grin at Jordí's approach. "So, my fat friend, I hope you've bid your farewells to northern Languedoc. Perhaps by the time you return, this will be part of France." He secured the saddle on the sturdy palfrey that would bear Jordí's weight on the road to Narbonne and motioned him to the waiting horse. He held the reins while Jordí mounted the saddle. "You're shaking like a child. Why so afraid?"

Sitting atop the mare's short, sturdy legs and square back, the monk avoiding looking at the sénéchal. "This is all so sudden," he said. "I hear these roads are no longer safe for small parties. Are we to travel alone?"

"These roads are unsafe only for those who would deny the will of the Christian Church and the Soldiers of Christ." Mauléon lifted himself lightly onto the horse he called Achille and drew alongside Jordí. The horse and rider towered over the monk and his palfrey. "And we have a long journey ahead of us, so there will be plenty of time for me to explain how you will best be of service."

Thinking of the words he'd read in the abbey of Saint-Gilles—

the warning about a falcon sent to slaughter the dove—Jordí shuddered. But Mauléon hadn't finished. "And whatever service we find for you, resistance will be met with the point of the same knife you saw slide into the archdeacon's chest."

Jordí couldn't get his brain to work fast enough to decipher what he should do, whom he could tell that Lucas Mauléon was Castelnau's assassin. He could only pray, pray for God's protection. It was not likely he could count on that of the Church.

Mauléon kicked out with the toe of his boot and dug it into the flank of Jordí's horse. The mare whinnied and shot forward. Jordí lurched in the saddle but regained his balance. He glanced behind to see the sénéchal laughing.

As they continued west, Jordí considered the calfskin pouch and the sheet of fine paper with the broken red wax seal folded within that he'd pressed under a stone in the nave of Saint-Gilles in the minutes after committing Castelnau's body to God. That velvety calfskin was now molded to the barrel of his belly, secured around his waist by a wide strip of cotton. It gave him some measure of security. Someday he would figure out how to use it to his advantage.

LE PÈLERIN, MINERVE—THURSDAY EVENING

Lia returned to Le Pèlerin as dusk crept over the valley. Slipping off her shoes in the foyer, she pulled her heavy heart up the stairs, sank onto the bed, and curled into a ball under a wool blanket.

Her suitcase sat tucked in a corner next to the armoire. It would be so easy to gather her few things, pour out the milk, toss the fruit, shutter the windows, and walk away. She could go anywhere. But nowhere she'd been before. No, it would have to be someplace new—one without familiar faces or any trace of the history she'd studied and thought she understood. Certainly no place where ghosts and memories could haunt her.

Lia had come to Languedoc in search of healing and for the only thing that made sense to her—the distant, ancient past. The past she could control, because she knew what happened in the end. But the past as she'd understood it was now a present that wrapped her in mystery and threat. What she thought she knew and could control through footnotes and translation was changing before her eyes.

A man from time gone by walked this world, as real as the sunrise, coming in search of her—or perhaps in search of rescue from a force that reason said simply couldn't exist. Lia balanced how it would feel to leave Raoul behind with her guilt and confusion over loving again.

The possibility of starting over loomed like a chasm. Where would she go that wouldn't be an ending? Languedoc—in the folds of these mountains, in these valleys of stone, with the history of these crumbling citadels—was her home. Rose and Domènec were her family now.

Exhausted, Lia drifted into a dream and found herself on a river bank along the Cesse. Before her stood Raoul, wearing the cloak of the man who had traveled forward through the centuries. Or had she traveled back?

What if we just disappeared, left this mess behind? her dream voice pleaded. *We could vanish into Greece, Morocco...*

He would follow us, Paloma. His hand caressed her cheek. *There would be no peace. But you don't have to be a part of this story. He found me through you, and he's using you to draw me out. I am here. You can leave. And when this is over, I will find you.*

She woke to silence. Before she gathered the energy to move her limbs and face the present, she replayed the dream, seeking the warmth in Raoul's skin and the assurance of love in his eyes.

He'd called her Paloma.

"I have to find him," she said aloud to the dark. "I have to find this man who is after Raoul. That's why I'm here."

She sat up and switched on the light. Taking her journal from the nightstand, she wrote down everything Jordí had said to her in the bistro, every word and phrase she could remember, his expressions and hesitations. Her questions and disbelief became acceptance and resignation as she wrote. She'd fallen in love with a man who should not be.

18

NARBONNE—FRIDAY

*D*ecades of sucking unfiltered Gauloise cigarettes had etched a web of wrinkles around Madame Isner's mouth, and lipstick bled into the tiny crevices. Those scarlet lips formed a moue of disdain when Lia set her bag on the counter of Saint-Just et Saint-Pasteur's administrative offices and announced she was there to see Jordí. Even though Lia spoke French as a native, tied her scarf just so, and wrapped her hair in an elegant chignon, Madame Isner sneered at her as if she'd walked in wearing a baseball cap and tennis shoes.

"Father Bonafé is not available," the secretary snapped.

"We had plans to meet today. I'm Lia Carrer. Father Bonafé said to come at ten." Lia checked her watch. "I'm a few minutes early. I'll wait."

"I know who you are, and you'll be waiting in vain. Father Bonafé is out of town."

"Out of town? But we had lunch yesterday. You called to remind him about a finance committee meeting, and he came back here."

"I did no such thing." Madame Isner sniffed. "Father Bonafé most certainly did not return here yesterday. At any rate, the finance committee meets every other Tuesday."

Lia imagined smacking the creamy, red smirk clean off Madame's face, and she clenched the strap of her bag to keep her hand in place.

"Do you know where I can find him or when he'll be back?"

"Most certainly not, Mademoiselle Carrer."

"It is *Madame*," she replied, acid dripping from her tone. "May I at least work in the Trésor until lunch?"

"Impossible." The secretary straightened a stack of papers, smacking the bottom edge against her desk. "No one is allowed to work in the archives without supervision, and I am the only administrator on staff. Not even I have clearance to access the Trésor. It is closed to the public until further notice."

Lia blew air noisily upward, ruffling her bangs, and slapped her hands on the counter. Madame Isner drew back, her mouth folding into a thousand tiny pleats as her lips pursed in distaste. "So be it," Lia said. "If you happen to hear from Father Bonafé, I'd be grateful if you'd ask him to contact me immediately."

"I suggest you leave a note for his mailbox. I am not his personal secretary."

Lia turned on her heel and left without another word. Back in her car, she pounded the steering wheel with the flat of her palms. *Damn you, Jordí. Where do I go now? I have no idea where you live.* She'd tried to leave a message earlier, but an automated voice informed her the priest's number was currently unavailable.

Out of ideas, she drove back to Minerve. On the doorstep of
Le Pèlerin sat a large mailing envelope with no name or address.

LE PÈLERIN, MINERVE—SATURDAY AFTERNOON

Lia drained a bottle of San Pellegrino and rolled her head from
side to side to loosen her stiff neck. Her eyes throbbed from
staring at pages of tiny, intricate handwriting. Photocopies of
letters or a private diary, written in a script and language she
was struggling to comprehend, were strewn across the dining
table. She'd worked on the translations late into the night and
started again just after dawn. None contained a salutation, but
two had been signed in the same name: *Manel*.

Even more intriguing were a few occurrences of Latin words
wholly familiar to Lia: *Militum Xpisti*—Soldiers of Christ. The
mysterious Knights Templar. Lia pressed finger pads gently
against her orbital bones and massaged her tired eyes. Then she
read again the note clipped to the inside cover of a file folder:

> Lia, the promised collection has been liberated and is now under
> lock and key in the Trésor. I've enclosed only a few of the docu-
> ments I felt confident sending through our scanner. The rest will
> need far more precise treatment, when the time is right. But I
> wanted you to have the first opportunity to explore. I will call
> soon. Jordí

How had Jordí managed such a coup? If these documents
were real, it would mean the archives of Saint-Just et Saint-
Pasteur, overseen by Father Jordí Bonafé, had grown from
small but important to perhaps the most critical mass of Cathar-
related history in France. And no one but he and Lia—and
perhaps the unknown "liberator" of the collection from the

institute, whom she suspected was Jordí himself—knew where these materials were and possibly the secrets they contained. It could take months, even years, to close the institute and comb out the bureaucratic and legal tangle. For the moment, these materials were their secret.

The archival room at Saint-Just et Saint-Pasteur did not possess a high-resolution, museum-quality scanner of its own. The only photo archive lab in the region worth its salt was housed at the Université Paul-Valéry in Montpellier. The documents' authenticity would have to be verified independently, but taking the materials to the university would mean admitting to their existence and where they had come from. Lia was aching to get her hands on the originals locked away in the Trésor. Whatever she was searching for, it had to be there.

Sighing, she gathered the papers into a neat stack and placed them in a binder. The kitchen clock read 2:30. She was meeting Lucas in Lastours at 4:00.

He'd sent an email that morning to say he was headed out to capture the castles in the late-afternoon light. His invitation had been breezy and noncommittal.

I don't know the châteaux very well. If you have time, I'd be grateful for the background while I shoot. The historical perspective always helps the visual one...

Still feeling delicate about how they'd parted in Termes, she had hesitated before finally sending a text. Meet you at visitor's center, 4:00, she promised.

The mystery of when Jordí had left these letters on her doorstep, why, and where he'd disappeared to would have to wait.

Part Three

···

The shapes wore away as if only a dream
Like a sketch that is left on the page
Which the artist forgot and can only complete
On the canvas, with memory's aid.
—CHARLES BAUDELAIRE

···

LE TEMPLE, NORTH OF PARIS—MARCH 1208

*I*n the hours before dawn, a thick fog rolled from the Seine through the Jewish quarter, settling on the plain just north of the city walls. The early morning chill permeated the citadel of the Knights Templar, save for a chamber deep in its interior.

The spacious room exuded comfort and elegance, betraying neither time of day nor season of the year. A fire blazed in the hearth, and a haze of smoke floated against the stone ceiling. Thick carpets from the Orient covered a floor inlaid with planks of polished elm.

Four men sat in a semicircle facing a hearth that was deep enough to hold them all within its brick hollow. Arnaud Amalric, the spider-limbed Abbot of Cîteaux, sat in his customary place on the far left and nearest the fire. Despite his years in the south, his skin was as white as a nun's kirtle. Vanity kept a cap of red velvet edged with embroidery and pearls on his skull so no one would see the bony knobs of his bald pate. Tiny blue veins streamed along his temples and the hollows of his eyes and just beneath the thin skin of his twitching hands. His fingernails were filed to perfect ovals and tipped in white.

Amalric's milky blue eyes roamed over Manel de Perella's long legs where they spilled from his finely woven wool robe, and the young man fought back a shudder of disgust. It was not the first time he'd drawn the wrong sort of attention from a powerful member of the clergy. Manel, the newest in this group of political intimates, had been named nuncio—papal emissary— after Pierre de Castelnau's murder eight weeks before.

Manel avoided Amalric's gaze and turned to the two men on his right. One filled his carved oak chair with dense, muscular limbs. Wearing a cloak lined and trimmed with fur, his face covered in a thick beard shot with silver, he resembled the gilded bear that was his insignia—the symbol emblazoned on his crest and embroidered on the front of his tunic. The bear was Philippe du Plessis, warden of this fortress outside Paris. As thirteenth Grand Master of the Knights Templar—warriors for the crown of France and the Soldiers of Christ—Plessis was one of the most powerful men in France.

The other man was introduced as Lucas Mauléon, the newly appointed sénéchal of the Aude and Hérault Valleys of Languedoc. Mauléon sat with his outstretched legs crossed at the ankles. His regal profile showed the sweep of a Roman nose that ended in a tapered point above his full lips and cheekbones that curved to an unlined brow above dark, almond-shaped eyes.

"My thanks to you, Lord du Plessis, and to you, Sénéchal, for meeting with so little notice." Amalric's thin voice pierced the room's hush. "The papal courier arrived with this letter as soon as the city gates opened. After reading its contents, our new papal emissary and I felt it could not wait. Father de Perella, the letter, please." Amalric motioned to Plessis.

Manel placed a parchment scroll tied with a leather string in the upturned palm of the regal man cloaked in furs. Plessis picked open the knot and unrolled the document. Amalric had broken the wax seal of the Vatican, but Pope Innocent's personal seal, a silver pendant, dangled from a small leather-reinforced hole at the bottom of the scroll. As he scanned the pope's words, Plessis's jaw tightened, and a thick vein on his temple expanded and pulsed.

"It is war," he said. "The pope has responded to Castelnau's murder just as we anticipated." Philippe du Plessis shifted his great bulk to address his coconspirators. "Our secret campaign is now publicly sanctioned by the Church. France is charged with eradicating the Cathars."

Though he'd read the letter, Plessis's authoritative affirmation of war was a hammer blow to Manel's soul. To hide his dismay, Manel swallowed deeply from a goblet of spiced wine and shifted in his seat. Amalric looked at him curiously but offered a wry smile to the Templar commander. "Your hatred of the infidels serves us well, Lord du Plessis."

"Hatred? Hardly, Amalric," Plessis said. "I hold them in contempt. I lost too many men in the battlefields of the Levant protecting the true faith to lose a single hectare to a ragged band of heretics. France would be united but for the south's determination at independence. We must respond immediately to His Holiness," he declared.

"I'll travel back to the Vatican," Manel offered. "I can leave today."

"There is no need for that, Father de Perella." Amalric's

dismissal piped on a reedy voice. "We can send the courier who brought this letter. He's lodged nearby."

"Then he and I will return together. As papal emissary, I insist. I've been away a month already, and His Holiness expects my account of all that's been set in motion since Castelnau's death." Manel was desperate to get away, not just from Amalric's clutches, but to find his cousin.

"I agree," said Plessis. "It would be best if the pope spoke directly with one of us, to look upon one of our faces and know our words are true. Father de Perella, Mauléon will escort you as far as Lyon, and from there, he will make arrangements for the remainder of your journey east and to Rome."

Ignoring Manel's protests against an escort, the commander of the Knights Templar unfolded his powerful limbs, rose, and seated himself at an escritoire set near the door. His bulk dwarfed the delicate desk that sat balanced on spindly, curved legs. His back erect, Plessis wrote in determined strokes. With obvious irritation, Amalric swept up from his chair and began pacing the room.

Manel planted both hands squarely on the chair's arms, preparing to rise. He glanced at Lucas Mauléon, and the sénéchal's dark expression chilled him. Mauléon was just a few years older, but the weight of battle experience was etched into his hard-set jaw and opaque eyes. As if reading Manel's mind, Mauléon tilted his head.

"Manel de Perella," he said in a voice low enough not to be overheard. "You came from the seminary at Sant Benet, did you not?"

"Yes, though I entered the priesthood in Rome."

"But still, you are a son of Catalunya, if I heard correctly?"

"My family is in the Val d'Aran," Manel confirmed.

"Precisely the name I was thinking of," Mauléon said. "You

would be acquainted, perhaps, with one Raoul d'Aran, formerly of the region you called home, who now resides near Lagrasse?"

Manel felt as if he were a mouse under a raptor's scrutiny. The room had grown close and warm. He was acutely aware of how near he was to the fire, and not just the one that snapped with orange flame a few feet from his boots. If this council discovered his deception, they could flay the skin from his bones or set fire to him in a public square to force a confession of conspiracy. Yet these men would never admit that their circle of power had been infiltrated. Retribution would be swift but secret. It would be final.

"Yes." There was no point in lying. "He is a cousin."

Mauléon nodded and propped his chin on the tips of his steepled fingers. "I'm curious about the priest who discovered the archdeacon's body." Manel tipped his head in confusion. "It appears he came from the same seminary as you. Jordí Baltasar Bonafé is his name."

"Jordí Bonafé?" Manel echoed with a gasp. No one had seemed interested in the fate of the young priest-in-training after his testimony had been recorded. And Manel, in his rush to prepare for his journey from the Vatican to Paris, had not thought to ask or even to wonder about the man's identity. "Yes, we were at Sant Benet together. I knew he'd been called to train as a priest, but I never imagined he'd leave Catalunya. Where is he now?" Manel's hand gripped the arm of the chair with an unspoken question: *Is he safe?*

The soldier raised one shoulder in a half shrug. "I heard he's been sent northwest. Poitou, perhaps, or Berry?"

How horrific it must have been for the good-natured young monk to discover the murdered archdeacon. At the seminary, Jordí had earned the nickname *Ósbru*—Brown Bear—for his round, dark body and his affable, lumbering countenance. Manel vowed to track down his friend, who was now so far from home and so close to danger. He burned to slip away from the greedy eyes of Amalric and the watchful gaze of the sénéchal.

The abbot provided his release. He rustled about the room, examining tapestries and handling the precious books and manuscripts Plessis had collected during his travels. The commander paused in his writing, irritated by the restless whispers of Amalric's shifting robes and turning of pages.

"Abbot Amalric, there is no need for you to remain." His deep voice rumbled. "If our young nuncio is to depart immediately, perhaps you should make haste for home and alert your household to prepare his horse and belongings for the long journey."

The abbot's face was a moon of contempt that shone white in the dim shadows of the vaulted chamber. Manel could almost hear Amalric's blood seething in his blue veins.

"Very well," he said through a smile that gripped his teeth. "You are quite right, Plessis." He then spoke to the young men still seated before the fire. "Sénéchal Mauléon, I bid you farewell and Godspeed on your mission. Father de Perella, I will see you momentarily." The heavy door closed with a thud behind him.

A smile flickered across Manel's face, but he was quick to straighten his features when he caught the sénéchal watching him. Plessis sighed and continued with his letter. The only sound was the scratching of a quill against vellum.

When he finished writing, Plessis dripped bloodred wax across the fold of the closed letter and pressed his seal—a bear in profile standing on his hind legs, claws extended and forked tongue lashing out—into the small pool. The correspondence to Pope Innocent III was ready; Manel was at last free to leave.

⌒⟿⌒

Manel picked his way through the melting mud pathways of the Marais. Though the sun had risen only an hour before, the neighborhood vibrated with activity. He flattened himself against a building to avoid being crushed by a cart full of winter vegetables drawn by a squat, disgruntled horse. The pitiful beast dropped piles of shit that steamed in the chill of the March morning. Beggars with shriveled limbs and rotting teeth pulled at Manel's cloak. He dispensed coins and touched the paupers briefly, blessing their doomed bodies and broken souls.

Manel loved the energy of Paris, even its stink and mud and decay; the city was so alive after the marble and stone confines of the Vatican that offered gossip but little life. He felt most at home here in the Marais, where the learned gathered and open debate was encouraged by the rabbis who governed this Jewish quarter.

Lost in contemplation, Manel failed to notice a trailing shadow as he followed rue aux Ours to rue Quincampoix. When he paused to give alms, the shadow blended behind the Jews in their black cloaks or melted into the gray walls. Manel turned into an alley, stopped in front of a wooden door, and rapped three times. He looked to his left, where the alley opened onto the larger road. Angry shouts of a hapless man relieved of his money belt by a pickpocket filled his ears. Passersby swept on, and no one took notice of a solitary priest standing before a closed door.

A small panel in the door slid open. Eyes the color of freshly turned earth peered out, their pupils shrinking to pinpoints at the flash of light. The panel snapped shut, the door opened, and Manel slipped inside.

LASTOURS—THE LAST SATURDAY IN MARCH

*T*his is one of the loneliest places in all of Languedoc." Lucas aimed his Nikon lens through the slit of a *flèche vitrine*—an opening in the side of the tower just wide enough to shoot an arrow through—to capture the raw landscape that punched with rocky fists toward the foothills of the Black Mountain.

"I'm certain this is haunted ground." Lia leaned into the wind that poured through Château Cabaret's ruined south end. "But it's the place where I feel closest to history."

Lucas joined her at the crumbling wall overlooking Cabaret's sister castles Régine, Surdespine, and Quertinheux, which stood sentinel on the spine of the ridge.

"I always imagine if I stand here long enough or visit during the full moon, I'll hear these stones speak." She dismissed the yearning with a shake of her head. "Not exactly material for my dissertation."

"Oh, I don't know, Lia. It sounds just right for the mystical Cathars." Lucas smiled from behind his camera; the shutter clicked and whirred. He finished and tucked the tripod under his arm. "Thank you for meeting me here."

As they walked through the ruins, she described the history behind the photos Lucas had framed and shot.

Each castle was comprised of a single tower surrounded by a stone wall. Perched on bedrock high above the Orbiel River and accessible by a crumbling footpath, the lonely ruins rose like four fingers bursting through a rocky grave. They were all that remained of a series of fortresses constructed in the eleventh century by a family that had derived its wealth from nearby iron mines. The castles became a Cathar seat of resistance until their inhabitants succumbed to a brutal siege in 1227.

Eight hundred years later, Lia could hear those lost souls keening through holes rent in the stone by war and the passing of centuries.

Black-green cypress quivered against a beryl sky, and the musk of thyme and the piquant resin of boxwood swelled with the warmth of the sun. The camouflage of silvery-gray garigue blended into the castle stone. They walked in silence down a steep footpath to the medieval village that had huddled at the base of Cabaret hundreds of years before. The waist-high walls zigzagging between oak and cedar trees were remnants of the homes of those who had loved, fought, and shared the lean times and the good.

They entered a bower sheltered from the wind and warmed by the sun's rays, which beamed between tree branches. Lia brushed russet-colored cedar needles from a level patch of wall and took a seat on the wide ledge. After leaning his tripod against the wall and tucking his camera away in its bag, Lucas sat beside her.

"You said in Gruissan that it would be natural for me to hope to see Gabriel again," she said. "I know I shut you down. The whole notion of reincarnation seemed almost offensive. I guess you could say I've had a change of heart. This agnostic historian now believes the Cathars were right."

Lucas blinked and frowned but allowed her to continue. Lia looked down at her hands, tightly folded in her lap.

"You remember my friend, the priest Jordí Bonafé, the one we were supposed to meet that day in Carcassonne? He's been something of a mentor to me, and I think he may be able to help prove that my theory about Castelnau's murder is right." Lia inhaled and then forced out her breath in a laugh. "I've had some odd experiences recently. You'd think me crazy if I told you what's happened, but I accept that there are spirits here in Languedoc—spirits from another time whose stories are part of mine. The suspension of disbelief doesn't seem like such a tall order, surrounded by the ghosts of history," she said in a weak attempt to sound convincing, sweeping her arm around the mystical space where they sat.

Lucas rose from the wall and leaned against a locust tree a few feet away, crossing his arms over his chest. "This *is* a powerful place, Lia, full of secrets and legends, but reincarnation?"

"Part of me is waiting for someone to reveal the hidden camera and the joke," she admitted, punching at the dirt with the heel of her boot. "But, Lucas, the truth is I haven't felt this clearheaded since before Gabriel was killed. And I feel him beside me, urging me on. Whether it's to love again or to uncover some truth in this strange history, I don't know. Maybe a combination of both."

"To love again?" he asked, an edge of scorn in his voice.

Lia pressed her chilled hands between her thighs and said the rest of what she'd come here to say. "The man I was expecting for dinner the other night saw your car parked in front of the cottage; he saw us kiss after dinner and misunderstood what was happening between us, Lucas. Which is nothing."

He flinched, and she winced at her lack of tact.

"Not nothing. That's not what I meant."

Lucas pushed away from the tree and waved away her words. "I know what you meant. I knew it last week. You can't blame me for trying." He flashed a smile that didn't reach his eyes.

Lia wanted to explain further. She wanted to say how untethered she felt, trying to reconcile her heart with the preposterous tales she should know better than to believe, but she knew more explanation would only humiliate the man before her.

The light had shifted while they'd talked, leaving them in cool shadow. "We should be getting back. They'll close the gates soon," she said.

They walked single file toward the visitor's center. "What does this priest friend of yours know about Castelnau's death that the rest of the academic world does not?" asked Lucas.

Lia grimaced. She'd said more about Jordí than she should have.

"Oh, I'm not sure he knows anything, really." She was grateful he couldn't see her face; she wouldn't have to hide the lie from her eyes. "It's just good to have someone else on the case, you know? But he's out of town indefinitely, so I'm on my own."

Lia waited for a reply but heard only the crackle of forest debris breaking under their tread. They passed out of the park and descended into Lastours, the still-inhabited hamlet that hugged a stretch of land between the basalt hills and the Orbiel River. Her thoughts turned from Raoul to Jordí and to the pile of documents she'd been working on since yesterday afternoon.

"*Militum Xpisti*," she said aloud, stopping so suddenly that Lucas collided with her back. He grabbed her upper arm, steadying them both. She turned, but her eyes looked past him as she searched and remembered. "*Militum Xpisti*," she repeated, oblivious to the narrowing of his eyes and ignoring his tightening grip.

"Lia?"

Her lips pursed in a small, secret smile, and she returned her gaze to his face. "Do you mind if we go our separate ways once we get back to the parking lot? There's something I need to follow up on."

"I have somewhere I need to be this evening myself. Maybe dinner later in the week?"

Lia nodded absently and turned out of Lucas's grasp. He let her go, and she missed seeing his hands clenching into fists and releasing as his feet moved forward. Her mind had already left Lastours and Lucas.

Militum Xpisti. The Soldiers of Christ. Knights Templar. *Le Temple*. Paris.

She knew where to find Jordí.

LIMOUX—THAT EVENING

Dusk seeped over the mountains as Jordí drove through Limoux. He'd feigned the call that ended his lunch with Lia two days before, but a real call—the one he'd been dreading—had come through a few hours before. Just as he'd been making preparations to leave Narbonne, perhaps for good, his past summoned him deeper into Languedoc. The sénéchal, now a photographer known as Lucas Moisset, demanded they meet at last.

Early Friday morning, he'd parked up the road from Lia's cottage and watched as she left to meet with him at Saint-Just et Saint-Pasteur. He'd had his hand on the car horn, prepared to stop her and tell her everything. But the moment had passed. His nerve had failed. He'd waited a few minutes more, until he was certain she wouldn't return, before hurrying up the sidewalk to leave the package on her doorstep. Then he'd driven to Lagrasse to see the past for himself.

Logis du Martinet had no tasting room, and the property's gate was locked, so he waited out the afternoon parked on an unused tractor path until he saw an old Jeep turn from the highway into the winery's long drive. The Jeep passed, and its driver merely glanced in Jordí's direction before he placed a hand on the haunches of a quivering greyhound beside him, forcing the dog to sit. But the priest saw the thick scar on the man's left cheek. *Raoul d'Aran.*

Jordí's destination this evening was the home no one knew he owned. Set outside Limoux, it was tucked deep in the woods on an unpaved stretch of Chemin du Rossignol. His blue Renault bumped along a dirt lane before emerging in a shallow meadow. Parked beside the house was a bronze BMW. Jordí's approach triggered the motion sensors for the front patio lights, but he didn't need the illumination to fit his key into the lock of his own home; the handle gave easily.

The main room of his L-shaped *mas*—a traditional farmhouse—was cold as a sepulcher and lit by the dim glow seeping through the windows from the outside lights. Jordí turned toward the sound of liquid glugging from a bottle and splashing into a glass and made out a lean, black shadow silhouetted against the dark blue window. He switched on a lamp near the front door, and Lucas turned, raising a snifter of Armagnac in a toast.

"A 1969 Château de Gaube. You have excellent taste. Can I pour you one?"

Jordí nodded, dropping his leather satchel to the floor. He began to shrug out of his wool coat, but he realized he could see his breath in the cold room.

"I thought I'd find snow in the mountains, not clear skies, but it seems the storm has pushed out to sea. We'll have a hard frost come morning. Shall I start a fire?" Jordí's voice carried a faint vibration of fear. He crossed the room as he spoke, rubbing his gloved hands together and taking stock of his surroundings. He hadn't been to the house in over eighteen months. A fine layer of dust dulled the gleaming wood and stone surfaces, but things looked otherwise untouched.

"A fire would be welcome. This should provide some warmth as well." Lucas handed him a glass filled halfway with amber liquid.

"Father Jordí Baltasar Bonafé, hiding in plain sight only a few streets from my office," Lucas said. He leaned against the edge of the antique oak cabinet, looking perfectly at ease in jeans, hiking boots, and a black sweater with a rolled collar. "I'm surprised by so little, but the sight of you catches me off guard. I was expecting a much younger man, one who had aged as little as I. It's ironic that a man so close to God would get the short end of the stick, don't you think?"

"Perhaps God showed me the greater kindness by disguising me from the Devil," Jordí replied.

Lucas ignored the slight. "You've remained a man of the cloth all this time?"

"Who can tell about the centuries?" Jordí waved his hand in dismissal and busied himself with the kindling piled at the hearth. "Where you and I come from, there's no such convenient construct as time." He touched a long match to the cedar sticks. The dry wood grabbed at the flame and snapped around the logs he'd left stacked in the fireplace nearly two years before. He settled his bulk into a worn damask-covered armchair and wrapped his trembling hands around the snifter of Armagnac.

"Perhaps my prayers that this life is the final one will be answered. What I hope for is to have a heart attack and land facedown in a plate of duck confît." He snorted and took a large swallow of brandy. "But here we are, wandering souls who have found each other at last. The hapless young monk and the feared Sénéchal Lucas Mauléon, with his unblinking, black eyes, who was, as you say, 'hiding in plain sight.'"

With one hand, Lucas dusted off a straight-back wooden chair and placed it in front of the priest. He folded his long torso onto the seat, his knees brushing Jordí's. "I was Lucas Mauléon long ago, Father. Now I am simply Lucas Moisset."

The tremor in Jordí's hand revealed itself in the copper shimmer of Armagnac as he brought the glass to his lips. He no more believed Lucas had left behind his identity as the sénéchal than he believed he would be canonized Saint Jordí when, *if*, he finally passed from this world.

"Why are you encouraging Lia Carrer to pursue her theory that Castelnau's murder was something other than an act of revenge by Toulouse?" Lucas asked.

"What does it matter?" said Jordí. "History recorded nothing of Lucas Mauléon. Or of poor Lucas Moisset. She has no idea who you are."

"Who I *was*, Bonafé. You must know what it's like, to be suddenly of this world with memories you don't understand, waiting for shadows to slip into the light."

"You were the falcon sent to slaughter the dove."

Lucas fell still, and Jordí thought of a great cat poised to strike. When he finally spoke, his voice was without inflection or emotion, too flat to be trusted. "What are you talking about?"

Jordí's mind raced. The letter Castelnau dropped in death was the only trump card he had left. Seeking to deflect Lucas's attention away from Castelnau, he slipped on the scree of his thoughts, scrabbled for purchase, and grasped hold of coincidence.

"Raoul d'Aran's wife. Paloma Gervais d'Aran. The dove that will haunt us as long as we walk this earth." Lucas's recoil was slight, but Jordí felt the electric tension where their legs touched. He readied for an explosion. The fire snapped. The pines whispered.

With studied care, Lucas set his glass on the floor. He considered the dark room beyond for a long moment before gently placing his palms on Jordí's knees. "What power do you think that name has over me, after all this time?"

Jordí spoke to the hands that spanned his thick legs. "Paloma Gervais and Bertran and Aicelina d'Aran are the reasons why our souls never left this earth." He looked into the sénéchal's eyes. "You tried to save Paloma, hoping to recapture her love after d'Aran's death, but you were too late. Guilt and the search for atonement are the consequences of those unfinished lives."

Lucas remained silent.

"But you have found her again, in a manner of speaking, haven't you?" Jordí prodded at the vulnerable spot.

"I've found Paloma?" A short, bitter laugh. "You're mad."

"Lia Carrer. You were there at the Institute for Cathar Studies just days after her husband's death. I recognized you immediately, though as you pointed out, time has not been so kind to me. You never once looked in my direction. You had eyes only for Lia. Lia, who so resembles your Paloma. She brings you back to the memory of the woman you adored. You're in love with her, aren't you?"

Jordí blinked. The chair before him was empty. Strong hands clamped his shoulders, grinding into the tender space behind his clavicles. Jordí was returned to the cold dawn eight hundred years before, when a soldier stood behind him, pressing a knife blade into the soft flesh at his neck.

"How is it possible that you and I are here when we were never believers?" Lucas growled in his ear. "We never belonged to the heretics' faith."

Back in the abbey of Saint-Gilles, a terrified Brother Bonafé had heard the gasps of a dying man floating through the nave: *I have seen the spirit of God*, the archdeacon had crowed, as his blood ran warm from his chest. *They are not heretics. They are the Trinity.* Philippe du Plessis had known of Castelnau's heresy. But he hadn't understood that truth did not have to be believed to be right.

Lucas's body shifted, and the grip on Jordí's flesh tightened. He removed the glass from Jordí's shaking hand and pressed a photograph into his palm. The priest brought it in front of his face, his eyes straining in the dark. He gasped and tried to pull away. "Where did you get this? How could you know?"

"What were you doing on that very road that day, Father Bonafé?"

The room grew warm, unbearably so, and Jordí began to sweat in the wrap of his wool coat. He didn't know. He'd never known. Raoul's own words came to him. "When I woke, I was," he whispered.

"My memories of this life began that day, not far from where this photograph was taken," Lucas said. His hold loosened, and he braced his hands against Jordí's clavicles, uncomfortably close to his neck.

Jordí nodded helplessly. "As did mine."

"It was, in fact, the first time I saw you. Though as I said, I didn't recognize you. I caught only a glimpse as you passed in your car. It wasn't until Lia said your name, the day we were to meet in Carcassonne, that I realized you've been here all along. Living with your own secrets."

"What secrets?" Jordí wheezed, although he knew the answer.

The muscle and bone behind him shifted. "Whatever it is you think you may know about me, remember that Lia has no idea what you've done either, Father. Unlike mine, history has recorded enough of *your* deeds to destroy you." Lucas's breath was hot against Jordí's ear. "Be careful whose truth you reveal. You may come face-to-face with your own." A blast of cold air pushed into the fire, and Jordí turned to see the front door wide open. Lucas had gone.

Lucas knew his truth. Yet Jordí still had history on his side in the form of a letter, carried through the centuries, to prove why Castelnau had been murdered and why the Cathars had been slaughtered out of existence. The very letter he told Lia had been lost to history.

He sat alone through the long night, wondering if he had the courage to reveal the truth, until the fire died out and he could no longer see the details of the photograph in his hand.

Well before dawn, Jordí drove to Narbonne. He spent several hours in his office at Saint-Just et Saint-Pasteur, sorting his affairs, and in the archives below, gathering the last traces of his past.

21

NARBONNE—EASTER SUNDAY

*L*ia made one stop before following her hunch to Paris. The sky blushed a rose garden's worth of pink and peach as she and the sunrise arrived together in Narbonne.

The cathedral doors off rue Gustave Fabre were unlocked. She slipped inside and inched forward as the door closed softly against her back. Mass would begin in less than two hours, but the only sign of life was the orange light flickering from thick, white wax cylinders on the altar. She skirted the nave's outer perimeter until she reached a hallway that led to the cloisters.

A breeze pushed through the cloisters' arched passageway, rustling a cluster of palms in the center of the manicured courtyard. Pigeons gurgled and cooed from their perch on a gargoyle with an eagle's head and dragon's wings. Through its open beak, the stone creature set loose an unheard, unending screech over Narbonne. Lia walked along the arcade to a wooden door opposite the choir. She grasped the black iron handle and whispered an entreaty. Then she opened the door into the cathedral's administrative corridors and moved swiftly to Jordí's office.

During that terrible week between Gabriel's accident and her journey to his family's home in Mexico with his body, she had come to the Trésor seeking solace. Jordí had brought precious tomes from the archives' inner vault to its cool, dimly lit reading room where Lia worked, and she had found comfort in the fragrance of old paper and leather and the sight of ancient script and illustrations. On her first visit, Jordí met her at the cathedral, and they stood in the doorway in front of his office while he patted his shirt and his pants before finally reaching up to palm two keys hidden on top of the door frame. He used one to open the door. The other, a skeleton, he slipped into the keyhole in the center drawer of his desk. From inside the drawer, he had withdrawn a metal ring crowded with keys large and small, using one with a large, square head to unlock the entrance to the Trésor beneath their feet.

The mismatched pair of keys was still on the lip above the door. As Lia let herself into Jordí's office, she replayed her conversation with the priest in the bistro, recalling the details of Castelnau's murder. She kept coming back to the letter the young priest had found near the archdeacon's body. Did he really leave it buried under a stone at the abbey in Saint-Gilles? Could he have carried it with him through the years?

On Jordí's desk, amid the chaos of correspondence, half-empty coffee mugs, and pastry crumbs, a Bible lay open, and on a tissue-thin page, Romans 2:16 had been highlighted in neon-yellow marker. She followed the words with her finger, speaking under her breath. "*On that day when, according to my gospel, God judges the secrets of men by Christ Jesus.*"

Lia fitted the second key into the lock of the thin drawer that spanned the length of the desktop and slid the drawer open. Sifting through the jumble of paper clips, pens, stamps, and business cards, she found no keys. She eased it back, but the old warped wood stuck halfway. Lia gave it a bump with her hip, shaking up the drawer's contents, and a glint of gold winked in the growing light. It came from the raised lettering of a business card. Lettering she recognized. *Lucas Moisset, Photographe Indépendant.* Behind the name was an etched watermark of a peregrine falcon.

She placed the card on top of the Bible, anger and confusion churning through her. Jordí. Lucas. "They *have* met." Lia's sharp voice flared in the dim office.

Jordí hadn't told her the truth about Lucas. He'd lied about the finance committee meeting. And he'd disappeared. "What else have you lied about?" she muttered. She shoved the desk drawer, but it caught on an obstruction. Cursing, she pushed again. There was a clink, followed by a hollow smack, and the drawer slid home. A set of keys lay at her feet.

Leaving Jordí's office with the keys cupped in her hand, Lia headed toward the Chapelle de l'Annonciade. The soles of her shoes squeaked on the cheap linoleum tiles. The hallway broke to the right and led to a cramped staircase. It was part of a much older floor plan, descending into the bowels of the cathedral to the Trésor, the disused wine cellars, and the crypts, where echoes were swallowed by stone and darkness. Steeling her nerves against the inevitable wave of claustrophobia, Lia descended.

Standing in front of a low, round door at the end of the short corridor, her bravado disappeared. The dark door glowered in the faint light cast by small sconces set in the walls. A chorus of whispers stirred the air, taunting her. *It's only the air regulator.* Impatience and curiosity overcame her hesitation, and Lia pressed on the handle, expecting the abrupt stop of a locked door. It gave freely.

The column of space on the other side was tar black. Her stomach dropped, and the jagged edges of Jordí's office keys stabbed into her palm. She released her clenched fist and dropped the keys into her front pocket. One hand groped for a light switch while the other clutched tightly to the strap of the backpack slung over her shoulder. She slid up the dimmer knob, and a calming glow seeped into the four empty corners.

The room was a perfect square, with space for two rectangular tables set one in front of the other and a pair of chairs tucked to the edge of each. No other furniture, not even a wastebasket. Of course, it offered nothing; this was only the reading room. Moving to the shadow of a reinforced-steel door in the far wall, Lia selected the key she'd once seen Jordí use and unlocked the door. Stepping inside the archival room, she guided the door back toward the threshold. Her throat closed as the steel sealed against the frame. She pushed on the handle, and a current of electric relief surged through her when the door opened. Not trusting she wouldn't be trapped inside, Lia dropped her backpack in the gap. The heavy door crushed the polyester, but the bag's thick straps held it open.

She raised the dimmer and a row of floor lights illuminated a strip of carpet between several low metal bookcases. Sconces glowed faintly on the walls of the cool, silent room. Despite the enclosed space, she relaxed. It was her first time in this inner sanctum of the Trésor, but she knew how to navigate the world of age-old documents. Secrets were confined to ancient script on fragile pages.

Walking down the center aisle, Lia peered between the rows. Protective glass covered the cabinet fronts, keeping out moisture and light. The cabinets were arranged by the five dioceses of the Languedoc-Roussillon region: Montpellier, Carcassonne, Mende, Nîmes, and Perpignan. The records of each diocese were divided chronologically by type of document—registers, leases, account rolls, court rolls, correspondence.

Where would she find a letter a young priest had hidden under a stone in the abbey of Saint-Gilles? Jordí said he'd left it in the church, where time turned it to dust. Yet what better place to hide something than in plain sight? It must be here.

Walking among the bookcases, Lia sought out the diocese of Nîmes, which still governed the abbey of Saint-Gilles eight hundred years after the death of Pierre de Castelnau. She located the cabinet designated for the parish of Saint-Gilles-du-Gard and pulled gently on the handle. Of course, it was locked. Lia pulled the key ring from her pocket. Around it were several small keys that looked identical. She ran her fingers along their sharp edges and fit one into the cabinet lock. It slipped in easily but didn't turn. She tried a second key, then a third. The lock clicked. She slid the glass front up.

Inside were archival binders covered in buckram cloth and set in protective slipcases, with numbers embossed in gold on their thick spines. A folio on top of the cabinet listed the contents of each. To have in arm's reach a trove of medieval documents she'd never before explored was intoxicating.

Three binders covered a span of time that included 1208, the year of Castelnau's murder. Two of these held tax rolls and deeds. The third was numbered, but its contents weren't listed in the legend. When Lia withdrew it from its case, something fluttered out and into the aisle. She noted where it landed and turned back to the cabinet.

The binder contained only a clear polyester envelope with a thin wallet inside. She pulled on the white cotton gloves she'd stashed in her pocket, wishing she could feel the material with her fingers but knowing the oil from her hands would mar the surface. She snapped open the envelope and removed the wallet. The caramel leather had worn thin in places and was streaked with fine black veins, like minute canyons that had collected centuries of grime. She imagined the many hands that had touched the finely tooled calfskin, fit for a nobleman.

One side of the empty pouch bore a brand Lia recognized immediately: one horse carrying two knights, bordered by the script *Sigillum Militum Xpisti*, the insignia of the Knights Templar. Philippe du Plessis would have used that signet. She returned the wallet to its protective envelope, certain she knew which letter it had once held. Then Lia turned to see what had fallen out. It lay in the middle of the center aisle.

It wasn't an ancient document. It was a photograph, one that had been printed from a digital camera. It showed an unremarkable stretch of highway bordered by low walls of stone and forest on either side, with evergreen-covered hills in the distance. The road could have been any in southern Languedoc, but something about the setting tugged at Lia's memory. She tucked the photograph into her back pocket and returned the binder to the cabinet, leaving it as she found it, locked, nearly empty.

Next, she visited the cabinets containing materials for the diocese of Carcassonne. It didn't take long. She knew those archives as well as any. She scanned the rest of the room, even peering into its dark corners. No unprotected piles, no boxes waiting to be unpacked.

Her search stopped. The ringing of the bells sank with muffled echoes to the depth of the Trésor, and Lia recalled vaguely that it was Easter Sunday. Resurrection all around her. She glanced at her watch. 9:00 a.m. Time to go. Sunday Mass was just beginning, and the cathedral would be packed with worshippers and tourists. She could blend in or pretend she'd gotten lost if caught where she shouldn't be.

The hallway was silent and dark. She crept back to Jordí's office and returned the key ring to his desk, rereading Romans 2:16 as she carefully closed the center drawer. She snorted softly at the verse's irony and dropped Lucas's business card into the small front pocket of her backpack. Yanking the zipper closed, Lia left Jordí's office. She slipped the mismatched pair of keys in place on the door frame on her way out.

❧

Lucas watched as Lia pulled her car around and took a left onto rue Gustave Fabre before easing his BMW into the street some distance behind her. She was forced to slow through the traffic vying for parking as the Easter Sunday Mass crowds grew. He followed her out of town and onto the A75. Southern France fell away as they climbed steadily toward Paris, Lucas cruising an easy distance behind, slipping into a parking space when Lia pulled off for fuel.

During a brief stop, as she walked toward her car from the market carrying a bottle of water and a coffee, the sun caught her, turning her copper hair to gold. In that moment, looking so distant, vulnerable, and pale, she was Paloma. And all the hurt and sorrow of a young Lucas Moisset and the regret of the soldier he'd become came pounding back.

❧

He considered the years of his boyhood in Languedoc, searching for clues that could tell him when and how he'd lost everything he loved. His mother, whom he couldn't recall, had died giving birth to a sister who hadn't lived past her first birthday. His father had been a drunken disgrace, falling to his death in an open well when Lucas was not yet twelve.

Hugh Gervais had extended a compassionate hand to Lucas after the boy's father died and brought him to live on the estate outside Limoux, and when Lucas was eighteen, he'd sent him to Agen to train as a knight. Lucas left with the certainty he'd won the heart of Gervais's only daughter, Paloma. But Lord Hugh Gervais had no intention of wedding Paloma to a penniless young man with a tarnished name.

When Lucas returned to Limoux from the battlefields of Anatolia, he learned in the village that Paloma, the girl to whom he'd sworn his love, had married Raoul d'Aran, a Catalan winemaker, and had given the foreigner a son and a daughter. And that Hugh Gervais had become a disgrace himself by pledging solidarity with the heretical Cathars.

Deprived of home and wife, Lucas wanted only to excise his connections to Languedoc and obliterate love from his heart. He dropped his Occitan surname to become Mauléon and rejoined the army of his former commander, Philippe du Plessis. The men were united again in battle, this time to eradicate the infidel Cathars from the south and unite Occitania with France.

Eight hundred years later, as he watched a woman in search of a truth she didn't understand, he realized that love had never been lost, but that he had failed Paloma when he could have saved her. Lia was his second chance. Yet once again, Raoul d'Aran stood in front of Lucas, barring the way to his future. And behind him, his past was catching up.

THE MARAIS, PARIS—MARCH 1208

*A*re you certain you weren't followed?"

"Le Temple was nearly empty. I would have noticed anyone near me. And the Marais was so crowded, no one could have found me." Manel moved to the fireplace and rubbed his gloved hands before the flames. "I don't have much time. I'm expected to depart from Paris this very morning." He turned to his cousin. "It's happened, Raoul. The atrocities Plessis and Amalric carried out in secret are now sanctioned war. I can't fathom why Toulouse had the legate murdered, knowing as well as we the price Languedoc would pay for his conceit."

"Then you must know that it wasn't the count who called for Castelnau's murder," Raoul replied. "Tell me what you know of Plessis's intentions."

Manel relayed the content of the council's meeting. "Anyone of the Cathar faith or seen as a sympathizer will be considered an enemy of Christianity and punished as such." He ran a hand through his wheaten hair. "I can't deny I'm relieved to be on the road again, away from Amalric, but what I wouldn't give to remain in France with you, my cousin."

Raoul approached the young man, whose smooth skin and bright eyes were little changed from the boy Raoul had known in the Val d'Aran. Manel, slight and clever, the second son of his mother's youngest sister, had blossomed into a scholar and a priest who sat at the pope's right hand.

"What risks you've taken." Raoul clasped his cousin's upper arms, looking at the cherished face he feared never to see again. "You're not safe, no matter what protection you claim from the Holy See. What you've done, whom you've betrayed—your life is forfeit if you're discovered. Yet you've never wavered."

"I accepted this role," Manel replied. "I'll see it through to its end. Then I'll leave the Church and return home. Or perhaps come back here and join the university. I'll change my name and lose myself among the poor, happy students." He laughed and broke away.

Raoul knew Manel would not leave Rome alive should his betrayal be revealed. He certainly could never return to Paris, where his radiant looks and linguistic genius were becoming known throughout the city.

"There is one more thing you should know, Raoul. A new sénéchal of Languedoc has been named. He knows of you. And now he knows we're cousins."

"I've heard nothing of this. Surely the Languedoc barons would have been informed!"

"He's only just been announced. In fact, he's accompanying me as far as Lyon before continuing south. His name is Lucas

Mauléon, a Templar knight. Apparently, he achieved some renown with Plessis's regiment in Anatolia."

Raoul acknowledged this with a caustic laugh. "Of course. One of Christ's Soldiers," he said, his voice seething with irony, "sent to prepare Languedoc for conquest by the pope's crusade and annexation by France's crown."

A sense of urgency inflamed Raoul. The threat to Languedoc, his adopted home, and to his young family, was imminent. He'd leave at dusk, before the city's gates were closed against the night. Mirò was stabled not far from the southern edge of town, near the Porte Sainte-Geneviève.

Anxious to be on his way, he scanned the small room and his provisions, which were packed in a constant state of readiness. The space he inhabited—nothing more than a bed, table, and fireplace attached to a larger house by a muddy courtyard—had been provided to him by a Jewish merchant sympathetic to the plight of the persecuted Cathars.

"You can't possibly return alone," Manel said. "The roads will be crawling with Plessis's henchmen. A solitary rider with an accent from the southern mountains will be vulnerable."

"Not to worry," Raoul replied. "I'll avoid the Rhône route and use the merchant road to Bordeaux." He plotted the course that would take the least time without catching him in a late-winter storm high in the central mountain passes. The one that wouldn't risk him crossing paths with the sénéchal. "I'll raise the alarm where I can. When the weather warms, the news can be spread across the Massif and toward the Alps."

"Send word to me through Father Anselm as soon as you can," Manel said. "I'll be in Rome within a fortnight." He spoke of a priest, one of several in a clandestine network of Catholics throughout Languedoc, who risked his life to offer shelter and pass along intelligence.

The cousins embraced, and Manel left the way he'd come. He returned to rue Quincampoix and continued south toward the Seine and the Île de la Cité. He didn't notice a hooded figure in the shadow of an arched doorway. Had he seen the man's onyx eyes, he would have known the sénéchal.

THE MARAIS, PARIS—MONDAY MORNING

Tucked in a side street between a hardware store and a coffee shop, near the intersection of rue Réaumur and rue Beaubourg, Hôtel Bailly was at the back door of Lia's beloved Right Bank neighborhood, the Marais. She'd discovered the hotel years before, during graduate school when she couldn't afford a more elegant address, and she returned to it each time she traveled to Paris.

When Lia apologized for not booking ahead, the man at the front desk flashed dazzling white teeth set against blue-black skin and said she could have nearly any room of her choosing. Her favorite, on the sixth floor, meant a panting hike up the conch-shell staircase to avoid an elevator smaller than a bathroom stall. But the room had a large skylight, a deep bathtub, and an oversized framed print of Van Gogh's *Starry Night* that made her feel melancholy and hopeful in the same breath. She remained in the room only long enough to leave her bags and use the toilet. Dropping her key at the front desk, Lia reentered the streets of the third arrondissement.

Her feet led her to the Square du Temple, just east of Hôtel Bailly. It was here, in the mid-twelfth century, that the Knights Templar established their European base. The area had been an insect-infested swamp well outside the city walls, but foresight and planning granted the independent knights tremendous wealth. By the early thirteenth century, when Pope Innocent III launched the crusade against the Cathars, the Templars owned vast tracts of Paris, and the Temple district had become an important financial center.

If she was in Paris when the weather was fine, Lia loved to bring a picnic lunch to the peaceful, groomed gardens of the square. Though nothing remained of the citadel of the Knights Templar, she imagined its imposing square tower surrounded by high crenellated walls; she could hear the hoofbeats of approaching horses and the clanking of armor and ringing of steel as knights practiced swordplay in the courtyard.

Lia settled on a bench that looked across rue de Bretagne to the elegant nineteenth-century buildings beyond. It was just past noon on Monday, and the park vibrated with energy. City gardeners in green coveralls turned over flower beds to work in mulch; the fecund aroma was thick with the promise of growth. The trees were grim and bare, but the sky beamed blue through the stark branches.

She didn't have to wait long. Jordí approached wearing a layperson's clothing: a long, black wool coat open over a dark suit, a gray shirt, and a gray-and-black-striped tie. He wore a charcoal fedora over his thinning hair. Dark sunglasses shielded his eyes, and he carried a cane that barely touched the ground between his footfalls. A bright red scarf added a splash of color to his somber attire. The sight of her friend filled Lia with equal parts relief and fury. Her multiple emails had gone unanswered for four days, but now Jordí breezed in, the epitome of Old World elegance. He strolled over and sat beside her.

"I never come this way," he said after a street sweeper rumbled by. "There's no reason to set foot north of the Marais, as far as I'm concerned." He peered around. "I recognize nothing of this place. I haven't been to Square du Temple in"—he paused—"about eight hundred years, give or take." His body shook at the joke. "Of course, things have changed a bit." He turned to Lia. "Yet you knew to look for me here." Not a question, but an acceptance of the inevitable.

"I'm learning to trust my instincts and accept the impossible." She tossed Jordí's words back to him with a rueful smile.

"Touché, Lia. I'm sorry I had to leave so suddenly. I'm sure it's been hard to accept all that I told you last week. Have you spoken to Raoul? Do you have the answers you seek?"

"You lied to me," she replied, sidestepping his question. "Madame Isner did not call you away from the restaurant."

He pursed his lips and gripped the top of his cane with gloved hands. "I left Narbonne to clear my head. Revealing the truth was unsettling. I needed to decide if my responsibilities lie with a past so distant it hardly matters anymore or with the present, where I feel as though I'm doing something of value."

"If I believed the past were too distant to matter, I wouldn't be a historian," Lia snapped. "Revealing the truth is my life's work. It's never too late, Jordí."

"Sometimes history is better left in the past, Lia."

"How can you say that? It was you who wrote me that email, saying you believed that legend could be truth."

Jordí acquiesced with a slow nod. "The musings of a lonely, bored old man." He ignored her gasp of protest. "There's no way to prove that the assassination of Pierre de Castelnau was a deliberate plot to start the Cathar Crusade, and what difference would it make if there were? The Church openly pursued the Cathars from the start. Their mistreatment of heretics has never been a secret."

"But there has been so little acknowledgment of what the Languedoc people suffered, from genocide to total loss of independence," Lia countered. "It's not about forcing an apology from the Catholic Church. It's simpler than that. It's about correcting history when the truth is known."

"Again, I wonder how will you prove such a thing?"

"I don't know," she admitted. "How do I take what's happening and turn it into believable evidence? This, you, Raoul." She gestured at him, at the air. "It's all impossible. If I try to spin historical fact out of tales of reincarnation, I'll be laughed out of the field. I'll never find a job. My credibility as a historian will be shot to hell."

And yet there she sat, in a place that could tell tales far older than the one in which she'd landed. "Knights Templar, Philippe du Plessis himself, wandered this very ground. It's possible, isn't it? If history has room for legends of knights and Holy Grails, could it not have room for men who roam the centuries? For a monk who witnessed a murder that changed the course of European history?"

An ambulance raced by, its siren shrieking. Lia waited as the siren's echo drifted away until she could speak without raising her voice.

"My only hope is to keep looking for evidence." She raised her eyebrows, staring hard at him. "Which I tried to do, incidentally. But of course the Trésor is—what did the watchdog say?—'closed until further notice'?" Lia mimicked the secretary's bark, and Jordí's lips twitched but stopped short of a smile. "When Madame Isner told me there'd been no finance committee meeting and that she had no idea where you were, I was pissed, Jordí. And frightened. You'd just hit me with the most devastating news since…" *Since Gabriel.* But she left that unsaid. The shame on his face told her he understood. "Instead, you left a packet on my doorstep and disappeared without an explanation."

"Lia, I—"

She held up her hand to signal that she hadn't finished. "I sweated over those translations this weekend before finally admitting how ridiculous it was. *Langue d'oïl*, dialects of Catalan, medieval Latin. You can read them as easily as I can read the back of a cereal box. You manipulated me, Jordí." Lia ran out of steam. There was too much she needed to know to waste time on anger. "But what's done is done. Now I need the truth. What does Raoul have to atone for, Jordí? He and I ran from someone in the old city, and he took me through that tunnel to protect me. Who was after us? You must know. Were they after me? Or Raoul?"

"I don't know, Lia." His lie slid forth, transparent and facile.

She sat back and folded her hands in her lap. The sounds of Paris at work and play seemed very distant, part of another life, another time. A tiny woman, wearing a thin cotton dress and frayed knit shawl, approached them clutching a bouquet of red roses. She smiled, her chipped teeth stained brown, her skin a legend of wrinkles. She spoke in a language Lia didn't understand but recognized as a Balkan tongue. Jordí began to wave the woman away, but Lia held out a two-euro piece, receiving a rose and a beaming smile in return. The Romani woman walked on, muttering.

"You took the institute's collection out of the Trésor before you came to Paris."

"Lia—"

"Don't lie to me. I know it's not there. Is it somewhere safe?"

His head snapped over. "How could you—?"

"I know where you keep your spare keys, remember?" she said. "I went searching for something, anything. A clue to this mess, to Castelnau, maybe a hint of where you were, though my first guess was right. I went looking for that letter." She thought of the empty wallet branded with the two knights and their single steed. "You know, it occurs to me that it could have been written right here, on the grounds of the Templar's citadel."

"The letter?" Jordí's hollow voice told Lia he knew exactly which letter she spoke of.

"The letter you found by Castelnau's body. The one Plessis wrote to warn Castelnau that he'd be assassinated."

"Plessis didn't—" Jordí stopped. "Lia, I told you. That letter was lost to history." His face sagged, aging as sorrow deepened the shadows under his eyes. They sat in the dead air of their unspoken truths.

Lia took a leather satchel she'd tucked against her left side and moved it between them. She opened the front flap and removed a thin envelope, offering it to Jordí.

"What is this?" he asked, setting it in his lap. He took a small case from his coat pocket and exchanged his sunglasses for reading glasses. He withdrew a photograph from the envelope and held it before his eyes. Then, he blanched.

"Where did you find this?" His voice descended to a whisper.

"In the archives. It obviously means something to you, Jordí. You look as though you've seen a ghost."

Jordí removed his reading glasses and pressed the pads of his fingers against closed eyes. The barrel of his chest heaved as he sighed. "This photograph is a message, Lia. But it's not meant for you."

THE MARAIS, PARIS—MARCH 1208

Lucas watched from the shadows as Manel left the alley. They would meet at Porte Sainte-Geneviève in two hours' time to begin their journey southeast. From Lyon, Manel de Perella would be accompanied by merchants, soldiers, and men of God traveling to the Italian provinces; many would go all the way to the Vatican and beyond. Lucas could send a letter with a knight in the retinue, spelling out his suspicions of the papal emissary's betrayal. Suspicions that could be delivered even as the Catalan freshened himself in his quarters before seeing the pope.

Lucas's mouth turned up in a sour smile. He would leave Manel be. Spies were useful, and not just those who reported to you. The spies who didn't know they'd been found out were the most valuable of all.

A glint of white caught his eye. A woman crossed the street to his left. Her head was covered loosely by a shawl of dark green wool, and her blond hair fell in a flowing tail across one shoulder as she bent to talk to the child at her side. She so resembled Paloma that Lucas nearly stepped into the street to hail her. She stood up abruptly, and he fell into the shadows. When he peered out a moment later, she was gone.

The sound of barking dogs erupted from inside the cluster of tall, putty-colored buildings across the way. Lucas moved swiftly up the confined street until he came to the passageway from which Manel had emerged. Just inside, tepid rays of sun dripped into a courtyard.

Two gray terriers streaked across the stones, followed by a man cloaked in black. His brown riding breeches were tucked into tall boots of worn leather faded to dull gray and patched with strips of brown. Lucas heard the sharp pitch of a young woman's voice, and the dogs dashed out of sight. The man raised a hand in farewell and turned.

Lucas fell back immediately, pressing his body flat against the wall. A pair of young women, their woven baskets full of vegetables, stared and giggled as they passed, and one whispered behind a raised hand. His black glare forced their eyes away, and they drew together, hurrying on. Lucas didn't linger either. Four long strides returned him to the street corner. He rounded it and edged his head out so he could just see the street ahead.

After he'd learned of Paloma's betrayal, Lucas tore through the Aude Valley from Limoux to Montpellier, determined to leave Languedoc forever. But he'd stopped in Lagrasse, tortured by the knowledge that Paloma was so close, praying to see her one last time.

He'd inquired about the d'Aran family in the village, and a stable boy had heedlessly raised his hand to point out Paloma's husband, who stood outside a smithy, engaged in animated conversation. Lucas had hissed at the child just as the boy opened his mouth to call out to Raoul d'Aran and shoved a coin in his hand to pay for his silence.

Lucas surveilled d'Aran from the shadows now, just as he'd watched him in Lagrasse, knowing the man had not traveled so far simply to visit with a cousin.

PARIS—MONDAY AFTERNOON

Lia plunged into the Marais, wandering without destination through the quieter streets, past rue des Francs-Bourgeois and down rue Quincampoix, where the shops were shuttered for the long lunch break. Her thoughts were leaves whirling down an alley, and she hardly noticed where her feet led.

She'd parted ways with Jordí not long before. He had hailed a taxi from the curbside, claiming an appointment at Librairie Loeb-Larocque, a rare books dealer in the thirteenth arrondissement. Before he climbed into the backseat, she placed a hand on his arm.

"You never told me how you died. Or why you've come back. Will you tell me what happened to you?"

His face was unreadable, his eyes hidden again behind dark glasses, but the corners of his mouth lifted in hint of a smile. "Meet me at La Colombe on rue Pecquay at eight. I'll finish my story over dinner." He tipped his hat and squeezed into the tiny Renault.

"Lia," Jordí called from the open window, and she turned halfway. "I do recall something else from Castelnau's letter. Two short sentences, written in a different hand and added at the bottom. The words made no sense to me at the time, so I thought little of them. But perhaps their very oddness cemented the words in my memory." He motioned her closer, and she knelt down. "'The bear is a traitor. A falcon flies south, and the dove will die.'" Jordí rolled up the window. The taxi jerked away from the curb and sped south from the curve of a roundabout.

Lia had repeated the words, committing them to memory. They meant nothing to her, but they sounded like a warning. What she would give to read that last piece of correspondence Castelnau had received. Important enough that he'd sought it in his final moments.

She was starving. She'd left Minerve at dawn, grabbing a horrid cup of coffee at a service station along the way, but she'd eaten nothing since the night before. The aromas of the Marais at lunchtime left her weak with hunger.

Weaving through the narrow streets, she found her way to the Marché des Enfants Rouges. The cafeteria, full of food vendors and kiosks of cheeses, produce, and charcuterie, hummed with activity. The fine day had routed workers from their offices, and the market—open on one side to the street—was warm with packed bodies. Lia queued at the counter of her favorite Lebanese vendor, where the orders were quickly dispatched. In ten minutes, she had a tray full of fragrant falafel, warm pita bread, and tabbouleh redolent of lemons and parsley.

Several tables and benches were arranged in the open court-yard outside the vendors' stalls, and copper columns radiated heat from propane burners. Lia found an open space at the end of a table and slipped in beside a young couple. He spoke French with a broad Australian drawl, and she replied in a husky Catalonian burr. The woman's beauty was intoxicating. Her flaxen hair was piled in a loose chignon, and a silk scarf was wound with practiced abandon around her neck. A cream jersey dress clung to her frame, hugging her breasts and the angles of her shoulders. She spoke with her hands; silver rings on her long fingers caught the light, and a stack of thin bracelets clicked as she gestured. Her partner leaned forward, struggling to understand her rapid-fire French, or perhaps he just wanted to soak in her aura. His replies echoed her words, repeating them to make certain he'd caught their meaning. He was unself-conscious and completely smitten.

Soon, the couple had eaten their fill. The Australian towered over the women as he gathered the remains of lunch. When he stepped away to dispose of their trays, the Catalan turned to Lia. As she looked into the woman's stormy-green irises, Lia flinched, and her heart skipped. It was like looking into a mirror.

"I love Paris," the woman said. "There is no city such as this for beautiful men and romance."

"He *is* lovely." Lia was lost in those eyes so like her own. "And I think the French lessons are going quite well."

"Just a little tutoring on the side" was her blithe reply. She tucked loose strands of hair behind her ears and placed her long, bejeweled fingers on the table. "What you seek is not in Paris, Lia." This time she spoke in Occitan. "The dove waits in Lagrasse."

Lia set down her fork. "What? What did you just say?"

At that moment, the Australian reappeared at the table. He held out a hand to his companion, and she rose like a sylph, gathering her bag and coat over one arm. She gave Lia one last look. "Return to Languedoc. The truth awaits you there." The man looked quizzically between the women, not understanding the arcane language. With a nod, the Catalan beauty moved past him, and they walked on.

Lia sat with her hands flat on either side of her tray, her appetite gone. When she could trust her legs, she rose and dumped what remained of her lunch in a nearby trash bin, adding the tray and utensils to the growing stack on top.

She passed through the Marais in a daze. At the intersection of rue des Lombards and rue Nicolas Flamel, a shadow emerged from an arched doorway and headed straight for her. Lia caught a whiff of roses as the figure approached. Details of a face came into view: wrinkled, leathery skin, a ruined mouth, and eyes grown old before their time. It was the Romani woman who had sold her a rose a short while before in the Square du Temple. As they drew side by side, the woman stopped.

"Go home, Lia. Go back to Languedoc." She too spoke in Occitan, her voice hardly rising above a whisper. She continued on without a backward glance.

Lia stopped in the recess of a large doorway and watched people stream past. The sounds of their conversations and the watery rainbows of their clothing and shopping bags were as distant as a vapor trail high in the sky. Gathering herself, she reentered the silvery March sunlight. Her feet carried her across the Pont d'Arcole to the Île de la Cité, where the Cathédrale Notre-Dame rose in monumental splendor. Turning left on rue du Cloître de Notre Dame, she approached the cathedral's east end. The sight of the massive flying buttresses ascending to the heavens, holding up the cathedral and the weight of history, lifted some of the leaden weight from her heart.

She sank onto a bench to watch the afternoon sun dip over Notre-Dame and turn its gray stone to platinum. This heart of Paris had been a site of ceremony centuries before the Templars constructed their citadel in 1140. From temple to basilica to cathedral, great houses of worship had stood watch as the city grew up from the swamps and plains around the Seine.

History vibrated, rejoiced, and clamored all around Lia. It was a thing she could touch, as warm and alive as her skin, as vital as the beating of her heart. *Go home. Go back to Languedoc,* the flower seller had muttered. *The dove waits in Lagrasse,* said the beauty with the Catalan accent that made a melody of her Occitan words. Lia felt no malice from these women; they seemed to be extensions of her own mind, her intuition revealing itself in human form.

By the time she returned to the hotel, silver strands of light were fading from the boulevards, and purple shadows burgeoned from side streets, subsuming the day. Lia climbed the winding stairs to room 602, weary from the morning's drive and footsore from wandering Paris's pavement and cobblestone.

She sat on the bed, massaging her aching toes, wondering if she had time for a hot bath before dinner, when the blood plunged from her head, turning her face to ice, her limbs to stone.

"That photo." Her foot fell with a thud to the floor. She pulled her satchel into her lap and rummaged in its depths. Her shoulder bag contained only her wallet, cell phone, and a notebook. She'd left the photo with Jordí. "Damn it," she cursed. "Damn my distracted mind."

She replayed their final moments together, when she'd given her impassioned defense of the importance of history. She hadn't noticed him secreting away the odd photograph, and she cursed again at her carelessness. No matter what the apparitions may have warned, she had to see Jordí and retrieve that photo.

Lia waited at the restaurant for over an hour, drinking a *pichet* of Burgundy before finally ordering a meal. Her texts and calls to Jordí's cell phone went unanswered. She lingered over her meal and ordered a Cognac, followed by a cappuccino. A trio of German businessmen watched her from the restaurant's bar, and one made his move while she sipped her coffee. Her waiter, discreet and stern, was at her table in a heartbeat, explaining graciously that madame was dining alone this evening, but he would be happy to show monsieur an excellent window table. Lia mouthed her thanks.

On her way out, she paused by the servers' station to express gratitude to her unlikely champion.

"It was nothing, madame. I sensed that you preferred to be left in peace." He peered at her over the top of his reading glasses.

"I was expecting someone, but he never showed."

"A grievous error." The waiter lifted the glasses to the top of his head and offered her a kind, tired smile. "No one should treat a woman with such disregard."

She couldn't help her very un-French grin. "I was waiting for a priest, believe it or not. Obviously, my feminine charms were lost on him."

He shook his head and sniffed. "I gave up on the Christian church long ago," he said. "I'm a Buddhist."

Lia received his smug irony with grace. "It's such a beautiful faith, Buddhism. Always a chance for rebirth and redemption, to do things better the next time." The waiter blinked, and his green eyes softened, as though he now saw a whole person in front of him, not just a customer.

"If the priest does make an appearance, he's a large man, but short, *costaud*." She held her arms out in front of her belly to emphasize Jordí's girth. "He's in his late fifties, looks very dapper—suit, hat, cane, maybe a red scarf..." She stopped when the waiter's mouth opened in surprise.

"He *was* here, earlier this evening, not long before you arrived. He said he was meeting someone, and I seated him at the very table where you were. Then another man came in and headed straight to his table. When I brought a bottle of water, they were arguing in whispers and waved me away. I took a few orders, and when I turned back, the table was empty. But your friend left this."

From a shelf below the computer where he'd been recording receipts, the waiter pulled out a basket that jingled with forgotten keys. Neatly folded on one side was a crimson-red cashmere scarf. A corner hung loose, weighed down by an embroidered white dove. Lia let the fine material slide through her fingers.

"Do you mind if I take this?" She draped the scarf over her wrist. "I'll return it to my friend."

The waiter assented, and a shout from the kitchen pulled his attention away.

"Wait." She held him back with a hand on his arm. "The man who was with the priest. What did he look like?"

"Tall, much taller than me. French, with a southern accent, like yours. His hair was dark blond. And his eyes—black."

Outside the restaurant, Lia withdrew Lucas's business card from her purse. She'd planned to confront Jordí with it when they met this afternoon, but his unexpected reversal on her quest into the truth of Castelnau's death had driven Lucas Moisset from her mind. The raised gold lettering of his name and title glinted in the low light, and the peregrine falcon watermark hovered beneath.

Lia then sent two texts. The first she dashed off to Jordí: Call ASAP. I know where that photo was taken. It took her several tries to find the right words for a message to Raoul. At last, she hit Send. She wished she could see his face when he read: I'm sorry. I believe you. I'm coming home.

She raised the collar on her coat and drew her scarf snugly around her neck. Trusting her instincts to see her safely back to the hotel, Lia stepped out of the shelter of light that glowed from the restaurant's windows and into the empty street.

NEAR ARQUES, LANGUEDOC—TUESDAY AFTERNOON

*L*ia left Paris before dawn. Neither Jordí nor Raoul had responded to her messages. When she stopped for fuel, she dialed Rose's number, just to hear a familiar voice.

"Lia! Four days and you haven't called me. Where are you?" The concern in Rose's voice nearly made Lia cry. She fumbled through something about a dash up to Paris for research, and she promised to stop by the farm as soon as she got back.

Then she sent a second text to Raoul, this time with an address and when she expected to be there. She had to admit, as the miles unrolled before her, that this second message was a test; she had tried not to read anything into his silence, but Lia knew that if Raoul didn't meet her that afternoon, she would have to let him go.

The hours seemed to drag on, but finally, she neared the turnoff to Minerve. She continued on and traveled south on the Route Alet-les-Bains, bypassing Limoux. At Couiza, Lia turned left onto the D613. Rounding a bend in the two-lane highway, she pulled the car into a small turnout blocked from the road by a low wall.

Burnished gold light illuminated the shorn fields, the white bones of the poplar trees, and the blue-green branches of firs and pines. Two wooden picnic tables were tucked next to the wall, but from the leaves piled on their tops, Lia guessed they hadn't been used in months. She walked back to the curve in the road, stopping where a dirt trail shot down from the embankment and connected on the other side before ascending again into the forest.

Two summers before, roadblocks had cordoned off this stretch of road from vehicle traffic, and fans had waited off to the side, looking for riders coming through. No one could explain why Gabriel had emerged over half a mile up the road, alone, from the wrong trail. No one had seen a black Mercedes on that stretch of the D613 or on the small roads that fed into the highway from Rennes-les-Bains. Lia knew her husband's case file held a report from a forensic pathologist that showed the likely rate of speed the Mercedes had been traveling when it allegedly hit her husband's bike. She'd wanted nothing to do with the details—they only brought her closer to the horror of Gabriel's death.

But as she stood in the sun on the empty road, she replayed the scene that haunted her nightmares: Gabriel flying off a mountain trail, hunched low, his body and the bike as one, fused muscle and steel. Knowing the road was blocked to cars and crowds, Gabriel, traveling at full speed but in complete control, wouldn't have slowed his descent. Lia imagined him glancing instinctively to either side as he hit the road, and she wondered how much warning he'd had, if he'd sensed the approach of the sedan before it was upon him.

The berm sloped gently to a copse of trees, and the trail picked up again. Lia had planned to come to this place since returning to Languedoc, but only when she was ready to say her final good-bye. In accepting Raoul's impossible reality, could that not mean Gabriel might return to her?

Lia stepped into the woods. The trees closed in, the air thickened with the nutmeg musk of forest floor, and her legs crumpled beneath her. She grabbed at the damp earth, closing her fists around clumps of fallen, dried leaves. She said her husband's name again and again, as if to will him back to this place where life had last coursed through his body. Then stillness fell over her. She sat on her heels and listened to the small birds twittering above, noticed the way the sun seemed to gather and embrace the tender, verdant leaves, felt the rebirth of the season. Lia knew she was finished with this place and the terrible images it held.

She pulled herself to standing and wiped the back of her hands across her damp cheeks. Bending over, she brushed the dirt and leaves from her jeans. The snap of a twig brought her upright. He came to a stop a few feet from her, his hands tucked in the pockets of a black leather coat.

"I didn't mean to startle you." Raoul spoke softly. "I saw your car parked in the pullout."

"How long have you been standing there?"

"Not long."

The sun dipped behind the mountains, and the shadows swelled. Lia hugged herself against the descending chill. "Did you see me crying?" she asked.

His small smile was a tender, unspoken yes. "Dom told me

about Gabriel's race a few weeks ago, in Barcelona. When you sent the text asking me to meet you here, I wondered if this is what you wanted to show me." Raoul approached. "I know what this place means to you, Lia. And I know those tears. I've shed enough of my own."

"I came to see for myself, to say good-bye if I could," she said. In that private moment, in that most terrible and beautiful place, Lia felt vulnerable but no longer wounded by memories. "I meant what I said: I believe you. I don't know if we knew one another in another life, and there is still so much I don't understand. But I believe your past is a part of Languedoc's history."

He took her face between his palms, the rough calluses on his fingers brushing her cheeks as he traced the outline of her lips. She closed her eyes and relaxed into the cradle of his hands. "Jordí Bonafé told me who you were, Raoul. But he hasn't told me everything." Opening her eyes, she asked, "Will you tell me the rest? Will you follow me home?"

"Of course. That's why I'm here." He turned aside and motioned her forward.

They walked back along the path toward their cars. She crested the slight rise to the side of the road and looked east toward Arques. As a wave of recognition washed over her, her knees went wobbly again.

"What is it?" Raoul pressed a hand into her back, sensing her unsteadiness.

Lia had seen photographs of the scene where Gabriel died; she'd read the police report. But what she saw before her now was far fresher in her mind than the hazy, jumbled details barely absorbed nearly two years before. It was the same scene as the photograph she'd picked up from the floor of the archives just two days earlier. Yet understanding why the photograph had been there in the first place and what message it held for Jordí did not come with the recognition. She felt only confusion and abiding sorrow.

"It's nothing," she said to Raoul. "Let's just get away from here."

The sun was low by the time they returned to Minerve. Lights glowed deep yellow from inside the tiny *épicerie* off rue des Remparts. Lia parked her car in front and grabbed a shopping tote from the backseat while Raoul pulled in beside her. She motioned for him to roll down his window.

"Would you stay for dinner?" she asked. "Nothing fancy—an omelet, salad."

"Of course," he replied. "Can I help?" He nodded to the *épicerie*.

"I just need a couple of things."

She returned a few minutes later with a carton of eggs, thin stalks of leeks, and a wrapped square of Pavé de la Ginestarié cheese. Heading to Minerve's northern edge, she drove slowly through the streets as she led the way to Le Pèlerin.

Inside the house, she motioned Raoul, who carried the shopping bag, to the kitchen while she turned on table lamps in the front room. Crossing the hallway, Lia saw him standing at the far windows that led onto the terrace. She kicked off her shoes and joined him, touching her palm to the cool glass. The windows reflected the gold and green of the river canyon as the setting sun shone its last. Raoul turned, scanning the kitchen until his gaze came to rest on her. He looked bewildered, as though he'd woken abruptly from a dream.

"The first time I saw you, you were standing in this room.

It was the morning I..." With a tiny shudder, he seemed to dismiss a thought. "I'd spent the night in a cave near the Cesse. I was injured and somehow I found myself in front of a pool, washing my wound." He touched his face, grimacing with the memory. "It was like looking through a window into a world beyond." He turned to Lia. "I thought you were a ghost. You were—"

"I remember." She smiled. An image of her own naked skin—what *he* had seen that night—flashed through her mind, followed by a rush of electric longing.

"I wanted to protect you," said Raoul. "But you vanished. Something changed at that moment. Something gave way."

In the living room, the creamy plaster walls and low ceiling crossed by timber beams glowed with golden light. Lia opened a bottle of mellow Savennières that tasted of honeycomb and freshly mown hay and set her iPod on a stream of singer-songwriters; acoustic Stephen Stills, Patty Griffin, and Laura Marling drifted through the warm air. They ate in front of the fireplace with their backs against the sofa and dinner plates perched on their laps.

Lia set her empty plate aside, refilled both wineglasses, and arranged herself in cross-legged fashion next to Raoul. His face in profile didn't show the scar, and for a moment, she could pretend he was unmarred by history, simply a man with whom she was going through the normal steps of learning to love again.

"Now that I have your undivided attention, I don't know what to ask first," she said.

He put his plate on top of hers and set the stack on the far side of his outstretched legs. "Whatever comes to mind. I'll do my best to answer."

"Where were you before you came back to Languedoc? Have you been…" Lia struggled for the right words and finally blurted out what she most wanted to know. "What have you been doing the past eight hundred years?"

A hint of a smile flickered across Raoul's mouth. "I have no memory of wandering through the centuries, if that's what you mean. I've tried to imagine what Adam must have felt, awakening to the world as a fully formed man with no past. Yet there must be some deeper consciousness, some continuation of the self in all of this. How do I have the languages, the muscle memory, the knowledge of how the present works when I can remember only the past? At least I have a past. I knew this place, that I belonged here, that I'd been called back through an inheritance to reclaim my home." He ran a hand through his hair and exhaled deeply. "There is no recollection. There is only an awakening."

"But you do remember something. You remember Paloma and your children. Your dreams must be memories."

"My dreams." The familiar gesture of his hand tracing his scar pulled at Lia's belly. "You're right. I remember the first moment I laid eyes on Paloma in Limoux. I remember my children, twins born two years after we married." At last, he was opening up, but Lia had to tamp down the sense of detachment from reality—they were talking about a family who had perished in a time nearly lost to all but legend and ruins.

"The Cathar Crusade was declared in March 1208, not five years after we married. I spent months traveling throughout Languedoc, trying to rally resistance against the northern invasion. After the burning of Cluet in July, I knew I could no longer keep my family safe. I sent Paloma and the children to the home of a trusted friend in Gruissan."

Raoul drew in his legs and rested his chin on his knees. "The day we said good-bye in October was the last time I saw my family. The sénéchal of the Aude and Hérault entered Gruissan the week before Christmas with a handful of soldiers and priests, and they burned the abbey of Saint-Maurice to the ground. I believe my wife and children perished inside that church—burned alive or suffocated by smoke. Paloma was five months pregnant."

His words hit like a punch to her sternum. Raoul uttered the cold facts, but his voice betrayed his anger and grief. His gaze into the fire was hundreds of years distant.

"My two worlds collided the morning I saw you in Carcassonne. Whatever separate consciousness I carry with me each time this…reawakening or remembering occurs, it joined with whomever I am in this present. I know that I died, Lia. I know what I've lost."

"Why do you think you've come back to this time, this place?" Her hands shook as she brought the wineglass to her mouth.

"You said it yourself, Lia. Our souls are lost to reincarnation until we find the path to redemption. I have something to atone for. I failed my family, and now I have a chance to redeem my past."

She shook her head, even as understanding rumbled through her like menacing thunder. "But that's just it. All of that *is* in the past. It's over now. We can live in the present," she pleaded.

"Lia."

He touched her face, and she turned her mouth into his hand. She'd been so afraid he would call her Paloma. She didn't yet have the courage to face the needle of doubt poking into her heart.

"I had no right to make you so vulnerable," he said.

He took the glass from her hand and drew her into his arms.

As they tightened across her back, Lia realized her own limbs were stiff with reserve. Raoul wasn't a dream, yet his existence shouldn't be possible. She willed herself to relax, to shove aside her disbelief and accept the love she held in her arms.

A little less than two years before, Gabriel had held her as they made plans for the future, dreaming of a new life in France. She listened for him now, and the question in her heart was answered by a calm, restful silence.

"Even after all this time, I haven't learned the fine art of mind reading." Raoul leaned back to look at her face.

Shyness overcame her, as though she'd been caught saying something aloud when she thought she was alone in the room. "If you can be here in the present, you and Jordí, why can't Paloma? Why can't you be with your wife and family?"

Raoul brought her hand to his lips. He kissed her palm. Her fingers traced his scar and ran into his hair. "I don't know, Lia," he said. Regret swelled in his eyes, and for a moment, she saw her husband shimmering there. "I don't. But I know Paloma is lost to me forever, just as Gabriel is lost to you."

25

LAGRASSE—OCTOBER 1208

*P*aloma entered the suite of rooms at the west end of the *longère*. In the gracious study, leaded-glass windows set in tall frames of worked iron and polished walnut bloomed with a luminous blue as the moon chased down the last of the autumn day. Raoul sat at a massive oak desk that stretched across the window bays, and several dripping candles burned to give him light. His hand moved rapidly across a piece of vellum, his writing punctuated by frequent dips of the quill into the inkwell before him.

Paloma's belly pulled tight. She feared she knew what he was writing. After the destruction of the cathedral in Cluet in midsummer, when dozens of Cathars and Catholics alike were burned alive, many Languedoc families prepared to flee across the Pyrénées to Spain or over the Alps to the northern provinces of Italy. The massacre had shattered any hope that the Church could be reasoned with. Men of God had abandoned the ways of mercy and love, choosing instead fear and destruction to save their property, while pretending it was the souls of their parishioners they cared for. As the reports of attacks throughout Languedoc increased, so had the frequency of Raoul's correspondence and his trips away from the farm. She sensed tension in the air, like lingering smoke from the distant city. Her family's days of peace in Lagrasse were coming to an end.

Her felt shoes glided noiselessly on thick wool carpets laid across the stone floors. Even so, Raoul turned before she'd taken half a dozen steps. His instincts were as sharp as the blade of the short sword that was sunk into a scabbard and sitting within arm's reach on the desk. Smiling, he held out his arms, and Paloma settled her petite frame neatly in the bulk of his embrace.

"I don't want to disturb you. You were writing so fiercely."

"I heard you coming down the hall, little dove. I was rushing to finish before you walked in the door."

"You certainly did not hear me coming down the hall!"

"Oh, but I did. You stopped Constansa to ask if she'd prepared your bath. Then you lumbered into the room," he teased. Raoul pressed his lips to his wife's neck, inhaling her scent of lemon balm mingled with the musky aroma of sweat. He flicked his tongue against her skin, and the salty tang made his mouth water. Her throat vibrated against his lips as she laughed.

"And did she? Did Constansa prepare my bath?"

"Can't you smell the lavender oil?" he murmured. "Let me show you."

As easily as if he were holding a child, Raoul stood with Paloma in his arms. She squirmed in protest, but he covered her mouth with his, their lips meeting in soft laughter. He carried her into their private rooms, past the bed, and into an alcove where a pool of marble had been set into the floor.

The room was an atrium that looked into a garden bound by a hedge of laurel and juniper. Raoul had seen the Moorish baths in southern Spain and constructed this haven for his wife, her one concession to luxury in their single-story *longère*. Carved from Italian marble, the pool was surrounded by a mosaic of tiles colored the cerulean of tidal pools, the green of sea foam, and the turquoise of the open sea.

"Should I leave you?" he whispered into Paloma's hair as he lowered her feet to the tile.

"Don't you dare," she replied. "But you must sit there." She pointed to a bench set against the wall, its seat covered by a cushion of lamb's wool. He sat and watched as his wife kicked off her shoes and turned her back on him, motioning to the ties that held her overdress closed.

He loosened the ties, and Paloma pushed the dress to the floor. Raoul caught it and smoothed the soft wool before folding and placing it on the bench beside him. He removed his boots and belt, his stockings, sleeveless *surcot*, and leather breeches. Paloma watched and waited.

When he'd finished and settled back into place on the chaise, she raised a foot, resting it on his thigh. He slid his hand up her lower leg. It was covered by finely knitted hose, tied just above her knee. He pushed up her shift, and she giggled as his thick fingers struggled with the tiny knots. She flicked a delicate nail at the silken cord and lowered her leg to the floor. The hose puddled at her foot; she did the same with the other leg. Raoul kneeled at her feet and gathered the hem of her shift in his hands, pushing it to her waist as his head rose inside her legs. He kissed the mounds of her calves, solid from daily walks through the hills above Lagrasse and chasing after children; he ran his hands over the outside of her thighs, taut and shaped from riding.

Paloma pulled the shift over her head and let it fall to the floor. She gathered handfuls of Raoul's hair and sighed as he braced her hips in his callused palms. Her young body scarcely showed the signs of a difficult childbirth three years before. A slight rise of her belly and the silvery strands of skin stretched tight on her breasts and thighs were marks of womanhood that Raoul loved to touch. He longed to see that belly become full again, her breasts swelling as they readied to feed another baby.

Paloma shivered, and her breath quickened as he flicked a tongue into the dark gold hair and licked the wet flesh between her legs. She arched her back, her hips pushing against him, and ran her hands up her belly to her breasts, kneading the flesh and catching her tender nipples between her fingertips. She tensed and cried out, burying her face in her hands as her body shook.

Raoul rose and lifted her. The bath no longer steamed, but the water was warm as blood, and he stepped down, his wife cradled in his arms. He settled her against a wide, rounded step and removed his under tunic, tossing it onto the tiles that lined the bath. He sat below her and pushed away from the step where she lounged, languid with pleasure.

"You are the most beautiful creature God ever made," he said, pushing the soles of his feet against his wife's.

"You don't believe in God," she laughed, flicking water at his chest.

"No, I don't believe in priests," he said. "But I most certainly believe in God. I have no other way to explain how blessed I am to have you. And the children." He pulled her toward him, and she wrapped her lean legs around his waist.

"Oh, I believe in God," Raoul said, his voice falling into a moan as Paloma sank onto him, laughing into his hair.

Before the water cooled, he carried her to bed, where they lay naked, warmed by the fire that heated the small chamber. Raoul traced circles on her hip and belly.

"Paloma."

"It's time, isn't it?"

"Time for what, little dove?"

"It's time for us to leave our home."

"I should have sent you and the babies away weeks ago. It was selfish of me to keep you here when I'm away so often. Yes, you will go to Duchesne's in Gruissan. I was writing to him when you came in tonight. He's proposed his home for your safekeeping. He'll soon leave for Paris, and from the outside, his house will appear sealed tight and empty. His stores are well-stocked and will hold you for weeks. I'm afraid you'll have to live in hiding, but it won't be for long—the winter, at most."

"What if I sent the children with Constansa and stayed here? Or traveled with you?"

"No, it's too dangerous. I would never put you at such risk. And those babies need their mother. You couldn't bear to leave them behind."

"I can't bear to leave you behind, Raoul." She kept her eyes fixed on the fire. "And those babies need their father. So does this one." She moved his hand from her hip to her lower belly, where the flesh rose in a slight mound from her pelvis. She heard Raoul's breath catch.

"Are you sure?"

Paloma brought his hand to her mouth and kissed his palm. "Of course. I haven't bled for three months. Sometime early spring, you will have another son or daughter."

LE PÈLERIN, MINERVE—TUESDAY EVENING

A log collapsed, dropping with a thud and the hiss of cinders, rousing Raoul from a light drowse. He pulled the blanket over his bare legs and rolled into the warmth of the woman beside him. Asleep, she sighed and tucked a knee between his. He propped up on an elbow and leaned his head into his palm to watch her as she slept.

Lia had changed since he'd first seen her the night of winter solstice. She was still lean but no longer thin or rigid with tension, as if one harsh word would snap her bones. Her ribs pushed against the fragile skin of her torso, but her belly had lost its concave impression. Raoul ran a featherlight finger from her navel up the hard line of her abdomen to the bottom curve of one exposed breast. It was full, as great as the span of his hand, high and firm on her chest. He circled the nipple, the petal-soft skin gathering and hardening as her body responded to his touch. The plate of her breastbone and the hard curves of her strong shoulders were peachy from the sun and sprinkled with freckles.

Her long curls spilled across the white cushion. The firelight played with the color of her hair; it was butter browned in a pan, wheat at harvest—a burnished tapestry woven through with golden thread. Here and there were strands of silver, evidence of a woman, no hint of a girl. Her face was smooth but for the faint lines between her eyes that deepened to furrows when she was angry or perplexed. The hollows under her eyes had faded, but he knew she wasn't getting enough rest. He lifted his hand, leaving her be. Lia slept on.

Raoul rolled onto his back and joined his fingers underneath his head. He thought of his Paloma, whose skin was the color of clouds at sunrise, pale cream and pink, her face sheltered from the sun by a bonnet as she walked in her gardens or held the children in her lap as she told them stories of princesses and faeries. It seemed not long ago that he'd been a father and a husband with a life that had a clear beginning and ending.

His thoughts unrolled in the silence as he considered the step from one life to the next, across an eight-hundred-year chasm.

On one side of that chasm was his past, filled with memories of his wife and children—so vivid he could see the silvery scars of childbirth on Paloma's skin, smell the milky-sweet scent of his babies' breath—and all the lives lost to a crusade against a people he loved and had sworn to protect.

On the other side was the present—the vineyards carved into the garigue, the curving black tarmac roads where once had been forest or plain, small villages that had grown into towns or disappeared altogether except for a ruined wall or a crumbling tower. He was returned to his land, land that had belonged to Raoul d'Aran, once of Catalunya, married into a Languedoc family.

And there was Lia, with her melted-sugar hair and honey skin, her eyes that flashed emerald in anger or passion or mellowed into the green of a forest floor when she was at peace. Lia's eyes that were Paloma's eyes. Lia's body, stronger in some ways than his wife's, yet more fragile for never having given birth in this lifetime. Lia, who looked so much like his Paloma he wanted to drink her in, to burrow under her skin so that he would never again be separated from his wife. Why did he tell her that he believed Paloma was lost to him forever?

Because he didn't want Lia to look in every face that passed for her husband. He wanted his to be the only face that mattered to her.

Raoul straddled a chasm that held in its depths something much darker, memories that stirred his heart and brought back his anger. In the remembering came the name of the man who had once taken from him all that he treasured: Lucas Mauléon.

The doorbell chimed, and Lia started awake.

"What the hell?" she whispered, willing the intruder away.

Raoul sat up, but she grasped his arm, holding back. "Just ignore it," she insisted. The bell sounded again, and the visitor held down the button, demanding a response.

"Wait here." Raoul gathered his clothes and dressed in haste, pulling on his shirt as he tiptoed to the front door to look through the peephole. "Short, round man in a hat, carrying a cane," was his stage whisper from the foyer.

"What?" Lia scrambled for her underwear. "That's Jordí Bonafé!"

"Should I let him in?"

"Don't you dare." She tugged on her jeans and yanked a sweater over her head. Stepping into the foyer, she waved Raoul back into the front room, holding a finger to her lips. Then she cracked opened the door just enough to see the priest.

"Jordí!"

"I'm sorry it's so late, Lia. I didn't put much thought into coming. I'm on the way home from Paris, and my car steered me here."

"I'm so surprised to see you. Will you wait just a moment while I finish getting dressed?"

"Of course."

Lia pressed shut the door and turned back to the front room. Raoul leaned against the sofa, and she entered his arms.

"I don't know if I can trust him anymore," she said. "I don't want him to know that you're here. Wait for me upstairs."

"Take him into the kitchen, and I'll stay in here. If you need me, I'll be a shout away." Raoul kissed her and whispered "I love you" into her open mouth.

She ducked back into the entryway and opened the front door.

26

NARBONNE—DECEMBER 1208

I lived in terror that Castelnau's assassin would return for
me," said Jordí Bonafé. "But the man who confessed was
torn apart by a mob, and war against the Cathars was declared.
I thought I was free. I tried to forget what had happened and
continue with my training to enter the priesthood." He hid
behind his mug of wine, swallowing the truth before he told
too much of it. Nearly a year after the murder of Archdeacon
Pierre de Castelnau, Jordí felt again the cold tiles grinding into
his knees and the tension clenching his belly. Sitting before his
dear friend Manel de Perella, under the grace of his kind eyes,
Jordí longed to tell all he had seen and heard that day and to
confess his betrayal.

King David's psalms of repentance came unbidden to his

mind: *You know my folly, O God; my guilt is not hidden from you. Deeper and deeper I sink into the mire; I can't find a foothold to stand on. I am in deep water, and the floods overwhelm me.* The words made a mockery of his secret life. The wine rose in his gorge, and he choked back his confession. Manel shifted, clearing his throat, and Jordí returned to the small room in a wayside inn outside Narbonne's walls.

"Two months after the murder, Abbot Bonnín introduced me to the new sénéchal of the Aude and Hérault, Lucas Mauléon." Jordí had told no one that the sénéchal and Castelnau's assassin were one and the same. His face flamed at the memory of how he'd pissed his robes at the sight of Mauléon, and he was grateful the room was illumined only by firelight. It was one thing to admit fear. It was quite another to explain why.

"I tried to send word to you that I had met Mauléon in Paris," Manel interrupted. "He knew we'd been in the seminary together, but he claimed not to know where you'd been sent. I learned only recently you never left Languedoc." Taking the pitcher of wine from a low table beside him, Manel refilled both tall cups of fired clay. "I've interrupted you enough, *Ósbru,*" he said with affection as he handed Jordí a cup of wine. "Please, continue."

"The sénéchal informed me that I was to depart from Saint-Gilles immediately. He escorted me here to the church of Saint-Paul. After the burning of Cluet, I was moved again. To Gruissan." He watched Manel carefully. The handsome priest kept a smooth countenance, but he couldn't keep the flinch from showing in his eyes. His pupils widened, black pushing into soft blue.

LE PÈLERIN, MINERVE—WEDNESDAY

The clock chimed midnight. Lia had remained silent while

Jordí took her back to the end of that wretched, bloody year of 1208, but this coincidence was too much. "Gruissan?" she burst out. "Where Raoul's family was killed! Why didn't you tell me this before?"

"Lia, there is so much I need to tell you. And I'm trying. Please, allow me to finish."

Although the questions hammered in her throat, she nodded, wrapping her arms around her knees and pressing her lips together. The priest poured out his story with downcast eyes, deflated in his wool coat, designing circles with his finger on the tabletop.

NARBONNE—DECEMBER 1208

"What of your dealings with the sénéchal?" Manel asked.

"I haven't seen him since we parted ways in Toulouse." Jordí's lie spilled easily, one more to join the many that had come fluidly from his mouth over the months. Bells chimed in the distance. He pressed his hand against his thick thighs and hoisted himself up with a sigh. "It's late. I must take my leave. I'll be expected at vespers." He looked around the modest room. "Manel, you should be staying in honor at the bishop's home and sleeping in silk sheets, not hiding in this dreadful hostel. Why are you here?"

"There is much I wish to tell you, but it will have to be some other time, my friend. And I would ask again that you tell no one you've seen me."

"Of course. You move at the will of His Holiness. I'd be a fool to interfere." Jordí gathered his cloak around his shoulders. "And what news of your cousin?"

"My cousin?" Manel echoed sharply.

"Raoul d'Aran is well-known in these parts. Married a local

woman and farms an estate in Lagrasse? I hear he and his family are no longer in residence there." Jordí fussed over the clasp of his cloak to keep from meeting Manel's eyes. "His wife's father is wealthy. Hugh Gervais of Limoux? A Cathar, it's rumored."

"Yes, I know of Gervais, but we've never met. Why do you ask after my cousin?"

LE PÈLERIN, MINERVE—WEDNESDAY

"You were with Raoul's cousin!" Forgetting her promise not to interrupt, Lia slammed her feet to the floor. "He was tied to the Vatican? He knew the sénéchal who killed Raoul's family!"

"Manel de Perella was Raoul's aunt's second son, his mother's kin. He… Lia, what is it?"

She bolted from her chair to the far end of the table where her research materials were piled in stacks. She pulled out a file folder and slapped it open on the table in front of Jordí. Inside were photocopied letters—the materials Jordí had left on her front porch—and the translations she'd started to create. Lia cursed herself for not having asked Raoul about the materials the previous night. But her mind and body had been elsewhere.

"Manel. You called him Manel." She rifled through the sheets until she found the odd one out: a page written in a different hand, in a dialect of Occitan or possibly provincial Catalan. "There are words I can pick out here and there. Look: *cosí.* That's cousin." She pointed farther down the page. "And here is Manel." Her finger punched at the paper. "Jordí, is this the Manel you're talking about?" Lia scattered the papers across the table, and several floated to the floor. "I've been struggling through these translations while you can read them as if they'd been written yesterday. What do they say? Who are they from?"

The priest sighed and patted the lapels of his coat. "I'll need to get my reading glasses from the car," he said.

"I'm sure that letter is from me. To Manel, my cousin. Your friend. Or so he thought." Raoul stood in the kitchen threshold, arms crossed over his chest, fists clenched against his biceps. Rhythmic pulses of his jaw betrayed his struggle for composure.

The priest started from his chair, but Lia placed a hand on his arm to steady him. With a sad smile, he patted her hand, lifted it gently away, and shook his head.

"Raoul d'Aran. It's an honor." Standing, Jordí pressed his palms together and bowed his head in a gesture of respect.

"Honor? What would you know of honor?" Raoul stepped around the corner of the kitchen island. "'Ósbru,' Manel called you," he spit at Jordí. "Your nickname at the seminary. The brown bear. '*The bear is a traitor. A falcon flies south, and the dove will die.*' Those were Manel's words to his steward. They were a message to me, to let me know my family had been betrayed. And by whom."

Lia gasped, and a scene where she had inserted herself between the two men flashed in her mind. The world slowed to a nightmarish crawl, yet it was spinning out of control.

"You were that bear, weren't you, Jordí?" Raoul advanced, and Lia stepped in front of him, pressing a palm hard against his chest. He stopped at her touch but kept his eyes on Jordí. "And Paloma, *my wife*. She was the dove." Raoul wore the same expression of pain and sadness she'd seen in her window three months before.

How many times had she wondered about Raoul's Paloma since the Cité at Carcassonne, when he'd called her by his wife's name? What she had looked like, what had made her laugh, how she'd been as a mother, a wife, a lover. *Paloma.* Such a beautiful name. Latin in origin, it meant dove. Paloma was the dove. She must be. She couldn't be.

"Jordí." Lia spoke to the priest without turning from Raoul. "The letter you found near Pierre de Castelnau's body. You told me it read, 'The bear is a traitor. A falcon flies south, and the dove will die.'" Raoul opened his mouth, and Lia gave a warning shake of her head.

"This is the truth," Jordí replied. "I know there is little reason to trust me, but I promise you, this is what I read."

"How did Manel know those words?" Lia asked. "How could he have repeated them to his steward?"

"I gave him the letter."

She snapped her head to the priest. "What? You told me you never returned to the abbey, that you had no idea what happened to that letter!"

"It's the rest of my story. It's what I need to share with you. Please."

NARBONNE—DECEMBER 1208

I have seen the spirit of God. They are not heretics. They are the Trinity. A dying man's final words. A letter acknowledging the truth. And in truth, death.

Jordí could stand his deceit no longer. He grabbed his friend by the arm and pulled him close. "The Gervais family are known heretics, but be aware it is Raoul d'Aran's agitation for a resistance against the Church that has put his family in grave danger. It's no secret the woman and children are hiding in Gruissan," he rasped. "A reward is offered for d'Aran's capture, and his life may be traded for theirs. If you have any way to warn him, do it."

From a leather satchel he'd strapped over his head, Jordí removed a thin wallet and spoke the only words that still had meaning for him: "And David said to God, 'I have sinned greatly, in that I have done this thing. But now, put away, I beg you, the iniquity of your servant; for I have done very foolishly.'"

He pressed the pouch into Manel's hand and whispered, "Castelnau was holding this when he died. I've held it too long, but I'm too much of a fool to know what to do with what's written inside. I am sorry." He kissed Manel on each cheek and backed away, his hand raised to stifle further conversation. Jordí passed into the dark hallway.

Outside the inn, he turned into an alley and pressed a coin into the palm of the boy he'd hired to keep watch over his horse. The boy dashed away and yelped as he nearly collided with a tall, cloaked figure. Jordí's departure was delayed for a few minutes more.

LE PÈLERIN, MINERVE—WEDNESDAY

"You fool, Bonafé," Raoul hissed. "You told Mauléon that my family was in Gruissan."

"Raoul, please. This is my story too." Lia's back pressed into his chest, her arm bent around his waist, and she held his body, rigid with anger, tightly against hers. "I'm in the middle of whatever is happening to you," she countered gently, turning into him. She held his face and forced him to look at her with his hard, furious eyes. His jaw clenched under her palms.

"It's all right, Lia." Jordí's smile was slight and sad. "His anger is no more than I deserve." Gray and old, he sagged into the chair. "No, Raoul." He remained still, his hands resting on his knees, and Lia sensed his withering regret. "Mauléon's network of spies was so vast, he likely knew even as you sent your family to Gruissan. I was sent to watch them, but I never meant to bring your family harm."

Raoul pushed Lia's hands away and tried to step around her.

His voice erupted in a snarl. "Did you wield a weapon against them? No, the murderer wasn't you. But your complicity makes you as guilty as the hands that set that fire."

The man who had held Lia with such tenderness and passion had flown away, leaving an empty shell, and she fought against a quivering despair.

"I know you have more to say, Raoul," she said in a low voice. "Just let me see this through."

"Then ask your confessor to tell you the truth. Ask him to tell you what happened to my wife and children."

"Let's sit," she murmured. "We can sort this out." She gently pushed down on his shoulders.

"I'll stand," he said, barely moving his lips. But his shoulders dropped and his knees unlocked as the tension began to seep away.

"Fine. But I want you over..." She looked around. Not the kitchen. Not near the knife block. She almost laughed, it was so absurd. "Just stay where you are." Lia pulled a stool from under the tall kitchen island and propped her feet on the seat of a dining room chair, creating a barrier between the two men with her body.

"Manel de Perella, the new papal emissary in Paris, your cousin"—she motioned to Raoul—"he knew this Mauléon. And Mauléon was appointed sénéchal by Philippe du Plessis after the murder of Castelnau?" She looked from one man to the other. They both nodded. "You'll have to excuse me for turning pedantic professor on you, but I know this history better than I know my own family tree. There is no record of Sénéchal Lucas Mauléon of the Aude and Hérault during the first decade of the thirteenth century," she said. "Nothing. In fact, there's no record of a sénéchal anywhere in Languedoc during that period. By 1209, Simon de Montfort was the law of the land."

"Mauléon wasn't in the position for very long." Jordí snapped his eyes to Raoul.

Lia wouldn't be sidetracked, not while she felt so close to untangling these threads of the past. "Fine. I'll concede for the moment that history just missed making a record of him." She thought of the archives Jordí had spirited away from the cathedral in Narbonne, of the shuttered doors of the institute in Carcassonne. "Or it hasn't yet been revealed. Jordí, you said Castelnau knew his assassin?" she asked.

"That is what I recall."

"So this assassin was the falcon. Castelnau was the dove. Not Paloma." She looked at Raoul. His face was a wall of granite— handsome, but distant and cold. His scar was a white snarl of flesh. "But there's more that you remember, isn't there? You just haven't told me." Lia recalled the cruel eyes of the eagle on the terrace railing and then the falcon etched into a business card. Although she had checked Raoul's fury only moments before, a sudden clarity drove her anger forward, like a cresting wave. She pushed off the stool, and its metal casters screeched across the stone tile. "Mauléon was the man in the abbey. Mauléon murdered Castelnau."

"Lia."

She wasn't certain which man said her name, and she didn't care. "You know, I think I've known for some time," she said softly, no longer speaking to the men in the room but working through what she didn't want to accept. "*The truth may lead you to things you'd rather not see* indeed. The truth was right in front of me, and I didn't want to see. Jordí, has he always been known as Mauléon?" Lia leaned into the table for support.

"Mauléon changed his name when he left Languedoc and joined the Crusaders," Jordí said, his own voice gentle as his eyes flicked between her and Raoul, cautiously watching their reactions. "He wanted to escape the legacy of his disgraced father."

She withdrew a business card from a pocket in her research binder and presented it to Jordí. "The first time I met Lucas, I made the connection between the name Moisset and the translation of falcon in Occitan. I think he wanted me to know. In some perverse way, he was trying to tell me. Lucas Moisset is the falcon in that letter."

Jordí closed his hand over the card without looking.

Lia paced to the terrace windows, wanting to throw open the door and scream her frustration into the wind. "Lucas Moisset is the Sénéchal Lucas Mauléon. Mauléon murdered Castelnau. He murdered Raoul's family."

In the window's reflection, Lia saw shapes moving, joining, separating in the room behind her. As he had in the Basilique Saint-Nazaire et Saint-Celse, Raoul moved with such speed, the empty space echoed with his passing. Jordí stood suddenly, and his chair toppled to the tile floor. Lia shoved past him.

"Raoul!" she called, though she knew it was too late. The front door was open wide, and the living room was infused with the scents of damp earth and rosemary. The street in front of Le Pèlerin was empty; Raoul had been absorbed into the dark.

"Dammit, Jordí, if he goes after Lucas…" Jordí, just behind her, grabbed her elbow, and she spun around in fury and fear. "You've known this all along!" she cried. "No one thought to tell me Lucas was a murderer? Are you and Lucas in this together? Am I some sort of bait? Is Lucas using me to get to Raoul?"

"Lucas means you no harm, Lia," Jordí said. "He's in love with you."

Her stomach dropped. She thought of the man she'd allowed to kiss her, the man to whom she'd revealed her love for Raoul.

It didn't matter that the blood on his hands was eight hundred years old. Lia felt ill.

"Yes, the falcon is Lucas Moisset." Jordí took hold of her upper arms, shaking her attention back to him. "Yes, Lucas assassinated Castelnau. But, Lia, listen to me. He did not kill Paloma and the children."

She wrenched out of his grasp and made for the door.

OUTSIDE NARBONNE—DECEMBER 1208

From the slit of window carved into the outside wall, Manel peered out to the muddy stretch of road below. He waited, his breath turning white as cold air seeped in. Just as he began to wonder where Jordí had gone, he saw the monk emerge from the alley on a small, sturdy mare. Manel watched the man's corpulent form sway on the overburdened horse until the pair turned a corner. He secured the shutter and emptied the last of the wine into his cup. Finally, he opened the leather pouch Jordí had pressed into his hand and withdrew a single sheet of vellum.

He knew the handwriting on the page the moment he held it to the light: the Latin script had been written by Philippe du Plessis. All, that is, but the final two sentences, which were

cryptic words inked by a hand he did not recognize. No longer
at the window, Manel did not see a shadow step away from the
alley and enter the inn.

⁓〜⁓

"It must be one of God's marvels that a land so vast and difficult
to travel could see the intersection of so many of my friends."

The wine caught in Manel's throat, and his aborted swallow
became a choking cough. He spun away from the fireplace, an
arm pressed to his leaking mouth, to see the sénéchal standing
in front of the closed door. Manel recovered his voice and his
wits. "What do you want?"

"To see the look on your face when I tell you I know
everything about your deception." A mocking smile curled the
sénéchal's lips. "Oh yes. I've known since the day the council
received the letter from the pope. I followed you through the
Marais and saw you enter and leave a residence. Your infa-
mous cousin, Raoul d'Aran, was just steps behind you." Lucas
paused, allowing the full effect of his words to take hold.

Manel blinked and swallowed but held steady, his arms at his
sides, one hand gripping the empty cup of wine. "How did
you find me?"

"I've tracked you since March and intercepted much of
your correspondence. Our mutual friend sent word that he'd
arranged to meet you on your way to…Madrid? Is that your
story? I thought it would be best if I were near at hand. Don't
look so surprised. You aren't the only spy in Languedoc.
Apparently, Bonafé didn't tell you everything."

"Jordí," he gasped. "But why would he—"

"Betray you?" Lucas finished. "Why would any man betray?
For power? Money? The threat of violence against those he

loves? That was the one that worked finally—threats to friends and family near and far." He turned slowly around the room, taking in the modest surroundings. "But I could ask you the same, Manel de Perella. Why forsake the Church? Why turn away from a life of influence and comfort and the certainty of your place in history? For this?" He swept out a hand, indicating the fusty room and the arid expanse of Languedoc. "You aren't even of this region. What does the independence of sheepherders and grape growers and heretics mean to you?"

Manel ached to sit; despite the courage in his heart, his body shook. The fatigue of travel had ground his nerves to dust. He straightened his spine, clenched his fists, and prayed for the strength to continue.

"I was forsaken," he replied, choosing honesty as a release from the secret life he'd been living. "Not by God, but by men who'd sworn to protect the weak and lift them up through the grace of the Church, men who'd vowed to live by Christ's example. I witnessed jealous lust for revenue and wicked contempt for those who dared question the sovereignty of the Church's rule. Something in me began to wither and die. The trusting boy became a soured man."

As his strength wasted away, he understood it was more than fear causing his shaking hands and blurred vision. It was more than the potent wine. Manel knew what would soon follow. Regret for not having done more, for being a disappointment in the end to his cousin and his cause, washed over him.

But with the possibility of death, either at Lucas Mauléon's hands or by God's mercy, there also came a placid release. "Is it so hard to believe that power and influence could be rejected in favor of compassion and justice? Is your heart that hardened to mercy, Sénéchal?"

Lucas snorted with derision. "You are talking to a soldier of the Fourth Crusade. Mercy will get you killed." He moved about the small room, fingering Manel's simple but finely made clothing, running his hand over the leather tooling that covered his Bible. "But what price do you put on the heads of your family?" he asked, as detached as if he'd queried whether Manel preferred the wines of Burgundy or those from Tuscany.

"My family?" Manel breathed. His skin shriveled in the grip of icy fear.

"Your cousin, Raoul. His wife, Paloma. Their children. Have you not heard? I have orders to find d'Aran. Others have been dispatched to arrest his family in Gruissan. But I'm certain you must know where I can find him. His family will be spared if he's captured."

Manel was stunned into silence. A wave of nausea rippled through his belly, and beads of sweat erupted on his skin, burning like hot oil as they trickled down. He knew he had only a few minutes more.

Lucas ceased his pretense at nonchalance and came to stand directly in front of Manel, his black eyes searching the priest's face. "As I speak, the abbot of Cîteaux is in Gruissan, waiting for me to either bring him this Catalan who is fomenting rebellion or to oversee the deaths of his family. I can't help the woman and her children if I don't find d'Aran." He gripped the priest's arms. "I am asking you to help me save Paloma."

"*Save* Paloma? Who is she to you?"

"I was once betrothed to her," said Lucas. "Long ago, when I was known as Lucas Moisset. Those children could have, *should have*, been mine. I thought I'd return from the Crusade a prodigal son, yet she didn't wait…" He exhaled a rueful laugh. "She was a wife and a mother by the time I arrived home. But does this mean I wish revenge? No, I could never wish her harm. Tell me where d'Aran is, Perella. I am his wife's only chance."

Manel's vision wavered, and the bile rose in his constricted throat. His legs could no longer hold him. He sank onto a bench before the fire, pulling at the neck of his long wool cassock.

"Lucas *Moisset*. The falcon. *You* murdered Castelnau."

Then the priest pitched forward onto his knees and vomited up the wine. Lucas sprang back in disgust, cursing as Perella slumped to the floor. His body shook violently, and his eyes rolled back until only the whites showed through his half-closed lids. Lucas knelt beside the man and slammed his fist into the table, splintering its top.

Beneath his anger was a tremor of fear. He'd heard the rumors of the priest's fits—some said they were evidence of his divinity and preternatural intelligence, that God spoke through the handsome priest at the moment he was overcome, or even that these fits were God in the form of man. Blood began trickling from Manel's lips, and Lucas cursed again. The priest had bitten his tongue in the midst of his frenzy. Lucas waited until Perella's body ceased to quake, but he couldn't rouse him. His eyes remained open and unblinking. His chest was still.

Lucas looked around the room for something to tell him where d'Aran might be. He found nothing but one sheet of vellum. The blood leeched from his face as he skimmed the script. He read it once more, slowly. Then Lucas folded the letter inside the calfskin pouch that sat on the table and rushed from the room.

Part Four

....

Death slue not him, but he made death his ladder to the skies.

—EDMUND SPENSER

....

GRUISSAN—DECEMBER 1208

Lucas held Paloma by the chin. She set her jaw and twisted away, but he dug his fingers into her skin and pulled her head back. Two priests in plain cassocks stood on either side of the door, watching with teeth bared in hideous grins.

Still holding her in his grip, Lucas groped for the chair behind him. Grabbing the wooden back, he yanked it around and sat before her, clenching her legs between his. Paloma defied her desire to shrink away and forced her spine to straighten.

"It didn't have to be this way," he said, his voice low and tired. Paloma tried not to listen. She trained her ears to the room beyond, where Bertran and Aicelina lay sleeping. "It's d'Aran I'm after, not you or your children. But by abandoning you here, he's left me no choice, has he?"

The sénéchal released her face and ran his knuckles across her jaw, where she imagined the imprints of his fingers flushed an angry red. To her horror, he laid a hand against the mound of her belly. He raised his eyes to meet hers, and Paloma saw a glimmer of light in their depths, a ripple of profound sadness. But the light extinguished, and she despaired. She swallowed with effort.

"Was I so different as a boy?" Lucas asked.

"You—" She faltered but tried again, this time speaking in a clear, unwavering voice. "You were such a lonely child." Even as she sought to appease him, a thread of empathy wove through the fear in her heart. She prayed the children wouldn't wake. "None of us felt our fathers' fists as you did. But you must know how much *my* father loved you. How much he still loves you. Please, let us go."

"I let you go once, never dreaming you'd betray me." He was all the more menacing for the softness in his voice. "I waited for you, Paloma. You know how long I waited."

Paloma recalled a young man's obsession, those eyes that followed her across the village square, a presence that always seemed to find her alone, in her garden, in her father's stables, or collecting apples in the orchards in early morning. Gracious child that she was, she'd treated Lucas Moisset with kindness. And with caution. She recalled too a young man falling at her feet and swearing his love. Before he left for Agen as a page, he'd pleaded for her secret betrothal, promising they would be wed when he returned to Languedoc a knight and a hero.

"I was a child," she replied, appealing to his remaining compassion. "I didn't understand what your love meant. But we were friends once. Dear friends."

He shook his head, exhaling a shallow breath, and Paloma despaired. Her words had bounced off his heart like stones thrown at a frozen pond.

"I know the promises we made. I remember as if it were yesterday. I returned to marry you." He stood and turned his back on her.

Paloma heard shouts in the streets beyond the house; she caught the odor of smoke.

Without warning, the sénéchal whipped out a long, booted leg, lifting the chair in front of her and sending it crashing into the cold hearth. One of the priests yelped as he dodged splinters of wood. Paloma reared back in her chair, and as she struggled to keep her balance, she heard Bertran call out. The children were awake. She froze before the man they called Sénéchal Lucas Mauléon—the boy she had known as Lucas Moisset— and willed her child to fall silent.

"It's too late for all of this," he said, ignoring Bertran's cries. "Our story has been written. Now yours is coming to an end. There's nothing more I can do."

"Sénéchal—Lucas—you can't mean this. Let us go, I beg you. We'll leave Languedoc. We'll vanish. We won't betray you."

Even as the words left her mouth, she knew they were the wrong ones. In one stride, he was in front of her. He pulled her up hard against him, forcing her to stand on her toes. She gasped but didn't struggle. To her horror, she began to cry.

"You won't betray me? You fool. Your betrayal began when your family adopted the heretic faith. I wouldn't have you now if you begged for me. I returned from fighting the infidels, risking my life for the Holy Church, only to learn I was betrothed to a Cathar whore." He bent his face to hers, pressing his rough cheek against her wet skin. His lips ran along her jaw, wiping away the drops of her fear. "It's too late," he whispered. "I can't save you."

"Maman?" At the sound of her son's voice, Paloma ripped away from the sénéchal with such force he stumbled back. She moved with the speed of a doe to Bertran's side and scooped him into her arms. Aicelina's little form appeared, and Paloma pulled her close as well. Squatting on her toes, she turned her torso to face Lucas Mauléon, her arms wrapped around her toddlers. Aicelina whimpered, and Paloma shushed her into silence.

For a long moment, no one moved. Then Lucas turned without a word and walked into the corridor beyond. In her head, Paloma screamed for Raoul; in her heart, she begged God for mercy. She heard men's voices, low and hushed.

The sénéchal reentered with two cloaked and hooded soldiers. One carried a torch, the other a dagger. Lucas stepped aside and motioned to the woman and children. "Take them to the church with the others." Paloma rose unsteadily, a trembling child in each arm. The men hesitated. "I gave you an order! Take them away!"

His bellow blasted the soldiers into action. A sentry reached for Bertran, but the boy screamed and buried his face in his mother's neck. Aicelina wailed.

"Please, let me hold them." Paloma pleaded. One of the sentries laughed, malice ripe in the cruel twist of his mouth, and stepped aside with a mocking bow. The other pointed his dagger to the door and moved in behind her. She forced her legs into motion, feeling nothing, not the weight of her children, not the chill in the corridor, not even the fear that had gripped her bowels moments before. Every fiber of her body sang for Raoul, willing him to hear her heart's cries.

ON THE ROAD TO NARBONNE—DECEMBER 1208

*R*aoul prepared to leave for Narbonne as the thin streams of apricot light faded from the western sky. He'd spent the day waiting out a sudden storm in a *cabanon* in a field north of the great salt marshes, just inland from the sea. But he could reach his destination in a few hours' ride, and if the stars in the eastern sky kept their promise and remained visible, he'd stay dry. Mirò whinnied a question at Raoul as he adjusted her saddle before dipping her graceful head to pull at the meager grass.

He was only a few miles but an impossible distance from his family in Gruissan, where he'd taken Paloma and the children in October, just days after the last grape harvest. Raoul had overseen the pressing before abandoning their home in Lagrasse for the anonymity of Languedoc's hillsides, coasts, caves, and sheepherders' paths. But this night would bring him to Narbonne, where many weeks before, he and Manel had arranged, through their small band of allies, to meet.

Raoul departed at dusk, heading west, following a course of his own reckoning, wishing he could see past the darkening horizon and into the future. As the moon rose like a bright silver button in the blue velvet of the sky, it was hard to imagine a more peaceful place. It was almost beyond comprehension that strife and despair flowed all around him. But Raoul felt it in his blood—his dreams were cursed with images of fire and the sounds of suffering.

By autumn, as word of the massacre in Cluet spread through Languedoc, men in plain clothes but riding the powerful destriers of nobles and knights began appearing in twos and threes on the roads from Toulouse and Béziers to Carcassonne and Narbonne and near the great citadels of Peyrepertuse, Quéribus, and Puilaurens. The forests and gorges seemed to swallow them, for no more was seen or heard after they passed through.

The land seemed to ready itself—not just for winter, but for some greater threat—and then it held its breath. Raoul's lungs pulled tight with Languedoc's tension, waiting for the sudden change that would force exhalation. And action.

One head turned as Raoul entered Manel's room near Narbonne's port on the Aude. He was a stranger, short of stature but lean and handsome, with dark copper hair and a scruff of beard shadowing his face. He stood beside an empty bed, stripped bare of its covering.

"Raoul d'Aran." The young man's voice was soft and full of sorrow; Raoul could see anguish in his eyes. Raoul did not respond, and his hand remained inside his cloak, poised on the grip of his short sword. "My name is Nicolo Carrer," the man said. "I am your cousin's steward." He stammered in *langue d'oïl*, his accent thickened by his native Italian dialect.

"Yes, he's spoken of you," Raoul replied in their common language as his eyes scanned the small room. "Where is Manel?"

Nicolo sank slowly onto the bed and studied his clasped hands. "Monsieur d'Aran. If I'd not known and loved Manel so well and had not already witnessed his fits, I would have sworn a demon had entered him. It was terrible." He looked up with dark, round eyes overflowing with tears. "But he didn't die alone. I was with him to the end."

Raoul sank to his knees, burying his wretched cry in the thick wool of his cloak. He wanted to flail out, destroy this room, destroy the sun as it rose over Narbonne. His beautiful, gentle cousin, brought down by a curse of God. He felt a hand on his back, a hand that gripped his shoulder and drew him up. Nicolo held out a cup of wine. Raoul accepted it and emptied the cup in one swallow.

"Tell me what happened."

The Italian nodded and cleared his throat. "Manel and I left Paris two weeks ago with merchants and holy men bound for Spain. We were traveling as horse buyers on our way to meet with breeders in Madrid. We arrived in Nîmes, and the group splintered as some headed east to Marseilles or Italy. Manel and I continued here, to Narbonne, where we were to wait for our escort south to Perpignan and across the Pyrénées. It was then Manel revealed to me that we would travel west, deeper into Languedoc.

"We arrived at this hostel two days ago. Manel had arranged to meet an old friend from the seminary in Catalunya. Bonafé, his name was. I went to find a smithy—my mare had a loose shoe. When I returned, the door to our room was open, and

Manel was on the floor before the fire. He looked asleep, but he…" Nicolo's voice broke. "He'd had one of his fits, one of the worst. He'd soiled himself and bitten his tongue, and I couldn't rouse him. These fits, certainly one as bad as this, rob every measure of strength from his body."

Nicolo inhaled deeply. "When he woke the next morning, he was confused, babbling about a letter that he insisted was here. I searched our belongings but found nothing. I tried to silence him, to keep him calm, but he raved about you, about your family in Gruissan."

Raoul ran a hand across his brow, squeezing his temples to check his anxiety. He returned his gaze to the young Italian and nodded for him to continue.

"I know he waited as long as he could. He wanted to see you, to tell you himself. But he must have known his end was coming. He insisted that without that letter, I had to give you his message in person."

"What message?" Raoul demanded.

"Your cousin told me, 'Say these words to Raoul d'Aran. Say them, and then forget you ever heard them.' And his message was, 'The bear is a traitor. A falcon flies south, and the dove will die.'"

Raoul repeated the words and shook his head. "I don't understand," he said. Nicolo's lips quivered, and Raoul hastened to add, "But no matter. It will make sense when I can think more clearly. Tell me about Manel."

Nicolo waved his hands helplessly. "He was overcome soon after. Merciful God, it didn't last long. I felt his life slip away."

Raoul cursed Manel's God and then thanked him for relieving the young priest of his suffering. He wished he could believe in Paloma's superstition of rebirth. Of all the souls who deserved a second life, his tenderhearted cousin certainly did.

Then in a heartbeat, the heat of Raoul's fury and grief snapped to ice.

Paloma, he screamed silently. *My dove.* A man one instant from becoming undone, he said in a strangled voice, "My family has been betrayed."

GRUISSAN—DECEMBER 1208

They stumbled through the streets, pushed on by soldiers. Torches flickered against shut doors and shuttered windows. No one peered out. The village remained closed to them, but Paloma sensed the terror behind the walls. A few streets away, cries echoed, shouts broke like thunderclaps, and then all was quiet. Dread thudded in her belly when she realized how alone they were. *Where are you, Raoul? Oh, my husband, you would know what to do.*

Saint-Maurice loomed ahead, a terrible hulk of stone turned the color of dried blood by the torchlight. The soldiers shoved her and the children through a door that led into the back of a chapel. The heavy door, bound with iron braces, boomed shut, and Paloma heard the click and rattle of chains. Iron against iron, iron against wood. The doom was thick in her veins, a mordant grip deeper than terror.

The stories whispered at the hearth and in the Lagrasse market of villagers burned alive in churches weren't gossip or fabrication. They were witnessed horrors of men killing their neighbors, cousins, and brothers. The thought of death by fire nearly sent her mad with panic. "We are lost," she moaned aloud, and Bertran whimpered under her crushing hold. Aicelina was silent with fear. Paloma prayed for quick deaths, for the smoke to overwhelm them before the flames could sear their skin.

She entered the nave, grasping her children's tiny fingers in her shaking hands. The dark, cold interior of the church echoed with the cries of babies, the sobs of women, and the pounding fists of men on the wooden doors of the nave and at the shuttered windows. She tried to count the souls trapped with her, but it was difficult to see in the shadows: more than a dozen, perhaps two. They were islands in their fear, no one working together to seek a way out. A woman began to keen, tearing at her hair and clothing, until another woman, perhaps a daughter, pleaded with her to be calm.

The crazed one sagged, and her wails diminished to gasps. The younger woman caressed her back, arranging the torn dress in a touching effort to preserve her modesty. The older woman pushed the other's hands away, rose, and looked directly at Paloma. Her voice was a mule's tortured bray, echoing across the dark nave.

"Those children!" Her arm shot up and she extended an accusing finger. "Unnatural creatures. It is a sign," she bellowed. "You are the devil's concubine, a witch. You have cursed us all!" The spittle flew from her lips, and her eyes shone with mad triumph.

The pale moons of the villagers' faces twisted in unison toward Paloma. She held her children tighter. The woman stumbled toward her, her torn shift falling open and her heavy breasts swinging free of the coarse fabric. Time slowed, and details came into sharp relief, even in the half-light: the woman's pockmarked face ravaged by boils and blemishes, her belly stretched and flaccid from childbearing. Paloma pitied her, pitied them all, trapped and helpless, now turning against each other in their fear. And still her accuser came with hands raised and fingers clawing at the air.

The woman lunged at Paloma, screaming in outrage. Paloma

stepped back, but the claw of fingernails ripped the chain bearing a silver cross from her neck. Off balance, the broken woman tripped and fell to her knees and remained there, weeping, while the villagers looked on, paralyzed by shock.

Paloma faced the crowd, standing to protect her children against this final insult. She'd been protected by Raoul's stature in Lagrasse from strangers' wild-eyed superstitions that her children, born minutes apart and as alike as rosebuds on a bush, were signs of witchcraft. And she'd been hidden away in Gruissan. Now she met the leering faces alone. Although it no longer mattered what these strangers should think of her; her end would be theirs. But she stood so that her last words would be ones of truth and courage, not mewling pleas for mercy, huddled in a corner.

"My husband is Raoul d'Aran of Lagrasse. He risks his life to save innocents threatened by this war." Her voice rang across the nave. "I am no one's whore, I am not a witch, and my children are as innocent as any trapped here. My family and I were brought here to hide in the safety of a friend's home. We were betrayed, as were all of you. By whom, I do not know, and it can hardly matter now."

Heavy thudding on the front doors startled the small band. Several of the women shrieked in fright, and the youngest children began to whimper again. There was no break in the ferocious rhythm. It became another element of torture, a senseless gesture to intimidate the already terrified. Some of the women cried, the tears running soundlessly down their pale cheeks. The men's faces were taut. They all flinched as the pounding continued, slow and steady, with the cadence of a funeral drum.

Paloma's nostrils flared as the acrid odor of smoke wound invisibly through the nave. She turned to look for its source, but it seeped in stealthily. Then she saw it on the far side: thin shafts of light through the panels of shutters shrunken by heat and rain. Tendrils of smoke caught the light, lazily spiraling up to the ceiling. The pounding stopped as suddenly as it began. The gathered group stifled their sobs and moans as they waited, and the nave grew eerily quiet.

"Fire!" a woman screamed, pointing to a row of narrow windows on the west end still in shadow and covered with boards. Smoke began to pour in, and with it, the first bright lick of flame, tiny but menacing. There was commotion as the villagers moved away from the windows. Paloma looked to the round moons of stained glass high in the north wall, where the dawn light was beginning to glow in the ruby, sapphire, and emerald panels.

MINERVE—WEDNESDAY

*L*ia shoved her feet into her running shoes, grabbed her bag and keys, and slammed the door behind her, leaving Jordí alone in Le Pèlerin. She raced up the street, but Raoul's Jeep was gone. She tried his number, but there was no cell service; the phone was useless.

She forced herself to stop and consider where Raoul would have gone. After Lucas? She had no idea where Lucas lived, and the address for his studio in Narbonne was a postbox. Then the response rang as clearly as if someone stood next to her, speaking the words aloud.

Logis du Martinet. Raoul's home.

Clouds weighted with rain hung so low she could almost touch their ragged skins. As she ran down rue des Célestins to the garage she shared with a neighbor, her footsteps reverberated in the mist, and the sound of her breathing filled the space around her head. The silent village unnerved her. Not even a cat sidled past. In the predawn, Minerve appeared abandoned.

The garage door creaked as she pushed it open. It escaped her grasp at the last moment, slamming up to the roof in an explosion of metal against stone. Clanging dread filled the air. She waited, her heart slamming in her chest. No sound followed. Even the car's engine turning over made her cringe, as if the noise might wake the dead from the peace of their eternal slumber.

Creeping through the canyons of Minerve's cobbled streets, she peered through the condensation on her windshield, looking for a glow from a kitchen window, a wisp of smoke from a chimney, the flutter of a bedroom curtain, a pale face peering outside to see who dared disturb the silence. No light, no smoke, no face. Lia pulled away from town, taking the right onto Route d'Azillanet.

She sped south down small roads that were just slivers on a map. The familiar modern landmarks had vanished. The army of wind turbines that kept vigil over the Corbières Valley was gone; what had been vineyards with glossy green leaves were fallow fields filled with dull, gray-brown stubs.

She picked up speed along the long stretch of road toward Lagrasse, but when she took the back way into the village, the tarmac thinned again and became hard-packed earth. Lia slowed, uncertain and anxious as the miles peeled away beneath her tires and fell into time.

Lagrasse was below her, tucked into a small valley through which the Orbieu River chortled with the mountain runoff of early spring. A left down rue des Tineries would take her to the center of the village. She veered right instead and onto a rough gravel road gouged with deep potholes. She gripped the steering wheel tighter as granite and limestone cliffs rose to her right and shadows shifted in the brush on the other side of the road.

No light was visible from Logis du Martinet. The iron gate shifted with the wind as it bounced open and shut against the latch, the bar vibrating in laughter at a private, sinister joke. Lia switched off the headlights and rolled down the window. Nothing could be heard but the wind, which scissored between poplar trees on either side of the rock-strewn lane. It was a dialogue of air that susurrated her name. She killed the engine and left the car a few feet from the gate. Lia checked her cell phone again: not only was there no signal, but the phone wouldn't even turn on.

"Shit." She shoved it into her pocket and slipped through the gate, sliding the bolt home. The camera system that had been in place during her earlier visit was gone. She was greeted only by the wind and the first plash of rain.

The handle on the arched door of the winery's entrance turned easily. Lia let herself in and closed the door against the weather. The silence was immediate. Brackish dawn light seeped in from the skylights that spanned the first feet of the long, vaulted room. Her eyes adjusted to the dimness, and the clumps of shadows reconciled themselves into meaningful shapes.

"What the hell?" She spun in place, taking in the inexplicable.

Raoul had kept his property spotless and the winery pristine. Each space where unbottled wine was stored—whether a stainless steel fermenting tank or the room of oak *tonneaux*—was a marvel of gleaming surfaces and polished wood. But now it looked as if the winery had never seen his steady hand. Muck streaked thickly across the skylights, and the brick walls were coated with the black fuzz of wild yeasts.

Gone were the enormous stainless steel tanks that had lined

the left side of the vast cave. Instead were giant vats of wood, but the vats had collapsed into chunks and splinters. The odor of rotted wood pushed against the intoxicating aroma of fermented grapes.

"Raoul?" Lia called out as she stepped into the vast, shadowy space.

The door to his office hung on broken hinges. The square window that faced his house was intact but filthy, and cobwebs trailed from its wooden casement to the floor. There was no desk, no computer, no light—just a table tilting on three legs and small piles of gray rubbish in the corner that could have been mice nests. Or worse.

She walked toward the back end of the *chai*—the storehouse—and turned left. The floor sloped down to a great, open space. A half-moon window set high in the wall at the far end overlooked the room. Its glass pane rattled with the wind, and she could hear the insistent percussion of the rain. Again, the room was familiar, but only by the shape of its bones. Where once there had been sealed and gleaming cement floors, a bottling machine, and crates of clear and green glass bottles, a floor of broken and crumbling brick with patches of bare earth showing through like open wounds now existed.

"Raoul?" Lia ventured again. Her voice echoed through the space. In the pressing darkness, her heart boomed and her chest tightened. The deeper she penetrated, the lower the ceiling slid. She descended several worn stone steps to face a small wooden door set deep in the wall. Here too the door had an iron handle set precisely in the middle. A vast cellar in disrepair, moldering and crumbling as if it had been left untended for centuries, yet the door opened soundlessly on well-oiled hinges. Lia peered in.

A small landing dropped abruptly to a spiral staircase that

looked carved into the earth's very core. She took a few tentative steps. The corkscrew was so tightly wound that only a few steps were visible before it twisted away. Two people passing would be forced to suck in and shrink their bodies. She could go no farther; her courage was at its end.

An image of the door flashed in her mind. She hadn't thought to prop it open, but she hadn't heard it close behind her either. Lia lunged back up the steps and slammed into the solid mass of the door. It held fast. There was no handle on this side. She moaned and slammed into it again. "No!" she screamed, and her stomach seized in panic. She scrabbled on the walls on either side of the door, pressing against the stone in a mad search for a hidden latch. She fell to her knees in front of the door, her face in her hands, keening softly, no longer able to fight the panic.

A stream of cool air, scented with rain, not ancient damp, pushed up from the stairwell. With the fresh air came a rush of understanding. By goodwill or evil, she no longer knew, but the certainty that she was meant to descend those steps pushed Lia from her knees to her feet.

Worn by the tread of thousands of feet and hundreds of years, the sandstone steps were smooth. The lip of each step had been rubbed away, curving and slippery under the soles of her shoes. Lia clung to the cracked and cold stone walls, allowing their tight spiral to brace her downward plunge. The thin stream of air rushed up to meet her. And there was light. A pearly glow, weak at first, growing stronger and more golden as she descended, allowed her to track her feet. She counted off the steps to keep calm. "...fifty-three...seventy-eight..." Her stomach roiled with nausea at the constant twisting, and cold sweat soaked into her sweater. Still she descended, like Alice tumbling down the rabbit hole.

GRUISSAN—DECEMBER 1208

The rotund young man yanked up his hood, pulled his body deep into his cloak, and edged his way around the nave. Most of the trapped villagers were gathered at the altar, lost in their fear and hysteria. A trio—a woman and two children—stood apart, beside a stone column. The woman's head was bent in prayer, her lips moving soundlessly.

Although he'd been sent as a spy for the sénéchal six weeks earlier, he'd yet to lay eyes on Paloma Gervais d'Aran. But he knew the descriptions of her slight frame and golden hair. Then there were the children, their delicate features so like their mother's and so similar to one another's.

He slipped through the shadows until he was at Paloma's side. Her son's eyes widened, and the man placed his finger to his lips. The boy squeezed his mother's hand and buried his head in her skirts. When Paloma lifted her head, she looked right into his face.

"Follow me. Quickly," he said. He wrapped a hand around her wrist.

"Let go of me," she hissed and jerked away, but his grip tightened.

"Paloma." He pulled her close and spoke firmly. "There is no time. If you want to save yourself and your children, you will do as I say."

"How do you know my name?"

The truth, offered quickly, covered for months of lies. "There are Catholic priests who act against this crusade. You must know this. One waits outside to take you and your children to safety."

"And the others?" Paloma nodded to the group. Most were on their knees now, praying, crying. The odor of smoke was intensifying, the silence beyond the church walls thick with doom.

"I'll do what I can, but you must leave now."

"If you know a way out, you must save us all!" She strained against his grip and opened her mouth wide as if to shout. In a flash, a short knife appeared, its point flush against the tender skin of Bertran's throat. Jordí dropped her arm and turned his body so Bertran was crushed between them.

"If I leave here without you, I'll be killed. If I let the others escape, we will all die together. There are guards posted everywhere, but you have the protection of Lucas Mauléon. Don't be stupid."

"Lucas?" Paloma gasped. "He is behind this? I will not come with you."

Jordí scooped Bertran into his arms, still holding the short knife in one fist, but the boy went rigid and began to squirm. Jordí clamped a firm hand over Bertran's mouth, the blade of the knife a hair's width from the boy's nose, and motioned with a jerk of his chin for Paloma to lead the way. His violence horrified him, but it would serve to save her life and the lives of these children. Inside, he roared. To Paloma, he said in a low, firm voice, "Move. Into the chapel."

Paloma leaned forward and nuzzled her son's cheek with her nose. "Quiet now, little man," she whispered in his ear. "You're with Maman. We're going to Papà." She turned, holding Aicelina's head firmly against her shoulder, and they slipped around the wood railing that separated the chapel from the nave.

In the center of the small chapel was a large stone sarcophagus that held the remains of the church's benefactor. It filled the space, leaving them nowhere to go. Paloma hesitated, and Jordí pushed her forward. "Behind. There is space behind the tomb."

A flight of steps opened at their feet as they descended into the gloom, and they were forced to feel for each step with their toes.

The stairwell ended abruptly. Jordí, still holding Bertran, pressed up tight behind Paloma. "By your foot, there, on the right."

Paloma stretched out her foot, shifting awkwardly under her daughter's weight. A hollow thump sounded. Her foot had met something other than stone.

"Tap quickly three times, and then twice more, slowly." Paloma did as she was told. Immediately, light appeared at her feet, a rectangle no higher than her knees. She hesitated.

"The others." Her voice broke in agony. "We must save the others."

"Save yourself. Save your children" was Jordí's harsh reply. "I've told you—it is too late. The others are lost. Now move!" She crouched down and released Aicelina, holding the child back while she sank to her hands and knees and passed through the opening. Jordí pushed Aicelina and Bertran after her. He squeezed through the hole with some difficulty and emerged, panting, into a passageway outside the church wall.

Paloma knelt in the mud, her arms around her children, pressing their bodies into hers. Before them stood a small cart, drawn by two chestnut packhorses, which filled nearly the width of the alley. The horses shifted, and their ears pulled back against their squat heads. The odor of burning pitch and sulfur was strong, and the air was growing thick with smoke that rose in the sky over the pitched roof of Saint-Maurice. The driver sat hunched on a short bench above the horses, and he spoke without turning his head.

"Into the cart, under the cover."

Bertran began to pull up the bottom edge of his tunic. Paloma bent to help him squat, and Aicelina began crying that she too had to pee. The driver let out an audible sigh.

"Better we all go now than in the cart," Paloma pleaded. Jordí turned to give her privacy and looked back when she cleared her throat. She stood in profile, her hands pressed into the small of her back. It was only then he noticed she filled out the front of her simple gown.

"You are with child. Dear God."

Jordí picked up Aicelina under her arms, and the child shrieked in protest. Paloma shushed and soothed her daughter, though her own voice quavered. She climbed in first. A patchwork cover of leather stretched tight over the bed of the cart, held in place by pegs tacked into the wagon's sideboards. It was dark and close, but fresh straw had been strewn across the bed in thick layers, cushioning their limbs from the slatted floor. Paloma was forced to lie on her side.

"Look how snug and cozy we will be," she said brightly to her children, as if it were a game. She clapped her hands and nodded to Jordí, who set Aicelina beside her and hoisted Bertran into the cart.

Once he was assured that they were inside and calm, Jordí yanked a thick skin heavy with the odor of cowhide over the end, matching up the holes in the leather to the pegs driven into the soft, weathered wood. He sealed them snugly as fingers in a glove.

"If you are stopped, show the letter and seal of the sénéchal," he said to the hooded man holding the reins. "Thank you, Father."

"We shall all be condemned to hell for letting the rest of those souls perish," growled a voice from behind the hood. "May God forgive us."

"I'll do what I can. Now, flee."

The driver slapped the flank of the nearest horse, and it started forward. He clicked his tongue and flicked the reins, and the horses moved in unison. Jordí watched as the cart passed into a covered alley and disappeared into shadow. He turned with a heavy sigh and kneeled down before the small rectangle of space carved into the church wall.

Smoke seeped from the opening. He coughed as he strained to fit his body in the hole. Half in, half out of the church, he felt hands clamp around his ankles with iron strength. He was dragged out and dropped in a pile of mud. Rolling over, spitting muck from his lips, he looked up.

Two years before, Jordí had walked from the seminary at Sant Benet to Poblet at the foot of the Prades Mountains to attend services at the Royal Abbey of Santa Maria de Poblet. The journey had taken three days, but the young monk and his fellow seminarians were carried by eager feet. They traveled to witness the services led by the famous abbot of Cîteaux, Arnaud Amalric.

Three men stood over him now. Two wore the uniform of men-at-arms. They flanked a tall weedy figure in a *surcot* of black velvet topped by a scarlet, hooded mantle embroidered in white and gold. Although this man's head was covered, Jordí knew his face. Resignation overcame his fear at last. Paloma and her children were safe. His last thought, before the flat side of a sword knocked him unconscious, was to wonder why Arnaud Amalric would bother to murder a lowly monk.

LOGIS DU MARTINET, LAGRASSE—TIME UNKNOWN

*L*ia emerged from the stairwell into a short passage. Lit by an unseen source, the corridor was a conch shell of glowing, iridescent stone. She had no idea how far she'd traveled. She tried to shove away the image of tons of earth piled over her, but her breath came shallow and fast, and her heart skittered inside a chest that felt too small to contain her fear.

An open archway gave into a vast, empty courtyard enclosed by high walls of solid granite. A fine mist fell in a curtain of silver beads from the pearl of open sky. It was daylight, impossibly, inexplicably, but daylight all the same. Relieved of the choking panic of claustrophobia, it mattered little to Lia where she'd come from or how she'd get out. She leaned against the wall, raised her face to the sky, and closed her eyes. She was beyond logic now. Calm flowed into her limbs, and her stomach unclenched. She couldn't explain this any more than she could explain how or why the wheels of time had spun Raoul, Lucas, and Jordí until their souls collided with hers. She was ready to let it go. To let happen what would.

A child's giggle broke through her reverie. She sprang away from the wall and looked around. Just outside an open threshold carved into the stone stood two children, three or four years old, with bare feet and wearing simple brown shifts. The boy's dark-blond curls touched the tips of his ears and sprang across his forehead to his brow. A lavender kerchief covered the girl's hair, and loose braids poured over her shoulders. The twins gawked at her with hazel eyes that made her think of the forest at sunrise.

Moments later, a woman cradling an infant stepped into the courtyard. She bent toward the children, whispered a few words, and kissed their dimpled cheeks. The twins glanced at Lia and then raced away.

"*Mei viste!*" Bertran called in Occitan. "Hurry up!"

"*Espera-me!*" Aicelina called after her brother to wait.

The woman approached Lia unafraid, her eyes glowing with tenderness and gentle curiosity. She was petite and willow-thin. A white wimple embroidered with flowers of gold thread covered her head, and thick waves of silver and gold cascaded over her left shoulder. Her eyes were the silvery green of the garigue in spring. But for the hair and height, Lia was looking at her twin.

"Paloma," she gasped. The walls amplified her voice, carrying her name to each corner of the empty space.

"I'm so glad you found your way, Lia."

"You know who I am?"

"Of course. I've been waiting for you."

GRUISSAN—DECEMBER 1208

The long December night wore on, but Raoul knew it was not too early for fishermen and scavengers to appear on the beach, where seagulls squabbled over crabs laid bare by the retreating tide. He led Mirò through the clinging sand, slipping and skidding over wet rocks strewn with seaweed. As they neared the village, he caught the aroma of smoke rising above the tang of shore debris. It carried an unnatural sourness, and he fought the urge to leap on his horse and pound across the sand, anxiety nearly subsuming his caution.

The village wall climbed out of Étang d'Ayrolle—the vast salt marsh that fed Jean Duchesne's fortune—and rose in an ever-tightening circle, protecting the village from the tides. Raoul had traversed this way before, when he'd brought his family to Gruissan in secrecy on an October night. Once Paloma and the children were safely inside and comfortable, Jean had locked the door and formally, publicly, closed his house, taking his family and staff to Paris. His stone manor had remained dark and silent, betraying nothing of the four lives sealed within. Raoul had left his family in Gruissan only two months before, yet it seemed an eternity ago.

He ascended a ramp built into the town's outer foundation and arrived at a recessed door. The wood, warped by the salt air, resisted the thrust of his shoulder before giving way with a scrape and groan of iron hinges. The odor of smoke was stronger inside the town's walls, and it carried a sickly note, a rotting sweetness. Mirò snorted, and her ears flattened against her great head. Raoul soothed her with soft sounds and led her through the compact doorway. Her flanks grazed the opening, her massive shoulders barely clearing the rounded arch.

Horse and man emerged into a covered alley. The sound of Mirò's iron shoes on the cobblestones echoed sharply in the sheltered street. The alley ended in a courtyard surrounded by tall buildings of plaster and timber—the homes of merchant families. A fountain of stone sat in the middle. Raoul scooped a handful of water and brought it to his lips—it was sweet and pure, sourced from one of the underground streams that poured down from the western hills. He left Mirò to drink and rest, not bothering to tie the reins. The horse would await his return and snap her powerful jaws at any hands that would try to disturb her. Raoul followed the scent of smoke through the quiet streets.

An old woman appeared from an opening in the wall that bordered the brick lane. A shawl covered her head, clasped at the neck by a gnarled hand. She stopped short and stood silently as Raoul approached, taking in his filthy, mud-strewn clothes.

"Grandmother," he said, extending a hand as a gesture of calm. "What has happened here? Has the flux come?"

Her eyes hardened, and she nodded her head once, twice. "Oh yes, it is a plague," she said. "A plague of men, a plague of priests." She spat on the ground, an ugly gesture from this tiny, bent creature. "Soldiers came—from Toulouse, I heard say—with priests among them, looking for the heretics."

Raoul's blood chilled. He wanted to grab her thin shoulders and rattle loose the story of what she'd witnessed.

"I live just here"—she pointed to the alley behind—"and I watched from the shadows as they passed. They weren't so many—a few men-at-arms, two priests. And a woman with child and two little ones I'd never seen. Such pretty creatures. One of those bastards took the little boy from the woman's arms as they passed. Carried him to his death, I'm sure."

Raoul felt as though his limbs had turned to molten iron; his blood pounded in his ears.

The old woman continued. "The lady, golden as an angel,

she stumbled just here." She pointed to a cobblestone kicked loose and sticking up in the street. "There was a man in black, neither priest nor soldier, who caught her and held her up. I must have made a sound when she stumbled, for when they paused together, he looked into this darkness." The old woman jerked her head back to the dim passage. "It was as if he could see past the shadows and into my soul. His eyes were as black as soot." She shuddered.

Before she finished, Raoul was twisting through the passageways to the center of the walled village. Saint-Maurice dominated the square, silent, black, and smoking.

LOGIS DU MARTINET, LAGRASSE—TIME UNKNOWN

*T*he front of Paloma's dress dipped low, and a thin silver chain with a cross pendant hung from her neck: the Occitan cross, each blunt side adorned with three raised points. Paloma gathered the sleeping baby to her breast and cupped Lia's cheek in one delicate hand. "Perhaps it's vain of me to say so," she said in a lilting Occitan, "but you are so lovely."

"Where are we?" Lia felt wobbly and light-headed. "Is this heaven? Are there others?"

Paloma's hand slipped from Lia's face to rest on her shoulder. "We're not always alone. But we don't inhabit a place in the way that you think of as living."

"Does Raoul know you're here?"

"Oh, dear heart, there is no *here*." Paloma swept her hand

around the hollow space of the courtyard. Then she gestured to the grass. "Let's sit for a moment. This child grows heavier every day." Her smile drew Lia as a sunflower to the sun. They sat on the lush grass, dry despite the recent rain. The baby, swaddled so tightly in linen Lia couldn't tell if it was a boy or a girl, pursed its lips and sighed but slept on. Paloma followed her gaze.

"Her name is Beatriu," she said. The Catalan version, but the same name as Lia's mother, Béatris. Long ago, it had meant *voyager, traveler*. Lia wondered where this little girl had been and where she would go. The daughter Raoul had never seen.

"Why can't you come into the present like Raoul?" Lia asked. "Why haven't you and Raoul found one another in some other time?"

"The children and I are already home, Lia," Paloma answered. "This is the only present that matters."

Her beauty made Lia's heart ache with a bittersweet longing. She was looking not only at Raoul's past, but also his future. She nodded, unable to speak past the emotion burning in her throat.

"There are layers to the soul that peel away in death," Paloma said. "At the very core of our beings is eternal life. Those whom death claims justly—when they have lived their natural, full lives in the glory of God—find peace. They are freed from the cycle of rebirth, from the bindings of a worldly existence." Her voice was a balm, her words slow and deliberate.

"Some souls linger because they lived or died in violence. They are condemned to this in-between existence until the balance of life is set right. There is no hell for a Cathar. There is only perpetual grief on Earth. And so our Raoul and Lucas Moisset and Jordí Bonafé remain suspended."

Our Raoul. As if she knew what Lia and Raoul had shared.

Yet instead of contrition at loving Paloma's husband, Lia felt embraced by the light and peace emanating from this exquisite woman.

"Why Raoul? What did he do that he needs to atone for?"

"Raoul was caught in a shadow of anger, doomed to the hell of rebirth. He believes we perished in the fire at Gruissan." Paloma touched Lia's hand, the connection softening the anguish of her story. "But he was wrong, for I lived to hold my children's children. We fled Languedoc and lived our full lives with Raoul's family in Catalunya. Then our souls found safe passage and eternal rest. Raoul has been searching for us since his own death, not knowing we were safe."

"And Lucas? And Jordí?"

A cloud darkened her sweet mien. "Whatever God's plan, He chose to bind these men to their fates in different ways. Jordí carries a burden of history for what he represents: his church, his faith. Waiting too long to speak of the crimes he witnessed. Lucas…" Paloma trailed off. "Lucas exists in a torture born of guilt and self-loathing."

"But they entered *my* time, *my* Languedoc? Why? How?"

"Their souls found a split in the fabric of time and slipped through." Paloma's explanation was delivered calmly, as if Lia would understand how the fabric of time had woven the distant past into her present.

"This is beyond all comprehension." The serenity that had come over Lia when she'd walked into this place of warm peace began to dissolve as she struggled to understand Paloma's riddle. The pieces tumbled together without falling into place, and questions inserted themselves between the gaps. Why had she and Raoul fallen in love? Why was she not spared the pain of giving him back to his time and his family? "Who am I in all of this? *Why* am I in all of this?"

Paloma trailed a finger over Lia's wedding ring. "You are the connection between the past, the world beyond the past, and the present."

"Because of my research? Because of what I've discovered about Castelnau's death? But Jordí has known all along. Why me? Why now?"

"Scholars such as you have kept our history alive," Paloma said. "But these Cathar traditions and beliefs have become myth, even among those who know them best. You will find a way to show the world that history has not always honored the truth of our beloved Languedoc's past." She placed a hand on Lia's arm. "But the past I speak of is yours, Lia. Past and present met on a summer day not so long ago, on a road near Arques. It was just a moment, a few heartbeats, and then crushing sorrow."

Lia's vision wavered. She saw a cyclist, broken and alone on a mountain road, and she cried out. Paloma drew her into her arms, Beatriu pressed gently between them.

"Gabriel," Lia gasped.

"Your husband," Paloma said, caressing her hair.

Lia pulled away, pushing the tips of her fingers into her temples to stop her tears. Her head throbbed with the impossibilities of Paloma's explanation and the pain of what she was reliving. She stood and took a few shaky steps forward. She could just see past the opening in the wall to the wheat fields beyond, where the stalks swayed in a breeze, drops of rain dangling from their tips and glinting in the sun. Paloma joined her, still cradling the sleeping Beatriu.

"Raoul's soul took purchase in your world at the moment of your husband's death. His soul touched Gabriel's and became connected to yours."

"I don't understand. What am I meant to do?"

"You have become Raoul's only way out of this half life." Paloma's voice was gentle but insistent. "Do you understand, my girl?" She drew Lia in with her free arm for a brief, fierce embrace and then leaned back to gaze at her.

For an instant, Lia saw the Romani woman in Paris offering roses and the gorgeous Catalan whose table she shared at the Marché des Enfants Rouges. But, more than anyone, she saw herself. "What about Jordí and Lucas?" she said, though her voice now sounded as if it came from a great distance. "What am I supposed to do for them?"

But Raoul's wife was speaking, pressing something into her hand, her words and touch fading into a pale blue light. Then Paloma disappeared.

GRUISSAN—DECEMBER 1208

Black streaks of char marred the outer walls of Saint-Maurice, and the wooden portico had been reduced to cinders. Thick pools of congealed tar and piles of soot-covered debris lined the perimeter facing the village square, and clouds of ash puffed in the light breeze. Raoul had seen this destruction before. He knew that piles of kindling and horse hair doused in pitch and sulfur had been lit below the wood-framed windows and at the solid oak doors at the entrance.

The interior of the church was shot through with light where slabs of stone had caved in and the plaster and timber frame had failed. Some walls were scorched, others left unscathed. Flames had chased through the wooden benches and railings, snatching at cloth tapestries and devouring the dry rushes spread across the floor. The extreme heat had turned the sacred space into an oven, roasting alive those not granted the mercy of dying from the thick smoke.

Fresh sea air poured in through gaping holes that had once been windows, mingling with the stench of burned flesh. The stained glass was now melted and hardened into lumps of muddled rainbows. Raoul waved and shouted at the crows perched on the altar and on the piles of charred and broken stone, and the murder rose as one with a thrashing of black wings, squawking in mocking protest. The birds quickly resettled, scuttling about on wiry feet and eyeing him with shining ebony pupils.

In fear and fury, he moved from corpse to corpse, trying not to gag as he pulled stone from crushed bone. Some bodies, overcome by smoke or flame, were entangled where they'd fallen. Raoul came across a man who looked to be asleep, his seated frame whole, covered only in a light dusting of ash and flakes of soot, his head dropped to one side, his eyes closed. But no Paloma. No Bertran or Aicelina. Or perhaps too many of them. Too many bodies scorched beyond recognition.

"Not everyone is here." A small man in patched breeches and boots worn thin at the toes stepped into the church from a gap in the wall. "We've been moving the bodies since dawn, taking them to a grave just outside the village. I'm the carter. It's my horses and wagon carrying the dead."

"How many were there? Did you know everyone here?"

"Guess I did. I've lived here all my life." The man gave a sorrowful glance around the destroyed nave. "We're missing sixteen of our village. I've found many bodies, but whether they are sixteen complete, I couldn't say." He stopped, taking in Raoul's fine clothing and well-made boots, the quality showing through the tears and stains of travel. "You're not from the village. Did you know someone here?"

"I'm looking for my wife and children. Paloma Gervais; my son, Bertran; my daughter, Aicelina. Did you see anyone brought to the church?"

The man was shaking his head before Raoul could finish. "It was before dawn. We knew the soldiers were here. They came in the night before, taking over the inn. One of them, they say it was the sénéchal, routed a woman and two children from Duchesne's home. Duchesne is—"

"Yes, I know who he is. Where is the sénéchal now?"

The older man ran a hand over his face, and his shoulders sagged with weariness. He spoke, but his gaze remained cast on the floor. "I don't know."

Raoul closed the distance in a few long strides. "I believe my wife and children were sent to this church." He grabbed the carter by the front of his rough linen shirt and lifted him to the tips of his toes. "Why are there no mourners? Why is no one here to collect their dead? This happened just yesterday, yet this cursed village feels abandoned. Where is everyone?"

"We're afraid, my lord. Who will risk being seen to mourn those branded as heretics?" The villager's eyes bulged and he remained teetering, cowed by Raoul's rage. "Most hide in their homes," he rasped. "We're just waiting for the soldiers to leave."

Raoul released the carter and held him gently by the shoulders as the man coughed and regained his breath. "My good man, I'm sorry. I'm desperate to find my family."

"We'll mourn when we're left alone. My son and I, we offered to take away the dead. We can't wait for the rats and crows to do it. But whether your family died here, I cannot say."

LOGIS DU MARTINET, LAGRASSE—WEDNESDAY

A trail twists through the stone cliffs toward Arques. At its end lies a broken man, his soul lifting away from his body, fluttering on a butterfly's wing, as fragile as a dream. An eagle, golden and sleek, more rare and precious than a happy ending, swoops down. His massive wings shelter the whispering soul. The eagle and the soul touch, share a breath, part. One into eternity, one reborn into the present.

The whimpering and scratching woke her. Lia lay motionless, curled on the floor, her knees drawn tightly into her chest and her cheek pressed against the cold stone. Her head pounded, and her body was cramped with cold. She opened her eyes in a squint and saw faint amber light seeping in from a gap at the bottom of the door. She raised her head. Deep shelves lined with wooden wine crates were mounted on three walls from knee height to just below the low ceiling. There was no opening to a stairwell.

The stream of air that flowed from underneath the door was cool but ripe with musty, fermented aromas. A pair of paws with clipped black nails scrabbled underneath the door, followed by a long red snout tipped with a damp black nose. Isis whined.

"Hello, sweet girl." The dog licked her fingers, sniffing rapidly as if trying to drag Lia's body out through the cool black of her nose. Her body collided with the door as she leaped up, her claws scratching at the wood. Then Isis was gone, but her frantic barking echoed through the chambers of the winery.

Lia pushed up on one arm, fighting a wave of nausea. She inhaled with difficulty and sat upright, resting her back against the door. The side of her face was stiff, and pain radiated from high on her forehead. She touched her hair, probing delicately until she found the thick lump at her hairline. She winced at the pain and pulled her hand away. The tips glistened with blood.

"Shit," she groaned. The blood had dried to a crust on the side of her face, but the wound still wept at its source. She wiped her soiled fingers on her jeans and pulled her knees to her chest. As she lifted her legs, Lia uncovered a sheet of paper that had been pressed underneath her body. She dragged it toward her with a heel until she could grasp it between her thumb and forefinger.

Staring at the script, she willed her woozy brain to make sense of the ancient letters. Two short paragraphs, one written in Latin, the other in *langue d'oc*—the old Occitan—both signed by Sénéchal Lucas Mauléon. The names of Paloma Gervais and Bertran and Aicelina d'Aran were legible to her unsteady eyes, but she lost the rest as tears welled. Isis's barking grew close again. Lia followed the letter's creases, the parchment still supple despite its age, and slipped it into a crack between the stone floor and the closet wall.

"Lia?" Raoul's voice rang through the old stone structure.

"I'm here," she whispered. "Raoul. I'm here." She rose with stiff limbs from the cold floor and began to pound on the door. Her head throbbed with each blow.

"I'm getting you out, Lia. Just hang on." She heard the scraping of iron against wood, followed by a rush of air and an embrace of warm skin and silken coat as Raoul pulled her into his arms and Isis pushed her smooth body into Lia's hip. The greyhound whined and disappeared into the closet.

"Your car was parked out front when I pulled in. I've been in the winery twice, three times, shouting your name. What happened? How long have you been in there?" Raoul held her at arm's length. "Jesus, Lia, your head. You're bleeding. Sweetheart, what happened?"

"Raoul, I don't...I..." Shining fluorescent bulbs burned into her skull. The steel bottling racks, the polished concrete floors, and the glass bottles glinted and threw beams of light into her eyes. All traces of grime and ruin had vanished. Lia looked up at the round window high above. Sunlight and shadow danced past its clean panes as the wind pushed the clouds along.

Lia looked at Raoul again and saw Paloma reflected in his eyes. She pictured Raoul gathering his children in his arms, their tiny bodies caught up in his embrace. Sorrow and joy suffused her.

"I came to find you," she said at last. "Raoul, it's Lucas. He didn't kill Paloma or your children. I don't know what he wants from us, but you have to let this go until we find out the whole truth. Please."

Raoul pressed a finger against her lips to silence her. "Shhh...
Lia. Never mind that for now." He pushed the hair away from
her face and winced at the blood. "Let's get this cleaned up. Are
you hurt anywhere else?"

"I don't think so. I remember opening this door, but everything was different," she said helplessly, gesturing around the
bottling space. She pointed to the closet. "The door locked
behind me, but I knew I had to go down." Lia grasped Raoul's
arm. "I thought the stairs would lead me to you."

Lia didn't tell him that her heart had cracked the moment she
saw Paloma. It had splintered when she saw the mother with
her children. She knew it would break when she told Raoul of
his wife—that in telling him, she would lose him forever.

"Hey, just stop. You're safe now." He held her upper arms
firmly, stooping to examine her eyes and her head. "That's more
than a bump; it's a blow. We need to get you to the hospital."

"No, please. I'll be fine. I just need some ice and ibupro-
fen." She shook her head, the motion causing her skull to spin
and throb. "There was no one around, Raoul. I searched for
you. I thought you'd gone after Lucas. I was so afraid I was
too late."

"I drove for hours but finally cooled off and returned to the
cottage." Raoul draped his jacket over her shoulders. "You
and Jordí had left, and I couldn't get through to your phone.
I called Dom and Rose, and they said they hadn't heard from
you. But something told me you were here. I arrived maybe
twenty minutes ago, and I've been looking everywhere for
you. Isis found you finally." At the sound of her name, the
greyhound was again at their side, nuzzling their hands with her
wet nose. Then she loped off through the winery.

Lia closed her eyes against the needle-sharp brightness of the
lights, and Raoul put an arm around her waist as he steered her

through the room. "It's ridiculous to stand here. Let's get you cleaned up. I want a doctor to see that head."

They walked through the winery, now restored to its pristine state, its modern equipment clean and shining within the ancient bones of the vaulted building, and emerged into the sunlight. The sky had been scrubbed blue. Although the wind still gusted and cold air from the mountains plunged into the valley, warmth radiated from the earth. It was the first of April, and spring was in full bloom. Raoul led Lia inside the shelter of his *longère*.

He sat in front of her, their knees touching. He gently wiped a damp cloth around her wound and down the side of her cheek, lifting away the blood. While they waited for the doctor to arrive, Lia told Raoul of her strange journey from Minerve. "It was as though I'd gone back in time. No lights on the side of the highway, no autoroute in the distance, the villages were completely dark. My phone was dead."

Raoul smoothed her hair behind her ears. She sucked air as he daubed a cotton ball moistened with disinfectant over the cut on her temple. "I'm sorry. I know this hurts." He dropped the cotton in the wastebasket and dampened another. She braced herself for the sting.

"And the winery, Raoul," she continued, trying to ignore the pain. "It was a mess. It looked as if no one had been inside in ages. It was filthy, full of old, broken vats. The floor was packed dirt and broken cobblestones."

"Your hands are so cold." He gave her a warm mug of tea and held his hand over hers to make certain her grip would hold. He'd already exchanged her damp sweater for a wool plaid work shirt. "You're in shock, Lia. Let's not talk about this anymore. Dr. Vanel will be here at any moment."

Sunlight cascaded through the windows over the sink and the panes set into the door, sending waves of heat into the kitchen. Lia swallowed the chamomile tea. The warmth seeped into her, and she began to feel drowsy. But she couldn't stop the questions from scraping at her. Or the guilt.

Two quick beeps of a car horn roused her. From the kitchen windows, she saw a white 1960s-model Peugeot convertible entering the drive. Dr. Vanel emerged from the car and stretched her long torso over the backseat to grab a large black satchel and white lab coat. With her Jackie O sunglasses, kitten heels, and pink sleeveless chemise tucked into white linen slacks, the doctor who made house calls throughout the Corbières Valley looked ready to do battle in a Parisian advertising agency. But Lia had heard tales of Marie Vanel delivering breeched lambs as well as human babies in the remote villages of the Pyrénées foothills. She was a daughter of Languedoc.

"It's quite a blow, but you're not concussed." The doctor placed a Steri-Strip bandage over the lump on Lia's temple and touched each end with her tapered fingers. "The stitches will dissolve, but avoid getting the wound wet for the next forty-eight hours. If you experience any dizziness or persistent headaches, call me immediately." She washed her hands in the kitchen sink. "And you keep an eye on her. Any muddled speech, any wobbly movements, I want to know." She wagged a finger at Raoul.

"Of course. Lia's staying put right here."

The doctor placed two small vials of pills on the counter.

"Pain relievers straight up." She pointed to one with a yellow label. "This one has a mild narcotic to help you sleep." She pointed to the other with a pink label. "I suggest you take two of the regular now and again in four hours. Wait until an hour before bedtime and take the sleep aid. A warm bath in Epsom salts will help with the aches. And stay out of closets."

Raoul accompanied Dr. Vanel to her Peugeot. From her perch at the kitchen table, Lia could see them talking. They glanced at the house once or twice, and Raoul pointed to the winery as if explaining her escapade. He opened the car door and kissed the doctor on each cheek, and she settled inside. After maneuvering a tight three-point turn, Marie Vanel gunned the engine and sped through the gate, scattering stones and leaves in her wake. The gate swung shut behind the dust.

Raoul stood with his back to the house, his hands in his pockets, head lifted to the sky, and Lia wondered how she would ever let him go. Love and dread, sorrow and hope surged through her. She longed for his touch, his reassurance that he would keep her safe and not leave her. But she'd already begun to say good-bye. His family was waiting for him.

She slipped out of her chair and made her way wearily to the bedroom. Perhaps it was just a few minutes later, but she was only vaguely aware as her jeans were pulled from her hips and a soft duvet was tucked around her shoulders. She fell away into dreamless sleep.

Lia woke hours later and managed to eat some puréed carrot and fennel soup and tender, sweet apricots. She sat with Raoul on the terrace, its stone and brick surfaces radiating the warmth of the setting sun, until fatigue plowed her down. Raoul led her through the house, drew a bath, and left her while he cleaned up from their simple supper.

She sank back in the bathtub, recalling her first night in Languedoc, remembering how lost in her own grief she'd been, how closed and distant she'd felt. Yet it all seemed simple. She'd known who she was—a woman alone, a widow determined to persevere through her grief but escaping a world that held such impossible expectations. In other words, she'd been running away.

Lia never expected—never even thought to want—to fall in love again. Her heart, her soul, her head all seemed to be charging in different directions. She'd experienced a maelstrom of passion, guilt, and bewilderment in the months since she'd arrived. Then love and desire. And now, full circle, back to grief and resolution.

The bathroom door opened wider, and Raoul backed in holding a tumbler of Cognac and a mug of tea. Lia sat up, and the water rolled in gentle waves, releasing jasmine-scented steam. He handed her the tea, and she heard a faint clink as he set his glass on the tile floor. He picked up a bottle of shampoo from the edge of the tub and pulled up a chair.

His hand, slick with shampoo, ran up the base of her skull, tugging her hair slightly to pull his fingers through the wet strands. She closed her eyes and leaned into his touch as he kneaded her scalp and worked the lather through her hair. The painkillers had dulled the throbbing pain to a flickering ache.

"Rinse," he whispered into her ear as he took the mug from her hands. She tilted her head back, and Raoul swirled warm water through her hair, careful of her bandaged temple.

When she sat up, he'd taken off his shirt. He pulled his belt tighter to release the catch, then unbuttoned and pushed his jeans off his hips. Grasping both sides of the tub, he climbed in gingerly behind her, sliding his legs on either side of hers. A cool breeze whispered through the open window and brushed their damp skin.

Later in bed, she stretched to face his sleeping form. "What will become of us?" she murmured to the dark. "Where do you want to be? In the past with Paloma, or here with me in the present?"

In his sleep, Raoul pulled Lia in, wrapping the length of his body around her. She curled into his chest. For the moment, it was the reassurance she needed. She slept.

LANGUEDOC WILDERNESS—DECEMBER 1208

Paloma was in agony. The baby pressed hard against her spine, and the wagon boards became crueler with every bump in the road. The roads were too dangerous to travel by night—bands of robbers would as soon use the sénéchal's letter of safe passage to wipe their backsides as obey it. All that day, the cart lumbered on, away from Gruissan, through the mud and unrelenting rain, its living cargo hidden under the tanned leather hides.

At dusk, they found shelter in a clutch of houses braced against a tower built of limestone bricks. The skies remained gray, the air cast in pearly light. Although the terrain was as familiar as her shadow, Paloma had no idea where they were. The light told her their direction was northwest, but when she asked the priest their destination, he would say only that they were leaving the coast long enough to skirt the marshes before rejoining the road to Spain.

Spain. Paloma despaired. Away from Raoul. Away from her father. Perhaps Raoul knew already of the burning of Saint-Maurice. His friend's home raided, a village church burned to the ground—this wouldn't remain secret for long.

Someone must know their fate by now. She must find a way to get to Minerve, to the cave near the river where she and Raoul long ago determined they would meet should she need to flee Gruissan.

The priest provided them with bread and pungent cheese mottled with blue and green mold. They dipped their bread in cool beer that tasted of summer's wildflowers. Later, they were left alone inside the tiny shack of an old woman with weather-beaten skin and tired eyes; the priest assured them they'd continue the journey at dawn. Paloma bedded down alongside the crone and tucked Bertran and Aicelina against her. She pulled up her knees and rubbed her heavy belly, praying the fire that pulsated from her lower back into her legs would cool so she could sleep.

The old woman extended her twig-thin arms under the blankets and placed a hand on Paloma's hip. She ground into Paloma's skin with the iron rods of her fingers, massaging the muscles of her back, hips, and buttocks until Paloma began to weep with relief. She wept with the pain of being touched with such care and understanding by a stranger. She wept with loneliness and fear. *Wait, Raoul. We are still alive. We'll find you. Just wait, my love.*

She felt for the cross around her neck. It was gone, torn from her in those moments of panic inside Saint-Maurice. Paloma pretended to take it up in her palm, to kiss its cool silver as she mouthed a prayer for her husband, for her children curled beside her, for herself. And for those souls who had perished inside that tomb of a church. Then she turned to the old woman, drew her into her arms, and whispered at length into the crone's ear.

When the priest returned to the hovel at dawn to collect Paloma, Bertran, and Aicelina, they were hours into their flight to Minerve, hidden once again in a cart that was driven by a stranger to whom Paloma had entrusted their lives. Tucked inside her cloak was a letter of safe passage, plucked from the sleeping priest's satchel. Paloma could entertain no thought of anger nor gratitude for Lucas Mauléon until she knew her husband's fate. Nor could she worry about what would happen to the priest who'd been charged to see them safely to Spain. His fate was beyond her reach.

LOGIS DU MARTINET, LAGRASSE—THURSDAY MORNING

*L*ia awoke to a room filled with the citron light of mid-morning. Through the open window came the drone of a distant tractor, and she pictured Raoul turning over the soil beneath the vines, releasing weeds from the fertile earth. She probed the bandage on her temple and prepared for the responding flare of pain, but the hours of deep sleep had soothed most of the ache in her head and muscles. Then she remembered.

"I don't want to be a part of this," she said to the bright, empty room. A muffled buzzing sounded: her phone, buried underneath her clothes. She scrambled for it, knocking the freshly laundered and neatly folded shirt and jeans from the chair beside the bed to the floor. The phone vibrated with a text message from Jordí: 3 Chemin du Rossignol, Limoux. Please. As soon as possible.

With a heavy heart, Lia gathered her clothes. A whisper and faint clink caught her ear. Scanning the bare wood floor, she saw a tiny puddle of silver next to her foot. She scooped it up, and a thin chain fell like water between her fingers, leaving the Occitan cross pendant in the center of her palm. Paloma's cross. The one Lia had seen her wearing in that world suspended below the stairs. How had Paloma's cross traveled with her?

As she dressed, Lia thought of their embrace, recalling that Paloma had pressed something into her hand in the moments before everything went black. She'd found that letter when she came to in the tiny room that drifted between the present and the past, but this… Raoul did not belong to her any more than he belonged to the present. He belonged only to this place, to Languedoc. To Paloma. Lia raised the necklace to her lips and made her choice.

The tile in the sunroom was warm beneath her bare feet. Opening the door to the terrace, she heard the tractor humming in the vineyards that rose behind the house. The sun shone on, oblivious to her anguish.

Nothing had changed. Everything had changed.

As Lia followed the sound of Raoul's tractor, she felt as fragile as a patch of ice over a swiftly moving river. At any moment, her heart could shatter and dissolve into the gelid water of her sorrow. Yet all around her, the earth surged with warm, vibrant life. The vines in the first flush of growth had turned the hillsides into shifting seas of green, and fields of mustard, poppy, and wild narcissus burst in riotous splashes of color. Aromas of thyme and almond blossom drifted in the breeze blowing off the Mediterranean.

Lia wondered what would become of the place after Raoul was gone but pushed the thought away. The common-sense worries of the property and its vines in flower, the tons of wine aging from the previous autumn's pressing, were more than she could absorb. She could do only what she believed was right and trust the rest would take care of itself.

Isis charged out of the vineyards, her teeth bared in a gleeful grin, and pushed her long snout into Lia's hip. "You'll come with me, won't you, girl?" Lia bent down and embraced the greyhound, pressing her face into the sun-warmed coat. Isis leaned into her, snuffling into her hair, and then sat back on her haunches and considered Lia with amber eyes.

"I won't leave you here alone."

The dog tilted her head, and for a fleeting moment, Lia wondered whose soul inhabited the wise and loving creature.

"What am I doing, Isis?" She stood and looked across the expanse of vineyards toward the distant Pyrénées, which were visible only as a blue smudge against the white sky of morning. "How can I let him go? How can I say good-bye again to love and a future? Please tell me it's going to be all right. Tell me *I'm* going to be all right." Isis barked and shot past her, up a row of vines. Lia shifted her features into a smile as the dog twirled in a frenzy of joy: Raoul was descending the hillside toward them.

"You're up early. How do you feel?"

Lia nodded her reply, not trusting her voice with the truth. With one arm, Raoul pulled her close, kissing her temple just outside the bandage. In his other hand, he held a small silver thermos.

"I thought I'd get an early start and let you sleep," he said as he filled the small thermos cap with steaming coffee. "I noticed new shoots on the Carignane and grenache that I've got to pull in the next couple of days. With this stretch of warm weather, flowering has taken off." Raoul's talk of vines soothed Lia's frayed nerves. If only they could stand forever on this hillside, watching the vines flower and their berries ripen from dull green to deep purples, reds, and golds.

They shared the cup of coffee, taking turns sipping at the hot sludge. "Sorry, I should've let you make it." Raoul grimaced. "Next time," he said, replacing the cup on the thermos and setting it at their feet.

Next time. The words pierced her. His future was not hers to share. Lia knew she had to do this now, before her heart failed her. "Raoul—" she began.

"There's so much I need to tell you," he interrupted, taking her by the waist and pulling her hips into his. "I brought you into this mess, where you have no reason to be."

An image of Paloma, the sun turning loose strands of her hair to gold, came to Lia, and her misery spilled out of her hot and wretched. Raoul cupped her face and slid his thumbs across her cheeks, catching the tears.

"But that's just it, Raoul. Don't you see?" she said. "It's *because* of me that this is happening. We're all connected. You. Me. Lucas." She hesitated. "Gabriel and Paloma," she said softly.

"Your husband?" Raoul leaned back, dropping his hands from her face. The motion pained her heart more than the lump pained her head. "What are you talking about?"

"Gabriel's death is tied to your"—she searched for the word—"your rebirth or awakening or whatever it is that's happened to you. He passed from this world, and you entered it."

"That's crazy, Lia. Are you saying that Gabriel was some sort of sacrifice for me?"

"I don't know, Raoul. I don't know." She willed herself on. "I understand only that I can end this cycle. I can bring you to Paloma. To your children. To the baby daughter you haven't seen. They were waiting for me yesterday. And they're waiting for you now."

He gripped her shoulders, the pads of his fingers pressing into the thin muscles beneath her cotton shirt. "Lia, stop this. Whatever happened to you, whatever you think you saw, happened because of that blow to your head. It was some sort of dream or hallucination. No one is waiting for me, and I'm not going anywhere. Just stop."

"What I saw yesterday was as real as this moment," she insisted. "Why can't it be real? Look around you. How can you explain this place? How are you possible? Lucas? Jordí? How is any of this possible? Yet here you are, flesh and blood."

Raoul's mouth was set in a grim line, but his eyes were soft. In them, she read her same love and desire and sorrow.

"Do you believe if you give me up, Gabriel will come back? Is that what this is? Trading one soul, one life, for another?"

Lia reeled. "No," she said simply. "There is no exchange. Gabriel is gone to me forever. I'm not making a deal with the devil or even with God."

She closed her fist over the cool silver cross in her pocket and lifted it between their faces. The pendant twirled, glinting in the sunlight, and Raoul caught it in his palm. His gaze clouded, and he pulled away for an instant, but it was enough. The understanding she'd seen in his face rang clear as a church bell. *Paloma.*

"Where did you find this?"

"Your wife gave it to me yesterday."

Raoul's eyes sharpened as he refocused his attention on her face. He pushed down her hand, removing the barrier of the necklace between them. "Paloma died in Gruissan with the children," he said, agony twisting his features. "I saw their bodies. I found this cross in her hand. Then I went to Minerve where we said we would meet. I didn't know where else to go. I had her cross with me when…"

You died, Lia finished his sentence in her mind. Whatever he felt for her, she knew it couldn't compare to the love of a husband for his wife and a father for his children. "No, Raoul. Paloma didn't die in Gruissan. She and Bertran and Aicelina escaped from that church. I don't know whose bodies you saw, but your family survived. They lived their full lives, and now they're waiting for you." She took his hand. "There's something I need to show you."

They walked through the vineyard as the sun spilled into the valley. Would the light ever be as rich and golden, the air as fragrant with forest, field, and sea? Would Languedoc ever be so sweet? Or so bitter?

Isis ran ahead, disappearing into the tangle of scrub and oak trees beyond the vineyards. Lia led the way into the cool, dark winery. This time, she wasn't surprised by the ruin of an ancient, neglected vault, the stifling odor of ferment and decay. As they passed the splintered vats and the gray piles of rubbish, Raoul protested, but she pulled him on. He grew quiet and tightened the connection of his hand to hers. They entered what had been the bottling room, full of gleaming machinery, but it was now a dark chamber, full of refuse. The door that had locked behind her, trapping her in a tunnel of time, looked insignificant and forgotten at the far end. Lia thought to grab a brick from a pile near the closet.

She pushed on the iron handle, and once again, the small, rounded door opened without a sound. She motioned for Raoul to enter. Before the dark and tiny space could swallow them, Lia set the brick on the floor and closed the door gently against it. There wouldn't be anyone to rescue her if the door shut fast behind her again.

"What the hell?" Raoul whispered, just as she had the day before, a lifetime ago. As her eyes adjusted to the dark, the tiny room took shape. It was as it had been: a thin stream of cool air poured up from some unimaginable depth along the corkscrew stairwell to the landing where they stood. For an agonizing moment, she wondered if, in making her choice, she had caused the inexplicable transformation of storage room to passageway between worlds. If she clung to Raoul and made him turn around, could that choice make all of this go away? Perhaps that's what it meant to have faith: complete acceptance, even in the absence of logic and reason.

"I can take you back to Paloma and your children," she said, her voice sounding hollow in the small space.

"You don't know what you're saying."

"Raoul, I do. Please believe me. We have to try." Lia nodded toward the stairwell.

"You can't be serious."

"I've never been more certain of anything," she lied. He took two steps and began to descend, winding out of her view, his footsteps absorbed by the soundless chamber of the stairwell. Her love for him grabbed and shook her so hard that she staggered on the step, clutching at the stone as smooth as the inside of a shell.

"Lia?" Raoul's face rose out of the darkness, and his solid form met hers, holding her steady. A light shone in his eyes, as though he'd brought hope with him from below. Warmer air pushed past, and Lia knew the end of the stairwell was only steps away. Her feet moved again despite the dizzying mix of exhilaration and dread. It appeared, just beyond a corridor glowing with light: the massive courtyard open to the sky above, with a door set into the thick stone on one side, slightly ajar, a golden field visible just beyond.

Raoul took a few steps into the courtyard. "What is this place?"

"I don't know what it is," she replied. "But I do know it's where you belong. Paloma is here waiting for you. She is so beautiful, Raoul. She looks like an angel. And your children. They are tiny and sweet." Dizziness washed over her, and she willed her legs to remain firm.

"Lia." Raoul steadied her again. "No."

She turned her face to the sun, which was at its zenith, and closed her eyes against the insistent gold. "There has to be a reason why we met. There has to be a reason why your soul was released into this world at the same time Gabriel's was taken. This." Lia turned in place, searching for Paloma, for the right words, for the reason she was letting her heart break. "This is the reason."

And there she was, standing with her hands clasped before her, her hair unbound and streaming like molten gold over a plain brown shift. "Paloma," said Lia.

Raoul turned.

Part Five

....

What would the world have been if we had not been.
If your eyes had not been, what would the world have been?
—NIZAR QABBANI

....

LOGIS DU MARTINET, LAGRASSE—THURSDAY AFTERNOON

*E*merging alone from the winery into the sleepy golden light of late afternoon, Lia felt disjointed and loose, a collection of broken parts. Her mind detached and floated above her shock. She reasoned out her next steps, putting one foot in front of the other before she collapsed with grief.

She called for Isis. "Please be here, girl. Please be the one good thing that remains." Like a four-legged angel, Isis flew out of the vineyards and into her arms. Lia sobbed into her dusty, light-red coat. When she'd emptied out her heart, she sat back and rubbed behind the dog's alert ears.

"If we leave now, it'll still be light by the time we get to Limoux," she said, and Isis thumped her tail. "Can I hold it together long enough to find Jordí? We have to try, don't we, girl?" She had nowhere else to go. No one, not even Rose and Domènec, would believe or understand what she'd done.

What *had* she done? How did a life just disappear? Could she get him back? In the silence that met her questions and prayers, Lia knew there was no going back. And there was no staying in Languedoc either. As soon as she heard what Jordí had to say, she would leave.

LIMOUX—SAME DAY

The afternoon light had deepened to burnished copper when the GPS announced she was approaching the turnoff to Chemin du Rossignol. The car bumped along a dirt road that led into the forest. Isis sensed they were close to the end of their journey and sat at attention in the backseat, her breath steaming up the windows. Lia slid open the sunroof to let the chilled mountain air pour in.

Parked in front of Jordí's *mas* was a blue Renault and a bronze BMW. "We have company, Isis." The greyhound bounded out of the car but stayed close to Lia, sniffing the ground. The front door opened, and Jordí stood silhouetted against the yellow glow of lamplight.

"You're alone," he said as she crossed a patch of stone and shrub that was his front yard.

"No, I brought my new best friend," Lia replied and motioned to the dog trotting at her side.

"Where is Raoul?"

She climbed the front steps. "He's gone."

Inside, Lucas stood before the unlit fireplace, hands in the pockets of his dark brown chinos. Isis let out a low whine and looked up at Lia expectantly. She placed a hand on the russet head, and the dog responded with a reassuring nuzzle.

"Jordí," she said without taking her eyes from Lucas, "Isis needs water."

"Of course." He shut the front door with a soft thump and passed behind her. A moment later, the sound of running water came from an adjacent room. He returned, set the bowl near Isis, and sat on a sofa without a word. The greyhound took a few noisy laps at the bowl and leaned her warm body into Lia's locked knees.

"So, this *was* a setup." Lia clutched her elbows, her body rigid with tension.

"I thought if we were all here, I could…" Jordí floundered. "That the truth would save us." His hands flopped to his knees.

"Your friend here thinks I'm in love with you." Lucas turned away from the stone hearth. "He appealed to my better nature."

"So you thought I'd come here with Raoul and then what? What did the two of you have planned for us?"

Lucas stepped in her direction, but Isis rumbled with a low growl. He stopped and spoke in a low, even voice. "You said something during your lecture—that night I first saw you. I'll never forget it: *History assumes the role of truth. We study the past to prepare for the future, and we become historians so the truth of those left behind will not be forgotten.*"

Lia nodded in recognition of her own words and waited for Lucas to make his point.

"I am the left behind, Lia. God took everything from me but my life—instead of eternal peace, I was cursed with eternal rebirth." He drew in a tight breath, and Lia's eyes flicked to his hands. They curled in, as if he clenched in his fists all those years of anger. His forgotten place in history. The damnation of reincarnation.

"Yet I have now returned to a world where the Cathar Crusade is a tourist attraction. Highway of the Cathars, Cathar

Country," Lucas snapped in disgust as he described the signs directing the curious to sites sacred and profane. "I have a right to my past and to my story, yet my history has been erased or rewritten."

"*Your* story? *Your* past erased? What about the thousands murdered in the name of the Church? Don't they have a right to the past and to their stories? Generations were tortured and died because your story was more important than theirs." Lia poked at the sore spots, seeking to lance the infection of lies and deceit. Her heart's desire was to get as far away as possible from Languedoc and the Cathars. But, for the moment, her head won. She would push aside her grief to hear Lucas out.

"The Crusade would have happened without me, Lia. It was an unstoppable tide."

"Persecution of the Cathars was happening before you played a role, yes," she conceded. "But it was you in that abbey in Saint-Gilles. Castelnau's assassination launched the genocide."

"I was a soldier following orders. I believed I had the will of God behind me."

"How many did you kill? Do you even know?"

"Yes, I know," he replied quietly, his black eyes round and without guile.

"Paloma? Bertran and Aicelina? Did you count them too? Paloma's baby? You must have known she was pregnant."

Lia looked to Jordí, expecting him to interrupt, to confirm that Lucas was innocent of the crime Raoul held against him. But the priest no longer seemed to be listening. He sat motionless, his face buried in his hands.

Lucas's mouth twisted in a grimace. "I tried to save them. I knew d'Aran could never leave Languedoc alive, but I was certain I could save Paloma and the children." He passed a hand over his face. "I had to create the illusion that I'd sent her to her death, so that later…" His arms dropped to his sides, his palms open in a plea for understanding. "I had spies in the network of priests who helped Cathars escape. But this time I used it for good. I arranged to send them across the mountains into Spain, to hide until the madness had passed, and I would find them when I could. But I was too late."

GRUISSAN—DECEMBER 1208

Lucas sat in front of a window that overlooked the Étang d'Ayrolle. His knees pushed against a pedestal carved in the form of a mermaid. Her arms stretched over her head, and she held a round of polished oak in her palms.

The walls of Jean Duchesne's library were lined with shelves enclosed by leaded-glass doors. Behind the ornately cut glass were volumes of leather-bound books that only the most learned could read and the wealthiest could obtain. But Lucas ignored the merchant's riches, absorbed instead by a sheet of parchment on the table before him that was held down by glass weights. A list of names spilled down its creamy surface: nineteen names under the heading *Gruissan*. With his eyes on the list of the deceased, Lucas picked up a bottle and pewter cup that sat to one side. He let the clear marc flow to the cup's brim.

"Nineteen, my lord abbot. Twenty, to be precise. The Gervais woman was with child." Rancor laced his rasping laugh. "Was this my test? Did I pass?"

"The actual count numbered twenty-one, Sénéchal. A last-minute acquisition for the Church."

Lucas raised his eyebrows in a question. The abbot picked up the quill and dipped it in a still-open vial of ink before him. He scratched one more name below Aicelina d'Aran's and blew across the sheet to dry the ink.

"We came upon a young monk entering the church through a bolt hole, one that your men failed to notice until it was almost too late. He informed us he was one Brother Jordí Baltasar Bonafé, late of Saint-Maurice of Gruissan. Very late, as it happens." He smirked, his face pale as a fish belly.

Lucas struggled to swallow without choking. His free hand, resting on his knee, twitched in search of the slim dagger in his boot. Instinct.

"Odd thing, though, Sénéchal." Amalric caressed his chin with long, white nails. "Brother Bonafé said you were Castelnau's assassin. That he was the same unfortunate clergyman who found the body of our beloved archdeacon. Such a wonder of coincidences!"

"Where is Bonafé now?"

"Oh, he confessed his intentions to spirit away the heretics from the church. So we helped him back inside to suffer their same fate." Abbot Arnaud Amalric's voice held a snake's hiss in its sibilant wake. "Though it took some doing—those Franciscans are always so fat. We made certain to seal off his escape."

Lucas's throat closed in horror. But the abbot hadn't finished.

"Father Raimond and Father Humbert said you put on quite a show, declaring your unrequited love for Raoul d'Aran's wife, tossing chairs about, frightening her children. So that's all done then? No weeping regrets for sacrificing the woman you loved? And where is d'Aran?"

Lucas didn't respond. He refused Amalric the satisfaction or suspicion of detecting his anguish.

"Not yet found?" Amalric smirked. "Time you were on your way, then. Curious that you knew the d'Aran family was hiding here. I was informed only days ago that the heretics were being protected by Jean Duchesne." The abbot helped himself to a cup of the piercing marc. "Although it's not likely we'll do more than excommunicate the merchant, if even that. The tax from his trade is too valuable," Amalric muttered into his cup before swallowing the wine with a shudder. He set down the cup and looked expectantly at the sénéchal.

"Let's not talk around each other any longer, shall we, Abbot? I don't have time for intrigue." Lucas pulled the sheet of names around to examine them again, running his fingers down the list. "I never told you of the archdeacon's dying words: *I have seen the spirit of God. They are not heretics. They are the Trinity.*" Lucas watched the abbot as he repeated Castelnau's rant, taking satisfaction as the blood rose in Amalric's white face. "I'd wondered all these months what he meant, until I read this letter." From inside his cloak, he removed a calfskin pouch and handed it to the abbot.

Amalric received it, the taut space between his brows wrinkling in puzzlement as he withdrew the vellum within. His face went gray the moment he opened the folded sheet, and a grimace twisted his bloodless lips. "Castelnau. What a fool. He should have destroyed this." He tossed it on the desk in front of Lucas.

"So it's true," Lucas said. "Plessis wrote to tell you that not only had Castelnau changed his mind about the heretic Cathars, but he also believed them to be divinely chosen. Castelnau believed the heretics to be the embodiment of the Holy Trinity. What greater blasphemy could there be than the pope's own emissary betraying his Church and his faith?"

"The archdeacon had requested mercy for the heretics." Amalric sniffed, rose, and left the table, bending slightly to examine Duchesne's bookshelves. "Clearly, he'd taken leave of his senses."

"And that's your script at the bottom, is it not?" Lucas pressed on. "Plessis is the bear. I am the falcon. Castelnau was the dove.

You sent this letter on to Castelnau as a warning that Plessis plotted his death and that I would be his assassin. Why?"

Amalric clasped his hands behind his back with a shrug. "We needed to broker the settlement between Toulouse and Baux, and I thought the warning would be enough to silence Castelnau's raving. The Church needed that peace."

Lucas snorted. "You mean, of course, the Church needed the money promised by Baux if the settlement went in his favor."

Amalric raised his palms in a twisted benediction. "Plessis was correct about one thing. The pope reacted to Castelnau's murder just as our famed Templar knight thought he would. But that"—he waved at the letter—"that is more dangerous than any crusade."

Amalric crossed to the fire and crouched in front of the small flames burning themselves out in the cold room. "It goes without saying, Mauléon, that only the three of us need know what happened in that church." He lifted an iron poker from the floor and thrust it into the fire, shifting the wood and raising sparks. "Hand me that letter. I'll destroy it now."

When the abbot turned to see Lucas's reaction, he was greeted by the soldier's empty chair. The table's surface held only one sheet: the list of the dead. The letter was gone.

Amalric's mouth twitched in a half smile, and he spoke into the air. "Never mind, Sénéchal. Soon there will be just two of us. I'm sure Plessis would agree that your service is no longer needed."

LIMOUX—THURSDAY

Lucas laughed without a trace of humor. "I took that letter with me. To do what with it, I had no idea. When I realized everyone I loved had died, I no longer cared what happened to me or what would become of Castelnau's heresy. And justice was done. Lucas Mauléon ended there, on that plain, in the very grave he'd had others dig for the souls he'd condemned."

"How did you die, Lucas?" Lia's voice was a whisper. As his grief spun out, her anger trickled away.

Lucas raised his left arm and pulled his shirt from his waist. He approached Lia, and Isis snarled, stopping him in midstride.

"It's okay, girl. Lie down." The dog's ears flattened, but she dropped to her belly and laid her head between her paws, eyeing Lucas from under pointed eyebrows.

Lia pulled Lucas's hands away from his shirt. His beltless chinos hung low, and she traced the thick, white scar that ran between his hip bones. She choked back the bile burning her throat. He'd been gutted. Her shaking legs began to give way, and backing up, she sank onto a wooden chair. The black shell of anger she'd been holding began to release and soften into compassion.

"Who did this to you?" she asked, looking up. Thin threads of golden light shone in Lucas's eyes, the black melting into a dark brown, suddenly so like Raoul's that her heart broke anew.

OUTSIDE GRUISSAN—DECEMBER 1208

*T*he bodies were burned beyond recognition. Raoul made out six shapes laid in a row. Some were merely a collection of pieces, and others had scraps of clothing clinging to their ravaged flesh and charred bones. It was impossible to tell if they had been men or women. Four were shrunken skeletons with tiny skulls. He knelt and grasped a foot that was bare of flesh, either burned away or picked clean by the crows circling overhead. *Children. Just babies. Oh God, could they be mine?* He sank to his knees.

A seventh mound lay apart from the row of corpses. Wrapped in a soot-covered blanket tied fast around the neck and the ankles, it was a body intact. Raoul, in a frenzy of fear, cut through the binding around the head and yanked back the covering. It was a fat young man, his skin unblemished by flame but bruised profoundly on one side. The wind teased through his hair, the tonsured cut indicating he'd been a monk. His eyes were closed and his face smooth; he looked as though he were enjoying an improbable siesta underneath the December sun. The right side of the covering, near his waist, was matted and soaked, nearly black. Raoul touched the fabric, and his fingers came away red. He returned to the burned bodies.

Wind roiled the clouds, and for a moment, the sun was revealed. Light pierced the haze and snatched at a silver chain half buried in the damp earth. One end hung from the blackened palm of a wretched corpse. Raoul brushed away the dirt, hooked the chain under a finger, and withdrew it carefully. The chain was fine and delicate as rain. Pendulating in the slight breeze was a single, squared cross, made by a silversmith in Carcassonne. Raoul had offered the necklace to his wife at the birth of their children. He enclosed the pendant in his fist. He touched the body before him, laying his hand on the blackened skull where tufts of yellow hair crumbled and scattered to the ground. Two small bodies were arranged on either side of his wife's.

"Paloma," he whispered. He ran a hand over the length of the skeleton, oblivious to the stench. He saw his Paloma's sweet face, her halo of thick, golden hair spilling across bare shoulders as she wiped a damp, lavender-scented cloth down her arms and across the nape of her neck.

His keen ears caught the pounding of hooves. A single rider approached the gravesite on the road from Gruissan. Miró stamped and neighed a question to Raoul, her withers twitching. He ran a hand down her muzzle and up to the white star on her forehead. "Hold steady, girl." Hidden from view by a rise in the road, he removed the short sword strapped across his back. He stood in front of the terrible grave, his hands behind his back, his legs spread wide.

A cloaked rider appeared; he was mounted on a great black destrier that could have been the brother to his own Mirò. The horse and rider slowed as they neared Raoul. The man dismounted. The sun, already at its highest point on this short day, seemed to fade around him.

He wore no armor, but he was protected from the winter wind by a cloak of finely woven black wool lined with fur. His face was pale, drawn tightly over cheekbones that pushed ridges against his white skin, and his eyes were dull wells of black.

"On behalf of the Church, I have come to affirm the dead." His head was bare, and he ran a hand through his long, dark-blond hair.

"The dead have nothing more to tell you," said Raoul. He flexed one hand, then the other, and regripped the hilt of his sword. "The innocent cannot confess."

The man dropped his steed's reins and walked along the shallow pit, peering down at the bodies. Raoul shifted his stance to keep his eyes trained on the intruder.

"What a price you paid for your glory. Oh yes, I know who you are, Raoul d'Aran." The man looked up, his face in shadow. "I loved your wife as you did. Did she never once mention me? Lucas Moisset?"

Raoul blinked but did not respond. His heart slammed to a halt, and his blood turned frigid in his veins.

"How little could these lives have meant to you?" asked Mauléon, sweeping an arm above the prone bodies. "You abandoned your wife and your children in the village, pretending they could live undetected while you played at being the savior of Languedoc." He moved to the far side of the pit, where the body of the monk lay exposed to chill wind and weak sun.

Heedless of Raoul's presence, the sénéchal dropped to his haunches and pulled the rough covering away from the monk's body. Raoul saw the source of the blood he'd touched earlier: the man had been sliced from one side of his belly to the other. "And one more on my head," said Mauléon. He tucked a thin leather pouch underneath the monk's demurely folded hands. "May God save your soul, Bonafé. And mine," he muttered before pulling the blanket back over the monk's face.

Raoul drew his right hand to the front of his body, his knuckles white around the hilt of his short sword, while he soundlessly pulled free the simple mace hanging from his belt with his left. He stepped closer on silent feet, his mind registering the location of his shadow, which ran close to his body in the minutes before the sun began its westward creep. He gritted his teeth, his jaw working in fury.

There was an upward rush of air and black shadow, a blast of horses screaming, and a bite of pain so fierce Raoul thought his face had been cleaved in two. He spun back, blinded in his left eye by a curtain of red. He used the force of his momentum to pivot, his arm swinging out and around, his blade whistling as it whipped through the air. But Raoul wasn't quick enough. His sword met a void. A booted foot slammed into his wrist and sent the sword flying. The sénéchal's blade rushed toward him again, but lower and crossways, aiming for his belly.

Time stalled. Raoul saw and heard everything with the clarity of an eagle, even as blood streamed warm down his face. The sun glinted off Mauléon's long, thin knife, Miró pounded the earth behind him in a frenzy of agitation, and Mauléon's battle-tested steed shifted but held his ground, waiting for some unknown signal to act. Beside them, the black bodies of the slain whispered in the wind.

Throwing his weight left, Raoul swung out his arm. The rounded bronze head of his mace landed with a dull crack on the side of the sénéchal's skull, and he collapsed without a sound. Raoul bent forward, his hands on his knees as he gasped and spit into the ground. The blood poured from the gash in his face, and his mouth was coated with its iron tang. He grasped Mauléon and pulled him onto his back. The sénéchal's eyes were closed and his chest was still.

As he yanked his short sword from the earth, Raoul felt rather than heard the pounding of hooves on the earth. Retrieving Mauléon's blade from the grass where it had slipped as he fell, Raoul wiped it clean and returned it to the sénéchal's hand. Without a second glance at Mauléon, Raoul pulled himself onto Mirò's back, thrust his feet into the stirrups, and whispered into her flattened ear, "Run, girl."

Lucas heard the falcon's cry, which pulled him from a thick blackness that was filled with pounding drums, drums beating inside his head with such force his gorge rose. He turned his head, and the motion nearly sent him underneath the black again. He rolled despite the pain and released the vomit that filled his mouth.

"Thrown from that infernal horse at last, Mauléon?" Lucas opened his eyes just enough to see two pairs of armed men dismounting. Each man wore a hauberk of chain mail over a quilted wool gambeson, a conical helmet that covered the nose with a thin strip of metal, and boots of tanned leather. They formed a circle around Lucas, hands resting on the hilts of their swords. None wore a mantle to indicate allegiance, but he knew each man by name. Just as he knew they were no longer his to command. One kicked the knife from his hand, breaking his fingers. Lucas closed his eyes to receive the final blows. The falcon called once more.

LIMOUX—THURSDAY EVENING

*T*he scar on his face. You were responsible for that?"
Lia asked.

Lucas closed his eyes and nodded.

"Why did you attack him?" Lia pressed, thinking somehow
that if she understood, she could turn back the centuries and
change what had happened.

"He'd drawn his weapon, Lia. My instincts overcame
my reason."

"How did Raoul die?" she whispered.

"I would tell you if I could." His cool, firm fingers closed
over hers. "When I came to, he and his horse were gone.
Soldiers surrounded me, and it was over soon after. My last
thought was a prayer: that God would grant me the chance

to beg Paloma's forgiveness should we meet in whatever lay beyond." He pulled back his hunched shoulders. "There was never a beyond for me. I never left Languedoc."

"They escaped." Jordí's voiced startled them. They'd nearly forgotten the priest still sitting in his own fog of memories. The room had grown almost completely dark while they spoke. The only illumination came from a small table lamp in the far corner. Jordí sat in shadow.

"No, Father," said Lucas. "Raoul and I met at that terrible place. We saw the bodies—*your* body. You were buried on that plain with proof of Castelnau's heresy and the riddle of his murder underneath your corpse. I know you tried, but no one left that church alive."

"Lucas, it's true. Paloma and the children escaped." Lia recalled Paloma's words. "She lived to hold her children's children."

"How do you know this?" Lucas grasped her hands, squeezing with icy fingers.

"In my car is the letter of safe passage Lucas Mauléon wrote on behalf of Paloma Gervais and her children," she replied, offering his very words as his own salvation.

OUTSIDE MINERVE—DECEMBER 1208

Four days after they were spirited away from Gruissan, Paloma arrived with her children in Minerve. She would not be separated from Bertran and Aicelina until they reached the village, where they could shelter with trusted friends. She left the children playing at Félix's hearth with a litter of kittens in the very house Raoul had helped to build, and she continued alone on horseback to the river canyon.

She dismounted at the top of the gorge and tied the horse in the shelter of a holm oak, Languedoc's flourish of evergreen in the deep of winter, and descended into the canyon. Paloma followed the Cesse, past familiar boulders half the size of a parish church. In the distance, she heard a horse whinny, sharp and short.

"Mirò," Paloma gasped. Frantic, she scrambled down a short slope to her husband's beloved mare. Mirò lifted and tossed her head at Paloma's approach, stamping in recognition as she caught familiar scents. The horse wore no saddle and only a loose rope bridle. Raoul was nowhere to be seen.

"He can't be far, Mirò." She rubbed the horse's forehead as Mirò pushed her snout into Paloma's cloak, snorting. "You're hungry," she whispered into the tangled black forelock. Paloma's stomach thudded in hollow despair. She lifted her skirts, stepping around a shallow pool near the river's edge, and ascended a rise toward the wall of the gorge, Mirò trailing behind.

Minutes later, Paloma's howl reverberated through the canyon, horrible and tortured. It silenced all sounds but the eternal chatter of the river.

LIMOUX—THURSDAY EVENING

Lucas held Lia's gaze as firmly as he held her hands. Lia caught a glint of warm gold in his black eyes before he let go and walked away, melting into the shadows.

He returned to her side and handed her an archival sheet. In the dim light, she could barely make out the cursive Latin scrawl on the priceless paper tucked inside. She skimmed it, struggling to decipher and understand what had been written. At the bottom, however, two sentences stood apart.

The appended words, penned in fine script, were easily read. They formed phrases she'd memorized a few days before. *Bears, falcons, doves.* Remnants of the past. With only this scrap of history to prove how those words had changed Languedoc forever.

"Plessis's betrayal of the archdeacon, followed by Amalric's betrayal of me. Those words told Pierre de Castelnau what I had come to do. But the betrayals ended in a field outside Gruissan."

"Where did you get this letter?" she asked.

"I followed a suspicion that turned out to be correct." Lucas gathered his bag and hung the strap from his shoulder. "Jordí told me you went looking for the letter and found that photograph instead. I never meant for you to find it," he said. "I am sorry. I'm sorry for what that photograph means."

Lia shook her head, uncomprehending. "That photo was of the road where my husband died."

"I know, Lia. I took that photograph and gave it to Jordí as a warning. When I threatened to expose his secret, he gave me Castelnau's letter. Maybe he thought we'd both agree to bury the past. But I'll leave it to him to explain."

Lia glanced at Jordí. Lamplight sparkled in his eyes and on his cheeks. He was crying.

"Lia," Lucas continued. "I didn't return to this world as Lucas Mauléon. I returned as I left, as Lucas Moisset. And I had no idea why I was here until I saw you. I thought you were Paloma Gervais and that I'd been given a second chance. But I know now that you aren't her. And that my chances are gone."

"What do you want to do?"

"To leave the past behind." At last, a smile without deceit, a hint of the man he might have been. He reached into his bag and handed her a manila envelope. She felt the flat, round shape of a computer disk inside. "You'll know what to do with this," said Lucas.

"Where will you go?"

"I hoped you could tell me," he said.

And Lia understood. His story had ended; he was freed from the burden of guilt over Paloma's death. The document to show his role in history had been found and was now in the hands of someone who could continue its journey toward the truth. Lucas Mauléon had died in that field long before; it was time for Lucas Moisset to be at rest. Lia saw Paloma. She saw Raoul walking toward his wife. She rose to embrace Lucas.

"Go and seek forgiveness," she whispered in his ear. She whispered of a stairwell in a winery, of a great hollow space within an abandoned fortress and a small door set in its mighty wall. She whispered of wheat fields and wildflowers spreading out beyond the door. Her whisper was the laughter of children and the rush of wind through the fields, warm and healing, as eternal as the Languedoc sun. She watched as he walked out the door.

"Where did you get this?" Lia sat next to Jordí on the sofa, holding the letter written by Philippe du Plessis and added to by Arnaud Amalric. "Where did you get those materials you left for me? Did they really come from the institute?"

He shook his head. "Months ago, one of my parishioners brought me a small wooden box full of documents he was certain were ancient; he was terrified of handling them, so in good sense and good intention, he brought them to me. That man was a notary, in charge of probating the estate of Hermès Daran of Lagrasse." Jordí nodded at Lia's sharp inhalation. "Yes, Logis du Martinet," he said in response to her unspoken question. "The notary himself had found the box in a closet inside the old winery. He admitted to me that the search for an heir had all but been abandoned and the estate was being inventoried. Anything of value would be sold to pay off Daran's debts. I convinced the notary that it would take months to verify the veracity of the documents' age and provenance. I haven't heard from him since, and I've stayed away from Lagrasse.

"With the memory of who I am and where I come from came the memory of what history those materials contain. It may even be that I put them there in some other time. Perhaps I've been waiting for the right person to come along who would know what to do with this." He touched the protective sheet she held, the ancient warnings passed between men with enough power to direct the course of history. "But I fear I put you in the middle of something that's bigger than we are. Once again, I made a dreadful error."

Lia considered the letter she held as the puzzle pieces of the past shifted and fell into place. "It would take me all night to decipher this handwriting. Read it to me. In French."

Jordí patted his pockets until he found his reading glasses. Before he began, he cleared his throat and said, "The night in Paris, when we were to meet for dinner, I had planned to tell you everything. But Lucas appeared, I played my hand, and I gave him the letter."

Lia nodded her understanding, and he read.

The letter wasn't long, just a few paragraphs. The blood emptied from Lia's limbs as Jordí spoke and rushed through again, leaving her hot and nauseated.

"Castelnau believed them, didn't he?" Astonishment thundered through her. "He believed the Cathars!"

"If this letter is true, yes," said Jordí. "And he tried to plead their case to Plessis."

"And Plessis wrote to warn Amalric."

"Who thought he could play both sides."

"Which he did."

"Yes. But in the end, who was right?"

"'*I have seen the spirit of God. They are not heretics. They are the*

Trinity.'" Lia repeated Castelnau's dying words. "He was saying
the Cathars, or reincarnation, were evidence of the Holy Spirit?"

"Lia, there is so much we don't know. One letter. One
man's memory..."

"But it all makes sense. Castelnau's murder makes sense!" Lia
exclaimed. "If he'd started spreading the word that he believed
the Cathars, that could have ripped the Church apart. It would
have changed Christianity." Visions of her dissertation becoming a book, a sensation, the ripple effect of her theory gaining
traction until it grew to a tsunami, flared before her mind's eye.
Then the visions sputtered and died out. "But these materials
are meaningless. Even when we have them verified, they'll be
meaningless without Raoul's and Lucas's stories, without yours.
Stories no one will believe. This is the truth, but it's not history." Historian and priest sat, weary and bewildered.

Lia smoothed the letter and placed it in her bag. She wanted
to ask after the rest of the documents, where Jordí had stashed
the box found on Hermès Daran's estate, but there was something else she had to know first.

"Jordí, what did Lucas mean when he said he'd threatened
to expose your secret? Was he talking about what you'd taken
from the institute?"

The priest dropped his face in his hands. His shoulders heaved
in a great, shuddering sigh. Then he looked to Lia. "There is
something I must show you."

He rose and walked to the front door. Isis bounded past him
when he opened it to the blue night. Lia followed, and the
three made their way to a stone shed with double wooden
doors behind the house.

LIMOUX—TWO SUMMERS AGO

*A*s he walked from the hotel to the starting corral, Gabriel Sarabias retreated into the mental space where only the race existed. He had ridden the roads and trails of the route between Limoux and Arques several times in the past weeks, until his body responded to each curve, incline, and descent with a memory born of intense training.

Placing in the top tier of the Tour d'Arques would guarantee him a spot in September's Trans-Pyrénées—the most prestigious multistage race in the competitive mountain biking circuit. He'd won the Trans-P three years in a row in the mid-2000s; now he was an elder statesman in the sport. Simply being among the hundred riders in the race had secured his sponsorships until he declared his retirement.

But none of that mattered now. He rehearsed each mile in his mind.

At the corral, race volunteers yawned and smoked and sipped from water bottles; some paced importantly in front of the early bystanders who were filling the sidewalks on either side of the starting line. Molten and pulsing, the Languedoc sun rose in a deep blue sky. It would be hot and dry on the trail, the altitude offering no relief, but Gabriel thought nothing of the breathless air. He'd trained all spring and early summer in the tinder-dry Sierras and southern Cascades—the conditions were second nature. He was prepared; his heart was calm, his mind clear.

His manager caught up with him as the corral began to fill with other riders. Together, he and Colin conducted the final gear checks in a silence punctuated by their athlete-and-trainer shorthand—one-word questions answered by nods or numbers. They would be in radio contact during the race, but Colin wouldn't see him until the finish line.

The route would take the riders along shepherds' trails paralleling the D118, dipping through villages on single-track dirt roads and deeper into the hills as they dropped southeast toward Arques. A few miles before the ruins of Château d'Arques, the packed-earth trail crossed the D613 and briefly reentered the forest before concluding in the village. Twenty-five miles of hard mountain road under the pounding summer sun.

In the moments before the starting horn blasted, a gasp rippled through the crowd of onlookers. Even Gabriel, so intent on the challenge before him, followed the hands raised to the sky. He peered into the cobalt, seeing nothing at first. Then, emerging from the top of the densely packed oak and gorse, two great birds swooped and screeched. They passed so closely overhead that he could see the black-and-white pinstripes of a peregrine falcon's underbelly and a flash of white and brown-gold of his pursuer—another bird of prey he couldn't identify. Gabriel smiled and tightened the strap of his helmet. The fighting birds seemed a good omen.

Gabriel let the pack pull away early, glad to be clear of the whirling legs and extended elbows of riders fighting for space. There would be time to regain ground as the sun and altitude climbed. He passed rider after rider as the race left the highway and began ascending into the hills. A few south-facing slopes were terraced into neat rows of vines. The trails were pock-marked by dislodged stones and eroded by runoff from the streams that erupted from underground caverns. He anticipated the places where he could surge, others where he knew to hold back, picking carefully from the map ingrained in his mind.

Fifteen miles in, surrounded by forest, Gabriel opened up. He ground past the final riders, barely registering the sheer drop of the cliff face to his left as he squeezed by, every sense in tune and in control. The forest swallowed the trail again, and he was thrown into shadows. Movement ahead alerted him to a cyclist stopped off to the side in a small patch of sunlight. Blood ran from a gash in the rider's knee.

"*Ça va*?" Gabriel shouted without slowing his approach. He recognized Iban Arroyo from Spain, who waved him on and continued changing a tire, likely blown by landing hard on the spike of a stone's edge.

"*La course c'est à toi, Gabe. Vas-y!*" Iban shouted his encouragement as Gabriel flew by.

He was in the lead. Colin's contact was infrequent, but he tracked Gabriel's progress via their two-way radio. When he did make contact, Colin spoke quietly as Gabriel passed rider after rider, holding him back until it was time to tap into those calibrated reserves. The final two miles of the trail before it met the road leading into Arques descended steeply, from granite hills studded with cedar and pine into meadows crowded with vibrant wildflowers and ecstatic bees.

He sensed the creature before he saw or heard it. His neck and cheek tingled as the falcon's wings sliced the air next to him. An eagle, screeching in fury, tore out from behind, and both raptors ascended like rockets. Gabriel snapped his attention away from the great birds and scanned for the slim break in the wall where the trail connected on the other side of the road. The gap was nowhere to be seen. The trail rounded an unfamiliar bend, and in that instant, Gabriel realized he'd ridden off course.

Cursing at being forced to slow, cursing Colin for not alerting him to his error, cursing the birds for distracting his attention, Gabriel coasted to the edge of the cliff. The black ribbon of tarmac came into view, and in the distance, he could see a break in the rock wall lining the road. The road was empty; it was not where he was supposed to emerge, but he estimated he was less than half a mile south of the race route. He'd take a chance that his error wouldn't disqualify him rather than give up his solid lead to find the correct course. He tried to reach Colin, but the radio was dead. In his adrenaline-fueled anger, he ripped out his earpiece and tore off the radio clipped to his jersey. He tossed the unit over the ledge and retook the trail.

Gabriel nailed his gaze to the yards just beyond his front wheel as he leaned into a series of hairpin turns and continued whipping down the mountainside. His eyes locked on the gap, and he prepared to launch over a drainage ditch, onto the road, and across to the trail.

A scream shot out of the hill above him just as his tires went airborne over the ditch. A second shriek followed in the echo of the first. His tires found the road, but the direction of his wheels was out of sync with his body. His torso pulled away from the turn. The bike worked against him, tearing away from the grip of his muscles; his cycling cleats snapped out of their pedal locks. Weightless, his mind flew free. Man separated from machine.

In the moments before the pavement claimed his body, the scene unfolded before Gabriel in stuttered slow motion. He saw streaks of black, russet, and gold as two birds descended with the force of bullets. They fell as one, locked in battle, indistinguishable and doomed. In the heartbeat between light and dark, his wife's face rose, her eyes the dark green of the Mediterranean in winter, full of sorrow and love. He whispered her name: "Lia."

The screech of car tires blended with the screaming of birds. Gleaming black steel collided with featherlight aluminum. The Mercedes tossed the bike high into the air. It flew across the road and landed, twisted and broken, against the base of a cedar tree. For a moment, nothing moved but a single spinning wheel.

The birds had disappeared into the hills beyond. The memory of their screams was all the driver could hear beyond the pounding of his own heart. He left the engine running but stepped out of the car, his legs jerking with adrenaline.

Inches from the car's front tires lay a cyclist on his back, his eyes closed, his face turned away. With difficulty, the driver sank onto his thick haunches. He could see no blood. He felt for a pulse.

The front grille of his Mercedes was unmarred, but the driver failed to notice a shattered headlight. He crossed himself and braced a hand on the fender to hoist up his short, stout body. His bulk cast a shadow over Gabriel.

He drove the short distance back to Arques, where he

stopped at a pay phone and made a brief call. As he circled through a roundabout on the other side of town, he heard the wail of approaching sirens. He pulled in close to the car in front, and both drivers waited as a police car, followed by an ambulance, flew past.

He drove onward without a plan. When it was time to stop for fuel, he saw the damage to the headlight. He took the small highways south, circling through the Aude Valley, until he arrived well after dark just outside Limoux.

The porch light clicked on as he coasted into the drive of his old *mas*, three miles outside town. He stopped in front of the wooden double doors of a shed behind the house. He labored to open the doors, rusty on their hinges, but at last, he pulled them wide enough to allow the car to pass through.

The next morning, he walked into Limoux and boarded a regional bus for Narbonne. No one at the cathedral knew he owned a Mercedes—he stored it in the garage behind his house outside Limoux and never drove it in the city. His one concession to worldly vanity gathered dust and spiderwebs, locked in a stone shed, its broken light a scar that would not fade with time.

LANGUEDOC—1209

Paloma returned one last time to her home in Lagrasse. There, she buried her husband in his vineyards, barren and shaking in the icy Cers wind—that winter assault from the faraway ocean. She took her children to Catalunya, carrying no possession from her old life but the necklace that had slipped from Raoul's hand when he'd died alone in a cave beyond Minerve.

MAS HIVERT, FERRALS-LES-CORBIÈRES—LATE THURSDAY

*A*s Lia pulled into the drive in front of Mas Hivert, the door opened, and shadows swept through the light that spilled onto the patio. Domènec embraced her without a word; Rose's arms encircled them both as Lia wailed and shook. Finally, they retreated inside the warm house.

Domènec prepared a pot of chamomile tea and they tried to convince Lia to eat. But the thought of food made her throat close and her stomach clench with nausea. All she wanted was to lie down. Exhaustion pulled at her, her thoughts collapsed, and her limbs seemed made of glass—heavy, but ready to shatter.

Rose brought her to a guest room and started water running in the tub in the adjoining bathroom. The bedroom's open windows faced southwest, where the sunset glowed over hills and acres of vineyards, and a breeze swirled through. Lia caught a whisper of sea in the air. Limp from the long day, she stripped out of her clothes and slipped gratefully into the hot water. When she heard the door click shut, the tears began to flow again.

She stayed in the bath until the water cooled and then watched it swirl out between her feet. At last, she heaved her tired body from the empty tub. The mirror over the sink revealed her swollen, red eyes and puffy lips. Lia felt small and alone.

A soft tapping on her door brought her out of her sad reverie. "Come in," she said, wrapping a plush yellow bath towel around her body and tucking the end under her armpit. Rose entered with her hands full of spare clothes and a thin cotton robe.

"Sweetie, would you like me to sleep in here with you?" Rose set the clothes on a wing chair tucked in the corner of the room.

"I don't think I'll be able to sleep. I'll try to read for a while."

Rose held out her hand. In her palm lay two small blue pills. "Valium." Lia shook her head. "Lia, please take them. You need to rest." Rose set the pills by a glass of water on the nightstand.

Lia lowered herself on the bed, and Rose sat beside her, taking her hand. They looked out to the turquoise that was giving up the day to the fresh spring night. At last, Lia spoke, telling Rose the truth, telling her all about the past.

"He was never mine, Rose," she said after her story was over and the sky had waxed to an endless black. "He always belonged to her. To Paloma." Lia took the pills from the nightstand and placed them on her tongue. The sweet coating turned bitter as it melted. She took a small drink of water and swallowed. The acrid pills burned her raw throat, and their taste remained in her mouth.

"And you belong here, Lia."

She lay back and curled her body into a ball, wanting to disappear into the ebony emptiness of the sky. The wind rushed in, cooling her bath-warmed skin. Rose lay down, wrapping her smooth arms around Lia's torso. When Lia's breathing deepened and slowed, Rose covered her with a thin duvet and kissed her damp face. As Lia drifted into the release of slumber, she heard Rose whisper, "Sleep. Sleep and forget, for as long as you can."

MINERVE—THE NEXT MORNING

She pulled the garage door shut behind her, but instead of climbing the road to Le Pèlerin, Lia walked toward the village. The ruin of La Candela drew her on. In the shimmering light, she counted four white doves nestled on a jagged outcropping of the stone tower. The air rippled with a cool breeze.

An eagle floated high above her. He broke with the air current's course and swooped down, gathering speed as he neared earth, and her heart soared. Lia wanted to shout with joy at his freedom, shout to let him know she understood. And she wanted to weep. She was bound to the earth, left behind to close the chasm of the past.

The eagle landed with wings spread at the top of La Candela. He cried once, shifting on his powerful feet, his claws clutching at the stone, before releasing his body into the wind. The doves rustled below, cooing in round tones, until they too rose, floating on wings white as hope.

The bag over Lia's shoulder contained two letters. Both had been written in that terrible year between December 1207 and December 1208, when Languedoc fell on the blade of a sword and split open into war. One letter warned of evil; the other offered safe passage to a woman and her children. Betrayal and forgiveness. The past not forgotten, the future in the form of new life.

This land wouldn't change, nor would its history. The battle against the heretics—one driven by intolerance and greed—had continued until the Cathars were nearly eradicated and Languedoc had become a part of France. But Languedoc's stories would live on. As would many of its souls.

In her hands, Lia held the mock-up of a book jacket. Large and in full color, it showed Château de Quéribus, isolated on a high, snow-covered peak, illuminated by a full moon. Arranged over the grand citadel in shimmering gold font, a title proclaimed, *En Pays Cathare: Une Histoire en Images*. Beneath the title, smaller print read, *Photographies: Lucas Moisset; Texte: Natalió Cloutildou Carrer*.

The eagle hovered, and the sunlight cast a halo around his suspended figure.

"*A diù siatz.*" Lia offered him an Occitan farewell before turning toward the cottage. At the corner, she looked back. The pinnacle of La Candela was etched black against the azure heavens. The skies above the bare tower were empty. The birds had flown.

Author's Note

The inspiration for this novel was born in the mountains, valleys, and villages of the Languedoc-Roussillon region. I wondered as I wandered through its ruined citadels and medieval towns, drank its wine, and whispered its language—*what if?* What if the Cathars were right? What if history just got it wrong? I set about to create my own version of events, draping layers of fantasy over a scaffolding of fact. Well, of *history* anyway. Fact is something else altogether, isn't it?

History tells us this: in January 1208, papal legate Pierre de Castelnau was murdered outside the village of Saint-Gilles, on the Provence-Languedoc border. The assassin was identified as an officer of Raymond VI, the Count of Toulouse. The powerful count, who governed much of the region, had been accused repeatedly of harboring sympathies for the Cathars; his second wife was a believer.

Within weeks of Castelnau's assassination, Pope Innocent III declared war on the heretics, and the Catholic Church launched a religious crusade in the heart of Europe. The enemy wasn't just the infidel in faraway Levant; it was the heretic within. By 1244, after decades of brutal sieges throughout Languedoc and through the systematic tortures of the Inquisition, the Languedoc Cathars were all but eliminated, making their last stand in the mountain fortification at Montségur.

I have chosen, for the reader's comfort and to bridge the distance between past and present, to use all modern French place names in the text. Depending upon their country of origin and station in life, medieval characters would have communicated in Latin, in *langue d'oïl*—the antecedent to modern French—or in *langue d'oc*. Characters from Catalunya would have spoken a dialect of Occitan known as Aranese. I have assumed, with the grace of fiction, the ease of these characters' transition between the Aranese and Languedocien dialects. Cathar followers in southern France were known as Albigensians, after Albi, a town northeast of Toulouse. They are now universally known as Cathars. For consistency, I have used Cathar and Catharism throughout the text.

This is a work of fiction. Some of the characters are historical persons, but their portrayals are entirely of my imagination, as are the events depicted here. All of the towns you will visit in *In Another Life* are real, except the village of Cluet. I have taken liberties with the location, names, and description of some existing sites.

So much of the Cathars' writings were destroyed during the crusade that little is known of their beliefs and practices; I have not attempted to re-create a Cathar lifestyle here, believing there is often a wide gap between what religion dictates and how people truly live. The Cathars held many beliefs we would consider mystical or paranormal. My imagination was sparked by those Lia explains, resists, and finally accepts as truth: reincarnation and the remembering of lost souls.

Reading Group Guide

1. We learn in the opening sentence that Lia lost her husband eighteen months earlier. Do you think there is an appropriate length of time for a spouse or long-term significant other to remain alone before thinking about being part of a relationship again? Discuss Lia's reasons for returning to Languedoc to heal and move on with her life.

2. Our faith largely shapes our views of the afterlife. How do your religious views affect the way you perceive death and what happens to the soul?

3. Lia was raised in Africa, by European parents. As a child, she identifies herself as African; later, she comes to regard Languedoc as home. Discuss her evolving cultural identity. Why did she never feel "American"? Discuss Lia's yearning for a home. Where do you think she belongs? How do you define home? Have you left behind a place that's left a significant impression on you? What do you think it was like for Rose to give up her home and family in the United States to make a life in France with Domènec?

4. Jordí and Lia discuss history versus the past. What do you think of Lia's assertion that history is what we can prove and the past is what we can only guess at? Lia states her role as a historian is to "[correct] history when the truth is known." What does she mean?

5. Lia has few long-term personal relationships. What about her past has made her reluctant to open her heart to others? Why was she so drawn to Rose? How did you feel about Rose's "meddling" in Lia's love life?

6. Discuss the tension between Lucas and Lia. Why is she attracted to him, and what about him makes her pull away? If she hadn't met Raoul, do you think she could have formed a deeper relationship with Lucas?

7. Do you think Lia and Raoul could have made a life together in the present? Do you think Lia did the right thing in returning Raoul to Paloma?

8. Why did Lia return Raoul to Paloma? Do you think she really believes Gabriel is lost to her?

9. Depictions of loving marriages are rare in literature— marriage is most often the source of conflict. *In Another Life* shows three loving relationships: Rose and Dom, Lia and Gabriel, and Raoul and Paloma. Discuss how Lia's marriage to Gabriel may have led her to return Raoul to his wife.

10. What do you imagine happens after the novel ends? Does Lia remain in Languedoc? Do any of the characters return to her? What becomes of Lucas? Of Jordí?

11. Forgiveness and atonement are two major themes of the book. Who do you think has the most to atone for, and why? Do you believe they each achieved redemption at the end?

12. Do you think the story ends on a hopeful note, despite the obvious tragedies?

13. Is there a true antagonist in the story?

14. Archdeacon Pierre de Castelnau was murdered for his potential heresy. Lia says, "If he'd started spreading the word that he believed the Cathars, that could have ripped apart the Church. It would have changed Christianity." Why was the archdeacon's change of heart about the Cathars so threatening to the Catholic Church?

15. Why did Jordí leave the scene of Gabriel's accident without identifying himself? How do you think Lia reacted when Jordí took her to the shed to show her his damaged Mercedes? Do you think he told her the truth?

16. Why does Lia mistrust religion? How does her skepticism change by the end of the book?

17. Who was responsible for Gabriel's death? Do you think Lia continued pursuing the lawsuit against the Mountain Cyclist Federation after learning Jordí's truth?

18. Can you relate to Lia's ambivalence at the beginning of the book, her grief and her loneliness? Have you and your spouse or significant other ever discussed what you would do if one of you passed away unexpectedly? Could you imagine marrying again? Do you think it's possible to hold grief and longing for one partner while falling in love with someone new?

19. The historical context of *In Another Life* may be one unfamiliar to readers. Before reading this novel, were you aware of the history of the Cathars in the South of France? If these events were unfamiliar, what was your reaction to learning of this religious/cultural purge?

20. *In Another Life* is based on historical events but uses paranormal events that border on fantasy. Discuss which events you believe are real and which the author created. What is the responsibility of the fiction writer to present a realistic representation of historical events?

21. Did Paloma's level of literacy and independence surprise you? Do you believe that women of that era could choose their husbands or be allowed romantic love?

22. What do you think is the emotional and symbolic significance of the falcon, the eagle, and the dove?

A Conversation with the Author

Who are some of your favorite authors?

I'm in awe of writers who can pair beautiful language with great storytelling. In no particular order: Kate Atkinson, Jane Austen, Colm Tóibín, Lily King, Louise Erdrich, Jhumpa Lahiri, Ian McEwan, Edna O'Brien, Michael Ondaatje, Tim Winton, David Mitchell. Poets Seamus Heaney, Richard Hugo, Leanne O'Sullivan, and Emily Dickinson provide insights into possibilities of language, imagery, and rhythm. Music is such an important part of my life, and singer-songwriters such as Tori Amos, Glen Hansard, Beth Orton, Damien Rice, Mark Knopfler, and Emmylou Harris are present in my writing, even if you can't hear them!

What advice would you give to aspiring writers?

Write every day. No excuses. Everyone has at least half an hour they can capture for writing instead of watching television or scanning social media. Schedule it, prioritize it. Read every day; read widely and deeply; study your favorite authors; study the craft of writing. Keep a notebook of words, sentences, passages that resonate with the reader and writer in you. Take classes, workshops; attend conferences. Observe the world around you with every sense. Make notes of conversations; what people wear and how they wear it; the sounds of their voices; aromas in the café, on the bus, in the woods; what your food tastes like; how skin feels. Pay attention when you are in physical and emotional pain, when you are walking on air. Write. Be deliberate. Be thoughtful. Submit your stuff for publication; learn how to take criticism and rejection. Revise. Edit. And write some more. Talent has only a small part to play in being published: grit, determination, and an indefatigable work ethic are far more important.

What is the most challenging part of being a writer?

In general, turning off the inner critic and believing that, in time and through many revisions, the story will sort itself out, the layers will deepen, and the thing you are working on will not be the piece of utter crap you are certain it is in its early stages or when you run into trouble (which is inevitable).

At this specific point in my career, my challenge is to balance many projects and many different roles: writer, editor, promoter of my work. Each demands a different set of skills and uses different parts of my brain and creative energy. Sometimes I must do all three in one day, but I try to balance my workload.

What drew you to this story, and why?

The Languedoc region itself. I attended university in France many years ago, and I make it a priority to visit France every couple of years. I have many France-based stories pulling at my heart. In 2011, my husband and I spent a few weeks in Languedoc, exploring all the places Lia visits in the book and many more. I was enchanted by its fierce beauty, the generous, proud spirit of its people, and I was enthralled with the history of Languedoc—particularly the history of the Cathars.

What kind of research or preparation did you engage in before writing this book?

Our time in the region was one long, wonderful research adventure. We visited every Cathar site we could and collected several books on this history of the area. Each night, I would read about the places we'd explored that day. I didn't know then that I was building the foundation for a novel, but that exploration brought me fully into the history of the Cathar faith and the crusade that ended their story.

A year later, when I began to write *In Another Life*, I knew that if I started with the research, I might never emerge from early-thirteenth-century Europe to write the actual story. I didn't want to delve so deeply into medieval history that those scenes dominated the narrative. My challenge was to create a balance of detail between the past and present; my goal was to give a flavor, an impression, of the medieval lives of Raoul, Paloma, Lucas, and Jordí without losing the reader in the details.

I started with my basic premise—an alternative history of the assassination of Archdeacon Pierre de Castelnau—and worked out the historical details as I wrote and refined them as I revised.

Several books were invaluable resources: *Montaillou: The Promised Land of Error* by Emmanuel Le Roy Ladurie; *The Albigensian Crusade* by Jonathan Sumption; *Medieval France: An Encyclopedia* (Routledge Encyclopedias of the Middle Ages) by William W. Kibler, et al; *Paris in the Middle Ages* by Simone Roux; and Jo Ann McNamara (translator); *Romanesque Churches of France: A Traveller's Guide* by Peter Strafford.

What is your writing process like?

You're going to groan when you read this, but I get up between 4:00 and 5:00 every morning. I read, journal, work on a blog post until 6:00 or 7:00 a.m. Then I run or swim or practice yoga, eat breakfast with my husband, clean house. By 9:00 or 10:00, I'm at my desk, in a café, or at the library, back at work. I typically work on one project at a time during the day. I work six to seven days a week, five to eight hours a day, knocking off in the mid- to late afternoon. I go for a walk or to yoga class, make dinner, read, go to bed. One day a week I reserve for writing "business." I don't schedule days off, but I take one when I need it.

Which parts/characters/places are factual, and which did you create?

Archdeacon Pierre de Castelnau; Philippe du Plessis; Abbot Arnaud Amalric; Raymond VI, Count of Toulouse; Hugh de Baux; and Pope Innocent III were historical figures, though I have completely fictionalized their personalities, physical descriptions, and actions. Castelnau was assassinated outside Saint-Gilles by an unidentified assailant, and the pope did indeed declare a crusade against the Cathars in 1208 as a result.

All the town and cities and street names in the story are real, with the exception of Cluet. Cluet is a fictional town, based on the city of Béziers, which was sacked in July 1209 by a crusading army led by Abbot Arnaud Amalric. The church of Saint-Maurice in Gruissan and its destruction are fictional, but the cathedral in Narbonne, the basilica in Carcassonne, Minerve's Candela, the chateaux in Lastours, Termes, the lovely small city of Limoux, and the sites and street names in Paris are places you can visit. You can even book Lia's favorite room in that hotel in Paris, if you find out the hotel's real name. And I highly recommend *all* the food stalls at the Marché des Enfants Rouges in the Marais.

This story has both historical and contemporary scenes. Did you find one or the other more challenging or enjoyable to write?

Of course, the historical scenes had the significant challenge of creating an authentic medieval setting. But I loved being in that world. The rhythm of the language is slower, richer, more lyrical—something I found that carried over when characters from the past became part of the present. Lia's scenes rolled out so easily. I felt such a strong connection to her healing process and the renewal of her sense of self.

This is your first published novel. What was your journey to becoming an author?

When I was six years old, I read Louise Fitzhugh's wonderful *Harriet the Spy* and decided that when I grew up, I would become a writer. I modeled myself after Harriet and began keeping a journal and creating worlds on the page.

Then life intervened. There was a thirty-year hiatus from the time I stopped writing stories as an adolescent to the first short story I penned as an adult. After undergraduate and graduate degrees, I worked for many years as a university study abroad program manager and adviser, then as a wine buyer. Over the years, I filled dozens of journals and did some professional and feature writing during my career as a university administrator, but I was so afraid that if I tried my hand at fiction, my dream of being a writer would be shattered by my own lack of talent and grit.

The impetus to begin writing came after personal tragedies in my late thirties and early forties. I realized I wasn't going to have the sort of life I imagined I would have. So I had to create and fulfill other dreams. I knew that if the second half of my life could be lived as passionately and authentically as I tried to live the first half, it would be as a writer.

In October 2010, when I was forty-one, I took my first writing class at the superb Hugo House, a writing center in Seattle. From there, I wrote and published my first short story in 2011. Other short stories and essays followed. In July 2012, I wrote the first words of *In Another Life*. In October 2014, when I felt the novel was ready to take its chances in the publishing world, I pitched it at a writer's conference. Three weeks later, I signed with a literary agent and received an offer from a publisher on the same day. And now you've just read the result!

Where do you get your story ideas?

I'm fortunate to have lived in some extraordinary places: France, Japan, central Africa, New Zealand, and I've traveled the world over. I draw many story ideas from these settings, their histories, and my experiences living and traveling abroad. My characters are often challenged to look at themselves and respond to the world differently because they are in unfamiliar surroundings.

In addition, I listen and observe the world around me. Story ideas have come from a passing remark, an overheard conversation, an expression on someone's face, a line in a newspaper article, a photograph. The stories are there for the taking.

Acknowledgments

Deepest gratitude to the many loved ones, writers, and readers who have so graciously supported my dreams through your encouragement, humor, and big shoulders.

Thank you to my editor, Anna Michels, and her team at Sourcebooks, for your vision, passion, and patience. Thank you to my agent, Shannon Hassan of Marsal Lyon Literary, for your steady hand.

To the earliest readers of *In Another Life*—Charlotte Mae McDonnell, Edith O'Nuallain, Marci Peterson, Sylvia Bowman, Melissa Denny, Chris Burt, Jeanie Murphy: you salvaged this from the rubbish bin and made me believe it was worth finding my way to The End.

Thank you to Candace Johnson, editor and cheerleader extraordinaire. You helped me to chip away at the stone until the shape of a story was revealed.

To Anna and Peter Quinn of the Writers' Workshoppe and Imprint Books in Port Townsend: thank you for celebrating and supporting Pacific Northwest writers and for all that you do to make our little corner of the Olympic Peninsula a haven of creativity.

So many writers have opened their hearts to me in fellow-ship and empathy, including Karen Gaudette Brewer, Margaret Grant, Bianca Bowers, Sion Dayson, Jeanne Gassman, Kelly Byrne, Cerrissa Kim, and the writers of the WFWA. I learn from your grace; I celebrate your art. Kim De, my first writing buddy, this would not be without you.

To the women and men of the BtCLBB: your enthusiasm and virtual hugs keep me going.

My love and gratitude to my family for their steadfast support.

This book is dedicated to my darling husband, Brendan. Your soul is my light; your heart is my home. Thank you.